RED LIGHT

Visit us at www.boldstrokesbooks.com

What Reviewers Say About the Author

"*Punk Like Me*…is different. It is engaging. It is life-affirming. Frankly, it is genius.…This is our future standing tall and, most of the time, alone, and this is the impact of this story. At a minimum it compels us to listen and to remember…This is a rare book in that it has a soul; one that is laid bare for all to see." — *Just About Write*

"Powerfully written by a gifted author in the first person point of view, *Punk Like Me* is an intimate glimpse inside a cool "dude's" head. … Glass makes it fresh, makes it real, and gets to the heart of the matter where there is nothing left but truth." — *Midwest Book Review*

"In *Red Light*…we follow Tori through love, lust and trauma…and we watch her come out the other side, a woman who has prevailed against much to become the person she truly wants to be. Whether you're looking for a sexy book with a plot that holds together, or a good book about a good character, with some romance and passion, then this book will definitely be worth adding to your 'to read' pile." — Erica Friedman, *Shoujoai ni Bouken: The Adventures of Yuriko*

"JD is a gifted storyteller with the ability to pull you into Tori's adrenaline-fueled life. [In *Red Light*]…Tori does few things half-heartedly and neither does JD Glass." — SX Meagher, author of *Arbor Vitae*, *All That Matters*, and the *I Left My Heart In San Francisco* series.

By the Author

Punk Like Me

Punk and Zen

RED LIGHT

by
JD Glass

2007

RED LIGHT

ISBN 1-933110-81-3
ISBN 978-1-933110-81-3

THIS TRADE PAPERBACK ORIGINAL IS PUBLISHED BY
BOLD STROKES BOOKS, INC.,
NEW YORK, USA

FIRST EDITION: JUNE 2007.

CREDITS
EDITORS: SHELLEY THRASHER AND STACIA SEAMAN
PRODUCTION DESIGN: STACIA SEAMAN
COVER DESIGN BY SHERI (GRAPHICARTIST2020@HOTMAIL.COM)

Acknowledgments

Beta readers: Lieutenant Christine Mazzola, EMT-P FDNY (medical control); Dr. Cait Cody, MD; Eva; Paula Tighe, Esquire; Ruth Sternglantz. You guys rock—and thanks for being with me every step of the way.

Thanks always to Willie Wright, EMT-P FDNY; Joanne Wright, EMT EDT; Linda Doering, EMT, Physical Therapist, Masters; Kathy Finkelstein, EMT RN; Dr. Pamela Carlton, PhD, EMT-P: for teaching so many to save even more.

Thank you, Cate Culpepper, for incalculably valuable advice.

Thanks always to Radclyffe, Shelley Thrasher, and Stacia Seaman for patience, for guidance, for support and confidence.

Dedication

To my sisters and brothers who ride the rig and answer the call, every time: **"We be of one blood, thou and I."** (Rudyard Kipling, *The Jungle Book*)

"I solemnly pledge to consecrate my life
to the service of humanity;
I will give to my teachers the respect
and gratitude that is their due;
I will practice my profession
with conscience and dignity;
The health of my patient will be
my first consideration;
I will respect the secrets that are confided in me,
even after the patient has died;
I will maintain by all the means in my power,
the honour and the noble traditions of the medical profession;
My colleagues will be my sisters and brothers;
I will not permit considerations of age, disease or disability,
creed, ethnic origin, gender, nationality, political affiliation,
race, sexual orientation, social standing or any other factor
to intervene between my duty and my patient;
I will maintain the utmost respect for human life;
I will not use my medical knowledge to violate human rights
and civil liberties,
even under threat;
I make these promises solemnly, freely and upon my honour."
Declaration of Geneva 2006

Shane, *te adoro*.

"I am only one, but still I am one. I cannot do everything, but still I can do something. And because I cannot do everything I will not refuse to do the something that I can do."

Helen Keller

I Don't Need a Hero

I don't drive around in a fancy car, though the rig I'm in cost a couple of good pennies. I don't carry a gun, because my weapon of choice in this battlefield is what I carry in my brain and what my hands can remember to do between the spurts of adrenaline that are causing microtears in my blood vessels. I've got an O_2 cylinder and a valve, some funky plastic parts, and a mattress on wheels.

I don't have any super powers. I've run into fires and back out again, looked down the barrel of more than one gun, had knives in my face and bullets over my head, panicked, checked and double-checked to make sure I haven't been stuck with a syringe that's fallen out of a pocket during a call.

I'm no fuckin' superhero—it's just my job, and I'm glad to do it, because I'm paying my dues, penance, like everyone else here.

Been calm while picking brains off a windshield and went for a long walk in the freezing wind to get the why out of my head. Held the hand of a little girl whose mom sold her for crack—and her mom laughed at her tears. Comforted the dying. Brought the dead back to life twice, and helped witness it start out wet and bloody—but I'm not the only one.

I'm part of a caste, born of Vietnam vets who wanted to do something good for the world when they got back, paramedical and paramilitary. Funny, they say the street is a never-ending war—and it took men and women who'd fought one in a jungle to figure that out.

We hear what people say: EMT, "Empty Mental Troll," "Extra Man on Truck," and maybe, just maybe, a few, but not the ones that belong, might fit those descriptions. We joke amongst ourselves: "Every Menial Task," "Eggcrate Mattress Technician," and even, for the lucky few, "Earn Money Sleeping."

We joke because we have to, because we live by a creed. We are bound beyond the Geneva Oath to protect, to heal, to serve; and we are sworn, sworn to each other, sworn to our city and to our people; and even if we don't get the respect that others who are similarly sworn get, we do just that. Heal. Help. Protect.

We serve the one true religion, follow the one true call: to save life, any life, every life, every time.

Yeah, and if you're one of us reading this, you know who you are, who we are: part of the brotherhood, the Brotherhood of Blood. *We be of one blood, Thou and I.*

If you're not? Don't worry. I'm around the block, just come back from someone's first day, worst day, or last day, and I'm having a butt while I sit in my rig, waiting for your call. Don't think you will? Most don't think so either, but…everyone does sooner or later; even we have to, whether we want to or not. No one ever wants to.

They say the members of the police department are New York's finest, and the fire department are the bravest. Know what they call the emergency medical services?

New York City's best.

AIRWAY

Will the airway stay open on its own? Does anything endanger it?

"God damn, I'm hungry and I am *never* going to remember all of this shit!" Roy groaned as we sat together in the students' lounge during a meal break.

"Chill, man. We got through Orson's class, we'll get through this, c'mon. Do it again: trace the path of a drop of blood from a toe and back," I urged him, his anxiety reflecting mine. I just hid it for the moment because we had to know this, inside out and backward, and I couldn't focus if I let him freak out. The only thing that betrayed my nerves was my hand running through the thick brown hair that I kept just shy of shoulder length—a family trait, both the hair and the gesture.

"Yeah, and she says men are evolutionarily inferior because of that whole excretion/reproduction thing," he reminded me, a worried frown creasing his almost coal-colored forehead.

"Dude." I laughed, because it was true, she had said that, and so had Baumel and Finkelstein and even the lab assistant in our first year. "I don't think she meant your brain."

"Don't be so sure about that, Scotty," he shot back, using my nickname instead of calling me Tori like he usually did.

"Okay, from the top, uh, toe." He grinned and closed his eyes to concentrate. "From the capillaries to the venules, to the veins, dumping into the inferior vena cava…" He went through the drill and got it right.

My turn was all about flow in the heart itself, from right atrium through to the tri-flapped valve, down to ventricle, up through pulmonary valve…yeah, the works. From there, we reviewed the tricky part of the basics: the pulmonary artery is the only one with deoxygenated blood (artery—away!), while the pulmonary vein is the only one that carries oxygenated blood (from the Latin—*veni*, "come, return").

There was more, and I was just pulling out another text with a diagram when Kerry announced her arrival by straddling my legs and swooping down for a kiss that was all fuck.

"Hey, baby," I murmured when she let me up for air.

"You hard?" she asked softly into my ear, her dark blond hair brushing against my lips.

"Mm-hmm," I answered, "and I've got an exam to study for."

Her light green eyes looked into mine. "Smile, baby," she said, smoothing my forehead with her fingertips, "you're scaring Roy."

Had I sat up straight, I could have peered over her head because, at just over five foot, Kerry was charmingly petite to my 5'9", somewhat lanky frame, but that would have forced me to change positions—and I was enjoying this too much. Instead, I put the smile she requested on my face and peered around her arm to see Roy for myself. He was studiously ignoring us by reading my notes.

"Are we scaring you, Roy?" I asked.

"Hey, Kerry," he said, glancing up for a moment, only to frown back down at my handwriting.

"Hiya, Roy," Kerry answered, still gazing at me.

"Not happy to see me?" she drawled, pressing her hips down and onto my crotch.

God, I couldn't do this now. I might have unintentionally said that last part out loud.

She was my girlfriend, after all, and normally I was happy to see her, except she just didn't seem to take this whole thing seriously. My class simply didn't mean to her what it did to me and Roy: a ticket out—out of student loans and scraping by on a dumb job at the supermarket while trying to maintain a decent GPA at our local City University, the College of Staten Island, otherwise known as CSI. Because it was local, some called it the College of Stupid Idiots, but it was what we could afford, tuition and commute-wise.

Roy worked at a 7-Eleven making the same close-to-minimum wage that I did at the local supermarket I'd worked at since I was in high school, even though I'd graduated three years ago. At least I'd finally been promoted to head cashier.

Now, at the beginning of our junior year, the pressure was on and coming down hard. Roy had a girlfriend and a brand-new baby girl just two months old, and while I didn't have the baby, I had the babe who needed to know I could take care of her; and I did, every way I could, since we'd moved in together about two months before. Not that we did too bad. I mean, Kerry was a bonds analyst for a major firm, but I wanted to do my part and do it right.

Still and all, though, there was that degree and its accompanying loans and debts—and the accompanying future Roy and I both wanted after the degree. I couldn't see a way to afford it. My student loans only went so far, and between the apartment and the money I sent my mom every week to help with my sister's schooling, I didn't know what I was going to do—I'd already maxed out on everything.

One of our professors had turned us on to this possibility: even on a per-diem basis, EMTs—emergency medical technicians—could get paid pretty well once they got seniority, and our instructors had told us that paramedics made even more. Plus, that training was two years of medical school crammed into thirteen months, which appealed to me. I could skip a whole year of medical school, take the MCAT before finishing undergrad—and go into the classroom with some real-world experience too.

But the only way to get on that train was to ride the bus, as our instructors affectionately (and sometimes not so affectionately) called the ambulance, as an emergency medical technician, BLS: basic life support.

That license was an express ticket to the end of the line, and tonight? We got that ticket punched—by earning our CPR cards.

As important as all of that was, Kerry was living and warm, her cunt separated from me by two layers of denim. I couldn't deny the body, and I slid down slightly in my seat so Kerry could ride me just that much better—better for both of us, and worse, because I really needed to know this stuff, and in another minute I was going to excuse us and take her by the hand to my car so I could—

"Okay, again: the four valves are…?" Roy asked, bringing my attention back to the matter at hand, the most important matter in the world. My cunt didn't agree, but again, it was rare that big head and little head were on the same wavelength, at least not when Kerry was around. That was something I still had to get used to.

JD GLASS

"The tricuspid, between the right atrium and right ventricle; the pulmonary, between the right ventricle and the pulmonary—" I began to recite from memory, but Kerry interrupted.

"Give it a rest, Tori. Roy, come take a drive and let's go grab some pizza—you've got another hour before class starts again."

I glanced around Kerry over at Roy—he had just complained a few minutes earlier about being hungry.

"Roy," I asked, "can you study when you're hungry? Wanna go grab a bite?"

He sighed and shut the books in front of him, shoving them against the pile on the center of the table.

"Can't study when I'm hungry, can't study when I'm"—his eyes rested on Kerry for a moment as she slid ever so slightly against me, and he grinned—"really hungry."

"Okay, let's go eat, then," I said, clapping my hands around Kerry's waist not only to hold her, but also to still her motion a bit—she was getting me to the point where I was going to cry if I didn't come soon. Maybe not cry, exactly—but I'd definitely get ornery, and Roy and I had a practical lecture after our exam. I wasn't looking forward to bandaging my fellow classmates while I fought down a raging hard-on.

"We can take my car," Kerry offered as I smiled at her. She ran her fingers through my hair—it was starting to get a bit long, I thought. I'd have to take care of that soon.

"No need, baby, we're just going to the caf," I said.

Kerry got that look in her eye, the one that meant she disagreed.

"We really do need to study—and we can't be late for the exam."

Kerry gave one final hard push against me, her way of making sure I wasn't late coming home, either, then stood.

"Yeah," Roy agreed as we collected our various books and papers from the table, including our all-important Brady books, the bible of emergency medicine, and tucked them carefully into our bags. "This is really important, Kerr."

"It's all right, guys. You just take it so seriously."

I stopped, my hands on the clasp of my bag, and straightened to stare at her, surprised. "Kerry, it *is* serious—people are going to put their lives in our hands."

She smirked. "Not tonight, they're not."

I shook my head. I didn't know if she thought her eight, almost nine years over me gave her an insight I didn't have or if she wasn't interested, but either way, she just didn't get it.

❖

We ate, we studied, then studied some more, and thankfully, the written and practical parts of the exam went well. Two hours later Roy and I had our shiny new cards to slip into our wallets, and we spent the following practical lecture learning how to say "it feels snug" whenever a triangle bandage was applied correctly.

From here on in, Bob, the head instructor, who was not only the founder of this particular EMT school but one of the founders of emergency medical services in the country, reminded us that we would each need to carry to every class an O_2 wrench or key (to open the oxygen tanks), medic shears (which were very cool because they could cut right through a penny), and our pocket masks (which would provide a layer of protection between the rescuer and the patient), as well as our stethoscopes.

Even though we used military time for everything, we also had to wear a sweep-hand watch so we could count respirations and pulses against the movement of the little wand, and I wore a Timex on my left wrist so I wouldn't beat up my favorite Mickey Mouse one my grandmother had given me years ago.

With all the equipment we had to start carrying, I was eyeing the utility belts that some of the instructors wore. I needed to get one soon, I thought; well, that and a decent stethoscope. Toys, I mused to myself, it really was all about the toys.

One of our toughest instructors, Kathy, who knew her shit down cold, had a Sprague Rappaport, a stethoscope I really liked. Instead of a single tube to transmit sound, it had two, plus it had two listening heads that she could switch over for pediatrics or to discern tones differently. When Kathy had let us try hers to listen for lung sounds and blood pressures, well, I was impressed with how much more I could hear with that than with my single-tube, single-head one. Sprague. Sprague Rappaport. That's what I wanted, especially after Kathy showed us all its different pieces and parts: bells and diaphragms and earbits. It was like a customizable hot rod for your ears. Maybe I'd eventually get one, in blue or something, but black would be fine, since it was really all about the improved function.

"Never ever *ever*," Bob insisted, his tone grabbing my attention from my equipment daydreams, and I watched as he pointed in the air for emphasis, "let rescuer number one become victim number two—not by accident, not by inhalation, and not by contagion. Gloves on, masks ready to go, and eyes open, people!"

At the end of the session I said good night to Roy, Bennie, and various other classmates, slung my bag over my shoulder, and walked out to my car.

Kerry sat on the hood of my '79 Grand Prix, black with a black ragtop, waiting for me. "Hey, lover!" She smiled at me as she slid to the ground.

"Hey, yourself." I grinned back, happy that she'd come to meet me earlier, that she'd waited for me until my class was over. I wrapped my arms around her. "You know…I don't have class tomorrow night," I told her, then kissed her.

"So," Kerry asked when we broke for air, "what are you planning— a threesome with that hot instructor of yours?" She ran her fingertips up and down my neck, a smirk playing across her mouth.

"I didn't know you were so into Bob," I joked back. "No, it's a surprise."

I cupped her face in my hands so I could see her wink back at me, her eyes as mysterious as a cat's in the lamplight. "I know how much you like my surprises."

Kerry reached under my jacket and ran her palms over my breasts, making tiny circles that made my nipples harden and my clit twitch.

I grabbed her ass and pulled her closer, massaging firmly because I knew she liked that, because it would shift and spread her pussy lips, force her clit to rub against whatever she was wearing. She wouldn't be wearing it much longer; I knew that for certain.

"Naked. Home. Now?" Kerry requested, a heated murmur against the skin of my throat.

Oh, God, yeah, I thought, definitely—we just had to get there first.

"I'll race you there," I almost stuttered as we separated.

Kerry gave me a knowing glance as she pulled away and sauntered over to her car parked several feet away from mine. The sway of her hips was meant as a preview, and I certainly appreciated it.

"I'll be waiting for you," she called as I slid into my seat. I hit the button and let the window roll down as she started her engine.

"You better!" I called back.

I broke no traffic laws on the ride home and slid into my parking spot, anticipating the one that waited for me once I got inside. After grabbing my books and bag off the seat next to me, I made sure the car was locked and hustled to the door, then up the stairs. I wasn't disappointed when I got inside—this was a race we both won.

❖

"That was fucking *nice*," Kerry sighed as she stretched languidly next to me, then curled up against my side.

"It really was." I kissed the crown of her head while she trailed her fingertips up and down my chest. She kissed my sternum, then stared into my eyes with an amused smile.

"What?" I asked, smiling back.

She stroked the fine hairs that had fallen back over my brow—my hair really was getting way too long.

"Nothing," she said, and kissed my chin, "I just love how your eyes shade—you get this dark green ring around the brown after you come."

"Really?" I thought the only time they did that was when I drank or when I cried, neither of which I indulged in too often, though I was finally legally old enough for the one and not terribly fond of the other.

"Really," she answered in a tone that meant there'd be no further discussion. She pressed her cunt against my stomach firmly, sending fire into my groin. Letting her tongue tangle with mine, I wrapped my arms around her and gently turned us over.

I nibbled on her neck, working toward that soft spot under her ear. "Ready for round two?" She'd already wrapped her legs around my waist.

Kerry reached over my ass and slid into me. "As ready as you are, babe, as ready as you are..." She sighed as she fingered my willing cunt. I was more than happy to return the favor.

❖

Even though I'd been scheduled for only a half shift, the day dragged, and I raced home to get ready for everything that I had planned for later. Kerry came home from work just as I was drying my hair, but we didn't have much time, and I told her so as I kissed her hello briefly, then rushed her to get ready.

"So…what's the big surprise tonight?" Kerry asked as she walked out of the shower. All I'd told her was that tonight was formal, formally funky: dress to impress—everyone.

I handed her a towel and checked my watch, my good one.

"Hurry, Kerry," I urged with a smile as she took the towel from my hands, "the car will be here in forty-five minutes."

"I like this on you—a lot," she murmured, and licked her teeth. She played with the collar of my jacket, a slightly fitted, oxblood red leather that hung about four inches down my thighs over a black turtleneck and black leather pants. I liked it too.

"Thank you." I grinned a bit self-consciously. I didn't want to let her get too close—we had to leave.

Kerry understood and slipped past me to the bedroom to finish dressing while I waited in the hallway. I was nervous—she didn't know it, but she'd meet my whole family tonight—and I had planned another surprise to take the edge off. Besides, Kerry really did like my surprises, usually. I just hoped tonight followed the typical pattern.

While I waited for her I thought about the impending meeting. I'd lived with my mother and sister until I'd moved in with Kerry. It had been one thing with the other girls I'd dated, casually or otherwise, but…Kerry was a little different. Honestly, I'd gotten tired of fucking in my car or at her place, and no way would I take her back home, that was simply too…I just couldn't do it anymore, and it wasn't because I had issues at home. My mom really didn't care about my being gay, and neither did my younger sister, Elena.

The only thing my mom had ever said to either of us about sex was that waiting until marriage was stupid and just don't "get pregnant," while her only comment about my being gay was that it gave her one less thing to worry about, one less potential disgrace for the family—I wouldn't bring home a bastard.

Otherwise, my mom didn't care about anything. When I was tiny we'd moved to South America, and there, she and my father had split. She brought us back here when I was seven or eight.

And then? My mom just…broke like a fucking porcelain doll—arms and legs in place, head shattered, only she said it was her heart. I'd always thought it was because my father had remarried and wanted nothing to do with his "old family." Fuckhead.

We had moved into her sister's, my aunt Carolina's, home, where she and her husband had created an apartment out of the basement for us so we could have our own family unity.

It was a beautiful place. They'd constructed stairs so we could have our own entrance, enlarged the windows so we'd have plenty of light, and really, we treated the rest of the house as if it was ours too. In fact, my aunt gave us girls our cousin's old bedroom—but it wasn't ours, not really, as my mom reminded me and Elena every day.

"This is not your home, girls," she'd cry from the sofa as tears streamed down her cheeks, "this is not your station in life." She'd sob, then sob some more about how one day someone would lift the curse they'd placed on her life.

And despite the light and the room and the unconditional and unquestioning love that my aunt and uncle and cousins gave us, all my mom did was lie on the sofa all day with the shades drawn. Some days she didn't bother to dress at all because she had headaches, her chest hurt, she had "too many troubles."

Oh, she had her moments, great ones, like when Elena broke her ankle playing in the schoolyard and my mother not only made sure Elena was well taken care of, but also somehow managed to convince the board to replace the old steel climbers with newer, safer construction and to lay rubber tiles on the tarmac. And the time a teacher unjustly gave me a detention and then lied to my mother, who pulled me out of school until he was removed from teaching.

She even belonged to some international legal association that asked her to come and speak from time to time, and on those days my mother shone. But really, all she wanted was to be brought back to her "place in life," her proper station, back to the respect she'd had as a prosecuting attorney, then later as a judge, and the inheritance that waited for the family back in South America.

She *hated* that I was becoming an emergency medical technician. Why couldn't I be more like my cousin who had gotten scholarships everywhere? Why couldn't I just go straight to medical school? My cousin could have if she had wanted to, or so my mom had told me more times than I could count, but instead, she'd started a very successful record label. At least, my mom said, my cousin knew her place in life, what she should be.

I sighed and shook my head. If I didn't work, who'd support my mom and my sister? And yeah, my grades were decent enough, but not enough for a scholarship—how could I get a scholarship if I didn't have time to study because I had to work? I *was* trying, that was for sure…

Fuck that for now, though, I thought as I checked myself in the hall mirror one last time. Everyone, the whole family, would be there tonight, and for at least one night, my mom would feel okay. She was great at these social occasions, situations where she felt she was again in "her place," the guest of honor. I suppose it reminded her of who she'd been in South America—known to the politicians, feared by drug cartels, and loved by the poor and the underclass.

❖

The car was waiting for us when we came out of the apartment building—nothing ostentatious, but definitely a nice black sedan with a uniformed woman holding a sign that said "Tori" in green block letters.

"She's hot," Kerry told me with a grin as we got in for the ride.

"Is she? I didn't notice."

"Really?" Kerry drawled with apparent disbelief. "What did you notice, then?"

"You," I told her, and kissed away the pout on those pretty lips, "and your little black velvet skirt, the cadet-gray jacket nice and snug over your…" and I let my hands show her what I meant.

Kerry sighed as she kissed me back. "So where *are* we going?" she asked, her fingers tracing down my neck. "Is it that very, very special that you can't tell me now?" She edged even closer and I gently took her hands in mine before they traveled anywhere else.

"You'll never get it out of me," I teased her back, still careful to avoid her hands when she tried to tickle me again as we sprawled across that luxurious backseat.

"Is this that Angel tour concert? The breast cancer fund-raiser with all those artists?" she asked excitedly, and rattled off the list as we pulled in front of a multilevel nightclub, Nox, that had private parking below it on Manhattan's East Fifty-seventh.

"Yeah, that's the one." I grinned at her. "Cool, right?"

Kerry seemed to be lost in thought. "Yeah...that is really cool," she answered almost absentmindedly before she gave me a dazzling smile. "How did you manage to score tickets for this?"

"My cousin's performing tonight." I was rather pleased with myself as the driver opened the door for us.

"Aha!" Kerry said, her eyes evaluating me. "And can I ask who that is?"

"Well," I drawled, "that would be part two of tonight's surprise."

She raised her eyebrows at me.

"We're invited to the after-party—I'll introduce you then." I grinned as we walked over to the door. I knew how popular my cousin and her band were. This *was* going to be cool.

As I cupped Kerry's face, I didn't know if I really loved her or not, but I knew I cared about her and really did love the way she looked at me like she did at that moment, with a mixture of amusement and affection.

She laughed and took my hand as I felt in my pocket for our passes. I gave them to Kerry, who promptly draped one around her neck, then did the same for me. "Let's show these people how to dance."

I agreed as the bouncer glanced at our passes and waved us in, past the waiting crowd and into the club.

It was a great show—four bands, then my cousin with a rockin' DJ in between sets, and honestly, my cousin was phenomenal. I'd attended her performances before when she was in town, but never in such an intimate setting—she rarely played anything smaller than a concert hall—and it was great to watch the way she interacted with the crowd, she and her wife, her partner, who played bass behind her.

When she saw me from the stage she waved and said, "Hey, Tori!" into the microphone.

I waved back and beamed at her—she was just way too cool.

Kerry tugged on my sleeve lightly. "You know her?" she asked in my ear, then stared back at the stage.

"Know her?" I answered in Kerry's ear as the people cheering around us made it almost impossible to speak. "Nina Boyd's my cousin."

Kerry faced me again, plainly shocked, and I smiled even bigger.

"That," she said, and pointed, "that's your cousin?"

"Yeah," I answered, still beaming, "can't you tell?"

She stared again at where Nina waved to the crowd with a smile, my smile. She tossed her head and her hair, same texture as mine only longer, a bit redder, settled around her shoulders as she laughingly agreed to "one more!"

Kerry scrutinized me again. "Yeah...I can," she said finally, "that's so...so...wow." She shook her head. "Any other surprises?" She grinned crookedly before returning her attention to the stage.

"Just one..." I whispered into her neck as I wrapped my arms around her. Kerry pressed her hips back against me.

"Oh..." she said, and wiggled harder. My groin jerked into her, an automatic response whenever she was that close to my cock, and she turned in my arms. "Is that for me?" A smile played at the edge of her lips, and her eyes simmered as they hooked onto mine and she rubbed suggestively against me.

I caught my lip between my teeth and let my breath hiss out. "Do you want to wait for it or do you want it now?" I asked her. I'd learned in the last few months that Kerry liked to live dangerously. I'd also learned I liked to help and, in fact, I enjoyed it.

"How about both?" she teased, kissing my neck, pressing her body even harder against mine.

The place was jammed with people. No one would notice if we left, and maybe we'd make it back for the after-party—maybe not.

"Let's go." I knew how to get down to the garage, as well as every quiet hallway along the way.

"I like the way you think," Kerry said as I took her by the hand.

We eased through the press of the crowd and out a side door to the hallway that led to the stairs—and the garage. As the door slammed behind us, Kerry shoved me up against the wall and began to jerk me off.

I bit her neck none too gently as I cupped her breasts under her jacket, then tugged on the hardened points beneath my fingers.

Fuck it. No one came down this hallway, and if they did, well, I didn't care.

"Now," I breathed harshly into her ear, "I'm gonna fuck you now."

"You better," she agreed as I pulled that tiny bit of her satin thong out of the way, letting my fingers glide along that thick, wet fold. "Fucking hot," I groaned, because the slip of my fingers along her waiting cunt, the feel of her clit so hard under my hand, fired my clit to bursting.

Her fingers slipped nimbly along my fly to release my cock, and she gripped it firmly, pumping me.

"You wanna play or you wanna fuck?" she asked, her eyes glinting as she reached around my neck to bite my lip.

I widened my stance so my groin would be level with hers.

She bit me again and her body lurched into me when I dipped into her slightly, so I could feel the tightening of her cunt around me, that slick tight feeling, the smooth entry that wanted me. When I took my fingers away I held them to her lips, and her tongue played around my fingertips as we both tasted her cunt. With my free hand I gripped the head of my cock and teased it between her lips, rubbing up and down, spreading that slickness, and as her hips started to rock, I let her clit ride my head.

"C'mon, baby…please," she asked, a throaty moan that made my stomach clench.

My dick was now against her opening, just the very tip inside her, and I pushed lightly, maintaining pressure without really entering. But that's not how I wanted to fuck her, and I knew for a fact she'd like what I had in mind even better.

"Turn around," I growled into her ear as I eased my hips away.

Kerry's breath caught a moment, and she grabbed my dick roughly before she did as I asked.

I slipped an arm around her waist, bent my legs, and eased up under her, and together we guided my dick into her waiting cunt.

"Oh, yeah…" one of us sighed as I filled her.

"That's…nice…" I huffed out as I felt myself sink into her.

The sounds of the band on the other side of the wall made it seem that "one more" from Nina had turned into "okay, another," which meant that we had some time, but not a lot.

When Kerry craned her head around, I leaned over to kiss her as I slid slowly in and out a few times and reached for her clit.

Over the course of the last few years since I'd really started dating, I'd come to know that there are women who like their clits stroked. Others like to be jerked off, and still others love that constant caressing pressure that rubs the hood along the shaft.

But when Kerry had my cock stretching her pussy from behind

with a deep, fast thrust, she liked the shaft of her clit stroked from below so the exposed head could fuck my fingers.

"That is so fucking good…you fuck me so right…so…fucking… right…" she moaned as my hips forced her against the wall and she grabbed my arms, pushing herself back into my chest.

My clit throbbed behind my dick as I fucked her, an exquisite, painful pleasure, and torn between needing more and giving more, I pressed harder on her clit, which swelled as it grazed my skin.

"Come, baby," I crooned into her ear, my eyes half closed as I felt the burn intensify, narrowing its focus from my groin to just my clit, "come with your pussy wrapped around my cock."

She gasped and ground down on me, and I knew that the combination of the fuck and the words was bringing her to the edge.

"So close," she groaned as she released my arm to reach for my shoulder, "so fucking close!"

Her fingers dug into the muscle as her body waved, then arched, rigid against me. The cry she wanted to let go strangled in her throat, and I tightened my grip around her waist so she wouldn't fall as she released my shoulder.

"God, Tori," she breathed heavily, her head leaning on my collarbone.

I kissed her neck as I carefully withdrew from her so-hot cunt and slipped my dick back into my pants. "You okay?" I nuzzled the soft skin of her neck. Her fine blond hairs tickled against my cheeks, as soft as rabbit fur, and I adjusted her skirt.

"Wonderful, baby, just wonderful," she answered. She threw her arms around my neck and kissed me with that sexy just-been-fucked languor.

"You didn't come yet, did you?" she observed softly, stroking my face with her fingertips and grinding my cock between us.

"Kerry…" I groaned in a low voice, spitting the words out between clenched teeth, "we…have to go…to the party." God, I was so hard.

But we really did have to go, and I caught her hand to stop her because the sounds beyond the door indicated that not only was the show over, but at least a few people would come out the door we were next to.

Kerry grinned, still firmly gripping me. "Well, stud," she asked, "know where there's a bathroom where we can freshen up?"

Breathing under control, heart beating madly, and cunt so fucking swollen it was painful, I somehow managed to nod.

"Yeah...this way."

"Good," Kerry answered, and flashed me the smile of hers I loved the most, a wicked gleam of teeth, "let's go."

We walked down the hallway to the promised bathroom: two stalls on one side, two sinks on the other, and black tile everywhere.

As soon as the door closed behind us, Kerry pounced, pushing me over to the far wall. "There's no way," she said, her voice throaty and harsh as she breathed into the tender skin under my jaw, "I'm letting you walk into any party with *my* hard-on," she finished as her hands worked quickly and once again released my cock.

"Nah, Kerry, it's all right, let's just—oh..."

Her fingers slipped under the leather strap and were barely inside my needing cunt as she knelt before me and took my dick in her mouth.

The sight of her blond head, hair hanging down so it obscured her face, sliding along the cock that had just been inside her did strange things to me as her fingers filled me and fucked me firmly.

I wanted to stop her so I could throw her on the floor and fuck her until we both couldn't take it anymore; I wanted to grab her and fuck her face hard.

But I did neither, and my fingers twitched as I touched the crown of her head and simply leaned back, the black tile cooling my head.

All I could do was groan and slip my fingers through the fine, light strands of hair as Kerry took the harness from me and replaced the pressure from my dick with the heat of her lips. My hips surged forward, and I let her swallow me as my cunt welcomed the third finger she slid into me.

"That's...that's fucking...yeah," was all I could manage, and Kerry's eyes flashed at me for a second before I gave it up and let the screaming need take over.

My eyes were half closed and my head still against the tile as Kerry fucked my cunt and I fucked her face, when the bathroom door opened silently and a dark head popped around it.

I looked across the floor into deep blue eyes that caught mine before they dropped to Kerry's head, then quickly returned to my face.

It was my cousin's wife, Samantha, and she grinned. "I'll see you at the party," she mouthed at me, then silently closed the door.

"Yeah..." I choked out, but whether I was responding to the question or to the expert head Kerry was giving me I didn't know and I didn't care because, oh yeah, she had my clit so tight between her lips, and fucking God, she had my cunt filled so good and...I was...I was gonna come, I was gonna fucking come, and I told Kerry so, cunt tight around her fingers, clit hard between her lips.

Kerry reached for my hand and I squeezed it as the end of the ride approached, but fuck it, no, fuck me...yeah, that's...there...*yes*.

I released her hand, and if Kerry hadn't wrapped an arm around my hips I might have fallen.

"Nice..." I sighed as I rode the last bit of come out.

Kerry kissed my clit one last time before she stood, and I steeled myself against the sensation of her fingers emptying my cunt.

"Just nice?" she asked coyly, her eyes glittering up at me.

"No," I bent and whispered into her ear before I kissed her lips, so soft and full after she'd gone down on me, "it was *fucking* nice."

❖

We made out a little more because we could, because we wanted to, and I'd always enjoyed the way Kerry kissed. It was an art form, and some days I was convinced it was half the reason we lived together.

Well, that and my strange family situation. Oh, shit—the party! And now, since we'd definitely been spotted, we'd definitely be expected.

Had anyone else seen us, a stranger, some other non-family member, I might have tried to skip the gathering. As relaxed as I was feeling, just thinking about my mother and what kind of mood she might be in was enough to cause the skin on the back of my neck to tighten.

But Samantha knew I was still around, which meant Nina knew by now, and while she would have understood if I didn't show, well, that was precisely the reason I had to. I totally admired my cousin. She'd always done her best to take care of me; she'd always told me I was her favorite little sister. I couldn't disappoint her.

"Kerry," I asked quietly against her lips—it really was a shame to stop kissing them, "do you want to go to the party?"

"After that, stud?" She kissed my chin. "I think we're ready for anything."

While we walked to the sink I glanced around. She had taken my rig off, after all. "Kerr, where—"

"In my bag," she answered with a grin.

Oh. I'd always wondered what she kept in that heavy bag. Now I knew at least one thing. Maybe one day I'd actually ask her about the rest.

Refreshed and renewed, I led us down the hallway and through a side corridor to the elevator that would take us up to the main floor—and the party.

I hadn't been to the club in a long time, probably since the semester and my EMT class had started, and when the guards nodded to us as we got off the elevator, I didn't recognize the place.

Nox was huge, an old warehouse that had been painstakingly converted to a multilevel club. Between the ambient music, the huge screens that appeared two stories tall that played various nature, space, and sky images, and the costumed workers with their angel-wing harnesses who walked so carefully around and through the swirl of people, this party was in full swing.

Someone came up, asked to examine our passes, and led us to a table—it was empty—but I knew where everyone would be: center floor and either talking, dancing, or both.

I searched the faces in the crowd. There…there they were, exactly where I thought they'd be.

Kerry set her bag down and took my hand.

"Ready?" I asked, and we moved toward the knot of people that were my direct genetic relations.

One thing, I mused as we approached, when the Del Castillos—the maiden name my mother and aunt shared—got together, we certainly were a pretty bunch. There stood my mom, dressed in an elegant deep sapphire blue gown that shimmered, and though her hair was streaked with silver, she wore it regally, pulled back in a chignon. I laughed at myself when I recognized that hairstyle and wondered if admitting that I knew its name would ruin my lesbian street cred. My mother held a glass of red wine as she laughed in conversation with my aunt Carolina, who wore a similarly cut gown in emerald green.

Next to her was my sister Elena, who chatted with cousin Nico, his hair similar in color to both his sisters' and swept back off his forehead. It curled slightly above the shoulders of his sharply cut black leather blazer as he grinned back at Elena.

I continued to look around. There—there was Samantha, shoulder-length brown hair with a shining honey glow that melted over the same formfitting black she'd worn on stage. The only other hint of color was the blue of her eyes and the silver wink of a charm—a miniature sword, a gift from Nina, if I remembered correctly—that hung around her neck. Next to her, back to me and recognizable only by her stance and the copper-touched sheen of the hair that flowed down her back, almost to her waist, stood my cousin.

Samantha glanced over and saw me, then nudged Nina, who turned.

"Tori!" Nina called, her voice delighted even above the din of the crowd as she waved me over.

I tucked Kerry's hand into my arm and let a genuine smile break across my face. Nina was the only other gay person in our family—and she was out and proud. I was looking forward to introducing her to Kerry, not just because I thought Kerry might enjoy meeting someone well known, but also because Kerry was more than just another girlfriend—she was the woman I lived with, was building an actual home, a life, a future with, and I admit, I was proud of us.

"I'm glad you made it," Nina enthused, and wrapped me up in a hug. Despite the width of her shoulders, she felt delicate somehow, like fine filigree steel, and as we ended the hug and parted so we could really see each other, I studied Nina quickly but carefully.

It wasn't simply that I was slightly taller than she was, either. To my eyes, hers were a touch more intense, the blue darker, the gray that surrounded them lighter, and she was pale or, at least, paler than usual—but that wasn't it, that could have been from the performance. No, something was different, something I couldn't put my finger on, something about her face, the delicate lines more pronounced, yet softer too, I thought as I kissed her cheek.

"Happy to be here," I said into her ear. Nina took my hand.

"So, introduce me to…" and when she saw Kerry, her eyes widened. "Kerry?"

I looked from Nina to Kerry in surprise, only to see my girlfriend with the strangest expression on her face.

"Yeah." She nodded. "You look great, Nina," she said as my cousin hugged her, an embrace I noticed Kerry was at first reluctant to return, but then did with an intensity that grew as I stared, shocked at their recognition, surprised at the strength of that embrace.

Samantha gave me a quick hello squeeze and stood next to me, her hands folded before her and wearing a pleasantly bland smile. Nina put an arm around Kerry's shoulder as they faced us.

"How do you guys know each other?" I asked, eyes darting from one to the other.

Kerry glanced up at me, then smirked at Nina. "We used to fuck," she said, then gave me the same smirk, her chin jutting a challenge as she faced me.

I stared at her, stunned as I heard Nina say, "Well, I wouldn't have put it quite like that." I looked a bit longer as Samantha murmured something to Nina about having to speak to whoever.

Kerry closed the space between us and put her hands on my chest. "Don't worry about it, tough guy," she smiled up at me as she played with the collar of my jacket, "it's way ancient history."

"Uh, okay," I answered, not knowing what else to say. I mean, all right, I knew Kerry was several years older than me, but it had never even crossed my brain that she and my cousin might have known each other. But stupid, stupid me—they were not only peers, they had much more than met. Of course, Staten Island was a small place.

"Ah, now there's my eldest daughter." I heard my mother's voice ring out in that unmistakably patrician tone she had when she felt good, and I fixed a smile on my face as I headed over to her, Kerry's hand once again tucked in my arm.

"Hello, Mom," I said, and kissed her on the cheek. "Hello, *Tía*," I greeted my aunt, using the word I'd always used—*tía* or "aunt" in Spanish.

"And is this the blond beauty who has stolen my child?" my mother asked, her gaze settling on Kerry.

Kerry had never, ever accused me of being a child, or young, or anything along those lines. Trust my mother to make me feel all of those, though, I thought as I held on to that happy mask I wore on my face. "Mom, this is my girlfriend Kerry, a senior bonds analyst at Dreyfus," I said, complete with appropriate arm motions, "and Kerry, this is my Mom, Mrs.—"

Mother interrupted me to take Kerry by the hand. "But you must call me Sophia," she prompted, "unless, of course," and my mother glanced at me again, her eyes appraising, "you and my daughter marry, in which case it would then be Mom or Mother or some such variation."

I tried not to let the shock show as my mother warmly embraced my girlfriend, then spared me a quick glance, an expression that I knew well, more calculating than kind. I could feel the nausea well up and wondered what she had planned.

"I'm very happy to finally meet you," Kerry said in return, and the rest was lost to me as I got caught up first in Nico's greeting, then Elena's. My head didn't stop swimming, though, and I excused myself and headed to the nearest bar after the words "college," "foolish pride," and "Nina could do it" floated into my ears in my mother's voice.

I'd rescue Kerry from her soon enough, I thought, but first? I really needed a drink to calm my nerves.

After I got the bartender's attention and asked for a scotch on the rocks, I thought about what my mom had said and all the things she hadn't tonight, but had before or would the next time we spoke. Damn.

My mom would talk about the family legend that had been repeated to me—hell, to all of us—since before I could walk. Remind me what we all had to live up to, the example that had been set, the path to follow, the path to the castle on the black mountain, because that's who we were: Del Castillo Monte Negron, and I was to never forget it, blah blah blah. She and her sister were Del Castillo, making me Scotts-Del Castillo and my cousin Nina Boyd-Del Castillo, and when oh when would I prove worthy of that blood, because we were both from the same castle that stood rooted on the black mountain.

And just look at Nina, my mom would add, look at what she's done.

Then she'd tell me all about how my aunt and uncle had made it very hard for my cousin when they discovered she was gay. In fact, she somehow found a way to bring that up whenever she was unhappy with me, her none-too-subtle way of reminding me that she was a great mom and that I owed her more than just my existence.

I wondered if Nina knew how close a thing it had been—two years before my mom moved us back to the States, before my dad split, Nina's parents had been going to send her to live with us during the off season and to boarding school that next fall. But it didn't happen— though I had been excited at the time that my cousin would live with us and was disappointed that she hadn't. Years later my mother told me it was because she'd told my aunt she'd be happy to take Nina in—my mom didn't care if her niece, who was also her goddaughter, was gay.

I took another sip and let it burn its way down. No, it didn't really surprise me that Nina was so stubbornly successful—look at our common heritage. I just wasn't sure how deeply we shared it, if I came anywhere near living up to it like she did.

Visually checking to see my mom and Kerry in cozy conversation, I could have sworn that one of them said the word "wedding."

I quailed, but made sure I seemed happy on the outside and sat down anyway. It was rather noisy, I must have heard wrong—no way could I afford one of those for at least a few years. Maybe after I'd worked as a paramedic for a while, or better yet, when I'd finished med school; at least then I'd have a real job.

As I held up my glass to a passing waiter for another drink, Nina sat down next to me, put an arm around my shoulder, and kissed my cheek. "Missed you, Tor, where've you been lately?"

It was an old joke—because Nina was almost never home. She was always traveling—touring with the band or exploring caverns and castles on journal-worthy expeditions with Samantha.

"Well," I grinned, "you know it's junior year, right?"

Nina nodded, smiling. "Yeah, and I'd guess you're getting ready to take your exams and figure out what med school you want and all that?"

I took a deep breath. "Actually," I began on a controlled exhale, "I've decided to become an EMT, while I'm finishing school, I mean," I hastily added.

Nina showed only interest so, emboldened, I continued and explained my plans: about working, becoming a paramedic, then taking the MCAT and working when I wasn't in school. I didn't mention that I'd maxed on loans or that I had to help out my mom and sister; I didn't need to share those details.

Samantha had come to sit with us in the interim, and she questioned me about the class, the things I was learning, the instructors and who they were.

"Oh, I know Bob. He used to work with my da in the fire department," she told me, her eyes sparkling, "him and…" She named a bunch of people, and some of them were instructors of mine too. It was nice, truly nice, to talk with people who seemed to care and be interested in what I was doing rather than trying to talk me out of it.

My mother cut in. "If she had the help, she wouldn't need to become a civil servant." Her lip curled on her last words, and her censure cut at and confused me. I knew that EMTs weren't the same as doctors by any stretch of the imagination, but they did work that mattered, and wasn't that what she'd always wanted for me, for Elena? Besides, judges were civil servants too.

I so wanted to disappear under the table, but Nina squeezed my hand. I stared at the tablecloth instead.

"But, *Tía*," she said mildly back to my mom, "Tori has a good plan."

Kerry's voice cut across the resulting silence. "You could help her out, though, so she wouldn't have to do such a menial job."

"Tori's sitting right here—why don't you ask her what *she* wants?" Nina asked coolly.

Thankfully, dinner arrived and everyone was spared—my gut told me this conversation would turn ugly real fast.

Sometime during dinner, Nina whispered intensely, her eyes shading a deeper blue from the gray, "Tori, you know if I can help, I will, right? You're my favorite little sister."

❖

Though more talking and dancing followed, other artists who'd either performed or attended made some little speeches, and I chatted politely and danced with everyone I was supposed to, the fun of the evening was dead for me, and I grabbed another drink whenever I could.

I admit, I hardly remember the ride home, although I do remember that Samantha reminded me that if I was ever in a jam, to call them, either one of them.

To be honest, I don't even know how I got into the apartment, because I was pretty wasted and way tired, but that changed in moments after I stripped and got into bed and Kerry crawled between my legs to blow me again.

It was nice, very nice, but I really needed to just fuck, and besides, I wanted Kerry to get off too. I stopped her before I came and decided it was time to play. Since as far as I could remember, my regular setup was in her bag, I reached over into the night table for something else— something we could share. I wanted to feel it and I was ready enough for this; it slid into me easily before I flipped us over and plowed into my girl. It was a hot, easy glide, but after the rhythm set, all I could think was that I had nowhere near accomplished what Nina had and no way was I going to ask for help.

I'd forgotten Kerry was there until her nails bit into my ass and I not only remembered she was under me, I remembered what she had said about Nina: "We used to fuck." God. That *look* on her face as she said it. The words played over and over in my head. Dammit.

I took Kerry's hands and stretched her arms back over her head. "So tell me," I curved the arc of my hips so my cock would rub along her clit as I pounded into her, "did she fuck you good?"

Kerry's head tossed as her body arched under me, her pussy smashing into mine. I worked her cunt over as her heels dug into my lower back.

"Uh…yeah…" she growled, her fingertips clutching at my hands. "What, Tori?" Her breath was a hot gasp in my ear. She was such a hot fuck I almost forgot—but I didn't.

"Nina," I breathed as my cunt tightened around the dick we both rode, "she fuck you good?"

Kerry's legs squeezed around my waist as she tried to pull me deeper. She gripped my hands desperately and bit my neck before she spoke again.

"Not like you, Tori," she gasped, "so shut up…" Her body surged under me and I felt the answering pressure build in my cunt. "Shut up and fuck me."

I let go of her hands to grasp her shoulders and dig deep into the fuck, into her, and her nails raked along my spine.

"I'm gonna come," I groaned, gasping also as I drilled into her, a pure power fuck driven by the spasms that gripped my cunt. "Coming inside you."

"Shit, baby," Kerry huffed out, her body rocking furiously against me, "me too."

I don't know. I mean, we came together, and she was as warm and sweet as she always was after, and I enjoyed, truly enjoyed, the feel of the woman I lived with, the woman I'd just fucked and made come and who'd made me come repeatedly, held closely, skin to skin, her head on my shoulder. But even though I murmured the right words and we exchanged the ritual tender caresses, I lay awake for a long time, eyes open in the dark, as I held her and she slept peacefully.

❖

We had a practical exam as well as a written coming up soon, but I'd decided not to stress too much. I studied a lot, and besides, maybe the class was doing something to my brain; it was certainly doing something to Kerry. She'd started to go off on me about our lack of time together, especially since the party.

Things were…strange, and maybe we did need more time, so I cut a few classes here and there, or simply left early. Maybe Kerry was right; between day classes, work, and the EMT training one or two nights a week, perhaps we did need some more "together." I wanted us to work. I wanted Kerry to feel secure with me, in me.

When Bob, the head instructor, asked Roy, Bennie, me, and a few others out of our class of one hundred some-odd to attend and participate in the disaster-preparedness drill, I knew I would go, for two reasons: One of our instructors, a paramedic called Roe, hinted that Bob chose the people for the drills specifically so they could get some "real time" and meet the people they'd eventually work with— and these were the people that Bob would eventually recommend for instructor training. Also, Bob himself, the former Navy Seal who had returned from Vietnam to be one of the first to form this tribe I was trying to join, had taken me to the side.

When he'd caught up with me in the quad during a break, he'd asked in his warm, yet brusque manner, "Tori, what gives?"

"What do you mean—did I fail my last practical?" I asked, alarmed. I mean, I knew I'd skipped classes, but I really was on top of my stuff—at least I thought I was.

"Nah, your grades are fine, but where you been, kid? Problem at home or something?"

His voice held a hard sympathy I respected.

"It's under control." I nodded shortly in reply, relieved my grades were fine.

"Okay, kid," he patted my shoulder and stared out across the quad for a few seconds, "because I want you here." He caught my eyes. "If you've got a, a situation, tell me about it, okay?" He gave me a quick smile that for whatever reason made me feel good, like he was a friend.

"I'll be here," I smiled back, "and I'll be at the drill site on Saturday."

"Good," he said, "now throw an old firefighter a smoke."

We lit up and chatted about different medical and trauma scenarios, some technical details of rope rescue, and interesting calls he'd had until it was time for the second half of the lecture. With a pat on the shoulder as we walked in, he advised, "Just remember: Improvise. Adapt. Overcome. No matter what, you'll get through every situation."

After two hours learning to do exactly that—makeshift splints, creative adaptations of found materials for litters, immobilization, and recovery-rescue—came the announcement.

"I want you to bring a windshield punch and a utility knife," Bob said to our small group after class as he handed us a paper with the address of the supply store. "Pick them up before the exercise on Saturday."

I looked forward to it, was even happy about it until I pulled into my parking spot. Kerry. Dammit. I was relatively certain Kerry wasn't going to be thrilled, but she surprised me when I told her.

"I completely understand," she said.

"Really? I mean, as soon as I get back, we can go do something, you know? It's just that Bob said—"

Kerry shushed me with a kiss. "Don't worry. When is it and when will you be home?"

I kissed her, then told her all the details, and while I thought that smile might have been just the slightest bit forced, I was glad she wasn't angry.

❖

The morning dawned sunny and bright, a perfect Indian summer day, ideal for being outside and working up a sweat, and I was careful not to wake Kerry as I grabbed my belt and equipment. Bob had said we might get a chance to play rescuer too, and I didn't want to be unprepared.

The mock disaster site was in the middle of a field located behind South Beach Psych, the local mental hospital, which was itself right behind University Hospital-North, one of the largest hospitals on Staten Island. I found a parking space and tramped down the dirt track in the field. As I got closer, I saw Bob, who waved me over.

"Yo, Scotty!" he called. "Come on and get moulage!"

I waved back and hustled, wondering what in the world "moulage" was. I soon found out. Two long tables held an assortment of bandages and rubbery plastic things that on closer inspection turned out to be burns, wounds, and protruding body parts like bowels and eyeballs. Lisa, Bob's wife, sat in a chair with a paintbrush and a cup of red liquid. My classmate Bennie sat in front of her, getting made up as an accident victim.

"Oh, hey!" She smiled up at me from her chair as Lisa painted carefully along her forearm.

I closely examined the plastic parts that were glued to her skin and guessed, "Radius-ulna fracture?" judging from the two sharp sticks that jutted out at odd angles.

"Needs more drip," Lisa commented almost to herself. "Hey there, Tori." She gave me a friendly glance, then focused on her art again.

"Okay," she said, finally satisfied, "you're in car six."

Bennie obediently got up and picked a path through the high grass to the next field. "See ya later, Scotty!" She waved, her ponytail flying over her shoulder as she marched through the underbrush to her site. I watched as her pocket mask smacked against her thigh where it hung from her hip-slung belt.

"Welcome to moulage." Lisa gestured to the now-empty seat before her with a hand full of red paint. "Next victim. Tori?"

I shrugged. "So…what am I going to be?"

"Ah," Lisa drawled, and pulled a slip of paper out of an inner jacket pocket, "you…will be an unconscious, facedown, backseat immobilization case—you're gonna lie between the benches and…" she continued reading, "your special surprise will be"—and she looked up at me—"a sucking chest wound."

When she was done with the magic of moulage, I was the walking wounded, complete with facial bruises and red stains on my shirt, a screwdriver stuck to it to re-create the puncture, and a little slip of paper pinned to it that described my presenting vital signs. I walked to my site, car five.

"Okay," Jack, one of our many practical session instructors, said when I arrived, "you get in the back here and…" He explained what was supposed to happen as I squeezed into an old Ford Escort. As I slid along the threadbare carpeting and settled on my side, I was relieved there was no glass on the floor. The hump in the middle of the floor dug into my ribs, and I adjusted my gear belt so that nothing would jab me or get in the way of the immobilization techniques that our rescuers might employ.

Feet popped in the window opposite my head as my favorite study pal Roy joined me; he was a passenger who'd been thrown from the backseat over the front, head resting on the dash.

"Hi, Scotty!" he said, his voice muffled as he stuck himself in place.

"Hey, Roy! How do you feel?"

"I feel snug!" he singsonged, and we both laughed from our uncomfortable positions in the car. Although it felt like longer, in five minutes, at most, we heard voices.

"They're in here!" a male voice called. Within seconds, someone reached in over my head and cradled my skull with their fingertips to stabilize my neck while someone else smashed through the back window. On a three count they rolled my body as a single unit an inch or so forward until they could place a long backboard behind me.

A collar slipped in place around my neck, and one by one, I felt the three straps that would attach me to the board—the first around my shoulders, the next around my waist, and the third around my thighs. My head was firmly affixed to the board and my neck locked in place, then I heard the crew give another three count before they pulled me out of the car.

Now they could examine my hidden injury; one of them took my actual vitals and checked what they were supposed to be on the paper. They administered oxygen (and it smelled like the inside of a vitamin bottle), stabilized the impaling instrument in place, and quickly semi-sealed an occlusive bandage with a flap over the supposed wound. The crew carried me on the board to a reviewing station, where the lead rescuer presented his findings.

There the reviewers scrutinized every aspect of the operation, from the snugness and stability of my head and neck, as well as the security of my attachment to the board, and reiterated the proper steps—airway first, always, then breathing. A patient with no airway and no respiration—well, it doesn't matter how competently they're bandaged and packaged if they're dead.

They also asked me if the rescuers were too rough, or if any had talked to me, introduced themselves, taken a moment to explain what was going on—medical and rescue care wasn't just the physical but the emotional too, or at least, that's what they were trying to teach.

Once the review was complete, I was released from the long board, free to visit the other sites and view the other rescues, including the much-anticipated demonstration of the Jaws of Life—a hydraulic-powered sort of pliers. But instead of merely cutting things, it could either slice right through the steel of a car rooftop or spread out a crushed-in door. That thing was amazing—and we demolished three cars while we reviewed its functions. Bob even threw me and Roy and Bennie leather work gloves so we got to handle it too. It was heavy and made me feel as if my very marrow was shaking to jelly, but was it ever cool.

"Nice toy, hey, kids?" Bob said as we rotated so others could learn how to use it too.

Strange. As much as we were enjoying ourselves and kidding around about playthings as well as learning how to use them, everyone undoubtedly knew how extremely vital this piece of technology was and what a difference it could make in saving lives.

Still, even with seven different scenarios and three cars to practice on with the fire department's new equipment, we were done early, and I was happier than I thought I'd be when Bob invited me and Roy and Bennie to join his team for lunch.

In full gore, we went to Mike's Place, a Greek diner (with no Greeks—go figure) not too far away. The staff was accustomed to the sight of the mangled and the medical eating together, and I got a plate of french fries with cheese to munch on while I soaked up the atmosphere and the banter that flowed around me. Every now and again, I'd catch Roy's or Bennie's eye, and we'd exchange these how-the-hell-did-I-get-to-sit-here glances.

❖

But even with the fun and the jokes, it was finally time to go home, and I was two hours earlier than I'd expected to be. That was great, because maybe I'd be able to make the missing time up to Kerry—she'd been so understanding.

I was in a great mood by the time I rolled into my parking space. The day was ahead of me, and I had the beginnings of a plan—maybe a trip to Manhattan, wander about the Village, then grab dinner in Little Italy.

After rounding the steps two at a time, I stripped off my jacket and hung it on the hook right outside the door, then keyed the lock to the apartment. I was so excited about what we could do and the fun we'd have, I was already there in my head.

The shower was running as I hummed to myself down the hallway, and I figured I might as well wash off the moulage. "Hey, baby," I shouted over the sound of the water as I stepped into the bathroom and reached for the soap, then turned the taps.

"Oh, hey, baby," rang out lightly behind me as she stuck her head out of the shower.

Whoa—that wasn't Kerry's voice.

I snapped my head around and gaped at a woman, a soaking wet and naked brunette, whose eyes widened as she caught sight of me.

"Aaahhh!" she screamed, a bloodcurdling pitch that made me wince.

And then I realized—I was still in moulage.

"No, no, it's just makeup, see?" I assured the scared, naked woman and popped off the occlusive dressing. Wait, who the fuck was this, and why the fuck was I trying to explain anything to her?

I needed answers and I wanted them now, as I felt my mind lock into a blank state, a logical state. First thing: where was Kerry? I stepped out of the bathroom just in time to meet her as she came running down the hall, wearing nothing but a T-shirt. Correction: my T-shirt. My favorite Ramones T-shirt with the presidential seal on it.

"Oh, my God!" she screamed. "What…what did you do to her?"

"Moulage," I answered shortly, "it's just fucking makeup."

"Makeup? Fuckin' makeup?" she spluttered. "It looks like someone died."

I took a quick glance at my shirt—she was right. "Glad I dressed appropriately," I told her flatly, then ignored her as I pushed past her into the bedroom. I don't know what I was thinking, if I'd meant to grab a new shirt or what, but I heard our "guest" in the hallway.

"I think I should go." Her voice rebounded against the walls.

"I think you should go too!" I called back as I ripped through a drawer searching for a new shirt. God, I didn't know how I felt. My brain was icy, numb, a numbness that tingled through my chest and made my fingers feel cold.

"She can stay!" Kerry yelled back. "At least she has a *real* job."

That did it for me. That was so unfair, just so wrong. I stood there a moment, not knowing what to do, breathing in and out while the ice instantly transmuted into heat, creating a steam that fogged my brain.

I don't know what I'd thought I was going to do before, but I knew I couldn't stay, not like this, not with my brain bleeding the way my shirt mocked.

I stalked out of the bedroom and passed Kerry in the hallway. "Guest girl" had apparently decided that discretion was the best route and hastily closed the bathroom door as I passed. She needn't have worried—I wasn't going to bother.

I didn't say a word, not to her, not to Kerry, as I strode to the front door. I finally surveyed Kerry as I grabbed the latch, and she was indignant and proud as she stood there in my T-shirt, eyes blazing with either tears or anger.

"You know, maybe if you'd spent more time with me, had a more normal schedule, and given that damn class up," she said, and this time I actually heard the quiet venom in her tone, "I wouldn't have had to look somewhere else."

I just shook my head, shut the door, and sped down the stairs, grabbing my jacket off the post on the way.

Shit. Shit. Shit. No way would this get fixed—what the hell was I going to do, I wondered as I walked on nerveless feet to my car.

❖

I had been trying so damned hard to get somewhere, to something, make myself someone, and it just wasn't good enough. It was never enough, not for her, not for my mother, and everyone wanted so much...

I could have forgiven Kerry's displeasure with my hours because I understood that she wanted to spend more time with me. And it was okay that she was a little into money. I knew where she came from, and besides, it was no big deal to me; I knew I'd get there sometime, anyway.

But I absolutely could not forgive cheating, no way.

Memory surfaced, sharp and painful, unbidden, and unwanted, of my parents—of my mother weeping hysterically while my father told her he had been sleeping with his secretary, how she wasn't the first, how he was leaving. She had clung to him and he threw her off him like she was nothing, then slammed out the door.

She had scrambled after him, and I had watched from the window as he screamed curses at her as he ran to his car, her right behind him. He obviously hadn't cared if he hurt her when she'd reached for the door handle and he'd pulled away. He hated her. He hated us. I hated him—but I wasn't going to turn into my mother either. I wasn't going to chase anyone who didn't want me.

No. Fuck around on me once, fuck around all you want because I won't be there. That was my philosophy.

Dammit all, though. I couldn't bear to stay with her, and I couldn't deal with going to my mother's—I'd hear over and over how my foolishness got me what I deserved. I slammed my hands on the steering wheel, once, twice. I breathed heavily and tried to control the heated pulse that raced through my arms, tingling through my palms where I'd hit the steering wheel.

I drove aimlessly until I reached Father Capodanno Boulevard and South Beach, then passed the drill site from the morning, and God— that seemed such a long time ago.

Finally, I pulled into the parking lot at the beach and cut the engine. As I got out of the car, the wind wasn't cold or whipping about too much, but I knew it would get stronger and cooler when I neared the water. I flipped up the collar on my jacket as I crossed the tarmac to the boardwalk.

Following where my feet led, I finally reached the beach, then the jetty. I climbed the rocks and walked out to the end, then sat, dangling my legs off the edge, staring at the water, the Narrows Bridge to my left and Brooklyn before me.

I sat there for a long time, letting the salt spray hit my face while the gulls wheeled and kept me company, their lonely high-pitched calls soothing my brain.

Nowhere, I had nowhere to go.

The sky changed color as the sun set and the water changed with it. "If you're in a jam," Samantha's voice played in my head, "call— either one of us." She'd then programmed all of their numbers into my cell phone.

Fuck. What else could I do? I had nothing until I had my EMT license—I barely owned the college credits I'd earned, considering how long it would take to pay my student loans back. Fuck. I hoped I hadn't already screwed myself over skipping classes. I stood and stretched, then waved good-bye to the seagulls as I walked back to my car. Before I drove off, I dug my cell phone out of my pocket, called my cousin, and left a message.

I almost didn't go—as I pulled over in front of their house in the Silver Lake section of Staten Island (and really, only five minutes from my apartment), I had a moment's doubt. What if Samantha didn't mean it, what if Nina didn't care? What if I was really as alone as I thought I was? But I pushed those thoughts aside. A promise was a promise, and I'd never known either one of them to go back on their word.

Still, I hesitated before I rang the bell, then forced myself to do it anyway. Samantha opened the door, her eyes wide as she took me in.

"Holy shit, Tori, what the hell?" She grabbed my arm and dragged me through the door.

It took me a second before I realized I hadn't changed since the practice drill.

"No, no, I'm fine, it's just moulage, you know, makeup," I protested against her probing hands.

"Christ, Tor," Samantha said, "let's get you cleaned up before you scare the shit out of Nina."

"Where is she?" I asked as we walked in.

"She's, uh, indisposed at the moment." Samantha led me to a bathroom. "Wash up, I'll get you a clean shirt."

❖

Washed and wearing a shirt of Sam's, a drink in my hand (scotch on the rocks, another family trait, only Nina did hers neat), and safely ensconced on their sofa, I sat next to Samantha and across from Nina as they waited to hear what I had to say.

"Oh, hey, you've switched to ice?" I asked Nina, glancing at her glass before I started.

"No," she smiled, "it's just ginger ale."

Interesting, I thought, and filed the information away in my head with everything else. I took a sip from my own glass, closed my eyes, and inhaled slowly.

I told them my sorry tale. "You know, maybe she was right," I concluded, musing aloud, "this was my fault. Maybe I should have quit the EMT class, or just quit some of my other classes so I could have spent more time…"

I glanced up and saw that Nina seemed ready to burst, but Samantha held up her hand and waved for peace.

"Ah, Tori, don't you know a vampire when you see one?" she asked me gently.

"Hey," Nina interjected as she stood anyway and ran a hand through her hair, "Kerry's not a vampire, not a real one, anyway." She grinned at Samantha, who grinned back, an amazing flash of light.

"True, that," Samantha conceded, "but, Tori," she turned back to me, pressing another scotch over ice into my willing hands, "*she* fucked it up, not you."

I sipped and considered.

"Let's go get your stuff," Nina suggested into the silence.

"I don't want to go back there," I said, shaking my head vehemently. They were probably still fucking, I thought, fucking in the apartment I'd helped pick, in the bedroom I'd painted, on the bed I'd goddamn bought. Dammit.

Maybe I should have quit school altogether and gotten a different job—like the one Kerry always said I could get in her firm. But that would have meant giving up everything I'd worked so hard for—

"Come on, Victoria, where's that Del Castillo blood?" Nina teased me lightly. One thing I had to admit, the Del Castillo blood was definitely prepotent: we all had such similar faces. Sure, we had different eye color, hair color, even different shades of skin, but we all had the same almost too-large eyes, the same curve of lip, the same bone structure.

There was, again, no doubt the Del Castillos were a very pretty bunch, and Nina was probably the prettiest of us all, I thought, though she was the only one who didn't know it. Hell, I considered as I sipped from my glass, maybe that's why she was the shortest of all the cousins, too. All that concentrated…whatever it was…became beautiful.

I shook my head and grimaced—I'd been staring at my cousin, the one who was about to save my sorry ass, and had caught myself admiring her lower lip, which was slightly fuller than mine.

"What do I need to go back there for, anyway?" I asked instead, trying to cover up that I'd been lost in thought about something other than my heartbreak. I didn't really feel heartbroken. I felt cold, and where I wasn't cold I felt nothing. The more I drank the colder I got.

My peripheral vision found Samantha smothering a grin at me.

Caught. Ah, well, at least Samantha had a sense of humor, and I grinned in return as Nina grasped my shoulder. She crouched before me and I stared at my drink, clunking the ice around in circles.

"You need your books, Tor." Her fingertips grazed my chin. "You need your notes."

Her eyes were such a light blue fading into gray at the edges, so unlike my light brown ones that were now probably ringed in dark, dark green since I'd been drinking.

I tossed my head away from her touch and shrugged.

Gulping my drink, I looked around me as I thought about myself and my life: fucked-up home, fucked-up academics, and fucked-up life while I sat on the perfect sofa—all clean lines and espresso-colored leather. Perfect.

Perfect Nina's perfect world. Perfect wife, perfect life, and then I remembered: she'd fucked my girlfriend first. Ex. My ex-girlfriend.

I had to know.

"When did you guys fuck?" I asked her and was instantly sorry. Still, as guilty as I felt, I wanted, I needed to know, and Nina knew exactly who and what I meant.

She pulled her hands away and stood.

"We were kids, Tori," Nina sighed, and ran her fingers through her hair, "and that's not what it was. We were just kids."

I nodded as if I understood. I did, but that didn't stop me. "Yeah… so?" I continued. "Did you fuck her? She fuck you?"

Samantha stirred next to me and set her glass down on the coffee table.

"Okay," she announced and stood, clapping her hands together, "this is where I excuse myself." She walked around the table toward Nina, who gave her an odd look.

"You can stay, Sammy. There's nothing you don't know." Nina gestured her back to the sofa.

Samantha shook her head and gave her one of her diamond smiles as she closed the scant distance between them. "I'm not worried about that, love," Samantha said softly, and put her arms around her. She kissed her softly, fully, as Nina returned the embrace.

God, they were so perfect together—it fucking killed me as I watched them, the fucking axe that drove through my ice, and once again I flipped from cold to heat because, as upset as I was about Kerry,

I'd never had what these two did. My jealousy moments before was petty compared to this.

Samantha murmured something into Nina's ear, who nodded in response.

"All right," Samantha agreed, and turned to leave the room. She stopped and pointedly stared at me. "You," and while her expression was very serious, she smiled anyway, "be nice. Nina's your friend, not just your cousin, okay?"

I nodded agreement, and Sam held my gaze a moment longer before she walked away.

I didn't love Kerry, not the way Samantha loved Nina, not even the way Nina loved me, and I knew I was missing something, a vital clue that would give me the answer I wanted.

Nina cocked her head to one side, her auburn-touched hair long and flowing, draping over her shoulders like a shawl. "What do you need to know, Tori?"

Samantha had shut off a light in the corridor as she'd exited to the stairs, and the shadow that reached back into the living room leached the rest of the color from Nina's eyes, making them flash silver as she neared. I stood to face her.

Her walk was catlike, almost predatory, and the dim light from a table lamp winked from the ankh that hung about her neck from an incongruously pink ribbon, part of the whole Angel tour cancer thing she'd done, I supposed. Dammit.

At thirty-one, Nina still appeared twenty, but her face—something was different, even as defined as it was, something was…gentler, softer, than I'd ever seen there before, subtle, but still more pronounced than I had noticed that night at Nox.

I shifted from one foot to another to dispel my growing unease, knowing that I shouldn't have asked about her and Kerry, but I couldn't back down, either. That would have been too…too humiliating. Of all the cousins, Nina was the one I loved the most, the one I was compared to, the one I wanted to be. Oh, hell, I'd practically grown up in her childhood bedroom. But not only that, we were *both* Del Castillo: we had the same blood, the same pride. No way could I back down.

Nina tossed her head again to clear the long strands that fell over her face and crossed her arms over her chest.

My expression, my stance were arrogant, and I knew it, but

even though I stood just that much taller than she did, she seemed completely fearless as she stared back up at me, through me, one brow arched perfectly as the color flooded back into her eyes and deepened. I wondered for half a second what color mine were, if they were mixed brown or if they'd shaded almost completely green as Nina read me, completely and correctly. I knew, because I knew her: same blood, same temper, but she'd always hid hers from the world better. Yet another thing she did more competently than I did.

"You wanted to know something, tough guy?" she asked me again. She was hurt, she was furious—I knew that, because I knew her.

"Yeah," I drawled, my own anger and frustration at the surface because no matter what I did she was better than me, so much better that she was willing to help me out of my sorry situation, which I probably could have avoided if I'd been more like her in the first place.

"I want to know when you fucked," I said, my voice sounding harsh even to my own ears. "I want to know how she let you fuck her tight—"

"Watch it, Tori," Nina warned, "have a little respect for both of us."

I laughed as I picked up my glass. "Respect?" I swallowed what was left and let the alcohol burn through me— maybe it would burn off some of the tension, take the edge off the arousal at the thought of *my* girl, wet and ready, waiting, wanting Nina's long fingers inside her, filling her, fucking her, probably as perfectly as she did everything else.

"Yes. Respect, Tori," Nina answered, her eyes flaring dangerously, "especially for yourself."

I chuckled mirthlessly. "Especially for myself?" I mocked, and put my glass back down. I straightened, closed the distance between us, and looked down at the sensual curve of her lip, then into eyes that had gone dark. "Respect this," I whispered, then kissed her.

The softness of her mouth surprised me, shocked me out of my anger, and I even forgot about it for about two seconds before the world flipped, and the next thing I knew I was on my butt back on the sofa.

"You're doing a *really* great impression of an asshole," Nina said, and I stared at her as she stood there, seeming as unflustered as if we'd just discussed what kind of tea we preferred.

She walked into the corridor, then returned a moment later with a pillow and a blanket and tossed them at me.

"Sleep it off—you're not a pleasant drunk. We'll get your stuff tomorrow. Good night." She didn't look back, not even once, as she left.

A mix of feelings warred in my head for dominance, from shame to guilt to yeah-that's-right, how-do-you-like-them-apples defiance as I watched her. But under, over, and woven within that reaction was the one thing I really hated to admit: she was right that I was behaving like an asshole.

I shook my head, disgusted with myself as I kicked off my shoes. Maybe I'd be a better person in the morning.

❖

Pain lanced through my head when the sun slammed into it through the bay window, and it physically hurt to open my eyes. Nausea jumped in like a jealous twin when my too-sensitive ears picked up a whirring sound from the kitchen.

It stopped moments later—the sound, not my head—and Samantha walked into the living room carrying a tall glass filled with something red and viscous.

"This…is for you." She placed it on the table and sat on the sofa across from me, then watched me, an amused smile playing about the corner of her lips as I struggled against the fierce pounding in my head to sit up.

"Hold your breath," she warned as I reached for the glass, "it's got a bit of a kick."

I looked at her blearily through the one eye that I could keep at half mast and nodded as I took the glass. I saluted her with it and, just as warned, held my breath.

It wasn't too bad as I swallowed. In fact, at first it was fine—maybe a little salty, but fine. Then the fire started. As soon as my eyes stopped tearing and the roaring through my sinuses settled to a dull red glow, I was not only completely awake, but I also couldn't have closed my eyes if I'd tried—they needed to cool down.

Samantha watched me, expressionless, as I choked and simmered. When the coughing and tearing ended and I could finally see her clearly, she stood.

"You know where the bathroom is—I'll wait in the car for you." She stalked away.

I nodded in agreement to her back, then felt around the floor for my shoes.

"Nina coming?" I asked.

She stopped and pivoted, her eyes piercing me where I sat. I never, ever, wanted to get that glare from her again because in it, I understood why she wore a sword around her neck. That look? Deadly.

"Nina's sleeping in—she's not feeling well, and we need to do this soon because she and I have an appointment."

"Yeah, no problem," I answered hastily as I stood.

"Good." Samantha nodded and left.

As soon as I'd taken care of morning ablutions—face and hands clean, breath minty fresh, as my cousin would say, only in this instance it was cinnamon, and head no longer pounding—I slung on my jacket as I hurried outside to meet Samantha, who waited, as promised, at the curb in her favorite automotive toy: a '74 Nova that shone like black oil in the early morning sun.

She pulled out of the drive.

"You know where it is?" I asked.

"I did know where to send the passes and the car, right?"

Oh, yeah. That was true—where the hell was my brain?

"Yeah, sorry," I said instead.

Funny, I thought. This was one of the oldest sections of the island, and one of the nicest, because blue-collar workers and educators lived side by side with local politicians, doctors, business commuters, and local entrepreneurs. It was politely eclectic and I loved it.

"Just a couple of things, Tori," Samantha said as she pulled into a vacant spot in front of the apartment building—my spot, in fact.

Those were the first words she'd said to me since she'd affirmed she knew the address. I blinked as I faced her—the sun was still a bit too bright for me. "Sure, Sam, what?"

She cut the motor and pocketed the key before she made sure she had my eyes on hers.

"If," she began slowly and evenly, "you *ever* lay so much as a breath on Nina that she doesn't want? I'll deck you if she doesn't."

I'd forgotten about what I'd done, and my ears burned with a combination of shame and anger—anger at myself at having behaved so...so...crassly. I couldn't think of another word, besides *asshole*, that is. "I need to apologize to her," I said, forcing the words past the burning lump of shame in my throat. I might have been wrong, but at least I knew how to admit it.

"Yeah, you do, and another thing, Tor?"

"Yeah?"

Here it comes, I thought, the speech about whatever it was that I was fucking up or playing the wrong way or just simply not smart about.

"There are two reasons you're nursing a hangover instead of a black eye," she said matter-of-factly.

Since that hadn't been what I'd expected to hear, I nodded in dumb surprise.

"Nina loves you and forgives you."

"Yeah, well I love her too. I mean—"

"Then you'll understand why I'm going to ask you not to do that again."

I began to protest—I wasn't ever going to do that again, but Sam held up her hands and went right over me. "I don't mean the kiss, Tori. I mean the angry third degree too."

"I'm really sorry about the whole thing. I was just…so…and then I drank on top of it and—"

Samantha finally gave me a tiny grin and actually put a hand on my shoulder. "I know, Tori, I know. But I need you to understand…" She leaned over, her gaze intent on me.

I stared back, almost mesmerized. Samantha's eyes snapped with crystal fire, and for the first time that day, I saw what looked like a real smile.

"She's pregnant," she almost whispered.

I stared in shock and the gears in my head engaged, sorting through all the things about Nina I'd noticed in the last month or so. And she hated ginger ale. She was a Coke fan through and through. The pieces all fit together with everything I'd been learning in class, and in that second I felt absolutely nothing emotional, only the answer, shining brightly in my mind like a trophy on the shelf, and I reached for it. "Second month?" I guesstimated.

"Eight weeks," Samantha agreed with a nod. A mixture of love, pride, and joy swam across her face, and I honestly couldn't think of anyone else who'd earned it more.

Then it hit me. My cousin, my friend, my role model, my secret

rival and big sister was going to have a baby. That—that was…
"Awesome, Sam!" I smiled and impulsively hugged her.

"Thanks," Sam grinned after briefly returning the hug, "but I'm not the one who has to give birth." She got out of the car.

"Ah, true that, but…I'm sure you had a hand in it."

I was pleasantly surprised to see Samantha blush and gaze down at the cement, which made me smile even more as I closed the door and stepped onto the sidewalk.

"Oh, hey, last thing?" Samantha asked as I approached the stairs.

"Yeah?"

"No one knows yet. Nina wants to wait another few weeks."

I nodded as I thought about that—it made sense to me. It was still early, and anything could happen. But again, in light of what my mother had told me all that time ago about Nina's issues with her parents, there might have been other reasons too. Either way, my cousin and her partner were more than entitled to their privacy; I wouldn't be the one to violate their confidence.

"Sure, I won't say anything."

"Thanks."

She clapped me on the shoulder and stared at the steps with me. "You ready?"

I swallowed. "Yeah, yeah, I'm gonna do this," I said, kicking the sidewalk a little.

Samantha pulled her cell phone out of her jacket. "Hit redial if you need me?"

"Yeah, sure." I dove a hand into my pocket to reassure myself of my phone's presence.

"Okay," I said, took a deep breath, and clapped my hands together. "I'm off."

I trekked up the stairs to get my stuff.

BREATHING

Is the rate and quality enough to sustain life?

Up in the apartment, "Tori baby, I'm so glad you're back," were the first words Kerry said when I walked in.

"I'm so sorry, stud," she said, following me as I walked through the apartment. "That was a total fluke, a complete and total mistake. I swear that'll never happen again."

I said absolutely nothing as I continued down the hallway, past the bathroom where—

"I just…you know how it is, bad experience, you make a mistake, but we'll be all right, we can work this out…I love you." Her hands eased around my waist.

"No…you don't," I said as I whirled around and caught her hands before she could embrace me. "You don't love me." Her gaze locked with mine. "If you did, you would have told me you were interested in someone else, you would have talked to me about something other than my being in class too much."

My heart hammered against my ribs, and my breath kept getting stuck in my throat. I relaxed my grip on her wrists as I watched her eyes fill.

"If you loved me," I tried again, shocked at the raggedness of my voice, "you wouldn't have done that in what was supposed to be our home." I let her hands go, and as I walked for the last time into what had been our bedroom, it hit me.

Home. She had fucked that girl in our home. I felt like…like I'd been robbed, like someone had taken something priceless from me, something that could never be replaced, a piece of me I didn't even know existed until it was gone, and now I missed it, I missed it horribly. That feeling grew and sent icy fingers down my thighs, throbbed in my stomach, and I almost threw up as I packed my clothes and equipment, then gathered my books.

I ignored Kerry when she walked into the room, the only sound the light thump of one of my books hitting the bed where I tossed my things. I refused to even look at her until she stepped up behind me, put her arms around my waist, and unzipped my jeans. Sex, as great as it was, wasn't going to fix this, not this time.

"God damn it, Kerry!" I spat, and pulled away from her, afraid to touch her. I was so angry I was afraid I'd hurt her, and I was so raw I was afraid I'd give in.

"Tori…please…it was a mistake, a stupid, stupid mistake…" I could hear her voice catch, and underneath it a memory played in my mind—my mother begging my father to stay—and the sound, the thought, the feel of Kerry's hand as it tentatively touched my back made me hurt, my muscles achingly rigid now with the effort to not turn around and catch her up in my arms, to let the press of her need against me, around me, in me, make me forget, make me forgive the unforgivable.

"I can't," I said shortly as I mechanically rolled some underwear, a few pairs of pants, and some shirts into my gym bag. I slung it over my shoulder, made sure my equipment was on top of my book crate, then hefted it. I had everything I really needed, and I carried my things to the door.

"We can talk when you come back for the rest of your things." Kerry's voice floated up behind me as I balanced the crate against the wall and grabbed the latch.

This time, I turned to see her, really see her, as she stood there. Her hair, pulled back into a simple ponytail, shone in the light that streamed in from the kitchen window, and her eyes were swollen—she was crying, had been crying. I ached, but as much as the desire to just throw my stuff on the floor and comfort her tore at me, I resisted—she was crying because of the results of her own actions, not mine.

My mother had forgiven my father once, and in the end? He'd despised her for it. That wouldn't be me, would *never* be me.

But it was terrible to watch Kerry cry.

"I'm not…" I swallowed and tried again. "I'm not coming back. Keep it all."

I forced myself out the door.

❖

"So…I hear congratulations are in order?" I asked when I saw Nina later the same day. She started for about half a second, then, to my amusement, arched a questioning eyebrow at her spouse.

Samantha shrugged innocently, then grabbed the full crate with my books and stuff from my arms. "We're going this way," she said cheerfully as she walked to the stairs.

I hugged Nina, then smiled at Samantha's back as I followed her up; I knew a dodge when I saw one. She led me to the room.

"This one's yours," she told me, then checked her watch. "Okay, we've got to run. Settle in, and we'll see you in a bit."

"Thanks, I—" But she was already a breeze blowing downstairs.

As I faced my bag and my books, I heard the door shut and wondered if they'd get pictures of whatever was going on with the baby. I unpacked, arranged my clothes in the closet, and put my tech equipment on the dresser. Done in minutes, I wandered about the house because I could, because I'd never really explored it.

Their bedroom took up the front of the house, and next to it was a smaller room. That one was empty, and from the shade of apple green it was painted, I assumed it would become the nursery.

As I looked into the sunlit space, I wondered what method Nina and Samantha had used to conceive their child; as a pre-med bio major, I knew they had lots of options, and as a lesbian, I knew what most of them were as well as what the new research was. Maybe I'd ask Nina sometime, I mused as I walked down the hallway.

My room, a soothing shade of periwinkle blue, was next, followed by the bathroom, and at the other end of the hallway was a room almost as big as the master bedroom—filled with bookshelves, an overflowing drawing table, two large computers with a scanner between them, and drawings all over the place. I counted fourteen guitars and another five bass guitars in three different racks strategically placed around the room.

I brushed the smooth and polished wood, the car-bright and candy colors of the instruments as I walked around. I probably had pictures in one of my albums of either one of them playing each one, I thought as I recognized three of the guitars from their last performance.

I finally walked over to the back windows that overlooked the yard, and when I peeked out, I could see an old but well-cared-for garden house in the back. A little slate path wandered from its front door to what I suspected was the kitchen downstairs.

Done looking out the window, I returned to the drawings that hung everywhere and inspected them and the shelves. The drawings were strong, sharp, filled with action figures and cityscapes; I wondered if they were concepts for their next album cover.

Then I wandered over to browse through the bookshelves. The books ran the gamut from encyclopedia sets to an enormous graphic novel collection, with a few autographed ones carefully framed and standing on the shelves. There were also books about Asian martial arts tucked in with what seemed to be old books about demons. That topic really caught my attention, so I picked one of those up, cracked it open, and settled into one of the comfy chairs in the corner to read all about something called "hounds."

The reading was fascinating: it described two kinds, ethereal and non, some of them human. Human hounds, while having no will of their own (they gave it up when they chose to become hounds in the first place), were set after prey, tracking them by the signature of their aura—I had to look that up in another part of the book—a trail they left, like footprints, through the energy field that surrounded the world.

It was all strangely heady. The hounds' prey were to be converted to thralls, living vessels of energy that fed—

"Hi, Tori," Nina's voice rang into the room.

Startled, I almost dropped the book, but managed instead to close it and put it on the nearest shelf. I stood.

"Hey, Nina, I, uh, I owe you an apolo—" I tried to say, but Nina cut me off immediately.

"You owe me nothing, Tori—just be the best EMT you can be, okay?" She smiled and hugged me, a real hug, to let me know we were okay. I shouldn't have been surprised, because that was Nina; she forgave me, and as far as she was concerned, it was over. That particular trait wasn't something I'd mastered yet, but maybe, someday, I would. I didn't think I was that generous-hearted, though.

"Do you like your room?" she asked as we walked down the hall together. She put an arm around my waist as we stood in the doorway and stared inside.

"It's great," I answered, and squeezed her to me lightly—I hadn't forgotten what Samantha had told me, and I wanted to be very careful.

"I'm glad. This is your home, Tori, for as long as you want."

Stunned, I faced her. "Nina, I'll pay you back, that's just…I mean, you can't—the baby—"

Her eyes glowed with what I knew now was not only her own good nature, but also the joy of the not-so-secret she carried as she held me tightly.

"You're family, Tor," she said, "and that's forever."

I was slow to return the embrace, because as much as I knew that somewhere in my head she was right, something in the way she said it told me it might actually be true.

"Thanks," I said finally, "thanks a lot."

❖

Sometimes I studied in the library/studio—and when Samantha read in a corner or played out her chops while Nina was working at her desk, either deaf to the world with a set of headphones and arranging tracks, or sketching out yet another cover concept, I remembered when I was a kid: Nina used to paint, and she'd even sit me on her lap so I could "paint" with her.

I asked her once why she stopped, because in my child's mind's eye she'd been so talented, but she smiled and shook her head.

"Goya, El Greco, and *Guernica*," was her only answer.

When I shook my head because I didn't know what she meant, she told me to take a break from blood for a moment and lent me an art text.

I got it—but I still thought she had talent, and I said so.

She smiled and hugged me in thanks.

❖

Time was getting tighter going into the finals and state exam, and two weeks before that most important test, we had to go on our ambulance rotations. We'd not only get some real field experience, but we'd also receive grades on how well we handled it. We had to pass the rotations because if we failed, we couldn't progress to the exam. Bob had made sure to emphasize this point: pass the rotation or return to the beginning.

We had a choice of hospitals and times and would do a total

of four eight-hour shifts. Mine were at night because I worked and attended other classes during the day, so I was assigned to University Hospital, North Site. I'd spend a day assisting in the emergency room, another on the bus, the next back in the emergency room, and the last night on the ambulance again. There were EMTs in the emergency room as well as on the bus, and Bob wanted to make sure we were exposed to both—just in case.

I stopped at the uniform and medical supply store; we'd also been instructed to wear the typical white uniform shirt and black uniform pants. After I spent more money than I expected and more time than I wanted to have one of the clerks measure my pants so they could be hemmed—otherwise I would have to roll them, which just looked terrible—I was ready to rock and roll: white shirt, black pants, work boots, and utility belt complete with all of the required tools. I had a cheapo stethoscope slung around my neck. It wasn't a Sprague, which I really wanted, but at least it worked, and it was a neat aqua blue.

I showed up at the emergency room promptly at seven p.m. and was directed to the nurses' station. Once there, I introduced myself to a harried nurse.

"Go get some coffee, um, Scott, Scotty? Scotts," she directed, stumbling over my name as she read it off the clipboard in front of her. "It's over there."

"Scotty's fine," I assured her as she waved me in the direction of the staff lounge.

I walked into a room the size of a closet, but at least it held a small counter with a coffeepot, a sink with a cabinet over it, and a tiny refrigerator.

I found a cup, then poured some coffee and almost spit the shit out. It was black, bitter, burnt rocket fuel—thick enough to walk on, and it smelled like gasoline.

I dumped the cup and rinsed my mouth in the sink, then tossed the rest of the poison down there too—no clog would survive that.

After searching the cabinets I found the makings for a fresh pot, so I set it up while I waited, and when it was brewed, a woman walked in, blue scrubs and gray eyes—and a charcoal gray Sprague slung over her shoulder, the bell tucked into the pocket of her shirt.

She was slender, sharp, angular: beautiful. The couple of gray streaks that streamed through her wavy black hair did nothing to detract from how very attractive she was—in fact, they added, because those streaks perfectly reflected the color of her eyes.

"Hey," she smiled at me as she walked over to the counter, "you make this?" She poured herself a fresh cup of java, then reached into the little fridge next to it for some milk.

"Yeah," I answered as she doctored her cup, "that other stuff was for shit."

She closed her eyes as she inhaled the steam that rose from her mug. "Smells great," she said finally, then took a sip and opened her eyes in surprise. "Nice!" She took another swallow. "Very nice. Oh, I'm Trace, by the way." She held out her hand.

"Glad you like the brew," I answered and reached for her hand. "I'm Tori."

She had a nice firm handshake and her skin was soft; her hand felt just the slightest bit cool in mine.

"Nice to meet you, Tori." She held the mug up in salute. "We'll have to keep you around here if you're going to keep making coffee like this."

I laughed and shrugged. "Actually, I'm supposed to be doing a rotation tonight, only no one seems to know what to do with me."

Trace leaned her hip back on the counter and frankly examined me. For one naked second, I could see the flash of appraisal, approval, and even attraction in her eyes, and I grinned to let her know that I'd seen it, and it was fine by me.

The look she gave in return let me know that whatever came next from either one of us would be totally okay.

"Well," she drawled, "you let me know if no one can figure out what to do with you—page me in respiratory therapy."

"Will do," I agreed. Nice. Very nice. An open door with a pretty woman. Every nerve in my body snapped to attention. The game was on.

Trace took another sip of her coffee, then put the cup in the sink. "You really do make good coffee," she said as she grabbed for the doorknob. "Oh, hey, when's your shift over?"

"I'm supposed to do eight hours, so I guess I'm here until three."

"Hmm, why don't you page me when you're done, and I'll treat you for coffee while you tell me all about your first time," she grinned, a sharp flash of teeth I instantly liked, "in the ER."

"Okay." I nodded. "I'll do that." Set.

"Cool. See you later, then?"

"Definitely." Match.

Well, that was cool, I mused as I sat there and played with my mug. It had been about four weeks since Kerry and I had—ah, enough of that, and enough sitting there. I checked my watch, the required one with the sweep hand, as I walked back to the nurses' station. Huh. I'd already been on duty for half an hour. Surely I could do something besides make a better supply of caffeine.

❖

"Hey, Debbie," I said, reading the tag of the woman who'd sent me to the lounge, "give me something to do. I'm supposed to practice stuff." I grinned. "And as much fun as the coffee room is, I'd really like to make myself useful."

Debbie finally peered up from her chart. "Great, then. Bed five, over there." She pointed. "Get his vitals."

"Will do," I said, and hustled over to bed five.

Bob and the rest of the instructors had been prepping us for this. If we were on a rig, we'd take vital signs and get an idea of the paperwork everyone had to fill out, the PCRs—patient care reports. If we were in the emergency room, we'd also measure and monitor vital signs, wheel patients around to X-ray and such, and if it got really busy? Help the triage nurse.

So with those duties in mind, I wasn't prepared to meet Mr. Wheeler—his name was written on the bag on the hospital tray table in front of him, in big, black Magic Marker letters: Mr. Wheeler.

"Hi, Mr. Wheeler," I said as I walked in, "I'm Tori Scotts and I'm—" I stopped cold. This wasn't Mr. Wheeler anymore. This man lay with his head back and eyes open, eyes that had the strangest cast. Before instinct prompted me to touch his hand, I knew. He was still warm, but Mr. Wheeler was dead, very dead, and I had no idea what I was supposed to do. Did Debbie really want me to take his vital signs? Did people do that in a hospital setting, just in case or something?

"I'm sorry, Mr. Wheeler, I've got to find a nurse," I said to the dead man. He couldn't have been dead long, and what if something was there, like a soul or something, and it could hear? "But I'll be right back," I told the corpse. I felt a little stupid, but what if, just in case... Besides,

I believed that whether or not some ephemeral, ethereal something existed, it would be very sad if a person left the planet disregarded and disrespected.

I walked back to the station, but Debbie was gone.

"Um, what am I supposed to do with the dead guy?" I asked the first passing nurse.

She stopped and stared at me a moment, then sighed, obviously exasperated. "This way," she snapped out. "Judy!" she called as we hurried down the corridor between bits of mechanical parts and stretchers. "I need a morgue kit!"

Like magic, one flew at her head, and she snatched it out of the air as she hurried over to bed five with me behind her. "We need to strip him and zip him," she said as she pulled the curtain back around.

"Huh?"

She opened the kit. "Take off his shoes and socks, and after we undress him, we're going to cross his hands and feet," she explained as I carefully unlaced a well-worn black oxford, "and we'll put him in this." She held up a white plastic shroud with a zipper that ran along its length. I'd seen them in class because every rig carried at least one morgue kit.

"Hey, Mr. Wheeler," I said as I took his shoes off, "it's Tori again. I'm taking your stuff off, and we're going to put it in this bag for your family."

I made sure I had gloves on before I took off his socks—dead or no, socks can be gross. I glanced up to see the nurse give me the eye as I continued to talk to the corpse.

I knew, because of all my classes, we weren't supposed to believe in such things as God or spirit. Everything was accident and evolution and that was it, no God, no one pulling any strings, but what if there was more? I was rather embarrassed, because I couldn't really let that spiritual sense go completely. I knew it was very unscientific, and one of my professors had said that to even *think* that there might be a God or some such thing was very ignorant, still, what if? And if there wasn't, then no big deal; I was just talking to the inanimate like people talk to the television. And if there was, well…better to err on the side of compassion.

"Well," I asked her as she efficiently stripped off his shirt, "what if he's, like, listening or something somewhere, you know?"

I looked up to see her smile at me across Mr. Wheeler. "That's not a bad idea, kid," she said, "it's not a bad idea at all." She started to talk with him too.

After I carefully crossed his hands and placed a bit of gauze around his wrists so the ties wouldn't cut into them, things got crazy.

Debbie tore the curtain back. "Scotty, we've got an MCI MVA coming in. Go out to the bay and help the crew."

"Right, okay," I agreed, but glanced back at the nurse I'd been working with.

"Got it from here, kid." She smiled yet again, more warmly than she had when we started. "Go play with the wreck."

"Thanks." I waved and ran off with Debbie to the ambulance bay. MCI was a multicasualty incident, MVA meant motor vehicle accident.

This…was going to be interesting. I wondered if I'd remember how triage was supposed to work, if I'd remember the basic stuff I was supposed to know. I wondered if I'd get so grossed out I'd forget everything and throw up my coffee.

As we waited for the doors to open, the first stretcher came in—and organized pandemonium began. It held a female in her fifties having a severe asthma attack brought on by the stress of the accident.

Next was a male, approximately forty, fully immobilized and complaining of a headache.

A sixteen-year-old male with an open tib-fib fracture of the right leg called loudly for drugs—and while in some respects I didn't blame him, under her breath Debbie told him to shut the fuck up, because we had more, all immobilized and ready for their dates with the X-ray machine.

Then the night really took off. Another male in his sixties with chest pain. A woman with nonspecific, wandering pain, but normal vital signs at least. A boy, aged two, whose sister had stuck a chicken leg up his nose and left the cartilage in his nasal passage as a souvenir. He didn't cry at all until I had to help hold him during X-rays, and I was certain those films showed more of my hands than they did of his head, poor kid.

Then the drunk driver arrived: fifty-year-old male, immobilized, well-bandaged head trauma, chest trauma, and obviously agonal, meaning distressed and difficult, breathing. Bennie had ridden third man on this call, and her face was pale but composed as we helped transfer the patient from the stretcher to an available bed.

The crash crew materialized like magic—I couldn't even tell at what moment they had been paged, and while I helped pass things to people and clear beds and stretchers, I got to watch as Trace dropped a tube down the man's throat and hooked him up for ventilation before he was wheeled into surgery.

Trace hung back a moment. "You're due for a break soon, you know." She grinned at me as she stripped off her gloves.

I glanced at my watch—one a.m. How had so much time gone by? "You sure?"

Debbie walked by just as I asked. "Yeah, kid, you're supposed to get a break—if you get a chance to take it," she said, sounding tired. She glanced around the ER. Except for the steady noises from machinery and the background hum of people talking, things had finally calmed down.

"Why don't you go for about forty-five minutes?"

I was about to agree when I saw Bennie stripping down the stretcher she'd helped wheel in, the two techs she'd come in with gone.

"Check me in ten?" I asked Trace.

Her eyes traveled from me to Bennie, then back again. "Sure," she agreed. "I'll come grab you in ten."

"Great," I answered and smiled, relieved. I didn't want to blow her off at all; I just wanted to talk to Bennie—she didn't look right. I held up my wrist and tapped my watch face. "See you in ten."

"Cool."

I hurried over to my classmate. "You all right?" I asked as I helped set the stretcher up with a fresh sheet.

"Yeah. Yeah, I'm fine," Bennie said, looking everywhere but at me as we wheeled the stretcher back out through the bay doors to the rig.

We opened the back of the parked ambulance and lifted it in, then slid it into position, locking it in place.

I observed her closely under that big square dome of light. Funny. I'd always thought of Bennie as young, just, well, younger than anyone I was used to being friends with, anyway. But in that moment and in that light, when I could really see her eyes, I realized I'd never think of her that way again.

Her eyes were a rich brown that made me imagine, well, I don't know really, they were just full and vibrant, and her ponytail flowed like honey over her shoulder. I wondered if she always wore it up like that or only for class and rotations. I wondered how long it really was when it was down.

I realized that after all these months of class together, I didn't really know her, and I wanted to, because she was smart, she was competent in class, and…she looked like she needed to talk. Maybe I could listen.

I spoke with that impulse. "Hey, Bennie, wanna grab a beer or something when you're done?"

She jumped slightly. "Oh. Where you thinking of going?" Her hair shifted as she finally turned those eyes on me.

"Not far—a little dive off of Sand Lane." I named the spot where the only gay bar on the Island was. I hadn't been there in a while, but if I was going to hang out, I wanted to be comfortable. "It's light, it'll be quiet, and we can grab a beer."

Something about her face made me think I'd read her wrong, and maybe I'd been misunderstood. This wasn't a come-on; it was just chat, that was all, chat and a beer.

"No one'll bother you," I told her. "It's midweek. It'll probably be pretty dead."

She smiled at me, a real smile finally, and I was surprised at how different it made her seem.

"Nah, I wasn't, I mean, I know the place. I wasn't worried about that," she said. "I just, well…I'm a little light this week and I gotta grab the bus."

I understood, I truly did. But still, that late at night? It wasn't really safe and I had a car—I'd drive her.

"Whattaya say I stand you for the beer and you get it next time?" I offered super casually, "and I'll give you a ride home?" I understood her pride. I had it too, and I didn't want to offend her.

I watched as Bennie considered.

"Fine," she nodded and agreed. "Okay."

"Okay?" I asked with a teasing grin, trying to catch her eyes with mine.

"Yeah. Okay." She smiled again. "Meet you back here in two hours?"

"Sure," I said, "no problem."

I checked my watch. It had been about ten minutes. "I'll see you later, then. I should get back inside."

"Later, Scotty." Bennie waved, and I walked back into the emergency room.

I met Trace by the nurses' station and followed her to the main cafeteria, which was empty except for the clerk behind the counter who doubled as a register person.

"It's not cappuccino, but it'll do for now," Trace said as we walked to an empty table.

"That's fine." I pulled out a chair and looked around me as I sat— Trace had picked a corner where the windows met, and here on the third floor, we had an excellent view of the ambulance entrance to the ER. The letters that spelled "emergency" glowed a dull red in the dark. I sipped at my coffee as I contemplated the sign, the shadows it cast, the word itself until it seemed to float apart into separate letters with no connection to each other.

"So...how's it going so far?" Trace's voice, a smooth burr, broke the silence.

I smiled in reflex when I saw her watching me with an expression I would come to know as a mix of humor and concern: it made the gray of her eyes darken.

"Well..." I took another sip, then launched into a recap of the events so far—from the boy with the bit of chicken cartilage stuck in his nose to Mr. Wheeler's last sock change.

Trace's nostrils flared slightly at that terminal tale. "She told you to do what?" And even though I'd just met her, it was obvious that she was upset.

"She told me to take his vitals. Should I have?" I asked, confused. Maybe that really was a protocol for the ER, make sure the obviously dead guy was really dead—but didn't they have machines to do that?

Trace shook her head. "That...was a bad call on someone's part," she said finally, her mouth a straight line. "That's not what's supposed to happen. You're supposed to be eased into this scene, not dropped head first into the whole mess."

"Ah...don't worry about it," I said, and grinned at her, because I recognized the element of care for me in that statement, "it had to happen sometime." We chatted a while longer and somehow, eventually, the conversation turned to what we both knew it would sooner or later: sex.

"I'm just talking sex—healthy, consenting adult sex—no strings," she said with a lifted brow and a very sensual twist to her lips.

"We don't know each other well enough for that," I said with a smile. She hadn't come on but had made a blatant declaration, and while I was definitely interested, I wasn't sure how to handle her—most women were a bit more coy, and I enjoyed that, the flirting, the teasing, the verbal foreplay, the game.

It wasn't that I couldn't have sex with Trace; it wasn't that at all. But I had just come out of living with someone, and while that wasn't what Trace was asking, I wasn't sure I wanted no-strings sex either. Then again, it was worth considering.

"I'm sure we could learn each other well enough, don't you think?" She let her gaze travel down my face to rest pointedly on my throat.

I could feel the pulse jump in my neck—she really knew how to play this game.

"But first," I took a sip from my mug, "are the preliminaries, you know." If we were playing, I wanted to up the ante, build the anticipation just that much more. I didn't plan to bed this woman this night, but I wanted to make sure she remembered me, because I probably would the next time.

Her hand lay on the table and I laid mine over it, running my thumb along its edge. "Victoria Scotts," I said quietly as I felt that smooth skin under mine, "and I'm very glad to meet you."

Trace exhaled softly as my hand touched hers and didn't pull away as she observed them. "Named and claimed, is that the deal?" she asked as her cool dark gray eyes met mine.

"Maybe."

I watched as she thought about my offer, then finally turned her hand under mine until she grasped it. "Trace…Tracy Elizabeth Cayden," she said finally, "and I'm very glad to meet you as well."

As I shook her hand again, I glanced at my watch. My time was up and I had to get back to the emergency room.

"Thanks for the coffee. Maybe I'll see you tomorrow—I'm doing ambulance rotations."

"You just might," she responded. "Tomorrow's an odd-numbered day and we're designated trauma. I'm on the crash team."

"I remember." I grinned. "But if it's a quiet night…"

"Page me in respiratory when you're done if you'd like," she finished for me.

"Will do." I stood to leave. She might not have known, but I planned on it.

The last hour of my rotation went quietly, and I spent most of it taking vital signs and writing them down on the various patient charts. I checked my watch: three minutes to go, three minutes until my rotation was done, three minutes until I met Bennie for a beer so we could compare notes.

"So…rough night?" I asked after we ordered our beers and found an even quieter spot in the nearly empty bar.

Bennie took a long pull from the glass bottle in her hand before answering. "Yeah," she said finally, then stared at the ground a moment, "yeah, it really was. You?"

I sipped at my beer and thought about it. "Mostly I was scared that I'd fuck it up, you know? I was afraid I'd forget shit, or that my brain would freeze up or something like that, at a critical point, but I mostly took vital signs—well, except for Mr. Wheeler and that drunk driver—" I shut up right there.

Even in the dim light, Bennie seemed green. I let the silence stretch, unwilling to push in any direction, just letting it flow however it wanted to or needed to.

"I was scared too," Bennie said in a half whisper, "and I was really afraid I'd forget everything. Man, Tori!" Bennie exclaimed. "He was almost fucking dead when we got there, and for what, you know? For what?"

Considering the damage that one earlier drunken driver had caused with that MCI MVA, I didn't know either, and we were both careful as we finished our beers to make sure there wouldn't be another idiot on the road before I drove her home.

❖

When I showed up for my ambulance rotation the next night and once again presented myself to the nurses' station, Debbie and I were old friends.

"Hey, Scotty!" She waved as I neared.

"'lo, Debbie." I waved back. "What's in store for me today?"

She gave me a big smile. "You're riding with Tigger and Trevor—the terrible twosome of the trauma trade." She said that last part in her best game-show voice.

"Okay," I drawled affably. This was going to be one hell of an adventure, I was sure—if I didn't screw it up.

Some of my anxiety must have reflected on my face, because Debbie tapped my arm. "You'll be fine, and you'll be with two of the best guys on the road—you couldn't ride with better," she assured me. "Come on, I'll take you outside to meet them."

All I could do was bob my head in agreement because here it came, the moment I'd *really* been waiting for as I stepped on the same tiles I'd walked over the night before on my way to the ambulance bay.

Through the glass doors I could see the backs of two ambulances and four uniformed figures chatting in a corner.

"Oh, here." Debbie stopped at the locker just inside the passageway. "Give me your jacket," she told me as she unlocked the door and reached inside. "Grab your wallet, and put this on instead."

She handed me the standard uniform jacket the hospital personnel wore, and I goggled at it.

"Don't want you to stick out, do we?" She grinned as she adjusted my collar.

"Uh…I guess not?" I hazarded, still struck dumb. I patted my chest to make sure my wallet was in place, then readjusted my gear belt across my hips so I could reach everything: holster with tools on the right so I could grab them easily, pocket mask just behind my left hip. I shifted the jacket once more so it fell comfortably.

"Let's introduce you to the guys." Debbie clapped me on the shoulder and we walked through the sliding door.

After I met Tigger and Trevor, they took me through the "one hundred"—the checklist of items the state required onboard, the items the city required, and the items the hospital required. This particular hospital was a "voluntary hospital"; they voluntarily linked to the 911 system by contract and agreement.

"Okay," Trevor said when they were done, "let's get started. You get to sit in the jump seat." He pointed at the seat that faced the head of the stretcher.

They hopped into the front cab, Tigger started the engine, and we pulled out slowly as the radio crackled to life.

"Five-five Eddy, what's your current status? Over."

Trevor grabbed the mic. "This is five-five Eddy, currently one hundred and en route to our cee-oh-are, over," he said crisply as we pulled out onto the main street.

"Redirect five-five Eddy. Respond to…" The voice continued,

giving a street location and the reported patient condition, which Trevor wrote down as Tigger turned the rig around.

"Hold on back there!" he advised, then flipped the lights and sirens on.

My blood pounded in my head. Where were we going? What would we find when we got there? What was—

"Hey, Tigger?" I called from the back over the din of the siren.

"Yeah?"

"What's a cee-oh-are?" I asked as we sped through the streets.

"C, O, R," he yelled over from the front, "stands for 'center of rove.' It's the actual cross street in the middle of the area we respond to."

"Oh. Thanks," I yelled back, adding that information to my mental file.

The first call was a fifteen-year-old male in a playground who'd severely twisted his ankle, if not broken it.

His friends clustered around him, and as I took the first set of vitals, Tigger quickly examined his leg and foot.

"That sneaker's got to come off," he said, shaking his head.

"I can't pull it off," the boy said, his words catching as he spoke. He had to be in pain, because the visible skin above the sneaker had already turned a reddish purple and was terribly swollen.

"I'm sorry, guy, but," and Trevor put his hand on the boy's shoulder, "we've got to cut your sneaker."

"But...but..." he spluttered, and Tigger sent me to the back of the rig to pull out splints while they handled the distraught patient. Trevor not only insisted I apply them, which was very cool, but he also had me present the patient when we got to the ER.

Once we transferred the patient off our stretcher, we cleaned the mattress pad and set it up with new sheets. I learned very quickly that this was SOP (standard operating procedure).

Next we responded to an MVA on a side street: a driver had run his car through a stop sign and T-boned another vehicle.

"This," Trevor yelled over the siren as we drove, "is what we refer to as an Allstate call."

"Why?" My throat was getting tight from talking over the sirens.

"Because," Tigger chimed in, "it's all property damage—you'll see."

When we got there, the driver of one car spoke to the responding officer, gesticulating wildly as he tried to explain himself, while the other driver sat in his seat, hands fixed firmly to the wheel. He knew who he was, making him oriented to person—he was Guy Carlotti; he knew where he was, so he was oriented to place—he said he was up shit creek because this was his wife's new car; and time—he knew the date. This made him "Ay and Oh times three," which was what I wrote on the PCR.

Tigger took tension on his head, meaning he held it between his fingers and lifted slightly—just enough pull to lift a six pack of soda is what we were taught—which was enough to relieve pressure from the head to the spine in case of a neck injury.

Trevor had me fit him for a cervical collar, which I slipped into place around his neck, and on a three count, we shifted the patient as a single unit so we could place the short backboard behind him, then fastened him to it, at which point it was safe for Tigger to let go of his head. We had to maneuver a bit to get him onto the stretcher, and the cops helped us, because Mr. Carlotti was no lightweight.

Once inside the ambulance, and at Trevor's subtle insistence, I got to perform the entire examination drill: A, B, C, D, E. Although the patient's blood pressure was slightly elevated, the rest of his vitals were within normal ranges, and except for his statement that he felt "a pain in the neck" that he said would turn into "a pain in his wallet," the examination revealed no bruises, no bleeding, no broken bones, no signs of internal damage, and he was able to wiggle his fingers and toes.

Again, the guys had me present the patient in the hospital: we had a forty-year-old male who'd been in an MVA. He had a slightly elevated blood pressure, or BP, and was complaining of neck pain. He was A&O x 3; his eyes were PEARL: pupils equally active and responsive to light; positive bilaterally for clear lung sounds; positive all four quads for nerve response, which meant he could wiggle his fingers and toes; and had no medical history to speak of. I may not have presented the information in the right order to the attending doctor, but at least I presented all my findings and left absolutely nothing out.

After we transferred him from the stretcher to a bed and Trevor got someone to sign off on the paperwork, we set up the stretcher and picked up a new short board on the way out.

There was another MVA. The driver RMAed—refused medical assistance.

Two asthma attacks. Check vitals, check lung sounds, administer O_2, monitor en route, then present paperwork and set the stretcher.

A fifty-six-year-old male with chest pain, a history of CHF—congestive heart failure—with visible jugular venous distension bilaterally. A check of his vitals revealed a rapid pulse and elevated BP.

We administered oxygen, and for the first time, when I listened for lung sounds, I heard rales: the distinct sound of cellophane paper crinkling that meant fluid in the lungs. The patient also had pitting edema, which meant that his extremities were so swollen that when I pressed a fingertip to the skin, an indentation stayed there for several seconds or longer.

Needless to say, we took him rather quickly to the emergency room.

After that call, things quieted down, and the guys drove to a Chinese food place off Bay Street where we picked up some food to go.

It was getting very close to the end of the shift. Tigger parked the rig on Edgewater, a large lot that faced the bay, and it was neat listening to them talk while we ate fried rice and smelled the salt of the ocean as we leaned against the front of the vehicle.

The radio crackled. "Five-five Eddy, come in."

Trevor grabbed the mic as he hopped in the front, and I clambered through the side door and settled into the jump seat.

"Oh, man!" Tigger groused from the driver's seat as Trevor wrote down the address and we pulled out of the lot. "It's Danny again. The skell probably ODed to avoid getting busted."

"Can they do that?" I asked.

"Sure," Trevor chimed in, "while we can override on the scene to declare the medical emergency and go to the hospital, the cop can choose between continuing the arrest afterward or letting it go as a medical."

"Saves 'em a lot of paperwork if they let it go," Tigger added.

When we got there, I had a feeling they were wrong about this being a medical override. Three patrol cars were there—one parked in front by the curb, another perpendicular to it, and another parked right on the lawn. And as we walked into the pile of sticks that was supposed to be a house, we passed a living room where two cops held a skinny, unkempt man who constantly screamed, "You ain't taking my boy from me—you ain't! You ain't!"

Another officer stepped out from the hallway. "This way," he said, and beckoned us over. "The kid's Danny Junior."

Suddenly, I was scared, scared that I wouldn't remember anything, that I didn't know enough, scared that whatever I saw would so throw me off balance that I'd vomit and forget everything, forget my job. I felt my head go light as the skin on my face tingled.

We entered the kitchen and stopped almost immediately. There, on the filthy, ripped linoleum that was covered in old food, dirt, and blood, lay the patient. Prone, head twisted to the side, a pediatric male approximately two, maybe two and a half years old—the back of his head matted in blood and suspiciously flat either from the crib or a fracture. A partially avulsed eye on the facing side. Multiple contusions over visible torso. Vomit all over the floor and a filthy Winnie the Pooh shirt. An incongruously fresh diaper.

His little lips gaped open and closed, open and closed, like a fish trying to breathe on land. My hands shook as I slipped my gloves out of my back pocket and over my fingers before I took another step and then...

A litany of orders blossomed in my head, and thought became action before I was fully conscious of it. I was the new man, so I set the regulator, then cracked the O_2 tank as Tigger passed me a pediatric non-rebreather air mask. I'd hold tension on the little head, because with this kind of damage, something in his neck had most likely been injured. Besides, I had the least experience, and this was something even the most rookie medical personnel could do. I carefully cradled his skull in my fingertips to take the pressure off his spinal cord. Airway. A full minute count for respirations, and I called the time and quality on them.

His breaths were irregular in quality, but he was breathing enough according to protocol, and we administered the maximum oxygen allowable.

Trevor soaked some sterile pads in saline, and Tigger produced a cup from somewhere and handed it to him. Trev first carefully covered the bulging eye with the soaked cotton, then with the cup, taping it firmly in place while Tigger oh-so-cautiously slipped a cervical collar around the little guy's neck. I spoke to Danny Junior the whole time, as did the guys. Every now and then I'd see the cops shuffle in and out of the room, or from the corner of my eye catch a pant leg shifting uncomfortably.

On the count of three we carefully turned and affixed Danny to a short board, still speaking to him, reassuring him that he was okay, that no one was going to hurt him. I watched Trevor's hands shake just the slightest bit as he secured the headrest to the board so I could take my hands away from Danny's head. Clear fluid slowly dripped out of one little ear.

A finger of ice stabbed my sternum as I caught Trevor's eye. That fluid wasn't a good sign.

Tigger told the cops what hospital we were going to go to and radioed ahead to alert the crash team as we moved the patient to the ambulance, and just as we got inside, Danny's hands, which had been balled into little fists, went slowly limp.

Tigger drove like a man being chased by the devil itself as the sirens blared over our heads. In the less than two minutes it took us to get to the emergency room, Danny's blood pressure had skyrocketed and his pulse rate had dropped, meaning bradycardia had set in—and then he stopped breathing.

I used a modified jaw thrust and a pediatric Ambu bag to force air into his little lungs, and the protocol that we had been taught—that no one rides the rails of the stretcher into the ER because we're supposed to use a slow, step-by-step progression—got trampled underfoot when Tigger ripped the back door open and Trevor urged me tersely, "Ride it in—don't stop, don't stop!" as I stood at the top of the stretcher, feet balanced on the aluminum tube that created the base, stomach pressed into the mattress for balance.

The crash team met us as we sped through the doors, and it was Trace's hands that met mine and allowed me to stop artificial respirations so she could drop a tube down his throat. Blood frothed on Danny's lips, and in that second we lost his heartbeat.

The flatline buzzer screamed in my ears, and the next thing I knew, a pair of hands grabbed my shoulders and yanked me away.

My head jerked, a sharp steel snap of muscle, to see who it was. Debbie. It was Debbie. "Come on, Tori," she said quietly, "your shift is over."

"But…" I gestured to the stretcher that had to be made, the paperwork that lay neglected on it. "I've got to—"

Debbie shook her head as she gently guided me back to the nurses' station. "You're done for the night—you're done with your rotations." She flipped deftly through the stack of paper behind the counter.

I was confused as I shucked my gloves, rolling one into the other to prevent contagion, and I dropped them into the nearest red bag. What the fuck? I had another two nights left. Had I really fucked it up so badly that they didn't want me back in the ER?

"What?" I asked, "I'm supposed to—"

Debbie pulled a sheet of paper from the desk, wrote something quickly, then thrust it at me. "You pass, Scotty, you pass. Call me when you need a job."

I took it from her hands and folded it slowly as I gawked at her. I was done? I passed? But what about the rest of my shift? What about Danny? I peered over my shoulder where the crash team had pulled the curtain and worked. The stretcher we'd brought the child in was gone, and so were Tigger and Trevor.

I felt Debbie's eyes on me. "It's okay," she said, and laid a hand on my shoulder. I met her eyes, cool and clear blue, which held intelligence and compassion. "Do you smoke?" she asked as she handed me my jacket.

"Uh, sometimes?" I answered, confused. I switched out of the hospital jacket I'd been wearing. What did smoking have to do with anything?

Debbie's hand traveled from my shoulder to pat my arm. "Why don't you go out by the bay, have a smoke, and I'll meet you in a minute?" She peered around my arm, behind me, where the crew still struggled behind the curtain to keep Danny alive. "It won't be long."

"Okay," I agreed, holding my jacket before me dumbly. I felt nothing. My brain didn't work. She could have told me to go do anything and I would have—I didn't even know how I breathed, just that it happened, air in, air out, an automatic response to signals sent by the lizard part of the brain: signals sent, received, and interpreted by nerves that I couldn't feel as I walked out the bay doors.

Several long boards rested against the wall, and a short board. The headrest was still affixed, and it was smeared with blood.

Tigger and Trevor had gone. They'd left a gaping space on the tarmac where the ambulance had been, and I don't know what I stared at as I finally lit a cigarette under the glare of the bay lights.

❖

I felt her before I heard her.

"Debbie said you'd be out here—would you like to get a cup of coffee?" Trace asked in a low, throaty voice that held none of the past night's banter, but an evenness instead, an evenness I could understand.

I exhaled quietly, still focused on the parking-lot lamp as I answered. "Sure." I tossed my cigarette to the cement and ground it under my boot. When I felt the light pressure of her fingers on my elbow, I didn't pull away, but I could feel my muscles automatically tense, as automatically as I breathed.

"Do you want to stay here, or should I pick you up when your shift is done?" My voice was strange, flat, a clipped sound in my ears as it floated out into the air.

Her fingers closed around my arm. "I'm off now. Let's go."

In my car, I followed Trace's directions, and instead of going to a café or a bar, I drove toward her place, a nice condo off the water along Father Capodanno Boulevard.

"Hey," I began, an urge growing in my chest that prompted me to speak, "do you mind if we stop at the beach on the way?"

"Why not?" she agreed, and patted my knee. Her fingers were warm along its inner curve as her thumb smoothed along the sharp delineation of bone and cartilage.

I tore my eyes from the road to glance at her. "Thanks." I made the turn. Seconds later, I pulled into the parking lot, found a space close to the sidewalk that led to the beach, then cut the engine. Trace hadn't moved her hand and I covered it with mine.

"Take a bit of a walk?" I asked.

Her eyes seemed almost colorless in the darkness of my car, as the light from the lamps on the boardwalk cast the rest of her into deep shadow.

"I like to come here to think too," she said softly as she unlocked the door.

"Thanks," I said again, because I had no other words, and I eased out of the car and waited for her just at the edge of the walkway.

It was cold and the wind whipped about, kicking the sand up, and we hadn't even gotten onto the beach proper.

We walked together under the boardwalk instead of over it, to the water, the water I could barely see as a black gleam on the horizon, but I could hear it, a steady thud that grew as we waded through the sand.

As we neared the hard-packed shoreline I let her take my hand, and the slip of her fingers against my palm stopped me from walking, brought me back from some edge I hadn't even known I was approaching.

I closed my eyes and just took it all in—the sound of the waves as they pounded, the smell of salt in the air, the harsh whip of the wind as it lashed my hair against my skin. I could feel the heat of Trace's body as she closed the distance between us to stand next to me, her shoulder nearly level with mine.

The warmth appealed to me, called me, and I put my arm around her to give some of that back, to get more of it. She let go of my hand to ease her arm around my waist.

"I really appreciate this," I said into her ear so she could hear me over the wind and the waves.

Trace shifted in response, her lips brushing against the sensitive skin behind my jaw. "These things...they're never easy," she said. Her mouth pressed into that spot, a blossom of heat in the cold that surrounded us. "Not the how, not the why, they're just not easy."

I understood what she said in the same place that told my hands what to do, in the same way I understood my ABCs, but the part that told me how to breathe put my other arm around her, found her eyes and traded the salty scratch of the wind for the surprising baby softness of her lips.

Trace leaned into me and I was so raw, I was aching, I was starving; and when her tongue slid along the roof of my mouth, I reached for her hips and pulled her to me urgently.

Her hands molded under my jacket and up my ribs, massaging along the muscles with a need that fired my blood. The heat that rose from my cunt threatened to take my head with it. Her leg slipped between my thighs and I needed more, more of everything.

"We can't do this here," I gasped, breaking away from that kiss that had returned me to sanity.

Trace's fingertips dug into my arms as she scraped her teeth along the exposed column of my neck. "I'm less than four blocks away," she murmured into my jaw.

Although her place was less than a minute away, it took longer than that to get there because we tripped along the sand—kissing, biting, allowing the hard rake of fingers to slip from cloth to skin and back again—and when we were actually in the car I drove with her hand held tightly in mine.

I'm not sure how Trace managed to open the door, reaching behind her that way, but once we were inside and the door slammed shut, Trace slammed me against it with a kiss that rolled in my mouth like the ocean as the nerves tingled along the skin of my back where it had hit the hard surface.

My clit strained against my clothes when the hard tips of her nipples pushed against my chest and my tongue met hers to explore the cuntlike softness of her mouth. My fingers methodically undid the knot that held her scrub pants up so I could slip my hands beneath the thin cotton and cup the bony prominence of her hips. When her thigh slipped between mine, my hands drifted from her hips directly to her ass, and I gripped her firmly so I could ease her along the flexed muscle of my leg. Hers snugged up against me perfectly.

"Oh…" I groaned softly, grateful for the pressure on my clit, equally grateful for the jolt of Trace's body against mine, for the slight, steady shudder that ran through her frame as her hips rode my thigh.

"Want more," she breathed into my neck. I didn't know if it was a question or a request as her teeth again worried the muscle.

She straightened against me, grabbed my shirt, and led me to the couch, her scrubs falling along the way as I kicked off my boots and her hands relieved me of my holster. The clang of it as it struck the ground seemed to hang in the air, a thin metallic whine that rang into the dark. I ignored it as my pants followed and we fell onto her sofa, a tangle of legs and shirts and skin.

Trace sighed, a sound that wavered as my fingers quested along her stomach to find the prize I wanted, and my lips marked her neck.

"Take what you want, baby," she urged when I finally held the slight rise of her breast bathed between my lips and the hardened peak between my teeth, "take what you need."

I stretched along her, above her, suspended. Watching the dark gleam of her eyes, I burned, burned with a need, a hunger that threatened to turn my bones to ash.

I took her mouth as I took her body: a sharp sudden thrust into slick, wet heat, a heat that seemed to meld with the burning of my bones when she tossed her head back.

"Yes...please," she moaned, and pushed frantically against me, on me, pushed so hard it had to hurt as she dug lines into my back, marking my spine as surely as I'd marked her neck. I could feel the skin split, the fluid rise and bubble behind her touch, and still I burned, we burned as her hands finished their trailblazing to grab my ass and she shoved her leg between mine, spreading me, anchoring me to her.

Burning. I was burning as my fingers filled her over and over, burning as my clit rode hard, even harder on the tendon of her thigh. Burning. There's the floor. Burning. Tiny limp hands. Burning. Little lips open and close, open and close until they stop, and then—

Trace grabbed my head and pulled me to her for a kiss that filled my mouth with blood and my blood with fire. She gave me no warning but the quickest glide of her fingers as they trailed down my ass to my thigh. She showed me the same mercy I showed her—none.

She filled my cunt completely.

I was the fire bleeding down the mountain, the liquid slip between her legs, the flame that took us both as she buried herself in me.

"Harder..." I urged, a harsh breath that scorched my throat as it flew out. And the burning...stopped.

❖

The night of the written half of the state exam started sanely enough—I picked up Bennie from the train station and drove to Mike's Place to meet Roy about two hours ahead of the exam. We figured we'd eat a little, chat a little, and review a lot before we took out our #2 pencils and answered the questions that would earn us entry into the practical exam.

We pulled out our Brady books and piled them on the side of the table, along with our notebooks.

"Hey, you guys hear about the dealer?" Roy asked conversationally as he poured sugar into his coffee.

"What, another dead or something?" I quipped as I picked at my cheese fries and waited for my cup to be filled.

"You mean...the one with the kid?" Bennie asked as she salted her eggs.

"Yeah, that one. What was his name?" Roy snapped his fingers to jog his memory, and the muscles clenched in my stomach.

"Wasn't it Dennis or something?" Bennie asked. "The one on..." She named the street I'd gone to with Tigger and Trevor.

"Danny—it was Danny!" Roy exclaimed. "Yeah, I was riding with Ray-Ray and Jack. Heard it on the radio."

I played with my coffee, fingers stuttering over the creamer tabs.

"Yeah," Bennie's voice sounded next to me, so suddenly I jumped. "I went in for the overnight ER rotation—heard they had a trainee with them. Hey!" She looked at me directly. "Didn't you ride that night?"

The fucking creamer burst in my hands, splashing everywhere but my cup. "Yeah," I said shortly as I tried to figure out what to do next, "I rode."

Roy threw me a sharp glance. "You?" he asked simply, his eyes warm and steady on mine.

I nodded.

"Hmph." He handed me a few napkins from the dispenser and pushed another creamer at me. "Heard you did good."

I wiped my hands with the offered paper, then shrugged. "They sent me home, so I'm not sure about that."

Bennie touched my shoulder. "That's part of their protocol," she said, her voice low and quiet. "Everyone who was on that was sent home as soon as they could be spared—and given two days off."

"Really?" I was surprised. I had just assumed that...well, that explained a lot, and the knot in my stomach started to loosen.

"Really," Roy affirmed, nodding across from me. "Oh, hey," he tossed a couple of sugar packets at me, "your coffee's gonna get cold."

I caught the sugar. "So long as it doesn't taste like that stuff they had..." and I launched into a recap of the first night. We also discussed where we were going to work once we got our licenses: private company, hospital, who was going to apply to the city. That? That was the real deal, as far as we were concerned, though a voluntary hospital was close enough if you could get it.

By the time we were done trading stories, laughing, and just generally being silly, we had forty-five minutes left to review, and we warned each other to be careful as we drove to the campus—Roy in his car, Bennie in mine. We'd already agreed that we'd meet the next night to review for the practical, which would be the following day: we were set up in groups, and Roy, Bennie, and I were scheduled to go first.

Once in the auditorium, I was literally the first one done with my exam. Three hundred of us, every other seat, and I surreptitiously peered about, trying to see if anyone else showed signs of completion. I reviewed my exam. I reviewed it again, then double-checked that I'd penciled my name in correctly and that my social security number was in the right place.

Finally, no more stalling—I couldn't take it anymore. Bob grinned at me as I tried to quietly scuff down the ramp to the front where he and the other instructors waited for us to hand in our paperwork.

I'm not sure if it was my hands or my chest that shook as I handed him first the exam book, then the test itself.

"See you at oh eight hundred, Saturday morning," he reminded me sotto voce as I gathered my books where we'd all been asked to leave them—in front of the podium.

"I'll be there," I stage-whispered in return.

My brain was blank as I walked to my car. Tomorrow. One last chance to review the practical aspects, and then the next day? The most important part of the exam.

I was so far gone in my thoughts that when I saw Kerry on the hood of my '79 Grand Prix, I smiled, because I'd forgotten, just for that moment, we didn't live together anymore.

"Hey, Tori," she said, her words low and measured as she slid to the ground to stand before me, still and proud under the light.

Her light blond hair drifted over her face, and as I stretched unstoppable fingertips to brush the strands back, I felt my breath hitch. There were at least a dozen things I could have said, and probably another dozen I could have done, but only one I could do. "Hi."

Her eyes once again winked at me—that mysterious green, light as new grass—except this time, I saw tears too.

"Miss you, tough guy," Kerry said, her words a half whisper as they tripped out.

Her skin was smooth under my fingertips, her hair as smooth and fine as I remembered it, and as that hitch in my throat turned to stone,

I realized exactly how much I cared for her. "Me too," I said. I wiped away the tear that escaped from her lashes with my thumb.

She turned her face into my palm, then threw her arms around me, and I reacted without thought or hesitation.

"Shh…" I soothed her as I held her against me. My heart pounded as my body remembered her, how she felt and fitted to me, on me, every way I had loved her and her me.

And…she cried, her shoulders shaking until all I could do was ease my palm along her back, murmur nonsense words, and kiss the top of her head until finally, finally, she stopped.

"Oh, I miss that sound," she said, her words still half broken by tears.

"What sound?" I asked gently and kissed her crown again.

Kerry sighed, a sad and wistful note in the crisp fall air. "Your heart, Tori," she told me, "that strong, steady beat…" She hugged me tighter and I closed my eyes and rocked her to me, against me, still rubbing soothing circles along her spine, her head against my chest. We stood like that for a long time.

"I got you something," Kerry said finally into our quiet, and shifted in my arms to dash at her eyes.

"You didn't have to do that." I loosened my hold.

Kerry dug into the bag that hung from her shoulder until she found what she wanted—a box about eight inches long, three inches wide, and wrapped in hunter green paper.

"For the ring around your eyes," she said as she pressed it into my palm.

"What…?" I asked as my fingers began to worry a neatly angled corner, and Kerry put her hand over mine to stop me while the fingers of her other hand stroked gently over my sternum.

"Promise you won't open it until after your practical exam on Saturday?" she asked, a slight, sad smile playing against the corners of her lips.

"Sure." I was touched that she'd come down, shocked that she'd remembered my exams and that she'd brought me a gift. It was an easy promise to make.

"Good." She kissed my cheek and I stared at her, bemused, as she walked to her car and opened the door. I simply didn't know what to say.

"See you 'round, stud." She waved with some of her usual grin and pulled out.

"Who was that?" Bennie asked from right behind me, and I fumbled the package I held as I whirled to face her.

"Kerry," Roy answered for me succinctly, as he half caught the box with me.

"Trouble?" he asked, as he shifted his own bag over his shoulder.

"Who's Kerry?" Bennie asked.

I sighed. "My ex, my ex-girlfriend." I stared at the spot where I'd seen her last.

"Well hey, then," Roy said, and clapped me on the shoulder, "you better put that thing in a bucket of water."

"Huh?"

Roy smiled brightly. "You know, bomb defusion?"

It took me a moment. "Oh. Oh, yeah!" I smiled back. "Nah, that's not an issue. We going to Mike's Place?" I deliberately changed the topic, tucked Kerry's present into my knapsack, then reached for a pack of cigarettes.

"Gotta spare?" Roy asked as I slid one out of the almost-full pack. He rarely smoked, and I'd practically given it up—not because anyone had asked me, but out of respect and concern for my beautiful cousin who would more than likely pass on that delicate Del Castillo face to my new niece or nephew.

Still, every now and again? It was better than drinking, anyway. At least I could drive without worrying about hurting anyone because I'd done something stupid.

We debriefed from the exam at the diner, and after discussing every possible scenario we could think of, we finally said good night to one another. Roy drove Bennie home.

Exhausted by the time I parked and got inside, I was thankful for the foresight that had prompted me to take the next few days off.

❖

I was dreaming, dreaming I was outside with my grandmother, her skin soft and warm as her fingertips held mine and I skipped along beside her down the sidewalk, kicking at little stones, scooping up dandelions. The sun was bright on our heads.

I don't know what made me glance in that direction, maybe it was the wink of glass embedded in the asphalt, maybe it was a flutter of movement, but I looked.

In the middle of the road, almost next to the Day-Glo yellow double lines, was a bird, a pigeon that walked forlornly with one wing held awkwardly away from its body.

I slipped my Nana's grasp and dashed into the street to save it, to take it home and nurse it like I already had with other birds, two mice, one kitten, and one rabbit.

My grandmother snatched me up and away over my wiggly protest before I took half a step.

"But, Nana," I pleaded, "the bird! A car—" One roared by at such speed it drowned my words of explanation and blew my hair into my face.

I began to cry hysterically while Nana held me tightly.

"Victoria!" she admonished. "You must never, *ever*, do that again!" Her arms tightened even further and swayed me with her while I sobbed harder. That poor bird!

"What would I have done if it had been you?" she whispered into my ear. "Who would save *my* little bird?"

I woke up with tears in my eyes, because she had been *so* real. I could still feel the silkiness of her cheek as it pressed on mine and the absolute comfort of her arms around me. A sob caught in my throat when I realized she'd been dead for the past eleven years—a long time, a very long time.

I glanced over at my dresser where my clock read six a.m. in unforgiving bright blue, then sat up and swiped at my eyes, all hazy dream sorrow gone, only to be replaced with nervous anticipation. Today was the day, today was the state practical exam. I jumped out of bed, rapidly showered and dressed, and as quickly as I quietly could, tripped down the stairs to the kitchen to grab some coffee before I left.

As I rounded the corner to the kitchen, I could smell the food cooking and knew Samantha and Nina were already up.

"Sit and eat," Samantha said as I stepped into the kitchen.

"I'm just gonna have some coffee. I'm a little queasy."

"Today's your practical exam, right?" Nina asked.

"Yeah."

"Well, then, it's going to be physical, which means you have to perform. No one performs well hungry," she said, "so have some juice and just pick at something."

She was probably right, so I sat down, Samantha passed me a glass of juice and a plate of scrambled eggs and home fries, and that was that.

I stopped protesting after the first bite—Sam made some mean home fries, and sure enough, I was starving.

"You know, I had the weirdest dream," I told Nina and Samantha while we ate. Sitting there and eating breakfast with them was a little like when we were kids and Nina and Nico used to watch us smaller ones. They made breakfast, and while we all ate, we'd tell each other what we'd dreamed.

Since I'd moved into Nina and Samantha's, on the rare occasional mornings when we all caught each other, we fell into the same habit.

"By the way, I'll get breakfast tomorrow," I offered, since they'd gotten it this morning.

"Sure," Samantha agreed, as she reached for the salt. "So, what was it, the dream, I mean?"

I recounted it to both of them.

Nina sighed and studied her plate before speaking. "Tori, you were eight when that happened."

"What?"

"Yeah, you cried yourself sick over it, and Nana took care of you. You don't remember?"

I frowned as I focused. "I remember...I *think* it was the first spring or summer we moved here...I was really sick and...yeah, you're right—I do remember that. Hey!" I smiled as it hit me. "She made you sing to me, right?"

Nina nodded and chuckled. "Yeah, she did, and you wanted show tunes, nothing but show tunes!"

"Huh! I did not!" I felt the burn in my cheeks and Samantha raised a brow at me.

"Well, there was at *least* one," Nina teased.

"Hey, 'The Rose' is a rock ballad, it doesn't count," I parried as I loaded my fork. I chewed thoughtfully for a moment and remembered another detail. "Or if you sing it in cartoon voices," I added innocently.

Samantha's eyebrows shot to her hairline as she goggled at her wife. "Cartoon voices?"

"She was *eight* years old," Nina countered. "Should I have explained to her about the heroin addict instead?" She smiled.

Samantha shook her head and took a hearty swallow of her juice. "Cartoon voices," she muttered.

We ate in silence for a few moments.

"Hey, Tori, you know Nana was kind of a rescued bird herself, right?" Nina asked.

"Huh?" I swallowed my coffee.

"Nana, you know, the *story*?"

I nodded. "Yeah, yeah, the whole castle on the black mountain thing, blahddy blahddy blah," I said dismissively. "I've heard *that* story about a million times."

"Well, I don't know it," Samantha chimed in.

"Oh, it's actually kinda cool, in a weird way." Nina faced her animatedly, waving a hand.

"Really?"

"Yeah," I agreed, "it *is* kinda cool, if you haven't heard it every day of your life."

"So?" Samantha asked.

"What?" I asked back.

"The story?"

Nina told her the family legend.

It was *really* all about our great-grandmother, Blanca Monte Negron. When she wouldn't let our great-grandfather keep his lover in the house, he stole her infant daughter, whisking her away to the working ranch high in the Andes Mountains. At gunpoint our great-grandmother took two horses and forced a *campesino* (a ranch hand) loyal to our great-grandfather to take her across the mountains in the dead of winter, then back to the city when she recovered her daughter. The fight for her daughter switched the *campesino*'s loyalties—and from then on my family considered his children and grandchildren as friends and cousins. In fact, they still lived and worked on the ranch back in the mountains.

At the same gunpoint our great-grandmother shot a would-be kidnapper who killed her husband during an attempt to steal her baby, our grandmother, and it was her—Blanca Monte Negron and that indomitable strength, will, and courage that had let her face and triumphantly overcome what should have been insurmountable odds for anyone, *especially* for a woman in that place and time—we celebrated whenever the clan got together.

Samantha choked on her coffee and with an uncharacteristic clumsiness knocked the rest over somewhere during the attempted kidnapping story.

"Are you all right?" Nina asked in alarm.

"Fine, just fine," Samantha croaked, waving her away. "What a waste of good coffee," she observed as she wiped the table.

I got up and brought her some more, and since no one was dying, which was a good thing because I wasn't licensed to do anything about it yet, I started to go.

"Kick ass." Nina smiled at me as I thanked them both and excused myself from the table.

"Yeah," Samantha agreed, "kick it hard."

I smiled nervously as I double-checked my belt and my holster. I had everything I needed and they each gave me a hug.

Samantha's hug was strong, steady, and sure, while Nina's was just as strong, but with an added something, something that made me feel secure. But there was another element, something off that set a buzz in the back of my head.

I visually examined her carefully, wondering if it was because she was pregnant. "You feel okay?" She did seem paler than usual.

"I'm fine, Tori. I'm not puking or anything," she laughed, "so go kick some."

❖

I was so focused on getting to the campus that it seemed I suddenly materialized in a parking spot.

My hands were a bit sweaty when I walked up to the registration table and was sent to my first testing station, but my nervousness disappeared as I fell into the role.

I went through all stations, covering a range of medical and trauma emergencies, and I don't remember any of them, except the difficult breather. I had a patient sitting in what's called posturing, or tripod, leaning his hands on his knees, raising his shoulders to maximize lung surface. That was an immediate hint, and when I asked for skin coloration, I was told the lips had a faint purple tinge, as did the fingernail beds. I was pretty sure I knew what this was, but I needed to know one thing for sure. I listened for lung sounds and asked what I heard: wheeze on exhale.

I smiled because I'd nailed it—and I knew it. "Asthma," I said, straightening, and ran through the treatment protocol.

Roe, the instructor who was running this station, smiled. "You know, you're the only one who asked about lung sounds? Good job, Tor."

At Kathy's station, I remembered her frequent admonitions during practical lectures (occasionally reinforced with a cuff to the head for the less swift) to describe the applied triangular bandage as having a "snug" fit for the state exam—or fail the station. If I failed? That wouldn't be the reason why.

I wasn't surprised when Bob asked me, Roy, and Bennie to stick around and play victim for the next three testing sessions, but I *was* surprised when Bob took us out to eat after the practical. As we waited in the diner for our food, I was bursting to know how I'd done, and I was certain Roy and Bennie had the same anxiety.

Bob grabbed a piece of buttered toast. "You're gonna give yourselves a heart condition," he commented mildly.

"Oh, no, this is a heart condition," Roe joked, and poked another of our instructors, Ray-Ray, next to her. "Ready?" she asked him, and quirking a grin our way, she picked up her coffee mug, holding it before her in readiness.

Ray-Ray grabbed his as well. "Any place, any time, Roe." He grinned back.

"Yeah, JVD race!" Joey, another instructor, called out. "I'll time it!" He stood, displaying his watch to all. Everyone except Bob joined him and grabbed their coffee mugs.

Bob remained seated and calmly ate his home fries. "Check this out, kids," he told us, indicating Joey with his chin. He wiped the egg yolks on his plate with his toast.

Roy, Bennie, and I just watched in confused amusement as Joey stared at his watch, holding his hand up for a countdown. "Three… two…go!"

Every tech, medic, and fire person there downed their coffee in swift gulps and almost in unison slammed their mugs back down. They stared at each other.

"Yeah…there it is!" Ray-Ray crowed, touching his fingers where his veins began to bulge out of his neck. I goggled at everyone else and, unbelievable but true, I could see the soft swell of a vein on most necks—jugular venous distension—except Roe's. The crew muttered good-naturedly as to what the exact nature of the winning prize was.

"Tori, what side's the blockage?" Bob asked sharply, quickly.

"Left," I answered, not even really taking time to consider as I reached for the home fries. They weren't bad, but Samantha made them better, I thought as I chewed.

"What else could it be, Roy?" He pointed with his toast.

"Late-stage congestive heart failure, both sides." He shrugged and buttered his toast.

"What about trauma, Bennie?"

She looked over her coffee. "Tension pneumothorax."

"And that's why," Bob started as he salted his eggs, "I'm comping you guys for the instructors' course."

I almost dropped my food into my lap. "We passed? Are you kidding?"

"Well, yeah, you passed," Bob grinned, "and notice you're the only students here?"

I nodded dumbly, as did Roy and Bennie. Even though it would be a week before we got our official grades, I had suspected that Bob and the crew would know who had passed and who hadn't before we even walked into the practical, but I'd been so nervous, I hadn't thought he'd tell us.

"I take the top two scores and scholarship 'em for the instructors' course. Since you guys scored the same, I used a little…discretion." He grinned. "All three of you are fee-waived."

That was fantastic news, and I felt really good about it, but I felt even better moments later when Trace walked in.

"Hey, how you doin'?" I asked as I stood, happy to see her. We'd spoken a couple of times since *that* night, but we hadn't really seen each other. "What are you doing here?"

"I know where you guys hang out," she said smugly, "so I'm looking for you."

We gave each other a hug.

"Hey, Roe, Ray-Ray," she said. "Bob."

"Yo, Trace," and "Hey," they returned.

Someone found a chair and everyone shifted to make room. Trace sat next to me and casually laid her hand on my thigh.

Bennie glanced at me sharply from across the table, and I smiled blandly as I covered Trace's hand with my own. Bennie could go get her own girl.

Trace's thumb stroked against the inside of my thigh, a very soothing gesture that reminded me that I wanted to know more about her, as talk at the table turned to our options once we got our cards in the mail.

"You guys might not even take the instructor course," Ray-Ray told us. "If the next academy class opens up in time, you guys will probably fast-track it."

The thought hadn't occurred to me, and I pondered it as the group reached the universal decision that the day was up.

"You kids, call me if you need a reference, wanna chat, whatever," Bob told us as we walked out the door en masse.

"Thanks," I said, Trace's hand warm in mine.

"Hey, yeah, thanks a lot," Bennie added.

"Hey, you're my kids, gotta look out for ya, right?" Bob told us with a grin.

He patted each of us on the shoulder, and we dispersed to our cars. Trace walked with me.

❖

"Drop your car off and spend the next two days with me," she said, draping her hands across my waist. "I want to celebrate with you," she added as she closed in on me.

Normally, I wouldn't, but the stirring of her hand on my leg and the electric scrape of her teeth along my ear made my mind up for me. Well, something did, anyway. Besides, I liked her and wanted the opportunity to show her.

"Howzabout I go home and change, then meet you back at your place?"

She agreed, and it seemed like two minutes later I'd showered, changed, and headed back out. Nina and Samantha weren't home when I left, but I figured if they needed to get in touch with me, they knew my cell number.

I got to Trace's condo a few minutes later and took a deep lungful of the ocean-scented air before I walked to her door.

It swung open before I could even think of knocking. For all of three seconds, I saw Trace wearing something other than scrubs, her hair soft and loose, before she twined her arms around my neck and pulled me inside.

"Missed you," she said simply, and pressed her lips to mine. I smoothed my hands along her ribs, then down the channel of her spine until they rested on her hips. Her mouth was wonderfully soft as I explored it and enjoyed the sensuous return of her tongue. It lit a pleasant fire that tingled from my thighs to my diaphragm.

But I didn't want to rush, not like last time. I reluctantly broke that kiss.

"So…you wanted to do some premature celebration?" I drawled, smiling into her gray eyes as I hooked my fingers into her belt loops. I shifted my hips and my groin brushed against hers.

Trace's fingers trailed down my neck, leaving a delicious shiver in their wake. "Kiss me like that again," she warned, "and it won't be the celebration that's premature."

I used the belt loops to pull her closer, so that she landed solidly against me. I dipped my mouth close to her ear. "I thought we might go slower next time," I whispered, then nibbled lightly on the delicately curled ridge.

Trace burrowed her lips into my neck, and she pulled my shirt out of my jeans as she led me to her room. "Next time," she agreed in that sexy, throaty buzz as we crossed the threshold, "not this time."

I kissed her to seal the deal and let go of her pants. Instead I undid the buttons of her shirt one by one, baring and smoothing the skin beneath, tasting her skin as it was revealed.

"Mm-hmm…" she sighed as I sucked on a spot in the hollow of her collarbone she was particularly responsive to, and she slid my pants down.

I flicked slightly to open her jeans and everything else just melted away, left to fall where it would as we stepped to the edge of her bed. She pulled me down on top of her and we wrapped around one another, her arms and legs warm and smooth along my body as I languidly tasted her tongue again.

I explored her further, trailing my lips and tasting her, drinking in her skin as I passed over the defined ribs, delicate, horizontal channels across her chest, my fingers clasping one slight breast, letting the hard tip slide between them and against my palm as I licked the underside of the other.

Trace shifted under me and etched a lovely line up my leg with her foot, sending a shiver through me, and ran her fingers through my hair, gripping strands that drew me to her until her breast was in my mouth and I played her nipple with my tongue.

"You do that well," she said breathily.

I glanced up at her. Her face held an interesting expression, a cross between arousal and something I couldn't quite define. It was time to shift gears. I stopped and slid back up her body, drawing her legs up higher around me, and let my tongue glide between willing lips. I eased my hips so my cunt rested against hers and rocked against her, a slow and calculated pace that she answered.

"Do you want to fuck?" I made my words a distinct and deliberate whisper against her ear. I could feel her cunt moving under mine, hot and slick as we rocked.

Her hands had dug into my skin, short sharp streaks that sparked into my spine, and I slipped a hand between us to swirl my fingers in the rich heat that bathed and licked at my clit. Hard. Wet. Open. My favorite combination of things. She caught her breath and exhaled with a shudder that snaked through us both.

"You want me to fuck you?" I asked again, and caught her throat gently between my teeth. I entered her slightly, just enough to feel the warm welcome of her.

"Uh…" she breathed, and bit my ear in response.

I closed my hand a bit as I slid into her, and once I filled her, I opened it again so that the upsweep of my palm would spread her lips farther and stroke against the sensitive underside and head of her clit. She jammed her hips up against me.

I groaned at the gratifying feel of that hard, hard push against my skin, her clit pressed against my palm, the sleek fit of her around me.

"Yes…" she answered, a soft sound that cut through the early afternoon silence and tickled against the light hairs on my neck. "I really *like*…the way you do that…"

"I like *doing* it," I told her, then kissed her again, fucking her as deliberately as I spoke.

Once again her hands moved on my ass, and Trace urged me on and in, and it was almost enough, just kissing her and fucking her, the blood surge in my clit moving in time to my fingers inside her, while she clutched at me and her legs pressed against my shoulders.

"God, yeah, fuck me, just…fuck me," she groaned, her body a wave under me, her fingers painting new lines up my back as I did her harder.

One hand came off me as the other slid back down, and finally her fingers came to my cunt, sliding along the fucking ache she'd built, and then I felt it; she must have gotten it from under the pillow or something, but there was no mistaking the skim of the cock that skated my wanting edge.

"Christ..." I groaned as she pressed it against me. I breathed hard—wanting, craving—and my head sank involuntarily. I rubbed my cheek against her neck. Oh...fuck. Yes...no...God. What...what would she want? "Do it," I told her, the words jerking out of my throat as she continued to play me.

She pushed, slowly, firmly, and for a moment I hung, once again suspended as my shoulders lifted and my back arched to meet her. The wordless sound that came from my chest led me deeper into her as she rammed me.

"Don't stop," she begged, "don't...fucking...stop."

"I won't," I gasped as her fingers worked that dick inside me. Oh, fuck it, I was slamming her hard, her cunt riding my fingers so easily that I added another.

"That's it," I encouraged when I felt that unmistakable squeeze, the crush that made me thrust harder, push deeper, past that resistance that builds as the body gets ready to come and come good while she fucked me, an unremitting, unrelenting push that left me ragged because the weight in my cunt told me there was another side to this, created a pressure I knew wouldn't be relieved until I had that part inside her.

"God...yes..." She bucked wildly as I strained against her, to contain her, to maintain the fuck strong, and steady, and deep, as her body slicked beneath me, and still she pumped me relentlessly.

"Oh, yeah...come," I urged, my own cunt ready to explode.

"Oh, fuck..." she moaned, and bit her lip so hard I watched the skin split. She held that dick within me and threw her head back. She clawed at my shoulder. "Yeah, that's...that's it, that's it!"

I fucked her and stayed deep in those last few moments, the cunt-kiss tight around my fingers, and I felt my own clench in response.

"God..." she finally breathed quietly as she settled under me.

I shifted and eased out of her, my blood raging because she still pressed that dick into me, the other part of it resting against the bed, creating a friction that was almost unbearable. I kissed the blood off her lip and gazed into her eyes, which had deepened to dark pewter, a fog gray ringing them.

"You okay?" I asked, my voice almost as gravelly as hers from choking back so much.

"I'm fine," she practically purred, and stretched a bit, resettling her long legs around me. "Do you wanna come?" she asked, a sly smile edging her lips. She began to pump me again, a slight, insistent motion.

"I…I don't have to," I groaned in response as I caught my breath. A slight breeze in the room brushed over me, raising a sting in the lines she'd drawn in my shoulder when she released it to reach between us, to stroke my clit between her fingers. She was driving me crazy.

She licked my neck. "Why don't you put that where it belongs so I can feel you come?" she asked, and guided me to her.

I almost cried with relief when that weight in my cunt eased, taken by hers, but still, I moved slowly. I *needed*, but she'd just come, which meant she'd be tight, and I didn't want to hurt her.

This time her kiss was totally full of sensuality, and even though she kept that hand behind me, holding everything firm, the other was gentle as she continued to rub my clit.

"Fuck me the way you want to," Trace said, her sensual low voice playing in my ear before she nibbled on it. "You're not gonna hurt me."

She thrust her hips against me to prove her point, and I wasn't going to, but I was so hard and she stroked me so good, and that cock begged me to bury it fucking furiously…driven beyond the edge of reason, I did.

❖

I didn't stay the two days. I'd promised I'd make breakfast the next day, and honestly, after I came, we drank, ordered in, took a nap, then fucked some more. I appreciated it, I really did, but…I can't explain it, I just had to get home. Trace was cool, she understood, and I left her with the promise that we'd be in touch in a few days.

I parked when I got to the house and practically crawled up the darkened stairs. I went straight for the shower, tired and sore, and needing to clear my head. Trace had left me feeling muzzy, and I wasn't sure if it was the champagne, the Chinese food, or just too much fucking, which I didn't really think was possible, because Kerry and I had really enjoyed marathoning it when we had the time.

Ah, Kerry, I reflected as I shampooed my hair. Sex with Kerry had always been fantastic, unpredictable, and had run through moods from soft and sensual, to playful, to please-baby-now urgency, but never, ever, had it had this edge to it, this uncontrollable fire that burned everything it touched.

My back stung in more than one place; in fact, it felt like my whole body stung as the soapy water sluiced off my skin, and I was more careful than I ever remember having to be when I wrapped myself in a towel.

Nina and Samantha were coming up the stairs as I closed the bathroom door behind me.

"Hey," I greeted.

"Backatchya." Samantha smiled at me, a smile that quickly became a crease between her eyes as she focused on me.

"Hi, Tori. How're you—holy shit!" Nina exclaimed, staring at my neck and shoulders as she approached me.

"Uh, Tor—" Sam began.

"I've got this," Nina interrupted her, taking me gently by the arm and leading me back to the bathroom.

"Yours," Samantha agreed, and waved acquiescence as I looked from one to the other in confusion. What the fuck?

"Nina, what?" I asked as I let her direct my steps. I was really tired and just wanted to get to bed.

She flipped the light on and turned me to face the mirror, her hands warm on my arms. She stood behind me.

Holy shit was right. I was covered in scratches and bruises, from just under the jawline to whatever disappeared under the towel. Named and claimed? Trace had staked me out as surely as if I'd been a gold rush tract—there was absolutely no mistaking exactly how those deep red marks, which were only beginning to blossom into the dark purple they'd become, had originated. Not even my arms had escaped her design.

"She scratched your face," Nina said, her voice taking on an edge that I knew was anger, as she pointed at my reflection. I craned my head at an angle to see. She was right; two clear red lines ran from my cheek to just under my chin.

Nina peeked down the towel behind me. "Turn around," she said, that edge in her tone even sharper, "and take a look at your back."

Shocked speechless, I did, twisting my head. I stared, and stared some more, because my back was well scored, some grooves so thoroughly etched that the edges still seeped red. I looked back at Nina and didn't know what to say.

"Tori..." She rubbed her face with her hand, then ran it through her hair. "Tor, I don't care if you get laid, I don't really care what you're into so long as you're okay, but Tori..." She carefully touched my shoulder. "Are you okay with this?" She stared up at me, her eyes a combination of deep blue center and gray outer edge. It struck me in that second how similar that gray was to Trace's, how that color fascinated me.

I sat back against the counter. "I...I don't know," I answered, thinking as I spoke, because I hadn't known how marked up I was. All I did know was that I had left there feeling strange.

Nina got some cotton balls and hydrogen peroxide from the cabinet.

"You don't have to know right now," she said as she moistened one and applied it to my cheek. It stung lightly as she drew it down. "Just don't let anyone touch your face," she said, and tweaked the tip of my nose. "That Del Castillo face is too pretty to get marked up."

I chuckled and let her continue to swab my face and neck.

"It's...it's weird, you know?" I said as she turned me around so she could reach my back. Ugh, that stung too.

"What is?" she asked as I watched her concentrate first on one mark, then another.

"It's just..." I sighed and tried again. "It's just so different, you know?"

"Hmm," was all she said. "Sit still, this is gonna sting a bit more." She dabbed at a point on my shoulder. "Different how, Tor?"

"Ow!" I exhaled sharply. She was right, that *had* stung quite a bit more, and I involuntarily flinched.

"Sorry, sorry. You've got a few like that."

"It's okay," I answered, tired and subdued. It was strange in a nice way, Nina cleaning up my boo-boos like she had from time to time when I was a kid. It hit me that Nina had never lied or exaggerated to me; she'd meant everything she'd said. She took care of me the way I used to take care of Elena, the way I still did, like a favorite little sister, which meant I could trust her, with anything.

"Different how, Tori?" she asked me again.

"I don't know, it's just so…it's not like it was with—" I shut up, because I didn't want to argue about my ex-girlfriend with Nina, not after the way I'd been such an ass about the whole thing.

"You mean, different with this girl than with Kerry?" Nina asked softly, soothing cotton along my arm.

"Yeah," I said, quietly. I was tired, confused, and uncertain.

Nina nodded. "That makes sense," she said, "different people and all." She took my chin in her fingers and inspected my face, then focused on my cheek again and dabbed at that too.

Her touch was so comforting and I was so tired. Good hands, I thought, Nina has good hands. It was an observation I'd made in class, during practical lectures. Some of my classmates, some of my instructors, they had this way of taking a pulse, or applying a bandage. They had a deftness, a knowingness in their fingertips that translated into a sense of security, a knowledge that the hands doing the work held strength, compassion, and competence. Nina had that sure touch; she would have made a good EMT, I thought, as I leaned my head back and closed my eyes. Very good hands.

"So what's her name?"

"Hmm?"

"This one who's so…what's her name?"

"Oh, it's Trace…" I thought a moment, trying to remember her last name as Nina applied another drip of peroxide to my face, "Trace Cayden."

The sound of the bottle smashing to the ground, the impact magnified in the tiled room, echoed alarmingly around and in my head, making my eyes snap open on Samantha standing in the doorway as Nina shook her head.

"You okay?" Samantha's face was a study in concern.

"Oh, man, I'm sorry, I'll get that," I offered, hopping down from the counter.

"I got it. I'm not that pregnant yet." Nina smiled at me, but her eyes were silver.

Samantha stepped into the room, and we collided as we both bent for the peroxide. She got there first and my towel slipped as I straightened. I caught it quickly, but not quite fast enough.

I heard Nina's sharp intake of breath, and the color drained from Samantha's face. Her lips set into a thin, grim line, but her voice was soft. "Let me see."

I shifted the towel and looked down for myself, and there, in the only spot of skin that hadn't been scratched or torn, across the bony parts of my chest and dipping between my breasts, was a bruise, a pattern.

"It's a cross—technically, an iron cross," Samantha said in the same low tone as she very gently covered me back up. She and Nina exchanged a glance.

Trace had put that there, not the first time, not even the second, but sometime before I'd left, when I'd let her lie on top of me and jerk me off. It had been a mind-blowing combination of drunken haze, cunt-throbbing thrill, and that knife-edge blend of pain and pleasure as she'd sucked on my chest and made me come.

Exhaustion swept over me and I yawned. "You guys mind if I go to bed? You can explain it to me tomorrow."

Samantha's expression cleared as suddenly as a cloud break. "Sure, and no worries about breakfast tomorrow, I've got it, okay?" She gave me a kiss on the cheek, a quick hug, then left the room.

Nina lingered a moment. "You feel all right?"

"Yeah, just really tired. Must have been the afternoon drinking."

Nina nodded. "If you want to talk..."

I smiled at her with as much cheerfulness as I could muster as we walked to my room. "I'll find you. Don't worry."

"Cool. Sleep well, then."

"Sure, you too," I said as I reached for my door.

"Hey, Tor?" Nina stopped me and placed a careful, warm hand on my shoulder.

"Yeah?"

Nina's eyes earnestly searched mine. "You...you know I love you, right?"

"Of course." From the way her mouth curved, I knew she wanted to say more even as she hesitated.

"I'd never violate your privacy or ask you, I mean..." She shifted her hand from my shoulder to touch my chin before she dropped it. "You'd tell me...if you had a problem, I mean?"

I was touched, truly touched by her concern. Things had gone maybe a bit further with Trace than I was used to, but really, I was okay.

"I'm fine, honest. It's just a couple of scratches, nothing to write home about." I smiled down at her as reassuringly as I could.

"Oh, hey," I asked as the thought occurred to me, "do you know if it's a boy or a girl yet?"

Nina shook her head and grinned at me. "Good dodge, Tori, good dodge. And to answer *your* question, there's a lot of movement going on, so no one's certain yet."

I nodded. "That happens. I guess, ah, you guys should get some rest, right?"

"We probably should, and you probably should too. Good night, Tori." She kissed my cheek.

"You too," I said as I kissed her in return, then opened my door.

That…was weird, I reflected as I took off the towel I'd been wearing and hung it on a hook next to my closet. Fuck pajamas, I thought as I went to my bed; my skin was too sensitive to handle even the lightest clothes. I sat on the edge of the bed and as I did, something on my dresser caught my eye—the present Kerry had given me, still unopened.

I pulled it down and stared at it, with no idea what it could be, but there was only one way to find out, and I teased the folded edges carefully, not wanting to tear the paper or rush the discovery.

Once the paper was off, I folded it carefully and put it on the night table. I held a box, a white box, and after slicing through the tape that held it closed on either end, I opened it.

On top of the carefully folded tissue paper lay a letter, which I pulled out first.

Tori, I read in the lamplight,

I know, I know, you'll say it's too soon, because you like to hedge your bets, but still I hope you're celebrating what I also know has been a very successful day for you. I know how hard you've worked for this and how much it means to you.

At first I was shocked, then I realized I shouldn't have been when I found out who you're related to. Well, it makes a lot of sense, Stud, you're a lot more alike than you think, and Tori? I'm sorry I hurt you, I never wanted to do that.

I know, I know, I pushed and I did things I shouldn't have, but as I watched you fall in love, first with your class, then with the ideas behind it, I realized, this is you, this is what you're going to do. Tough guy, I can't stand the thought of getting a phone call one day telling me you got hurt.

You deserve your chances, you deserve the best, you deserve a lot more than me.

You've got good hands, Victoria Scotts, and you're going to do great.

I miss you, I love you, and I hope you'll be careful when you're out there.

Love always, Kerry.

After I'd finished reading her note my chest hurt in ways I didn't know it could, and my eyes stung, sharper than the etchings on my back or shoulders did. I reached under the paper and felt with careful fingers, removing what I found.

I don't know how long I sat there with it in my hand while I buried my face in the other and cried.

It was blue. My favorite shade of blue. A Sprague Rappaport.

CIRCULATION

Is there life-threatening hemorrhage? Control bleeds. Treat for shock as necessary.

Trace called me two days later. "How're you feeling?" she asked in that throaty purr that stirred me.

"I feel...fine," I answered, "though that first shower was a bit, uh, sharp."

"Ah well, at least you could *walk*," she laughed, "and you look great naked."

Even though I knew she couldn't see me, I could feel the warm rush of blood race up my neck and flood my face. I didn't know how to answer, because I still didn't know how I felt. I remembered, quite vividly, how savagely that fuck had gone under her urging, but a part of me couldn't help but think the entire time that it had to hurt and I would never, ever, have done something like that with someone else, except that I had, with her, and the memory throbbed through my groin to swell my clit to a pounding urgency while guilt tugged at my head and killed my words. I couldn't reconcile the guilt and the memory of the fuck, which seemed to go against everything I'd ever known, the polar opposite of what my instincts usually were, but instead dug deeper, to another place, a different level, a level that I'd never visited before—and when I was in that place, I felt so out-of-fucking-control good, but in a very frightening way.

"I think I still owe you a dinner," Trace drawled into the silence, "and at the very least, that cup of coffee."

"We never did get to that, did we?" I laughed.

We arranged to meet later that night, and it was a nice evening. She made cappuccino quite well, and we supposedly watched a couple of movies, which we really ignored instead and talked about life in general, and of all things, school in particular because it turned out Trace had gone to the same college I went to, and we'd had quite a few of the same professors.

The talking evolved into closer physical proximity, which evolved into our wrapping around each other in an extremely sensual make-out session, but as tempting as Trace was at that moment, and she was the first person in a long time who almost made me come with my clothes on, and as much as she said it would be fine if I blew off work the next day, because, hey, I'd be working on the rig soon enough, I still had to get up, still had to deal with that checkout line.

When I asked her not to mark my face up again, she laughed and agreed, then left me a clearly visible ring of red marks around my neck.

And…I still wasn't entirely comfortable with what we, no, what I, had done, the last time we were together. I still couldn't even begin to find the words to describe it, but I didn't feel right. I was glad she didn't push it further—I don't think I could have said no.

My EMT card came in the mail about three days later, and it took about that long for the lightest of those first marks to fade.

Nina winced every time she glimpsed a bruise, and her eyes would flash silver at the sight of the scratches on my face because they looked worse on the second and third days than they had on the first—thankfully they were the ones that faded quickly. Samantha could barely look at me, and when our eyes did catch, she'd glance quickly away but not before I'd catch the grim line her mouth would set in. All in all, it made me feel pretty bad, and I was glad it was cool enough out that I could wear turtlenecks.

"Mail for you." Samantha pointed with her chin when I popped into the kitchen after another long day of smiling at too many people, making correct change, and dropping singles into the safe for the other cashiers at the supermarket.

"Thanks," I said to her back and poured myself a cup of coffee.

"Sure." She sat at the table to review the sheaf of papers she held and had nothing else to say to me, for which I felt a vague sense of guilt. Ever since that morning, night, whatever it was with Trace, this stilted feeling had existed among all of us.

I took a sip of my java and sighed. Maybe I could talk with Nina about it, I thought as I thumbed through the mail.

Credit-card offer, magazine offer, bank come-on. No, no, no, I told each envelope as I neatly shredded them with my fingers. Cell-phone offer, student-loan-consolidation offer—I had enough of those. A plain, white, legal-sized envelope. The upper left corner said "New York State Department of Health" in black letters. The envelope felt weighty, like it held more than one piece of paper.

Surprised, even a little scared to see what it contained, I stared at the paper in my hand. Yes, Bob had said I'd passed, but still, what if something had gone wrong, what if I'd screwed up a major section? I held a tremendous part of my future in my hands.

I took a deep breath and let it out slowly. It *was* here, it *was* in my hands, and I had to know if everything I'd worked so hard for had been worth it. If I hadn't passed, if this wasn't my license, I would improvise and adapt. I would absolutely overcome. But first, I had to know.

My fingers went numb as I split the envelope's seam and pulled out the paper, a thin cardstock, really.

Victoria Scotts, I read, along with my social security number, *test score: 98.*

Please tear off this card.
Victoria Scotts, EMT-B.
Expires on...

"Hey, whatchya got?" Samantha's voice sounded so suddenly behind me I jumped. I still don't know how she always managed to move so silently.

I held the paper and its attached card before me as I faced her. "This." I couldn't help but beam as she took it from me to read for herself.

"Tori!" she exclaimed, a smile breaking out across her face. "That's just too cool!" She clapped my shoulder. "Congratulations!"

"Thanks," and I laughed because I couldn't help it—I really had done it. "I'm official."

"You sure are." Sam grinned at me. "So, what are you gonna do now?"

It was a good question that deserved a good answer, and I'd given some thought to it for a while, especially since I'd broken up with Kerry.

"Find a job until I get called for the academy, take a leave of absence from school to try to catch up on some of my loans, find a place, and pay you guys back," I said in an almost breathless rush.

"Sounds good," Samantha nodded, "except you don't have to pay us anything, and you don't have to be in a rush to go anywhere. This is your home, Tori."

My breath caught on a huge weight I hadn't even acknowledged existed in my chest, and I stared at the ground.

"Hey…hey, Tori." Samantha touched my chin lightly and raised my face to hers. "Tori, you don't have to go anywhere—did you think we wanted you to?"

Her eyes were wide and brilliant blue, and they looked at me with such care that I could only nod as my eyes sparked.

"Aw, man, I'm sorry." Sam pulled me into her arms. "I'm really sorry, it's just…sorry."

I didn't know what was wrong with me, but the moment Samantha had me enfolded, I started to cry. Oddly, I'd been on the edge of tears for days, and I never, ever cried, except for those rare occasions when I dreamt of my grandmother, and even then, I banished the tears as soon as the dream dissolved.

I was still crying when Nina got home, and I couldn't stop when she had me tucked up at her side on the sofa, head held securely against her shoulder while she kissed it and stroked my back. She held me with the same loving firmness my grandmother had, murmuring soothing words, and the sound of her voice reached through the nameless hurt and transported me back to the first time she'd spoken to me like that.

My father had come bursting into the house, screaming and yelling, demanding to see my mother, and I don't know what possessed me, at nine years old, to defy him, to attempt to forbid him from speaking to my mother that way, but I did. He cuffed my head so hard my ears rang, and between the time he'd hit me and drawn his hand back to do it again, Nina had run in and snatched me up.

"She's just a baby, Edward," she said over her shoulder, omitting the *tío* or "uncle" honorific, a deadly insult in and of itself. He chased her as she carried me in her arms. I buried my head into her shoulder, my safe spot, until she was in a corner, and she put me gently down, her body between me and my father as I clung to her waist.

"She's just a baby," she repeated, and stroked my hand in a soothing gesture where it gripped. "You've done enough."

"*Cobarde!*" *Coward!* my grandmother said, more contempt in her voice than I'd ever heard, and as I peeped from behind Nina's waist, I could feel my eyes widen as she smashed the broom she wielded on my father's head.

"Take Victoria to your room, right now!" my grandmother ordered as she rained more blows on my father and he danced away from her and toward the back door she was obviously herding him to.

Nina obeyed and once again scooped me up. Up in her room, I suddenly felt the shock of my father's anger and the pain in my head, and I started to cry.

She gathered me onto her lap and into her arms, her head over mine as she spoke the same words she did now.

"It's okay, *hermanita*, it's all right…I've got you," she said, over and over. "I'm not gonna let anyone hurt you."

Like then, I clung to her and cried even harder; it would be a long time before I could puzzle out why.

❖

I finally got a job working per diem at a private ambulance company. I'd applied at every hospital first, but University Hospital had a hiring freeze, the local Saint Vincent's was "full-up" at the moment, and the other ones I went to wanted more experience. I heard "Sorry, outta luck, kid" at least three different times from three different emergency-response coordinators.

I stopped at the emergency room back at University anyway to say hello to Debbie and chat.

"You just keep coming back," Debbie said and smiled, "because you'll do well here."

It took some doing to get my first job at that private company, though.

When I first went and interviewed, Marco, the dispatcher and the one who held the key to my future employment, said, "Sure, no problem. Call me in a week and we'll get you a start day, probably next weekend."

That was fantastic, so I gave my notice at the supermarket, happier than anything to give up that apron and cash my second-to-last check.

I stopped by my mom's to give her the cash for Elena and entered quietly.

After I put the envelope on the table with a little note, I was about to step out again when my mother's voice surprised me.

"Let me see you." Her voice may have been sleepy, but it was still commanding.

I hastened over to her sofa and gave her a kiss hello. "Hi, Mom," I said in Spanish. "I didn't want to wake you."

She shifted over and made room for me.

"Sit, Victoria. You haven't visited in a while. What have you been doing?"

"Work, and I've been interviewing for EMT positions."

My mother grimaced as she sat up, and I helped her because she'd been suffering from back pain the last few times I'd seen her. She worried me; such a sedentary lifestyle couldn't be healthy.

"Put the light on?" she asked. "I want to look at you."

I reached over for the lamp, unsure of what she'd look for, but I knew that she'd see a lot, and it usually wasn't something I expected.

"You seem thinner," she said finally. "Are you eating, *querida*? Is Nina not feeding you?"

I sighed. "Of course she's taking good care of me. She and Samantha are wonderful."

She patted the sofa next to her. "Sit with me, *hija*. I want to talk with you."

As I sat next to her and she took my hand, it struck me how frail her bones felt, how delicate my mother was. Yet I knew she had once been made of steel, famous for the justice and compassion she showed. She'd been jailed in a stone room with no plumbing whatsoever and nothing to sleep on but her own jacket for protesting military juntas, had refused a police escort when she had received death threats from the drug cartels, and even after my father had left her, she had still walked proudly, at least for a while.

My grandmother had told me about that time, and she'd told me that my mother had never expected my father to really leave forever.

I couldn't imagine what it had taken for her to move here, to this country she didn't like, to this house with my uncle she didn't get along with, just to make sure that Elena and I had something in our lives, to be near our aunt and cousins, to get a good education in a country where being a divorced woman wouldn't be held against her or her children. But her depression and the U.S. requirement that she basically redo her entire degree, then retake the bar exam on top of that because she was a foreign national, were too much for her.

Yes, it was true, she hadn't really "been there" all the time for me or for Elena when we'd been children, but she'd made sure that we'd be around people who were, people she trusted: her mother, her sister, her sister's children. Her family.

It didn't matter what she did or didn't do for the last however many years, because I realized in that moment that not merely my father's remarriage, but the loss of her sense of self, of the profession she loved, topped by the death of my grandmother, had knocked her to the ground, shattered her steel.

Suddenly, I was filled with emotion I could only describe as this: she was my mother, and when she couldn't do something herself, this once-so-proud woman had sacrificed what was left of that pride and asked for help. I loved her and was proud of her for what she'd done—the best she could.

"You know, *amor*, Nina was always the queen of your grandmother's heart, even mine. She was the first, and she was always the best at everything. But you, *mi hija*," and she squeezed my fingers gently, "you were always my princess, my beautiful princess. I wanted such things for you…" She sighed. "Things I'm sorry I couldn't give you."

"No, Mom, you've done great, you've—"

"Hush, Tori, let me say this now, while I'm clear, while it's just you and me and we have this time, where I can be your mother and you can be my princess."

She smiled at me, the smile I remembered from when I was very small, and her eyes were bright with tears. Nina's eyes, I thought, she and Nina have the same eyes, while mine were all my father. I wondered if it hurt my mother to see the resemblance.

"Nina was a queen dethroned, and you a princess in exile, but look at you! Look at what you've done. You've found a way to do everything, gracefully. My princess has been the man of the house, and for that, Victoria, I am so very sorry."

Tears rolled down her cheeks and I impulsively hugged her, my mother, her body so frail in the circle of my arms. These moments when she was my mother, just my *mamita*, were rare, and I treasured them.

"I love you, *Mamita*, and you've always done your best for us. How could I not do that too?"

I felt a lot better, about work, about Trace, about everything when I went back home. I realized as I drove that the little kid part of me had never given up hope that one day my mother would come back, leave that world in her head that hurt her so much, and take not just comfort, but joy in how much Elena and I loved her. Maybe that day wasn't too far away, I told the little girl in my head as I sighted into the rearview mirror; maybe, someday, it would come after all.

❖

I got fed up after three weeks of Marco's "Tell her I'll call her back" every time I phoned. I'd quit my job for this one; I needed an income.

It would take something clever to get him on the phone, and I had a plan as I listened to it ring in my ear.

"County," a female voice answered.

"Hi, can I speak with Marco, please?"

"May I ask who's calling?"

I had the answer, the only thing I could think of that would get any guy on the phone. I took a deep breath. "Tell Marco it's the mother of his child."

Hold music came on and less than two seconds later, he picked up.

"Hello? Who is this?"

"Hi, Marco, it's Tori, Victoria Scotts. You said you had a start date for me?"

"Oh, man!" Marco laughed. "You had me scared!"

"Yeah, and you had me working, remember?"

"Yeah, yeah, I did," he admitted. "Okay, kid, when can you start?"

"As soon as you want. I was ready to start a few weeks ago."

He sighed. "Tell you what. Start in two days. Come in at six a.m. and we'll get you trained, okay?"

"Great. Thanks!"

"Yeah, kid, just make sure you get the blue uniform pants. You defibrillation trained?"

"Yes." I remembered the practical lessons and the jump of the practice dummy as the electric current passed through it.

"Good. Make sure you've got the right patches on your shirt. I'll see you in forty-eight at oh six hundred."

I'd already ordered my shield with the state seal and my license numbers on it, and I picked it up that day, along with the blue uniform pants, after I spent about two hours waiting for them to be hemmed.

It took another half an hour for me to patch my sleeve, the New York state orange and blue tombstone on the side.

Rising before the sun, I made a pot of coffee, and Samantha came down while I waited for it to brew.

"Morning," she said.

"It sure is."

"You know, Tori, Nina, and I were talking and, well, the garden apartment out back—you want it?"

I gawked at her. "You guys had enough of me?" I finally managed to jokingly splutter.

Samantha smiled. "No, silly, you're always part of the family. This is your house too. We thought you might want your own space, though."

"Wow" was the only coherent comment I could come up with.

"Oh, uh, how much do you guys want for it?" There, now that sounded like a very responsible and intelligent question.

Samantha studied the tiles on the floor before she spoke again. "I occasionally need to travel, and I'd really appreciate if you'd just watch out for Nina."

She watched me carefully.

"That's...that's a given, Samantha." I would always do that, because I loved my cousin. She'd always looked out for me, and I wouldn't do any less for her.

"Okay," she nodded, "that's my only concern. So...do we have a deal?"

"Yeah, yeah, we do." I shook her hand.

"Oh, by the way? I need a new sparring partner now that Nina's, um, well," Samantha grinned, "you know. You up for that?"

I grinned back. "Well, I don't really know much about it, but I'll give it a shot."

"I'll teach you, and it'll be good for your back after the days you're going to have."

"You might be right," I agreed. "You might be right."

❖

I drove over the Narrows Bridge into Brooklyn, found the ambulance garage and a parking space, then walked in. After I introduced myself at the window to the dispatcher, Barbara, she picked up a phone, hit a button, and yelled, "Marco, the fresh meat is here!" She had an interesting accent, which I soon learned was West Indies.

She put the phone back in its cradle and smiled broadly. "Welcome to hell, Ms. Scotts. I'll be your personal tour guide for a few days."

"You can call me Tori or Scotty. You don't have to call me Ms. Scotts."

Barbara leaned out the dispatch window. "Now you listen, Ms. Scotts. I may not be a big-time EMT or paramedic like you, but I know my medical, I know my patients, and I know how to give and get respect. Excuse me." She held up a finger and sat back down, then grabbed a portable radio off the desk.

"Where's my pick-up, six Charlie? Mrs. Sherman is an old lady, over."

The radio crackled back at her. "We're pulling up, Ms. Barbara, pulling up now, so keep your wig on."

"You keep your mouth shut and I might let you keep yours," Barbara retorted as she ticked something off in the ledger before her. "Now don't drop anyone, over."

Laughter trickled back through the static. "Ten-four, Barbara, and we'll see you in thirty minutes with your coffee, over."

"Shoulda been twenty," she grumbled back, "and don't forget my sugar." She clicked off and grabbed the phone while she looked back up at me.

"Marco!" she yelled into it. "You get your ass here so we can get this girl trained!" She slammed the phone down.

"You—come back here." She crooked a finger at me.

I walked through the door into the office, and she pointed to a clipboard on the wall. "Find your name, sign in for the very second you walked into the garage, and give me your driver's license and EMT card," she said and held her hand out while she picked up the radio again. "Ten Oscar, where are you? Over," she asked into the microphone.

I pulled my wallet from my back pocket and handed her the cards as she snapped her fingers at me. Then I found the appropriate clipboard. There was my name, Victoria Scotts, with "per diem" and "6 a.m.–3 p.m." next to it. I signed in what I hoped were the correct spaces and put my time in as 5:45 a.m.

"Lazy piece of shit," Barbara grumbled. "That's why Marco has no mister to his name." Barbara glared at me, then just as suddenly smiled. Since her expression seemed to be directed past my arm, I looked behind me to see what had caused it.

A woman walked past the dispatch window and through the door with an arrogant slouch, her hair a solid brown and slightly longer than mine, her belt hung just so over her hips, a sullen-red stethoscope flung around the collar of her jacket, and a bright orange tech bag slung over a shoulder.

"Ah, Ms. Barbara, my love, when are you gonna tell that lazy-ass husband of yours about our hot affair and let me take you away in style?" she deadpanned as she signed in on a clipboard.

"What? Leave all this glamour behind? Maybe when you get your big-time medic job with the city," Barbara joked back as the phone in front of her lit up like fireworks on a hot summer night and each line screamed for attention.

"Hey, as soon as they call me, I'll come get you." The woman laughed, then turned her attention to me. She appeared to be almost six feet tall and very fair skinned, with a dusting of sprinkles across her cheeks. She was very pretty, and I estimated her to be about twenty-five, maybe twenty-six years old. And boy, she had some shoulders—I wondered if she'd developed them on the job. The name tag above her breast said "Scanlon."

"Fresh meat?" she asked me, a friendly curve lighting her face. Dark brown eyes inspected me from an expression that read "good people." I liked her right away.

I shrugged. "Maybe."

"Nice Sprague, good color."

"Thanks." I smiled and held out my hand. "I'm Tori Scotts." I didn't know if she had good hands yet, but she had a good handshake. "But everyone calls me Scotty."

"Well, Scotty," she answered, "I'm Jean, and everyone will tell you I'm the psycho dyke bitch, so just leave me alone and we'll be fine," she said with a smile that told me not to take her words too seriously.

A blond guy with a crew cut came through the door and trudged over to the sign-in wall.

"Well, Jean," I answered as he walked past me, "I'm just a dyke EMT."

"Cool." She nodded, her smile even brighter. "Very cool."

"Oh, great, *another* one?" the guy muttered from the clipboard where he signed in.

Barbara wheeled her chair over and shoved my cards back at me. "Chuck, you're just jealous because she does better work with her pee-pee than you," she snapped at him as I tucked my licenses back into my wallet. "And you? Just a dog."

I tried hard not to laugh when Jean barked, then snapped her teeth at him. Chuck just shook his head and scowled.

"You, Ms. Scotty, you ride with Ms. Psycho-Bitch Scanlon and Up-Chuck here," Barbara jerked a thumb at him, "and I want you back tomorrow for the ten a.m."

"Okay, sure."

"Oh, Barbara, I thought it was you, me, and my pee-pee tomorrow at ten," Jean teased with a dramatic eye roll.

"I'll pick the position, you pick the color." Barbara grinned at her, then glanced around at all of us. "Well?" Her expression changed instantly from mirth to mock fury, "What are you all still doing here? Get out of my office!" she snapped, and we hustled out as the phones rang madly.

❖

The days passed quickly, and I crawled into bed at the end of every shift, grateful to sleep. Most of the work consisted of medical transports, dialysis patients that needed to be monitored to and from their appointments, hospital-to-hospital transfers (and some of those were very interesting because of the complications involved), as well as true emergencies from nursing homes or the occasional flag-downs from MVAs.

I met some of the other crews on a few shifts and worked with quite a few of them as I rotated through. Chuck had been right: just about all the girls were gay, and at least half of the guys too. It was amazing to watch: affairs ran rampant between crews, within crews, inter-shift, and high drama exploded whenever certain pairs, gay or straight, ran into others either in the emergency room or at a dialysis center.

The day crews tended to be circumspect about who was with whom, but those overnight crews? You could always tell which new pairing had formed and which had ended by watching the schedule change: a new person to the day with weepy eyes over the next week or so, contrasted with a happy new person on an overnight. Well, it didn't take a brain surgeon to figure out the logistics. Besides, the overnights were almost dead quiet, which left plenty of time for two bored people to become friends, and more, if that's what they were into.

A night rig could park almost anywhere it wanted, so long as it wasn't too far from the base or out of range for a call from dispatch.

One night during dinner I told Trace about the crazy relationship dynamics at the base; I'd picked her up after her shift and had the next two days off.

"It's a lot like junior high school, but instead of who held whose hand, it's sex," I said.

"So, anyone you're interested in?" she asked with a sly smile.

"What?" I was incredulous and certain my reaction reflected in my voice, if it wasn't obvious on my face.

She put her fork down and slid out of her seat to glide over to me, her hips a dangerous sway as she neared. My heart began to pound, and I wasn't completely certain if I was afraid or aroused.

She threw a long leg over mine and sat down.

Her touch was delicate when she took my chin in her hands. "I don't care," she said softly, then kissed me, "who you fuck," she finished as she first rolled my now-hard nipple under her palm before she let her hand rest on my crotch.

My clit was even harder under the pressure of that hand as she unzipped my pants for access, then began to jerk me off in earnest as her tongue tangled again with mine.

I couldn't help myself or my reactions, because she had me so wet and so ready, and I reacted automatically: reached for the knot of her scrubs, eased my hands beneath the thin cloth to stroke her clit with one and explore her more intimately with the other, and slipped my fingers along the sodden furrow and gently teased her.

"Really?" I asked breathlessly, "you don't care?"

"God…" she groaned as I entered her fully and her cunt held me, a suck on my fingers that made me swell under hers. "I don't," she whispered hotly in my ear as she played my clit expertly and teased me in return, making me squirm beneath her while I pumped her firmly, "so long as you think of me—"

Oh, my God, she was making me wait, wait for her to fill me. "Trace…" I growled in her ear. "You're killing me—"

"Yeah?" Her voice was a harsh whisper as she slid partly into me. "You want this, baby?"

I inhaled sharply and pushed against her, then stilled my fingers slightly. "You stop…I'll stop," I promised as her cunt tightened around me, urging me to continue.

"Mmph…can't have that." Trace shifted her hips off me and slammed back down, on me, in me, grinding her hips against my thighs.

"Shit…yeah!" I agreed because she felt good, everywhere.

She rode me in earnest and I stayed buried in her cunt while her clit slicked along between my fingers and she took me where I needed to go.

"Gonna come…" The words ripped out of my throat.

"Good," she groaned. Her cunt tightened around me further, and I swear her clit throbbed harder, bigger, as she fucked me.

"Come…come any way, with anyone, you want," and she breathed between each word, "just think of me."

"Thinking of you…right now," and I did.

❖

We managed not to wreck any furniture, and Trace had me again before midnight, flat on my back and riding my dick, and this time, she held my arms back over my head as I fucked her, which was…different. It wasn't bad, it wasn't bad at all, but I still had that faint red bruise on my chest, and this time when she bit me, in the hollow next to my collarbone, she drew blood.

I still came and so did she, before I did, anyway, something which left me both glad and relieved. Coming before she did always made me feel…wrong…but despite that relief, something was…off.

"You'll like that even better next time," she promised as she lay on top of me, my cock still inside her as she ground slowly against me.

I didn't mind the break because this had been our third or fourth time; I was starting to get sore. "Yeah?" I was still enjoying the aftershocks and the rebuild of the tension, the slick ride of her skin on mine, and the renewed tightening in my groin that hardened my clit.

"Yeah." She kissed me, her mouth tasting of my blood as her fingertips scratched up, along the sensitive skin of my arm. "I want to *fuck* you," she said in my ear as she held my wrist firmly.

"What?" I wasn't sure I'd heard her, because the easy glide and the embers it sparked had already blazed, had become a burn, an almost urgent thrust, the red heat threatening to become something I couldn't control, while the pain that shot through me equaled the thrill.

"Fuck, Tori," she whispered hoarsely, "I want to *fuck* you, fuck you until—"

I'd never been so relieved to hear my cell phone ring.

"I've got to get that," I breathed, and twisted to reach for my pants. That's when I realized she'd tied my wrist. My first instinct was to panic, but instead, I forced myself to breathe.

"Trace, I have to answer that." I kept my voice steady as my phone chimed again. "This late at night it can only be my family or work."

"Can't you call whoever it is back in a little while?"

All I could feel now was the discomfort deep inside, and a rising sense of frustration. "No. I can't." I clipped my words so I could control them, contain the emotion. "If it's my family, someone's ill. If it's work, I'm still per diem—I have to answer."

Trace kissed me, the metallic iron taste still on her tongue.

"All right," she sighed, grabbed my phone, and held it up to my face.

"Scotty."

"Hey, Scotty, it's Marco. I need you to come in as soon as you can. We're down a medic on the overnight team, and we can still ride them with an EMT. Figure you'll end about eight or nine a.m."

"Sure, give me an hour to get there."

"Great," was the last thing I heard him say as Trace took the phone back and snapped it shut.

"You've got to go."

"Yep."

Her nipples brushed past my face as she untied me, and we exchanged no words as I stumbled for the shower. While part of me couldn't believe I had to go back to work, because my muscles screamed with exhaustion, I was also more relieved than I can ever remember being that I could leave without making any excuses.

As I washed off, I could really feel how sore everything was. Parts of me were too sensitive to even touch, and when I did I noticed a red smear.

Blood. She'd left me bloody. I should have stopped hours ago, I thought, angry with myself as I painfully rinsed.

I dressed quickly because I had an extra shirt there and walked out into the living room, ready to go.

"Hey, this is for you," Trace said as she came out of the kitchen and handed me a paper bag, "because you can't find anyplace to eat this late." She kissed my cheek tenderly.

I'd been ready to say good-bye, to find a reason to maybe not see her again quite so soon because whenever the sex twisted like that I always felt so odd, but the kiss, the considerate lunch, and the hug she wrapped me in softened my edges, muted my emotions to a hazy confusion.

I kissed the top of her head and hugged her back. "I'll call you tomorrow."

It was cold outside, and I was glad my uniform jacket had a lining when I got into my car and keyed the ignition. Fuck. My car wouldn't start. I tried again, and after some hopeful sounds, it died again.

Trace knocked on my window. "I'll drive you."

"Fuck," was all I said, shaking my head in disgust at my car. I checked the dummy lights on the dashboard. Nothing. My battery had probably died.

"Come on," Trace urged, "we've got twenty minutes to get there."

I checked my watch: she was right. I had no other option.

"Thanks, thanks a lot," I said as we pulled up.

"Don't mention it." She patted my thigh.

I hefted my orange tech bag from the backseat and got out, slinging that familiar weight behind me.

"Don't forget your food," Trace said as she came around the car, once again handed me the paper bag, then caressed my neck and shoulders.

"Be careful?" Her face was pale, almost ethereal, in the streetlight, her eyes dark, dark pewter and her mouth a bruise against her skin.

"I'll be fine. We don't get a lot of flag-downs or things like that." Irresistibly drawn, impelled, I kissed her, I couldn't help it, and her lips were baby soft against mine, her tongue tender and sensual in my mouth.

"Hey, hey, hey, if you're gonna do that, you have to share," Marco's voice cut in.

I waved him away behind my back.

"Marco, this is Trace," I said when we finally stopped for air. "Trace, Marco."

Trace held her hand out. "Pleased."

Marco took it in his and, instead of shaking it, he bent over and kissed it. "Pleasure's all mine."

I backhanded his shoulder. "Hey! I don't share!"

I glanced at Trace, who seemed amused as Marco rubbed his arm.

"Hope lives on." He smirked. "Hope lives on. Okay," he clapped his hands, "say good night and get your ass in here, Scotty. You're riding with Jean. Nice meeting you, Trace." He grinned at her and disappeared into the garage. "Jean!" he bellowed. "Where the hell are you?"

Trace pulled my collar up around my neck to keep me warm. "You don't have to share, not if you don't want to," she murmured into my ear, "but I can. Do whatever you want." Then she kissed me again.

"I've got to go," I said finally. "I'll pick up my car later."

"Want me to pick you up after your shift? I can call in late."

I considered her offer for about half a second. No, as much as I enjoyed kissing her, I knew that if she picked me up, we'd end up fucking, and I wasn't ready to go through another round just yet, which in some ways was really strange, because I was almost always up for sex. Kerry and I had gotten along so well mainly because we'd matched each other in appetite.

"I'll get a ride with one of the rigs. I'll be fine."

"All right."

"I'll phone you after I get off," I called as she opened her car door.

Trace flashed me a smile, that wicked gleam of white I liked so much. "Just think of me when you do!"

I shook my head and went inside.

Jean, who was a medic, had already completed the "one hundred." Those who provided ALS, advanced life support, used the same general equipment as those who gave BLS, basic life support. But medics carried additional machinery, needles and IV fluids, and, more importantly as well as dangerously, drugs. Occasionally someone jumped and rolled a crew in a rough neighborhood, hoping to find morphine for recreational use.

However, as an EMT I just had to sign in, jump aboard, and tuck my tech bag in the back. I stowed the snack Trace had made for me in the front console.

"You don't mind if I drive as long as everything's quiet or the calls are all BLS, do you?" Jean asked before we climbed into the cab.

"No, not at all, works fine for me." I got into the passenger seat. "I prefer to tech anyway." That was true. I preferred patient care. If I'd wanted to drive all the time, I could have gone for a commercial truck license.

"Cool, cool." Jean nodded and keyed the mic. "Hey, Marco, we're gonna go sit off the Belt Parkway, under the Narrows Bridge, okay?"

"Yeah, cool. Bring me coffee when you come back to base."

"With or without sugar?"

Marco grumbled something. "Light and sweet, please, just like you in the morning."

Jean laughed. "Yeah, right. Ten-four."

The ambulance swung out of the garage into the night.

We didn't get many calls, but the ones we did get were strange. An elderly female patient, approximately eighty, from a nursing home had a prolapsed uterus. She'd borne eight children, and she was old, nothing else.

Transporting her was a bit difficult because we had to find her a comfortable position, well, that and we had to cover the exposed organ with dressings moistened with sterile saline so it wouldn't be abraded by contact with anything. Apparently, that sort of prolapse wasn't uncommon in women past a certain age, especially not in those who'd had four or more children, but it was still strange to see.

Next a male patient had somehow managed to fall out of his bed in the hospital and fracture his hip; his family understandably wanted him transferred to another facility and were so upset by the mishap that they wouldn't let anyone, not the nurses, not the doctors, care for the patient, aged fifty-three. His left hip bulged, he writhed in pain and cursed while his wife and someone we assumed was his son wrung their hands and looked on. They wanted him out, and they wanted him out now.

Since this was a hospital transfer, neither Jean nor I had expected to do anything other than evaluate vitals and monitor them, and had brought up only our tech bags and portable oxygen. Jean ran back down to the rig for the appropriate splints while I performed the initial evaluation.

The way this relatively young man cursed everything and everyone, we knew his airway was fine, but I checked everything in case I discovered something overlooked or hidden. He'd fallen hard enough to break a bone, and he could have hit his head and didn't remember, could have cracked a rib, or anything else.

When Jean returned we immobilized the fracture, and as Jean took tension from me on the injured site so I could fasten the first tie-down, I noticed, *good hands*. Jean had good hands.

That call took us almost two hours because the family wanted to go to a New Jersey hospital.

Jean decided we'd stay on Staten Island on the way back; most of our calls were from there, anyway.

"Mind if I eat?" I asked as we parked under the other side of the bridge, ironically almost directly across from where we'd been earlier.

"Nah, go ahead. You worked day today too, right?"

"Yeah, I did," I pulled the sack out of the spot I'd stuck it in, "so bio fuel is not a bad idea."

Jean snorted as I dug into the bag. An apple, a bottle of Gatorade, and a plastic container. Trace had included a fork and napkins and, underneath, two cookies. Chocolate chip, very cool, and among my favorites.

"Want one?"

"I'm all right." She laughed. "You probably need it more than I do."

"What?" I asked as I opened the container. Oh, awesome. Chicken cutlet and pasta. I was starving and done in moments, while Jean occasionally chuckled in my general direction.

"What's so funny?" I asked again as I uncapped the Gatorade.

"You." Jean smirked as she flicked the hair away from my neck. "That." She touched a spot with a gentle fingertip, then leaned back against the door and regarded me smugly.

I touched the spot and reached for the rearview. Dammit, large and fresh. I hadn't even noticed when Trace had done it, and I hadn't worn a turtleneck despite the cold because I'd forgotten, I'd been in such a rush.

I settled back down in my seat. "So…what?"

"So…that thing is so fresh you must have come up on the downstroke to answer the phone."

That was so close to the truth, as grateful as I had been for the phone to ring, that I could feel the heat rush to my face. But it was absolutely none of Jean's business, and something about the casualness of her tone pissed me off.

"Whatever," I answered. I hunkered down in my seat and closed my eyes. I was tired and had already started to learn to catch a nap whenever I could.

"Ah, come on," Jean cajoled, "you can tell me about it. We've got hours of nothing ahead of us. She have her legs wrapped tight around your waist while you fucked her and got called in to work with me? Or better, was she blowing you, lips nice, fast, and firm on your hard-on while you picked up the phone? No, no, not to leave a mark that fresh there…"

Every word she said brought a very visceral memory to the forefront of my brain, with an accompanying rush of blood to my groin. I hoped to hell the silence meant she'd stopped. I was wrong.

"I know! She was riding you, her lips on your neck and her pussy nice and snug on your cock, and you had to go and answer the phone."

I couldn't take it anymore. "Will you please shut the fuck up?" I opened my eyes and sat up straight. Now that was just wrong—respect for myself, respect for the woman I was sleeping with, and Jean's commentary lacked both.

She laughed at me. "Are you fucking stupid? No, wait, you were fucking *and* you were stupid."

I was wide-awake now, and the heat that blossomed in my neck had nothing to do with embarrassment or sex. It was anger, pure and simple.

"I'm serious, Jean, just shut up."

"Aw, what's the matter?" she taunted. "Are you still hard? Still wet? Need a hand, because you were so fucking hard you couldn't drive your car to get here after Marco's call-us interrupt-us?"

I shook my head. "What the fuck is wrong with you?" I was so mad I unlocked the door and stepped out into the brisk wind that blew off Raritan Bay, hoping it would cool and clear my head. Jean had infuriated me, but her educated guesses were surprisingly on target, and just thinking about fucking had me so hard…and it all combined with the confusion that I felt about Trace.

I leaned against the fender and decided I needed a cigarette. Jean climbed out of the truck and rested next to me as I lit it.

"Come on, Scotty." She pushed my shoulder lightly. "It's *cold* out here, and you could be in there with me. Hell, you could be *in* me, because thinking about you hard and wet has got me going, and I *know* I could get you off."

I looked at her as I exhaled and said nothing, because I didn't know how to answer something like this—this whatever it was she presented me.

It was understandable: people spent hours together, locked in a little box, struggling with huge issues or sometimes plain old boredom. Sex as stress relief I understood but…this was so far out of left field, I decided it best to assume she was joking.

She brushed the hair off my forehead. "You're not wearing anyone's ring…doesn't your girlfriend share?" Her expression changed, the sardonic twist of her mouth replaced by a gentler expression, almost wistful.

It was my turn for angry sarcasm. "Actually? I just found out that Trace, in fact, *does* share. I'm not sure I know how to handle that." I twisted my head away from that easy touch and took another drag.

"Trace."

The name floated out almost tonelessly, and Jean's hand dropped as if she'd lost all nerve function within it.

"Trace Cayden?" she asked in the same monotone.

I glanced at her sharply. "Yeah. I take it you know her?"

Jean shook her head, her hair haloed behind her in the wind. "I'm sorry. I shouldn't have…just finish your cig and hop in. Don't freeze out here." All the mockery, the taunting, the mirth—they were all gone from her voice as she jammed her hands into her pockets and let herself into the driver's seat.

I'd calmed down and was puzzled by Jean's sudden change. Besides, it was really cold, and I didn't want to smoke anymore.

I got back into the ambulance where Jean had thoughtfully turned up the heat.

"Thanks for that." I pointed at the registers as the warmed air blasted us.

"Yeah, it's nothing," she said, and stared out over the dashboard.

I was tired, I'd been really angry, and when I thought about it, I wasn't sure I wanted to know any more than I already did. I closed my eyes to nap.

"We lived together for three years," Jean said quietly, barely audible above the air vents. "It ended. I moved out about a year ago."

She had my attention, and for the second time that night, I opened my eyes and sat up. We were warm enough, so I lowered the heat. Besides, I really wanted to hear what Jean said, because she sounded so lost, and I could hear that strangely sad note clearly despite the rattling of the vents.

"I'm sorry. You, uh, you want to talk about it?"

Jean snorted and angled her head to peer at me. "You really are a nice kid, aren't you?" She smirked.

"Maybe." I shrugged. "I guess it depends."

"Oh, yeah? On what?"

I grinned at her in an attempt to lighten her mood. "On how you define 'nice,' and how you define 'kid.'"

Jean gave a half laugh. "Look, let me do you a solid, okay?" She grinned, some of the humor back in her face. "Maybe someday, you'll do me solid." Her eyes sparked at me, but there was something sad in them all the same.

She stared at her hands on the steering wheel and huffed out her breath, collecting herself. Finally she faced me.

"Trace…she's fuckin' bad news, really bad news."

I shifted a bit. "Well, she's kind of intense, but I wouldn't say—"

Jean waved a hand in negation. "You tell me how you're gonna handle it when she's fucking scarred you permanently, and believe me, she *will*. You think you can even be normal again when you've come with her riding your cunt and her knife at your throat?" The words tumbled out of her lips, terse, urgent.

"Think again, kid, think again. You're gonna cry for the days when all it took to make you come was a pretty girl and a steady hand."

I stared, shocked, not because Trace hadn't already marked me, albeit not so permanently, but because I could easily picture those things, could feel that there were places Trace was pushing toward; and I was fascinated, because I'd never seen such emotion come from a person speaking about their ex the way Jean did. Some people were angry, some were sad, and others were okay with it, but Jean?

She gave off waves of cold anger and self-loathing, which explained more than she wanted, I was sure.

"I…I don't, I don't know what—"

"Look, I'll prove it to you if you don't believe me," she said and unzipped her jacket.

She unbuttoned her shirt and showed me the scar. Keloid thick and white, just to the left of center on her chest, exactly where the curve of her breast rose. Two lines, perfectly matched in size and perfectly perpendicular to one another, crossing dead center, with little arms on each end.

If I hadn't been trying so very hard to focus on the fact that the pattern matched, in exact miniature, the one that had appeared under my skin and had yet to completely fade, I would have noticed more strongly the same light dusting of sprinkles across the pale, pale skin of her chest, and that the curve of her breasts was perfect from what I could see—but that wasn't the point of this exhibition.

"It doesn't say 'Jean,' now does it?" she remarked, her voice low with a bitterness I'd never heard before as she covered it back up. "It's a cross, an iron fucking cross, a *T* for Trace, and she put it there—because I was 'hers' and she said she loved me, like she could ever love anything." She gave a short, hoarse laugh, then leaned over.

"Believe me, once she owns you, once you feel like you're nothing without her—she'll dump you for someone new, and fresh, and innocent." She looked me up and down. "Just like you are, for now."

Whoa. That…was a lot of information to absorb, and what scared me was how much it jived with what I already felt, and I shifted uncomfortably.

"Fucked till you're raw?" Jean asked nonchalantly as she sat back. "Yeah, you're gonna want to use a good lube next time, it'll take a few days. Grab a few tubes from the back shelf. We can always pick up more."

I shook my head and said nothing. There was nothing to say.

Suddenly, Jean started laughing, then grabbed the mic and keyed it. "Marco, I have a problem."

"Yeah, what's that?"

"Scotty's giving me a hard-on."

I understood. She was joking, but only just, and I smiled as I shook my head. She *was* fucking crazy, but I was starting to think I knew why. She was also fucking funny.

Laughter floated back through the radio. "So? Ask her if she'll blow you. Hey, Scotty, you there?"

Jean handed me the mic.

"Yeah?"

"I'll give you a hundred bucks to blow her, and I'll give you both an additional time and a half for the shift if you let me watch."

He had to be joking and I laughed. That was fucking ridiculous.

Jean grabbed the mic from me. "She says she won't," she complained in an exaggerated tone. "What should I do?"

"Did you show her your tits?"

"Yeah, but she won't blow me."

"Put Scotty back on."

Jean smiled and handed it to me.

"Yeah, Marco?"

"What's the matter, Scotty, you don't like tits?"

I laughed harder. "I like 'em just fine, thank you," I told him, "but I told you before, I don't share."

"That's right, that's right, you've got a girlfriend. Okay. Hey, Jean?"

I handed the mic back to her.

"Yo!"

"Go in the back and jerk off or something."

"Well, since you said I could, I will. Ten-four, Marco, thanks for being a pal. I'm gonna go in the back now and do that."

She hung the mic up and got out of her seat.

"You're not seriously gonna do that, are you?" I was still smiling.

"Sure, why not?" Jean said in that same humorous tone. "I'm working with a hot girl who's getting me all sorts of crazy and has a girlfriend that wants her to fuck around, but she won't do me. What would *you* do?"

She shifted into the back of the rig, and the only other sound besides the engine was the unmistakable scud of a zipper along its track.

"Dude, you're not—"

Jean appeared back in the hatchway, smiling, her jacket unzipped. "No. I'm not. I'm just playing with you. You're probably beat, though. This is your sixth shift in five days." She settled back into the driver's seat. "Go rack out in the back on the stretcher. I promise to wake you if anything happens."

"Yeah?" It sounded like a good idea to me.

"Yeah, grab some z's. I promise not to come in and molest you or anything." She grinned rakishly.

I could feel the corner of my mouth quirk. "All right."

Once I was in the back, I racked out on the stretcher, put my hands behind my head, and closed my eyes.

"Hey, what's the matter with your car?"

I sighed, because it seemed like I'd never get to sleep. "I think the battery died."

A beat. "If we're quiet all night, we'll take the rig over there at seven, see if we can jump-start it, and if not, I'll give you a ride home later, okay?"

"Sounds good."

More silence as I settled in again and considered. It couldn't have been easy for her to tell me those things about herself, and it had to hurt her even more to show me that scar.

"Hey, Jean?"

"What?"

"Thanks—for everything."

"No problem. Don't mention it."

I finally got some sleep.

❖

My car did, in fact, have a dead battery, so Jean and I jumped it with the ambulance and my car started just fine, though she did follow me to the repair shop to make sure I didn't have any problems on the way.

We worked together quite a bit after that, with me either as third man on the medic bus or with her doing BLS with me. We didn't speak about Trace again, but we did talk about work, the year of experience necessary before we could take the paramedic class, what volunteer hospitals might be hiring—and we'd stop by during free time on our shifts to inquire. She eventually got a per diem at Saint Vincent's as a paramedic, which was great. We also talked about ourselves.

I told her about my mom and Elena, about growing up in my cousin's bedroom, about Nico and Nanny, and how they were like older siblings. I even told her a bit about Nina, and how I normally never spoke about our being related so no one would think I was just trying to get by on her name, and how weird it was, because she was family to me, but something different to the rest of the world, except for Samantha.

Jean vaguely knew Samantha from when they were kids, because Mr. Scanlon was a retired firefighter and had worked at the same station as Sam's father, Mr. Cray, and was probably the last person to speak with him before he'd been killed in the line of duty, a death Jean told me was *still* under investigation. I wondered if Samantha knew that, but I wasn't going to bring it up unless I had to.

Jean had met Samantha at family events at the station and had even attended Mr. Cray's funeral when she was ten—which was how I found out Jean was in fact twenty-five and about to be twenty-six.

She wouldn't tell me when her birthday was, though.

"Hey, if I tell you that, you'll get me a card or something, and I might start thinking you like me, because you know, we're lesbians, and we're all like 'hey, she said hello, what does *that* mean?' and I'm already half crazy about you, and I'll be wrong because you really hate me and it'll drive me to drink, and then I'll become an alcoholic and ruin my life because I'll end up homeless and have to camp out on your doorstep and your cousin will have me arrested for stalking and then I'll waste away and die in jail—you wouldn't want that, would you?" she said all in one breath.

I cracked up as she grabbed the mic.

"Barbara, she's doing it to me again!" she complained through my laughter.

"What?" Barbara's exasperation reached us through the speaker.

"She won't declare undying love and affection for me even though I'm sittin' here with my heart in my hands. She's laughing at me!" Jean concluded, her voice playfully aggrieved.

"Did you say 'heart in' or 'hard-on'?"

"Uh, I was pretty sure it was 'heart,'" Jean answered. "I haven't shown her my hard-on yet."

"Show her your pee-pee, kiss her, and *get off my radio*!"

I was laughing so hard I was crying, and I couldn't sit right.

"Why do all the pretty girls laugh at me?" Jean asked no one.

But in addition to the kidding, Jean told me about growing up in Brooklyn, her older brother, Patrick, whom everyone called Pat and who was a cop working in Manhattan, and her dog, a female golden retriever she called Dusty—because she liked to roll around in everything she could.

After work, she introduced me to Lundy's, a Brooklyn icon in Sheepshead Bay, and way too many shellfish at the raw bar, after which we'd grab a beer and walk the pier. Jean lived close by in Manhattan Beach, because it was a great place to do the two things she was really into outside of work: scuba diving and cycling.

I promised Jean we'd ride together when the weather got better, because I liked to cycle too and knew some really good routes, and Jean promised to teach me how to dive, something I'd always wanted to do but never had the time for.

I introduced her to black and tans and the burgers at Peggy O'Neills in Bay Ridge, a place I'd discovered by accident with Roy and Bennie one day after class when we felt like taking a drive and visiting all the private ambulance companies we could find.

The place was so much fun to hang out in, because of the food, the live music, and the occasional very competitive dart games, that we had all started dragging friends there, and we often ran into Bennie, who was working with a different private company, or Roy, who'd managed to snag a per-diem spot at Bayley Seton Hospital—affectionately nicknamed Barely Breathing Hospital.

Both Bennie and I had goggled at him over a beer and waffle fries when he'd told us, and he shrugged. "You know, it's a guy thing," he said. "It's not for any other reason."

I hated to admit he might be right about that, but I couldn't come up with any other reasonable explanation, and I had to let it go. We'd all applied to the city, though, and, like Jean, were waiting for that to come through.

I saw Trace a few times over the next weeks but, between the facts that she hadn't asked me before she tied me up and that I was so sore it hurt to piss, combined with Jean's story, I begged off staying too long because of work.

Barbara pulled me to the side one morning as I signed in on a clipboard.

"What's the deal between you and Jean?" she asked point-blank.

"We work together, why?"

Barbara scowled.

"Aw, come on, you mean that whole on-air thing? Jean's just playing, you know that," I said. "She jokes like that with everyone."

The truth was, Jean did have a bit of a rep as a pick-up artist, and she did joke like that with just about everyone. I'd witnessed more than a few exchanges between her and other crew members or hospital staff, and Chuck and a few others had told me I was pretty much the only female on staff who wasn't married or straight she hadn't slept with, which seemed to be the only distinction I held as low man on the totem pole.

I didn't know if that was true or not; not only was it none of my business, I didn't care because Jean was absolutely great to work with, and besides, we had fun hanging out.

"No, not with everyone. In fact, not with *anyone* anymore, and definitely not on air," Barbara clarified. "It's just you, so you better not be leading her on or something."

"What? That's…that's not—" I spluttered, and Barbara's expression softened as she interrupted me.

"Look, Jean…she's good people, you know?"

"Yeah, I know. She's great medical personnel too."

"She's one of the best, and she doesn't belong here. She should work for a hospital or for the city, but just because she's tough on the street…" Barbara sighed, then started again. "Look, the Ms. Psycho-Bitch thing, that's a game. She's good people, good-hearted, and I don't want to see her hurt."

I shook my head. "Look, Barbara, that's not my game. I like Jean, I think she's cool, and I don't go out of my way to fuck people over."

Barbara nodded. "Just…just letting you know. You seem nice enough, Tori. You get along well with everyone, the hospitals and the patients like you, but you never know, and I just—"

"You're taking care of your buddy, I understand." I smiled. "I'd do the same. But Barbara, I wouldn't play with anyone like that and, really, Jean's just joking around."

"I wouldn't be so certain of that," Barbara answered as she ticked something off on one of her endless ledgers. "I wouldn't be that certain at all."

I wondered about that comment as I readjusted my tech bag on my shoulder.

"By the way, Ms. Scotty, would you like to know who you're working with today?" Barbara asked without looking at me, her tone once again all business.

"Actually, yes, I would."

Barbara glanced up and beamed at me. "We've saved the best for last—get through today, and you can get through anything. You're on eight Danny with Lara. Have a great day!" She waved me off like she was Miss America as I walked to the rig.

❖

"Hi, I'm Lara. I'm bisexual, I'm born-again, and I'm into anal sex," she introduced herself, holding a hand out.

I stopped counting bandages for the checklist to say hello and shake it. "Nice to meet you." She had a good handshake, at least. "I'm Tori, everyone calls me Scotty, and I'm not, I'm not, and I'm not."

Lara laughed. "We gonna get along just fine, I think, just fine. You a gay girl, Miz Thing?"

"You know, I'm feeling pretty cheerful right now, and," I looked down at my chest, "last I checked I was a girl, so yeah, I guess you could say that." I grinned.

Lara chortled. "Yep, you and me, we'll be just fine, I think."

Lara was hell to work with. She drove slower than snails on quaaludes, and I wanted to scream with frustration as we inched down the street under the L line in Brighton, Brooklyn, as she searched for the right bank to cash her check in.

I couldn't even nap, because she regaled me with tales about herself, her fiancé Pierre, and her girlfriend, who was a "fine, just *fine!*" woman named Cerise, and she expected a response to everything she said.

By ten that morning, I knew more about her sex life than I knew about mine, by twelve in the afternoon I had a thorough academic overview of every way she and Pierre enjoyed anal sex, and by three I wanted medication—for myself. It wasn't that I had issues with discussing sex per se; it was just that this was so...*raw*, and from someone I didn't even know.

"Yeah, you know, I got the religion about two, three months ago, and you know, you're not supposed to do the dicky-pussy thing before marriage, but it don't say nothing about anal sex before marriage, so, since Pierre and I got engaged and he got the religion too, we do that now, and we'll save the pussy for after that day," she told me conversationally as she drove.

"Uh-huh, yeah, I get that," I answered briefly, hoping like anything she'd get the hint and simply stop.

"And you know, 'ccording to the Bible, and you read it real careful-like, you know, you can suck all the titties and clitties you want, just so long as you have a man and a baby. Read it, you'll see, I'm not making no lies."

"Yeah," I agreed, unable to believe that I was actually hearing what I was hearing. I'd never heard anyone, *ever*, speak the way she did, say anything like that, even with the crudity that passed for normal around the job. "I'm sure."

"But I love my Cerise, and if Pierre so much as even thinks I'll let her touch his willie, he can go look for it in the trash. Pussy is so much better and hers is so fine, hmph! But you know, the Bible and all."

I looked out the window and prayed for a flag-down, or an extra-super-routine dialysis transport. I even prayed for a personal aneurysm, because I was pretty sure that listening to Lara was not only rapidly dropping my IQ, it was also making my brain bleed; I was expecting blood to come gushing out of my ears, nose, and eyes at any moment.

"Um, what was that, Lara? I didn't quite catch that," I said as she made a sound that I now knew meant she was waiting for an answer. "The radio, you know?" I excused weakly.

"I was saying, you know, I think it's the rest of the world that's crazy, and I'm normal, you know what I mean? They're the wackos, out there," she said, and took both hands off the steering wheel to gesture when she faced me. "You and me, we're okay."

I could feel my whole face stretch with the alarm I felt at our imminent violent death by vehicular manslaughter, but I was careful as I leaned over and grabbed Lara's wrist to place her hand back on the wheel.

"Uh-huh, I agree with you, Lara, you're right," I said as I settled back into my seat after I was certain someone was actually driving again. What was it we had learned in tech class about EDPs, emotionally disturbed people? Don't fuck with their delusions. I was definitely with an EDP, and I wasn't going to fuck with whatever she said—she'd already let go of the steering wheel twice.

"In fact, Lara, you're so right that if you want me to call you Jesus, I will. I will call you Jesus. Is that okay, Jesus?"

She cracked up so hard I was afraid we were never going to make it through that intersection alive.

"Oh, my, you are so funny, Scotty!" she guffawed and punched my arm. "You…are such a card!" and she punched my arm again. "Jesus," she exclaimed, "you called me Jesus!"

For the rest of the shift, I was very sorry I'd said that, because she'd chuckle every now and again, say "Jesus—what a card!" and punch my arm. I didn't know if I'd ever be able to use it again.

"Hey, you diddling Jean?" Lara asked me when we finally got

back to base, thirteen hours later instead of eight because we'd ended up with a rig down and too many extra calls.

"What?" She was the second person to ask me about Jean that day.

"I was just wondering, you know, everyone is."

"Really? Why's that, you think?" I asked dryly as I removed my bag from the back of the vehicle.

"Well, she's not sleeping with anyone else. Hell, I asked her if she wanted to just two, three days ago, and she told me she was involved with someone. I asked about you, she said you were seeing someone and…you work together a lot, you the one she talks about on the air, so—"

Ah. I got it. She'd added two and two and come up with twenty-two. Wonderful.

"And she talks about how we're *not* having sex," I reminded her.

"Well, you a gay girl, she's pretty and tall—she got herself some *nice* titties—you pretty with a nice body. Why don't you hook up?"

I shook my head in negation, slightly irritated by the comment about Jean's body, especially since I'd seen the part she'd referred to, and I didn't want to *think* about that view, which, of course, now that I'd been reminded, was exactly like trying not to think about blue elephants. That and…it was wrong, somehow, to talk about Jean like that. And I didn't want to ponder the implications of what Barbara, and now Lara, had told me. "Lara, I *am* kinda seeing someone, and it's—"

"It's nothing," Lara said. "Jean likes you, you like her, you should do something about it. Hey, look, it's none of *my* business, but—"

"No, it's not."

Lara continued as if I'd said nothing. "—but if I was *you*, I'd grab a chance at her with both hands, you know what I'm saying?" She leered.

"Yeah, I hear you."

"No, you don't, cuz, that other girl, what is she, like a sometime thing or something?"

I shrugged. I didn't want to answer that question despite the fact I'd spent the day listening to Lara's most intimate details, none of which I'd wanted to know and most of which I hoped to forget.

"You and she, you'd be good together. I know these things, I truly do," Lara insisted as we walked into the dispatch office.

I penciled in my hours and faced her. "Lara, it was an interesting day," I said as I shook her hand. "Thank you."

"Why, you're welcome, Scotty." She beamed. "I had a most excellent day too."

"You have a great night," I told her as I put my hand on the door, "and you take care."

"You too. Oh, and Scotty?"

"Yeah?"

"You think about it, what I said about you and"—she waggled her eyebrows at me—"her, you know? It's got good feeling to it, I know these things."

I smiled at her. "I'll think about it," I promised. "Good night, Lara."

❖

I was given a regular shift the next morning, with Anton, who was a driver and not a tech. He informed me as we pulled out of the garage together for the first time that riding with Lara was the standard acid test for new techs and medics at the company before they were given a permanent shift: if the person survived both it and her report? Well, I had a regular shift and days now, didn't I?

Besides, despite the bruise Lara had left me as a souvenir of our day together, my arm functioned exactly as it should have, even if it was a bit tender.

Anton and I got along well, though when things went south and down—and plenty of times they did—he was muscle, not backup, which meant every decision was up to me, from vitals to treatment, and if I needed help I had to instruct and direct him.

It was too bad, because Anton had a decent brain and cared about people: he would have made an all right tech.

But the fact that I'd been partnered with a non-tech meant Marco, and more importantly, Barbara, thought I had the necessary skills and knowledge. Still, I learned a lot (some of them little things, like calling the bathroom "the facility" or "facilities"), and as my neck and shoulders strengthened, because I had to do a lot of lifting, my instincts sharpened.

I knew, for instance, that a patient with no legs in a closed room didn't slip and fall in a shower and break their hip. I also knew that if their lips were blue and the paperwork mentioned a history of kidney failure, and their skin was clammy, then contrary to the report the orderly furnished me, something more than just COPD, or chronic obstructive pulmonary disorder, was going on.

I practiced what I'd learned: to look for the little things, the small clues, the color inside the lips and the eyelids, rebound tenderness of an abdomen or rigidity in one of its quadrants; to look at the extremities and really check for ascites, which was swelling of the hands and feet as well as abdomen in right-sided congestive heart failure; and to listen very carefully to not only what the patient or their family told me verbally, but also to their body. Sometimes the stories didn't match, at all.

Which was how I ended up on a call that started out as an emergency pick-up at a private home for a suicide attempt.

Anton and I got tapped for an extra shift because there was no one else to work it, and we had the least seniority.

"Yeah, she took too many of her epileptic barbs," a slender, short man said as he led us into the apartment. "She was trying to kill herself!"

We had many protocols for psych calls, especially suicides. Only an active attempt required a call to the police department. These people had called a private ambulance, which meant they wanted no record on their insurance files since they were paying in cash.

"Where is she?" I asked, expecting to find a blue-faced corpse.

"Here, here." He led me to the bathroom. "Honey, the ambulance people are here!" he called as I followed him down the hall.

Female patient, approximately forty, conscious and sitting on the edge of the tub. She had a black gash on her nose, her lip was split in two places, and when she opened her mouth to say hello, I saw black between her teeth. There were brown-black stains on the gray sweatshirt she wore.

"Hi, I'm Scotty. I heard you may have accidentally taken one too many barbiturates for your epilepsy?" I asked carefully as I pulled a blood-pressure cuff out of my bag. Anton waited anxiously in the doorway with the stretcher and the portable oxygen tank.

I evaluated her respirations, her pulse, and her blood pressure. What the man had told us made no sense at all compared to the signals her body gave.

Her pulse was high but within normal range, her breathing also at the high end. It didn't *seem* like a downer OD. Her blood pressure, however, was higher than normal, and her pupils were constricted and nonreactive to light.

"Is that what he said?" She sounded weary and resigned.

"Yes."

I noticed the same dark stains along the waistband of her gray drawstring sweatpants. "Did you lose consciousness and fall?" I asked, keeping my tone even.

"She got her period!" the man called in from the doorway.

"Hey, Anton?" I called over my shoulder, and caught his eye. I nodded with my chin. "Would you take the gentleman to fill out the paperwork in the hallway while I finish my assessment?"

As the guy tried to protest that he wanted to stay, I answered flatly, "It's protocol." No way would I let him interfere with my examination. I didn't have to be an EMT to know that most women don't bleed on their shirts or up the front of their pants and along the waistband when they are menstruating, but a bloody nose could leave that trail.

"Whatever he says," my patient said as I finished my exam. "What, I tried to commit suicide? Sure, whatever."

Between the evaluation and the history, an ugly picture developed, and every instinct in my brain and body screamed the answer at me. She hadn't tried to commit suicide; he'd beaten her bloody, and despite the fact that she was alert and oriented to person, place, and time, I suspected a concussion and the force-feeding of a few uppers, either that or she was still adrenalized from the fight to have her eyes react like that, but nothing, nothing at all, even came close to being a symptom of barbiturate overdose, although her pupil reaction was a narcotic one.

Either way, OD or head injury, she was getting supplemental oxygen, and I helped her get comfortable on the stretcher. She wouldn't let me perform the rest of the exam, which would have required a head-to-toe evaluation; I didn't wonder why.

When the same guy who had called us, whom I started mentally referring to as "jerk," tried to climb into the back of the rig, I told him he wasn't allowed, that protocol required he sit in the front, which was true. *If* he had told the truth, and *if* she had OD'd, then she *might* go into arrest, and I *might* have to do CPR or whatever, which meant he *couldn't* be back there.

And the same reasoning and protocol followed when he tried to come into the emergency room; he would have to go in the front door and fill out her paperwork and wait, just like anyone else, since this was a potentially life-threatening emergency.

I reported my findings as well as the presenting story to the receiving nurse. "This is what they say, this is what I found," I concluded.

The nurse reviewed my notes, glanced over at the patient, then fixed her eyes on mine. "You think he beat her?" She pitched her voice low so the patient wouldn't hear us.

"Her face is all gashed up, dried blood on her clothes...and she refused a full assessment, so yeah, yeah I do."

She nodded. "Okay. Thanks, good job," and she handed me back a signed patient report.

I had a cigarette outside in the bay while I waited for Anton, and all he could talk about was the jerk's annoying whine as we rode back to base. I agreed with him, and when we finally parked the rig, I put my feet up on the dash and slept for the rest of the shift.

When I got back to the house, I found a note on the kitchen table.

Tori, there's a full meal for you in the fridge, and yes, you have the other *turkey leg.*

I smiled, because Nina had drawn a little picture of a turkey leg and a smiley face next to it—we always split them at family holiday meals. She got one, I got the "other." My mom always said it was because we had the "right of primogeniture."

We're staying over at a friend's in Manhattan tonight— do you remember Fran? You'll meet her again sometime if you're ever home!

By the way? The only thing left to do in the garden house is hook up the gas. Let me or Sam know if you want to go furniture shopping. Dude, your place should be totally ready in a few days!

Don't stay up too late reading. Miss you, stranger.
Love, Nina and Sam
PS: Happy Thanksgiving!
PPS: You have our cell numbers if you need anything.

I'd completely forgotten it was Thanksgiving, though I should have remembered—Trace had called me earlier in the week to ask me if I had plans.

Staying away from Trace was hard, I reflected as I found the promised meal and, more importantly, my "other" turkey leg and the pecan pie.

And I hadn't stayed too far away, either. I still met her for dinner on occasion, and when I'd drunk too much the last time I was there we'd ended up having sex that thankfully didn't leave me marked in any way—well, not too badly, I mentally amended. In fact, it had actually been really nice, and not just the first time either. It had only gotten weird later, after however long it had been and she lay half on top of me, that she'd asked me if I'd given any thought to, uh, sharing.

I told her quite bluntly that I hadn't, and she dropped the subject.

❖

Jean left the company a week later; her acceptance to the academy had come through, and in seven days she started what would be several weeks of training to "do it city-style," as she put it.

Barbara put herself in charge and took up a collection among the crews, and Marcus treated us all to dinner and drinks at Peggy O'Neills on a night a great Irish band was playing.

We were all a little trashed, and I can't speak for anyone else, but as happy as I was for Jean, and I really was because this was a hell of a career step for her, I was a little down too, because I'd miss her. She'd been great to work with, great to learn from.

The jokes, the food, the banter, everything was tremendous fun, and the music was grand; but when I looked at my watch, I knew I had to go. I still had to get up the next day for work, and just as I was about to say my good-byes, Jean stood.

"I just want everyone to know"—she paused, with a pint held above her head—"that it's been real, it's been fun, it hasn't been real fun, and you all kiss lousy!"

Everyone good-naturedly groaned, laughed, and protested.

"I'd like to amend that!" she added. "There's an exception. Scotty, why don't you tell them who it is?" Her eyes sparkled at me across the table.

"No, no. I've no clue." I really didn't.

"Hey, c'mon, Scotty, tell us," Chuck asked.

"Yeah, Scotty, tell us," Barbara seconded with a quickly hidden smirk.

"C'mon, Scotty, yeah!" everyone started insisting.

"Okay, okay! It's you, Jean, I've seen you kissing that mirror!" I saluted her with my beer.

"I can't believe you *told* them!" She laughed. "That was supposed to be *our* secret! And hey, I only did that so you'd know I was good at it."

"Hey, you asked mc to tell 'em."

"What do I have to do?" She spread her arms. "Do I have to walk across the table on my knees?"

She pushed her plate aside. "Excuse me, Chuck." She leaned on his head and jumped up on her chair. "I've shown you my tits, I've poured out my heart…"

She did it, I couldn't believe she did it. She knelt on the table and crawled over. "I'll even give you my beer," she said as she carried the glass, held like a torch before her.

"Did you show her your pee-pee?" Barbara asked while everyone else hurriedly moved their beers and food out of her path.

Jean paused. "You know?" She tapped her chin thoughtfully. "I haven't." Carefully holding her beer up with one hand, she began to pull her shirt out of her pants with the other.

"Do I have to show you that too?" she asked me from three feet away.

"Yeah, show her!" somebody encouraged.

"Hell, show us!" another voice said.

"That's not necessary," I told her as she fumbled along her belt.

Finally I reached over and held her hand as she reached the top button of her fly. "Stop," I said, looking up at her on the table. It was a very good thing, I thought, that it was solid oak.

"Stop," I repeated quietly as her eyes shone down on mine.

The whole table quieted, waiting to see what would happen next. She put the beer down.

"You're out of your fucking mind." But I couldn't help smiling as I said it.

"Yeah, yeah, I am," she agreed, nodding. "I'm the psycho bitch… but I really like you."

She covered my hand that still held on to the edge of her belt with her own and leaned down. "I really like you a lot."

"And now all of Bay Ridge knows you like me too."

"Everyone knows it but you, everyone but you." She got off the table and stood before me.

She still smiled, but her eyes, her eyes held something that sparked, a deeper glow that told me there was more that she wanted to say. I spoke to that glow.

"I like you too, Jean," I told her eyes, and reached for her face. As I stroked the smooth skin of her cheek, I could hear her sharp intake of breath. Then I kissed the spot my fingertips had traced. "I've got to go." I grabbed my jacket and waved my good-byes.

❖

Considering the drive home and the fact that beer was "something you rent," as Roy, Bennie, and I often joked, I decided to visit the facilities before I left. Jean and I bumped into each other as I came out of the bathroom.

"Hey, sorry," I said as I banged into her arm.

"Sorry," she said at the same time, and we laughed.

I leaned back against the wall as we smiled at each other. She had very light lines in the creases around her eyes when she smiled, and they added character and depth to her beauty.

"I'm gonna miss you," I blurted, then bit my lip before I said anything else I didn't want to.

"Yeah?" she asked, almost a whisper, as she angled in closer. I had this insane urge to kiss her as she wrapped an arm around me and her chest brushed against mine when she reached into my back pocket and pulled out my cell.

"You can call me whenever you'd like," she said into my ear before she straightened. It must have been the beers, because the few inches between us seemed really far.

She focused on my phone. "There. You've got…my home number, my cell number, and…my e-mail address." She pressed a last button and held the phone by her shoulder. "Don't lose it. I don't know when I'll get out to this part of Brooklyn to visit the base."

I stepped into the space that seemed to yawn farther even as I moved into it and reached for my phone. I wrapped my fingers around hers. "I won't." I glanced at the quirk of her lips.

When the urge hit me again it didn't seem so crazy—a compulsion that started as a pressure in my chest and jumped in time to the heartbeat in my neck—and when I kissed her, I hit the button on my phone that she still held.

Her lips were wonderfully soft and I loved, absolutely loved the way they moved with mine. They felt so good I wondered why I'd waited so long to find out.

She jumped when her phone rang, and I reached around her waist to retrieve it from her back pocket.

"Now you have my number," I told her as I handed it back to her, "so you can find me if you want to."

As she released my phone and I put it back where it had come from, she stared at me, an expression I couldn't read in her eyes.

She put a hand on my waist and cupped my cheek with the other. "Kiss me again?"

Her mouth was delicious, with that sweet beer taste, and the play of her tongue was elegant, skillful, but with a tenderness in it too, a sincerity that made my heart race and my stomach tighten with need as her fingers grazed through my hair and I held her tightly.

She leaned her head against mine, then nuzzled against my neck as we held each other. "Hey." Her voice was low with concern. "Are you okay?"

"Yeah, I'm fine. You?"

She nodded against my skin, then kissed it, a whispery touch that made me close my eyes. "We should go talk somewhere, not here." Her fingertips drew me even closer, and I sighed at the feel of her long, lean body pressed against mine: solid, and real, and strong.

"Where do you want to go?"

She chuckled softly into my hair. "I'd like to take you home, but that's probably not a good idea. Everyone still wants to get me drunk."

We separated though we remained touching, her hands on my waist, and I slipped my fingers through her belt loops.

"Actually, I do have to get going. I'm on tomorrow."

Jean smirked at me. "Think they'll think we're fucking in the bathroom?"

"Uh, considering all your forlorn complaints to dispatch on air? I doubt it." I grinned at her.

"Can I walk you to your car?"

"Sure, I'll meet you outside the door."

"You're not gonna leave?"

"Like you couldn't call me anyway?" I teased.

I waited outside for about a half minute before she came out.

"Where are you parked?"

"This way." I pointed, then shoved my hands into my jacket pockets to keep them warm, and Jean walked quietly with me.

"Are you still seeing…?"

"Trace?" I finished for her. "Sort of." I leaned against my door.

"I thought so." She gazed at the ground. "Listen, Tori, I know Trace's okay with the sharing thing, but," and she gazed at me, "I'm not."

"I'm not either," I said, my breath frosting in the air.

Jean rested against the car and brushed a strand of hair off my face, then pushed it behind my ear. "If I'm with you, I want to be with *you*, not you and anyone else. I want to *know*," she closed the distance between us, "that when I touch you, you're not thinking of someone else."

We had our arms around each other and I kissed her neck, the skin almost too warm in the chill that surrounded us everywhere but where our bodies met. She shivered slightly under my lips.

"Tori, I don't want to be your rebound from Trace, either. I want you to call me when you're free, when you know what you want, and if it's Trace, that's fine too. We can be friends, that's okay. I just want to know you, Tori. I really like you."

I could feel the pressure of her fingertips through my thick jacket, and I didn't know what else to say or do. Trace…even if I was okay with her offer to "share," it didn't matter, because Jean wasn't. And that was wrong somehow, wrong in a way I couldn't name—to fuck Trace and want to…what did I want with Jean, anyway?

I wanted to hear her laugh, really laugh, for no reason other than she was genuinely happy. I wanted to brush the hair behind her ears and feel her skin under my fingers, then run them through her hair again. I wanted to hold her, like I held her at that moment, but I wanted to feel her move under me, over me, with me, and I wanted to wake up next to her and do it all over again. But more than anything, anything else I could think of at that very second, I wanted to kiss her again, to feel the promise of her lips and the fulfillment of the tenderness behind it, and I wanted that so much it scared me.

"I'm sorry," I said. "I shouldn't have—"

"I hope you're not sorry you kissed me. I didn't think I was *that* bad."

I chuckled. "No, it wasn't bad at all. In fact, I…" I pulled back to look at her.

"You need time." Her voice was soft and low.

"I…I don't know what I'm doing," I admitted, my voice just as quiet.

Jean kissed my forehead then stepped away, and I instantly missed her warmth. "Can I give you a word of advice?"

"Sure."

She took a deep breath and stared at my car a moment before gazing at me. "Trace doesn't—she doesn't have any safe words. She doesn't…she doesn't play that way."

I just stared, waiting for her to explain.

"Christ," Jean muttered as she rubbed her forehead, "you don't even know what I'm talking about. Look, let me put it this way. She doesn't ask, ever. She'll push, she'll retreat, then she'll take it any way she wants it. But she'll never, ever ask you if it's what you want. And, Tori? Make sure you're okay with that."

I nodded. "I'll be careful."

"You need to be," she said solemnly.

Awkward silence grew between us.

"Hey." Jean's usual smile appeared and her tone lightened considerably. "Will you run away with me if I show you my pee-pee?"

I laughed, relieved, glad to be on normal territory again. I shook my head. Typical Jean. "Good night, Jean."

"Hey, just say the word and I'm yours." She smiled. "Good night, Scotty."

I watched her walk away before I opened my door.

"Yo, Scotty?" she called from the corner.

"Yeah?"

"Call me if you need me?"

"I will," I promised, and slid behind the wheel as she disappeared around the corner, her arrogant slouch a fading shadow on the sidewalk.

I decided to actually have a cigarette before I drove off. I definitely wasn't feeling any sort of buzz anymore, but I certainly wasn't feeling any type of sane, either.

Safe word. Huh. I couldn't think of a single one that could possibly apply to Trace; in fact, the words "safe" and "Trace" had not, could not, and would not ever go together, I thought as I drove over the bridge.

Trace. What did I know about Trace, really?

I considered her as I paid my toll. Nothing. She was hauntingly pretty, she was damn good at her job, great hands actually, and she didn't like to drive too often, said it was a waste of gas and polluted the air when she could walk during the day or take the bus door to door in the evening.

Her parents were alive and lived somewhere in the Island, maybe somewhere in the South Shore? I wasn't sure.

We never went *out* anywhere—unless that first visit to the beach counted. She…didn't really eat meat, but would cook just about anything with protein when she made dinner for us because she said I was still growing. She liked to make me breakfast when I stayed, but then she liked to fuck afterward.

She would say she loved my touch, but only if it was directly sexual or leading to sex or right after. Anything else she'd move away from unless she initiated it—casual hugs, that sort of thing.

She was appealingly intelligent and had very interesting ideas about ecology, world hunger, and poverty; I'd woken up a few times to walk out to her living room and find her crying over a documentary or infomercial on needy children somewhere in the world. I'd shut the set off and wrap her in my arms, rocking her until she calmed and quieted. Only at those times, when she was crying, I reflected, did she actually let me hold her. And that always evolved into sex.

No matter how I examined the entire situation, I found it strange, especially when coupled with the desperate way in which she always wanted to fuck, not just have sex, but *fuck*, repeatedly: she had to come at least three times before we'd stop. Well, that might sound like fun, and maybe, when this had started, it had been, but then it would get weird; she was always pushing, pushing for something…

Damn, though. When I wanted to end it altogether with Trace, she'd do something, say something—a touch, a look, a tear-filled confidence—that would shake me, wreck me, make me need to either bask in the embrace, give in to the sensual, or ease her pain; and somehow, my feelings would twist and overlap one another until, eventually, someone was bleeding, usually me.

The scratches, the bites that drew blood, the bruises she left on me, or the way she tied my wrists after holding them for so long—that and the insistence, the insistence on just one more, always, still bothered me.

Yet…something about her called me, because she *hurt*, so badly my chest squeezed, and I kept thinking that somehow if I cared enough, I could fix it, I could help, somehow.

And then…there was Jean. I smiled to myself, a lightness growing in me. I knew so much about her: how she loved her family dearly and saw them at least once a week, how her dog substituted as a pillow sometimes and ate slippers instead of chew toys—in fact, Jean bought Dusty slippers for that very purpose. So many things, like she loved a good black and tan with a burger, medium rare, at Peggy O'Neills after a long shift, and sometimes had to be dragged away from the raw bar at Lundy's; her favorite color was red, cardinal red specifically, not fire engine red.

She had a scar on the outside that I instinctively knew was probably nowhere nearly as large as the one she carried inside, and…she liked me. And I liked her too, maybe too much, I thought, considering that kiss we'd shared, the memory of it sending a pleasant tingle under my skin as I parked in the driveway. What I liked about Jean best was, well, everything. I liked that she was crazy, I liked that she was so good at what she did, I loved the way she walked and talked and stood, and I couldn't think of a single thing I didn't like, I mused as I trooped as quietly as I could up the steps.

It would have been nice if I'd been able to say something to her other than "I like you too." In fact, I would have liked to take her out for a nice dinner, go see a roundball game, because she shared my obsession with the New York Liberty, and maybe grab a drink afterward. But I couldn't, because no matter what Trace said about sharing, even if Jean had been okay with it, I wasn't.

❖

As I entered my room I found an envelope taped to my door and held it carefully, trying not to crush it as I placed my bag in a corner and paid scrupulous attention to where I placed my jacket and uniform; I had taken off my boots by the back door in the kitchen. I was mindful of the fact that I walked in and out of hospitals all day, and I didn't want to track something into the house that might negatively affect Nina and my developing niece or nephew.

Ugh, I had to shower, and I put the letter down with my stethoscope on my night table. I didn't know what I wanted to do most as I quickly soaped and rinsed: call Trace tomorrow, never call her again, or just let everything drift.

Since I was thinking in strange directions, why not call Kerry while I was at it and see if I could work that out too? At least I knew where we stood, and hell, Trace wanted to share anyway.

Truthfully, the thought made my skin crawl as I scrubbed it. I wasn't a cheater like my fuckhead father, and I wasn't going to become one. I hadn't been enough for Kerry somehow and she'd needed someone else, and here I was being a jerk, because maybe Trace thought she wasn't enough for me in some way; maybe that's why she needed so much reassurance, said it was okay if I went outside of "us" for something.

Maybe I'd let her insecurity rub off on me, and yes, Jean was great, and she was pretty and...I owed Trace something, didn't I?

Nina had stuck a sky blue Post-it note to the back of the envelope. *"Miss you—any free days coming up soon? Love, Nina."*

I smiled as I put it back down and toweled my head. Yeah. I missed her, and Samantha. I missed Bennie and Roy, I hadn't visited my mother or my sister, and I knew I would work over Christmas and the New Year because I still had no seniority. I sighed as I sat down on the edge of my bed.

When I wasn't at work, and I was there most of the time, I'd spent my precious free time with Jean, or got lost at Trace's, because even though I saw her occasionally, those occasions would last two or three days. This had to stop; I needed to know what we were doing, where we were going. We never discussed "us," and I sometimes got the impression that Trace would be perfectly happy if I stayed there forever so long as I was ready to fuck when she wanted, hold her when she cried, or be petted like the dog the rest of the time.

Insane. The entire situation was driving me insane. I had to talk with her about the things that bothered me, explain to her, make her understand that I didn't need to add someone else to my life and that she didn't need to fuck me half to death to keep me. If that didn't work, didn't help, I had to break it clean, I theorized as I slipped my finger under the envelope flap.

But when I pulled the contents out, I didn't think about any of that, because as of that moment, all bets were off. I read the letter once, I read it again, and my fingers shook as I read it a third time. My name had come up in the lottery, and I had to report for a written and a physical exam to enter the next academy class.

Assuming those went well, I was invited to the next six-week class: I'd start the second week of January.

DISABILITY

Identify priority patients: is the pt. Critical, Unstable, Potentially Unstable or Stable? Apply spinal immobilization as necessary, consider the need for ALS. If the pt. is Critical, Unstable, or Potentially Unstable, begin packaging during the rapid assessment while treating life threats and transport ASAP. Notify as necessary; continue evaluation en route.

Trace and I never did have the discussion I'd wanted, because the moment I'd said, "Trace, I really need to talk with you," at the door to her apartment, she started to cry, silent tears that made her eyes almost colorless.

"You don't want to see me anymore," she said quietly.

The tears and the words made me want to crawl, because I'd considered that possibility, because I didn't want to see her cry, and because I'd really wanted simply to see if we could work something out, something that had a direction, something that didn't leave me feeling so fucked up.

I spent all of ten seconds trying to explain, then I ended up trying to reassure her, which became an attempt to comfort her, and that inevitably became sex.

One really strange, fucked-up incident occurred after Trace and I had that aborted conversation. I'd taken a week off between work and the academy, we'd gotten fucking trashed at her place, and I remember...bleeding. Bleeding and fucking anyway. I remember my left forearm had been sliced nicely somehow—something broke, I think, a glass, maybe a bottle, I don't really know, but I had a two-inch gash that still itched...and then...I remember...not much.

I don't even know how I got home whenever I did, the next day, two days later, whatever it was, which I admit was a dangerously stupid maneuver on my part, but I do know that I'd gone to the house instead of my new apartment, and that after I'd finally gotten clear of the *worst*, the absolute *worst* hangover I'd ever had (I actually vomited four times, which had never, *ever* happened before) my brain had unfogged, completely.

I was more than vaguely embarrassed when I noticed the gash on my arm had been neatly cleaned and wondered how much of a mess I'd been in when I got home and whether Nina or Samantha had fixed me up yet again. After I'd showered and dressed, I found Samantha making one of the largest breakfasts I'd ever seen and, come to think of it, that's when she'd buttonholed me to a time for sparring, then invited me to join her and Nina upstairs for breakfast. I happily accepted.

We watched some silly movies together and joked about a bunch of things, and I noticed, really noticed, that Nina was finally starting to show—and she was absolutely stunning. Her eyes were almost completely blue, the silver a thinner, luminous ring around the edges, with that something, that indefinable something so obvious that I understood exactly why Samantha couldn't keep from touching her all the time. I could barely restrain myself.

She laughed when I asked, but allowed me to take her vital signs anyway, because I was curious to see if they were in range, and because, well, she still looked pale.

Sam flashed an unquestionably concerned glance my way, but everything I found was normal. We all settled down again, and as we laughed at the on-screen antics and teased each other about who was getting what for Christmas, I couldn't help but ask myself why I hadn't spent more time with them. This was the longest Nina had been home in years, and I'd been wasting time doing what? Fucking? Where in the hell had my head been?

I don't know what did it, but suddenly, I was fine with Trace, with everything—it was supposed to be about sex, healthy, consenting adult sex—that's all it was supposed to be, exactly what she had said in the first place.

Maybe, just maybe, I'd figured it out because I was finally able to start sparring with Samantha midmornings before I left for class, though that was a misnomer. Our sessions were more like martial arts lessons.

Maybe I'd had time to think because I had a three- or four-hour commute each day to Queens, added to an eight-hour day, or maybe it finally hit me that the first and not the second thing I'd done when I'd gotten that letter was to call Bennie's cell, then Roy's—not Trace's.

They'd both gotten letters too, and we arranged to travel to Fort Totten, Queens, together for the written and the physical. Although I had a few anxious moments afterward, both exams were relatively easy and we were informed that we'd start the afternoon classes in eight days, from three p.m. to eleven p.m., and I wondered what schedule Jean's medic class was on, since our sessions overlapped by a few weeks.

But whatever it was, I realized I'd mistakenly thought what Trace and I had was actually a relationship, and I chalked up that error in judgment to having recently come out of one. And...I'd discovered something.

So I was three weeks into a six-week stint at the academy and fucking my brains out because I'd already done my clinical rotations, seen my first two of what would be too many gunshot wounds, one emergency childbirth, several car accidents, and a dozen epileptic attacks, and now had an entire weekend free.

I'd done my rotations in Brooklyn, and since University North's emergency room was designated trauma, that's where one of the gunshots and two of the more severe car-accident patients went—and Trace had been on the crash team for all of them.

It had been easy to pick her up after the shift, easier still to drive to her place and, revved from the night I'd had, reach under her jacket to pinch and roll her nipples in my fingertips as she tried to open the door, simpler still to undo that knot that held her scrubs up and slide a hand down, down under the soft cotton and into those tight, hot folds, her clit hard and pulsing under my fingers as I dragged that slickness back and over that firm pulse and pressed my cunt against her ass.

"Get the door open," I hissed into her ear as I did her hard and slow, jamming my hips firmly against her, "unless you want to come out here—the first time."

I heard her sharp gasp as she shuddered against me, her hips jerking to my hands.

I bit her ear, scraping the tender flesh between my teeth. "C'mon, baby, don't you want my dick inside you?"

"Huh..." she breathed and kissed me, a fierce, hungry kiss, as her clit throbbed under my fingers.

"You coming, baby?" My voice was thick as it came out of my

throat, my own clit swollen to pounding urgency as my cunt buffed her ass.

"Yeah…" she choked, her cunt a hot flood.

This…was what I'd learned. If I was amped and took the edge off by touching her first, we'd fuck the rest of the night, day, afternoon, whatever, without my being too marked up after. Yeah, she'd still scratch and bite, but she'd do it impaled on my hands or my cock, and I was fine with that. She was fucking hot and fucking good, and so long as I set my alarm on my cell and didn't stay there, we were fine. This was not a relationship—I couldn't let myself go there with her or I'd get fucked up again.

Trace seemed to be absolutely fine with that; in fact, things seemed to have gotten much better, friendlier even, because we actually talked about things, mostly work. Then…we'd fuck again, eat, come a few more times, and I'd leave.

I also refused to drink with her at all. I told her it was because we got tested all the time at the academy, which wasn't exactly true, but it seemed that's where all the "issues" with her had started, and the not drinking appeared to make them go away.

Besides, even though I really couldn't remember how it got there, I had a clear red line on my arm to remind me I could have killed myself or hurt some innocent civilian and…I hadn't forgotten Jean's words: there was no way in hell I was going to let things go there, no matter how hot a fuck Trace was.

I let her rest for about twenty seconds to catch her breath and find the right key, then moved over her clit again, her cunt now really slick and wet from coming, and her hard-on growing under my fingertips. Neither one of us knew then it would be the last time we'd fuck.

"Jesus Christ! What are you doing to me?" she asked.

"Getting you ready," I drawled.

She got the door open and it took no time at all to get where we needed to go, which was naked, in her room.

We were both on the thin edge of insane when I sat on the edge of the bed and pulled her down onto me, onto my cock, the force of her body on mine driving deep.

I held on tightly to her hips so that she moved to my rhythm, and she jerked me off as she came. I blew my load about a minute later, and then it was time for the next one.

"Christ Tori—don't stop—don'tfuckingstop!" Trace gasped under me, her fingers digging into my lower back, tearing the skin in burning strands that sang as they stung, and I drove my dick into her.

Unable to speak as my lungs worked with my thrust, I drew in air to shove it back out, hot and harsh along our sweat-drenched skin.

"Coming…" she gulped and scraped her teeth along my neck, her breath catching as she slammed up to meet me and I fucked her hard, the way she liked it in those final moments.

I was still hard, but didn't think I was going to come again, until she stroked my clit. "Shit…" I groaned as the combination of the firm, knowing touch and the fuck did me in.

"Come, baby," Trace murmured throatily into my ear, "come inside me."

I leaned harder into that touch, my clit burning and my cock so deep in her as I moved she cried out again.

I couldn't even breathe anymore, never mind speak—choking for air, body shuddering, every neuron twitching in time with the spasms that racked my cunt.

"God…" I finally muttered as I rested my head on her shoulder.

Trace chuckled. "Didn't expect that, did you?" Her fingers outlined my neck and skimmed along the slope that led to my arms.

"No, actually," I breathed finally and kissed her neck.

"You've really got great shoulders," she purred, and massaged the muscles. Her touch felt so good I didn't want to move, and Trace's legs relaxed around me in a sensual embrace that smoothed along my legs while I nipped lightly at the soft skin of her throat.

"Thank you," I murmured as we shifted again to lie even more comfortably and I dragged the comforter over us. She kissed my head as we lay there, quietly drifting as she drew repeated soft patterns through my hair and down my back.

My cell phone went off about half an hour later, and Trace kissed me drowsily as I got up. I grabbed my clothes and stumbled into the bathroom to shower and dress.

"Coffee 'fore you go?" she asked as I stepped out of the bathroom.

She looked great with her hair pulled back in a loose ponytail and wearing one of my T-shirts and, from the way her breasts were outlined under the cotton, nothing else. She had fabulous legs and my shirt barely covered her anywhere. Fuckin' sexy.

"Yeah, sure," I grinned, "one for the road."

We chatted for a bit, about my rotations, about technical aspects of dealing with sucking chest wounds, and she gave me a friendly kiss and hug when I shrugged my jacket on.

"Call you?" I asked as I stood in the door.

"Whenever you want." She smiled.

❖

As I drove home I was really glad it was early evening; I wanted to spend time with Nina, and I wanted to speak with Samantha.

Something...I don't know...something wasn't *right*. I just couldn't nail it down. Nina's vitals were fine, and I tried not to annoy her every time I saw her with how-are-you? and how-are-you-feeling?, but it was hard.

As I drove, my cell phone rang and I hit the loudspeaker key.

"Scotty."

"Tori?" It was my sister Elena, and she sounded very upset.

"Elena, what's the matter?"

"Tori, it's Mami—she says it's heartburn, but she's all gray and sweaty. Tori, she's got her hand pressed to her chest and she's in pain—she doesn't look right."

I checked my mirrors to see where traffic was going and set my turn signal; they lived on the other end of the Island, and the hospital was near them.

"Elena," I said slowly and carefully, "I want you to call 911, tell them everything you've told me, and tell them you're family of a member of service, okay? Do whatever they say, call me back if you need to—you can leave the phone on speaker, all right?"

"Tori, I don't know what to do!" Elena's voice was edged with tears. "Should I get her some water?"

I cut down the next street and, after a quick check across the intersection, gunned the engine.

"No!" I said, too sharply. "No," I repeated a bit more gently this time, "just call 911. Do whatever they say, and in the meanwhile, while you're waiting?"

"Yeah?"

"Is she still talking?" I asked as I cut across Hylan Boulevard, one of the busier main roads. I decided to side-street it the rest of the way; there were no lights until I got close to the end.

"Mami...Tori's on the phone..." I heard Elena speak. Then silence.

"Elena!"

Nothing. My chest grew tight and cold.

"Elena!" I called again.

She picked up the phone. "Tori, where are you? She won't talk to me anymore, she's just—"

"Elena, hang up with me and phone 911—now, Elena!"

I glanced up at the corner I'd just passed. I was five minutes away. If there was a unit free, it would be sitting less than two minutes from there.

"But, Tori—"

"Elena, now! I'll be there in five minutes!"

I clicked off, focused on the road, and cut off some asshole in a white Camaro. Who still drove Camaros, I thought as I waved an apology, squeaked through the remaining two lights, and left rubber on the road when I jerked the car around the last right to park on the side of the house. A rig was in front.

As I ran up the walk I noticed who it was: University South, ALS. A medic unit, thank God, because unless Elena was exaggerating, and she wasn't prone to that at all, our mother was very likely having a cardiac incident.

The screen door slammed behind me, and two quick strides took me through the house to the basement door, which was open. I slipped down the first few steps, grabbed the railing, and vaulted the rest.

"Elena?" I called as I landed and whipped around the corner.

"Tori!" She came running up and threw her arms around me.

"Shh, Elena, it'll be okay," I said as I kissed her head. Elena trembled against me and I rubbed her back.

"Come on, sweetheart. Let's see what's going on with Mami."

"Okay," she sniffed into my shoulder.

I took her hand and we walked into the apartment.

Two medics already had our mother on a stretcher, a non-rebreather mask with oxygen running, an IV drip started, and leads running to her chest. Elena clearly hadn't exaggerated; Mom was covered in a sheen of sweat over skin that looked ashen, like wax.

"Hi, Mami," I said as I walked up to the stretcher where one of the medics knelt to evaluate her blood pressure while the other read the monitor.

I could see it was an effort for her to raise her eyes as I kissed her forehead. Her skin was cool and clammy under my lips, and her hands appeared swollen.

"I'm just going to take your watch off so you're more comfortable. Okay, Mom?" I told her cheerfully as I did so. The band had started to cut into her wrist. I pocketed it and got out the crew's way.

"PSVT," the medic by the monitor said.

"BP a hundred over sixty," the medic who'd been evaluating the vitals said. "Adenosine?"

"Yep. Hi, Scotty."

I glanced over at the familiar voice. Holy shit—it was Jean. I hadn't even noticed.

"Jean! What are you doing here?"

"Well, I wanted to send you an early Valentine, and I was in the neighborhood, so…" she quipped as she loaded a syringe, then angled it into the port on the IV line. She flashed me a warm grin. "Actually, I got called for a per diem at University."

That made sense; per diems were hard to get, no one gave them up unless they absolutely had to, and they were always a source of income and references, if needed.

Jean grew sober again. "Scotty, does your mom have a cardiac history?" She studied the monitors, and I watched with her as the other medic adjusted the oxygen tank for transport.

"No…" my mom managed to moan out from under the mask.

"Okay, Mrs. Scotts," Jean said, "we're going to take you to the hospital, okay?"

My mother shook her finger back and forth in negation, and I ached to see her, famous for her words, unable to speak.

"Tori will come ride in the back with me, right, Tori?" Jean gave me that warm smile again.

"Yeah, Mom, I'm coming with you. Elena's going to take my car." I handed my sister my keys, and her eyes, so like mine, were large as she nodded in agreement.

"Uh, Scanlon, protocol—" the other medic protested as they moved my mom to the stairs and I walked behind them.

"Burns, she's the member of service," Jean interrupted.

"Oh."

I helped them carry the stretcher up the narrow stairway.

"Hey, just like old times, right?" Jean grinned at me.

I snorted. "Yeah, just like 'em."

Once in the rig, I sat at the foot of the bench so my mother could see me while Jean worked.

"Saint Vin's?" called Burns from the front.

"Redirect," Jean called back. "U South is closer."

"Saint Vin's is cardiac today," Burns reminded her.

"I want the closest ER," she said as she did whatever voodoo magic medics did, "and run lights-only."

Jean was breaking protocol to go to the closest ER, which was about two minutes away, instead of the designated cardiac center, which was about ten. I was relieved because from what I could see, my mom's eyes had closed, her skin had gone from ashen to milk white, and her face had developed the mask, where the skin appears to be stretched too tightly over the bones. I hadn't looked or asked Jean what her vitals were, but I knew enough to realize Jean thought what I did: time was critical.

"Hey, Mom, that's not too far away." I rubbed her foot—it was cold. "Oh, and hey, since Elena's driving my car, we'll bring you home very quickly."

She bobbed her head and gave me a weak smile. I glanced at Jean, who was still doing the voodoo she did so well.

"Anything I can help with?"

"No, just fine," she drawled. "Why don't you fill us in on who... what you've been up to?" She smirked.

I chuckled anyway. Trust Jean to make jokes. But it was the right way to go, and as we rode to the ER I talked about my classmates, my instructors, Bennie and Roy, and the couple of funny things I'd seen on my rotations.

My mom didn't open her eyes, but she did try to nod in all the right places and occasionally managed a weak smile.

Things were a blur when we got to the ER, but I helped take the stretcher out of the rig, which was the least I could do.

The receiving nurse was about to protest my presence until she recognized me. "Oh, hey, Scotty," she smiled, "didn't recognize you out of uniform."

"Me either," I said as my mom was set up in a bed and a twelve-lead portable monitor attached to her. I held her hand and told her what they were doing so she'd be less anxious.

Eventually, I really had to leave so a proper evaluation could be performed, but I knew I could come back in as soon as they were done, since such were the perks of being an EMT.

I stepped outside the bay to have a cigarette, wanting to clear my head before I tried to find Elena in the waiting room so I could let her know what was going on. Not that I knew much at the moment.

The rig we'd arrived in was still there.

"Hey, Tor." Jean's voice sounded behind me.

"Hey, Jean, thanks for everything."

"Yeah, don't mention it," she laughed, and clapped my shoulder, "not unless you want to get me fired or something."

I gazed directly into her eyes as I chuckled. "Not hardly. But thanks, truly."

"You'd do it for me," she said, her voice low and sincere.

"You're right, I would."

Silence stretched between us. "So…I heard you're at the academy now?"

"Yeah, I started three weeks ago. I'm going three to eleven," I answered. "You?"

"My last week, next week—I'm ten to six. Maybe I'll run into you during a break or something?"

"Yeah, maybe, that would be cool, right?" I don't know why I said that. That…sounded monumentally stupid, but her hair had grown since I'd seen her last, and she'd taken such good care of my mom, and she was so pretty and tough and…the last time we'd seen each other, she'd told me she liked me. And I'd kissed her, a kiss I hadn't forgotten, as much as I'd tried to.

"It would be." She nodded. "We get a couple of breaks, about every hour and a half. I go outside, by the grease truck. You know, the van sitting out by the lot with the guy that sells the coffee and the sandwiches? But I don't stay very long, because it's too cold."

I laughed. I knew the spot she was talking about. "Yeah, I go there too, but you know, if you go down a level, where the phones are?"

I was grateful for cell phones because there were only two public phones in the entire building, and they were on the landing of the first sub-level.

"Yeah?"

"There's a room off to the side where you can hang out; people have left books and board games and stuff—I discovered it when I got lost trying to find the facilities."

She laughed. "Cool, very cool. You *would* find something else when you get lost. Maybe I'll see you there sometime?" she asked, a slight curve lifting her lip.

"Maybe." And suddenly it hit me, I was standing out there because my mother was inside.

"I've got to go find my sister. I've got to go."

"Oh, yeah. Hey, look, I'm on for another few hours. I'll check in from time to time?" Jean's face was the picture of friendly concern.

"That'd be great, thanks," I said, walking back to the bay doors.

"I'll see you later, then," she said as I punched the key code that would slide the door open.

Elena was pale and anxious when I found her, tapping her feet nervously as she sat in the waiting room.

"Tori, is Mami okay?" She stood and threw herself into my arms again.

"She's okay right now, Elena," I comforted. "I'm going back inside in a few minutes to find out more." I held her tightly, because I was as scared as she was, but she was counting on me to do something.

"Did you talk with the desk clerk?" I asked her softly.

"No," she sniffed against my shoulder. "I didn't know what to do. I brought Mami's pocketbook, though, and left a note for Aunt Carolina."

"Good girl, you did a lot. Come on," I said and rubbed her arm, "come with me." I took her hand and took her into the ER to see our mother.

By the time she was admitted and a bed found in CCU, I'd found a moment to call Samantha and left a message to have her tell Nina what was going on. My mother was Nina's godmother and they'd always had a special bond, but I didn't want to leave that sort of a message for her, all things considered. So when I stepped out into the corridor from CCU with Elena, the entire family—aunt, uncle, cousins, including Nina and Samantha—was there and waiting anxiously.

"Victoria, what do they say?" my aunt asked as she approached. Her eyes were wide and worried.

I hugged her and explained to everyone what Elena and I knew, which wasn't much except that she was stable at the moment and she'd be evaluated further. I strongly suspected that my mother had had her first cardiac incident and that it was due to CHF, congestive heart failure.

It was a long night. Aunt Carolina refused to leave the room, which was absolutely her prerogative, so I alternated with everyone else visiting my mom or waiting outside.

Everyone finally left very late, and for a long while, my mom and I were alone, surrounded by the hisses and beeps of the machinery that measured and monitored her body.

"How's she doing?" Jean asked quietly behind me as I watched my mother sleep.

"She's stably unstable." I sighed softly as I held my mother's hand. The skin felt so fragile, the bones so thin.

Jean put a warm hand on my shoulder. "She'll be okay, Tori, she's a fighter. She didn't lose consciousness, she didn't want the oxygen, and she didn't want to come here. A real fighter."

I covered her hand with mine briefly and raised my eyes to hers. "Thanks. I'm glad you think so."

"I've got a gut feeling," she said, a light curve gracing her lips, "and," she glanced down at her watch, "I've got to go."

I gave my mom's hand a kiss, then stood. "I'm glad you stopped by."

"Yeah, me too. Maybe I'll see you in Fort Totten?" she asked from the doorway.

"Maybe. Be safe."

"You know it," she said and cockily grinned, a bright flash in the darkened room, then left.

❖

They kept my mom a week, a week I spent back in my old room so Elena wouldn't be too scared or lonely, a week with my mother, as soon as she could speak, mad at me for not telling her that her beloved goddaughter was pregnant, which I tried to deny, but my mom kept insisting she could see. Honestly, I was relieved and grateful for both her discovery and her annoyance with me, because they meant she was feeling much better.

Besides, when she stopped smacking my arm, she was very excited about being a great-aunt, and happy that she knew something my aunt didn't. Ah, sibling rivalry, I thought, mentally rolling my eyes. I was so glad Elena and I weren't like that.

Roy and Bennie were great. They did all the driving during that time because I'd left Elena my car in case she needed it, and luckily the lectures, both the didactic and the practical, were rather easy; but then again, we'd been trained by Bob, and his class was considered one of, if not *the* best in the country.

The next week, we had EVOC, emergency vehicle operation course, which would begin very early during the day and then, the following week, our finals.

I spent five days, from six in the morning until three in the afternoon, out in Floyd Bennett Field, standing on the beat-up tarmac of the old military airfield, freezing my ass off, picking up traffic cones, and waiting for my opportunity to drive a rig, rev it up, weave between cones to create a dangerous sway (because the way these vehicles are weighted with oxygen, they tip much more easily than one would think), correct the sway, then floor it and push that mother as fast as it could go to the feather wall, a super-abrupt breaking stop that had to be corrected into a left turn. If you did it dead-on right, the vehicle hopped, and man, I loved making that thing hop! Of course, if you did it wrong, you'd roll the vehicle; we'd been told more than one instructor had ended up on disability that way.

"See that?" Roy asked me during a break, pointing to the adjacent runway field where cop cars and ESU—emergency services unit—trucks were put through their paces at high speed. "That's what I want to do."

Bennie and I both nodded. Rescue...now *that* was elite. The thought intrigued me: jumping into the water, rappelling down ravines and buildings to extricate...and if I got my diving certification... definitely interesting. The three of us discussed it as we rubbed our hands and huddled against the wind, then ate our sandwiches in the warmth of Roy's car.

It didn't make up for the cold, though ever since then, I've never felt the cold nearly as bad as I did those days, and I have yet to see a line of cones without either wanting to weave between them or joyously knock them over.

❖

We were on our way home from EVOC in Roy's car when we saw it: a van passed a motorcycle and clipped it, sending the rider ass over head into the guardrail. The van never stopped, but we did.

We stepped out with our tech bags, and Roy pulled a short board out of the trunk. The victim had tumbled so that he sat nearly upright against the freezing metal, his bike about twenty feet away.

He raised a hand to his helmet. "Don't move, just stay still!" we all cautioned him as we approached. I dialed 911 as Bennie and Roy introduced themselves.

His helmet was cracked and blood poured from his nose and lip, but he was conscious. The ugly swelling of his thigh and the subsequent scream that erupted from him when he tried to move his leg made me think, yup, broken.

We didn't have a lot of equipment, but we knew how to improvise, adapt. We knew how to overcome. Among the three of us, we had him evaluated, immobilized, and ready for transport when the responding crew got there.

They were a little surprised, maybe, that some academy rats had stopped, and they asked for our names, but hey, that was the job, that was what we were supposed to do—stop and give aid.

❖

I admit to being nearly unbearable in the days leading up to finals, and I hid in my apartment, studying. Even at the academy, we were done with our lectures and had to spend hours in a classroom doing nothing—I studied with Roy and Bennie or slept at my desk while other classmates read the paper.

I was so bored that when Lieutenant Griggs came in to announce a break, I almost knocked my chair over in my haste to run out of there, anywhere that wasn't too hot and stifling.

Though I wasn't the first one out the door, I certainly wasn't the last, and my next destinations were the female-designated facilities, the grease truck for some coffee, and a cigarette. I hoped that the combination of the caffeine jolt, the nicotine buzz, and the ass-freezing cold would wake me up enough to get through the next few hours before I drove all of us home. I couldn't believe we were getting paid to sit there and do absolutely nothing! How many crossword puzzles could a person do in one day, I wondered as I skidded around the corner.

I smacked right into her.

"Whoa, there!"

"Oh, geez, I'm sorry," I said as we overbalanced. She hit the wall with me on top.

Jean's eyes sparkled down at me. "I always knew you'd fall for me." Her lips formed a delicious curve.

"Did you now?" I asked dryly as I righted myself.

Her smile widened for maybe a heartbeat, then her expression became serious. "How's your mom?"

I sighed. "She's better, thanks. Home now, actually. Looks like right-sided CHF."

Jean nodded. "Yeah, thought so. But she's watching her meds and all that, she's doing okay at home?"

"Yeah, she's doing okay for now."

An awkward silence grew between us because those few moments of having her body so solidly against mine forcibly reminded me of her lips, of the sweet taste of her mouth, that dead-on perfect kiss. "So…I thought you were done last week?"

"This week's my last week. We do exams tomorrow, find out where we'll be Friday."

I nodded like an idiot as my face and neck grew hot and something akin to hunger thrummed through my body, threatening to erupt through my skin.

Suddenly I recovered. I had to go to the bathroom, have a cig, and get some coffee. "You on break?"

"About another fifteen minutes."

"Me too. Meet at the grease truck in five?"

She smiled. "Cool. Yeah."

I managed not to damage myself or another human being as I stepped out of the building and down the steps that led to the open space where the grease truck sat and a bunch of classmates, both from my class and Jean's, huddled around the open flap by the coffee urn.

I was careful on the slate flagstones that had lined the walkways of this fort since the Revolutionary War, because it was so cold and dark already; night had fully set, and a touch of ice dotted the ground. I recognized Jean's back as I walked over, then watched her detach herself from the milling crowd. She carried two large Styrofoam cups.

"This is for you, light and sweet, right?" She smiled.

"Thanks—you remembered." I was surprised as I took the cup

from her. The heat felt good against my bare hands, and I ripped the plastic lid and took a sip.

"Well, yeah," she laughed softly, "we only spent like, what, every day, for eight or more hours together for a few months? Some marriages don't last that long."

I laughed a bit self-consciously. She had a point, and I was pretty sure I was living proof of it. We found a clear spot along the low-lying wall that surrounded part of the building and started to chat, about anything, everything.

Bennie and Roy strolled over, then a few of Jean's classmates, and we were having a great time, discussing instructors and dumb classroom mistakes, and right before our break ended, we somehow all agreed that we'd meet that coming Friday at Peggy O'Neills in Brooklyn to celebrate the end of our classes.

"Wait up a sec." Jean caught the back of my jacket right before I reentered the building.

I let the door close again.

Jean glanced down at her hands and took a deep breath, then let it out slowly and it steamed in the winter air.

"You, um…you still seeing Trace?" she asked before she gazed at me, her expression indiscernible in the false twilight of the nearby arc lamp.

I thought about how to answer. "We're not dating, if that's what you mean," I said finally. It was true, we weren't dating—just the occasional fuck, which was something I'd been trying to stop too.

"Oh," she said, sounding surprised, "I thought, I thought that—"

"No, no." I caught her sleeve. The muscle in her arm was solid under the layers she wore. "I made a mistake, that's all."

When I realized I was about to run my thumb along the hard ridge of her bicep I dropped my hold. I wasn't thinking at all, I'd been going to pull her closer, and—

"What kind of mistake?" Jean asked softly as she neared.

I laughed a little self-consciously. "The mistake I made last time— fucking doesn't mean you're involved."

"Heh," she snorted, "I've made that mistake myself. But," and she tapped my shoulder, "I've learned from it." Her tone was as light as her touch.

"Oh yeah?" I asked, forcing my tone to match hers. "What was that?"

Her fingers moved from my shoulder to brush the hair I'd let grow for far too long away from my face, and they were so soft against my skin.

"You don't have to love someone you're fucking, but you do have to love them to let them fuck you."

"Ya think?" I asked, maybe a touch too sarcastically, and Jean dropped her hand, tucking it into her jacket pocket.

"I *know*," she said brightly, "and believe me, the more you love? The more fucked-over you get."

"Well, that *I* know too." I laughed as I opened the door again and stepped inside to return to my nap. I had no doubt of what Jean had said: I had my mother as living proof.

❖

About twenty minutes before we were allowed to finally leave from our very last class (our exam would be on Monday), we learned that we'd all be sworn in the next Friday at an official ceremony, assuming we all passed, and that would be when we found out what borough, which station, and what battalion we'd be attached to, as well as what shift. That was great news, but at that moment, we were beyond delighted to just be done. Bennie, Roy, and I practically sang as Bennie drove to Peggy O'Neills, and we got even giddier as it started to snow.

We got lucky enough to find a parking spot right around the corner and could hear the live band playing in utter earnestness as we approached. A traditional Irish tune set to a modern beat blew into our ears as I opened the door.

Roy, Bennie, and I stamped our feet, hung our coats up in the vestibule, and entered the bar proper.

It was past midnight and it was jammed; half our class was there, as well as a few of my buds from County, Bennie's from Access, and Roy's from 911.

Jean, waiting her turn for a shot at the dartboard, waved us over, a pint in one hand.

"Hey, we saved you seats!" she yelled, and we cut our way through the throng to the table.

Bennie nudged me as we walked. "You didn't say anything about dating a medic," she half shouted into my ear.

"We're not dating, she's a friend!" I half shouted back.

Bennie smirked. "You better fix that soon, or I'll ask her out myself."

I was shocked to feel the blood rush into my neck, and I tugged at my collar to give myself room to breathe. I stopped walking.

"Hey, don't let me stop you." I tried to smile. "Do what you want."

Roy grabbed my shoulder. "Hey, put it back in your pants, guys," he gave a teasing grin, "because I think we're about to get a show." He jerked his chin toward the band.

"Hey!" one of the guys on stage spoke into the microphone, his *very* Irish accent apparent from the first syllable. "Pat says his sister's a hell of a singer, so we'd like to bring her up here to do the traditional, ever-classic 'All Through The Night' with us, for all of the new members of New York's best. C'mon, Jean," he paused and stretched a hand to her, "will ya do it?"

The band began to clap, and we all followed suit as a tall young man whose face was so like Jean's he could only have been her brother pushed, pulled, and otherwise dragged her to the stage. Jean laughed and held her beer carefully above her as she stepped up onto the platform.

"Here, Pat," she said into the microphone and handed him her glass, "and if you drink my beer, I'll have to kill you, even though you're my only brother and I love you."

"Don't forget I'm armed!" he called.

"Don't forget I'm crazy, and crazy beats armed, every time." She turned around and spoke with the guitarist, who nodded, then spoke with the bassist, who also seemed to agree.

He leaned into the microphone. "All right, then, there's been a change. Still a classic, still traditional, though technically not Irish, but Scottish," he gave Jean a mock scowl, "but since she requested it," he shrugged, "here's 'Will Ye Go, Lassie,' and…" Jean nudged him.

"Oh, right, then. This is for Scotty, lucky dog, you." He smiled widely at the crowd, then stepped back.

Everybody laughed as the band clicked in the tune and I said hello to Barbara and Chuck as we found our seats. Roy waved a waitress over.

"I've got the first round," he told me and Bennie as we reached for our wallets. "One of you can get the next."

I thanked him and waved to Jean as she waited for her cue, and she gave me a quick grin.

Having grown up surrounded by Nina's music and voice, I was curious to hear Jean's.

"Oh the summertime is coming, and the trees are sweetly blooming," she sang, a melodious alto that suited her perfectly. *"And the wild mountain thyme grows around the blooming heather...will ye go, lassie, go?"*

The beers arrived and I took a very thirsty sip.

Bennie leaned into my shoulder. "And she sings, God...*look* at those fucking legs, they reach all the way to my neck!" she said into my ear. "There's *no way* you haven't thought of it, and she's a medic—man, I'll bet she's got *great* hands."

I put my glass down and stared at Bennie. That was just...wrong. "Bennie, don't...don't talk about her like that. She *is* a great medic, okay?" I returned to my beer.

"And we'll all go together, to pluck wild mountain thyme all around the blooming heather...will ye go, lassie, go?"

Roy leaned over on the other side. "You know, Tori, you never gave me shit about Aileen and the baby, and I never said word one to you about Kerry or your booty call—"

I stared at him. "What?"

He waved a hand. "It's not like nobody knows, but look, just look." He pointed to the stage where Jean still sang. "She's singing that for *you*, no one else. I hope you're listening."

I focused on the stage and saw Roy was right—Jean's eyes kept returning to me as she sang. She was amazing to watch; she moved with confidence and grace, and as much as I hated to admit it with Bennie sitting right next to me after that comment, her legs were incredible. Then again, so was everything else about her.

"I will build my love a tower, near yon pure crystal fountain...And on it I will build all the flowers of the mountain...will ye go, lassie, go?"

Bennie chimed in again. "I'm telling you, if *you* don't ask her, *I* will."

This time I glared at her. "Look, I'm not stopping you from doing whatever you want to do. Jean jokes around a lot, okay? You know what? I don't have to explain myself." I pushed my chair back.

"I'm done. I'll call you guys Sunday and we'll work out the drive, all right?"

Bennie grabbed my arm as I stood. "At least wait until she's done, that's fucking rude."

"Oh, so now you're the expert on fucking rude, right?" I spit back. "First you talk about her like...like"—I was furious as I cast about my mind for the right words—"like she's meat or something, then you bug me about asking her out. What the fuck?"

"Calm down, man, I'm just teasing you," Bennie cajoled and tugged on my sleeve. "No one's trying to insult anyone, okay?"

I pulled my arm away, sat back down, and folded my arms across my chest. "Yeah, fine, just don't, okay?"

Bennie held her hands up for peace. "Hey, here," she pushed my beer closer, "relax, man."

I glowered at her another moment as I reached for my pint, and Roy wisely ignored us both.

And just as suddenly as it came, the heat left my body. What was I getting all crazy for? Bennie was good people, and I knew that. If she wanted to ask Jean out... "I'm sorry, Bennie, just the stress or whatever, you know? Sorry."

Bennie smiled. "Drink your beer and relax. We're off for a few days, so enjoy it, you know?"

She was right, and I took a sip and enjoyed the rest of Jean's performance, then stood up with everyone else when she was done to clap enthusiastically. She had a very good voice, and I wondered if she'd ever thought of doing anything with it.

Her brother Pat gave her a big hug as she came off the stage, then handed her a fresh beer.

"You might have guessed this ugly so-and-so's my sister," he joked as they neared. Jean punched his shoulder and I held out my hand.

"Nice to meet you, I'm—"

"Tori Scotts, or Scotty," he answered for me with a smile as he took my hand. "I've heard *quite* a bit about you."

"All lies, I'm sure." He had a good handshake.

"Oh, so you *do* know my sister," he said and grinned again, which earned him another smack from Jean, this time on his ear.

I laughed, like I always did around Jean, and everyone introduced themselves as she wiggled around the table to find a seat and pull it up not quite next to me and half behind me.

Bennie shot me a quick smirk that earned her a scowl, so she volunteered to get the next round, and we got food to go with it.

The rest of the night flew by, between the beers and the music, the dart games that began to get dangerous when Roy pinned someone's hat to the wall—I grabbed Jean's wrist when she aimed at her brother Pat's ass.

"But I'm a medic, I know how to fix that!" she protested as she tried to throw it anyway.

"It's called 'darts,' not 'dodge,'" I told her, and we both laughed as she tried to escape. I put my arm around her waist to catch her, and the next thing I knew, I was staring into her eyes.

I forgot we were in one of the straightest, most Irish bars in all of Brooklyn when I dropped her wrist to reach for her face; I didn't think of anything except how smooth and warm her skin was under my fingertips.

I don't know what happened to the dart because the band had started to play "Whiskey In The Jar," Jean closed the distance between us, and surrounded by friends and peers, I kissed her.

I fell in love with her mouth all over again, stunned by the realization that I'd been aching to feel it for so long; I was lost, wonderfully lost in the completeness of the moment.

It wasn't until the rousing rendition of "Irish Lullaby," which signified the end of the night (it was four a.m. and even the bartender appeared exhausted) and required group participation, that we finally came up for air.

"You've got a great voice, you know," I told her as I held her.

"Thanks, but it's not like your cousin's," she said, and I smiled as I watched the light pink that spread across her cheeks.

"Well, whose is, right?"

We finished the last verses together, and Roy stood next to me, belting his heart out, which garnered him a quick, bemused glance from Pat.

"Hey, my last name's Mulligan. Haven't you ever heard of Black Irish?" Roy joked, and continued singing as Pat cracked up and couldn't continue.

"Did you drive or can I give you a ride home?" Jean asked as the song ended and the party broke up.

"I'm supposed to go with Bennie and Roy, I've got the toll tonight," I said regretfully. I would have liked to spend more time with

Jean, give in to the tide that pulled on my blood, but then…I didn't really want to hear the speculation from Bennie when we saw each other next. That kiss had been very public, but everything else—*if* there was anything else—I wanted to keep private. "They're probably waiting for me."

"I totally understand."

We separated though we remained touching, her hands on my waist and my fingers through her belt loops. Although I doubt she did it consciously, when she moistened her lips it was one of the most sensual things I'd ever seen.

I didn't want to let this go, didn't want to let things just…hang… between us.

"I'm free for a few days, if you want to…you want to do something?"

Jean flushed and glanced down before speaking. "Actually, tomorrow my parents, they're having a bit of a dinner party for me, you know, because, well, they're all proud and stuff." When she looked at me, her grin was so charmingly self-conscious I wanted to kiss her all over again.

"Doyouwannago?" she asked in a rush.

I *had* to touch her. I took her face in my hands and kissed her, a delicate glide of my lips on hers. When she again granted me entrance to her mouth, I could have sworn that I knew exactly how it would feel to have her ride my tongue, and the sensual image was so strong I thought my knees would give as her hands wreaked havoc along my neck and shoulders; I could literally feel her heart beat against my chest.

"So…that's a yes, then?" Jean asked, breathing hard, as hard as I was, and I couldn't help but repeatedly brush her long strands of hair behind her ears.

"Just tell me when and where. I'll be there."

Bennie and Roy were already waiting in the car when I finally walked out of the bar with the time for tomorrow and Jean's parents' address written neatly and folded into my wallet.

As I slipped into the backseat I caught the quickest of grins between Roy and Bennie.

"Thought you might get a…lift…from Scanlon tonight," Bennie commented, peering at me through the rearview as we pulled out. I could see the smirk trying to work its way out from the corner of her mouth.

"What, and have you remind me every day for the rest of our lives that I skipped out on the toll? Not on your life."

"Doesn't matter," Bennie retorted, laughing. "Roy owes me twenty, donchya?"

"Yeah, yeah," he grumbled good-naturedly and fumbled for his wallet. "You won, fair and square."

"Knew I would." She laughed harder. "I told you."

"Do I wanna know what this is about?" I asked from my perch in the back as we flew over the bridge.

"Yeah, you do," Bennie said.

"Definitely not," Roy said at the same time.

"Now I really want to know." I looked from one head to the other expectantly.

"Shit." Roy sighed dramatically.

"No big thing," Bennie said as we turned down my block. "I just bet Roy a twenty that you'd ask Jean out by the end of the night."

"What?"

"Yeah," Roy sighed again. "I thought you might wait a few days, but she"—he jammed his thumb in Bennie's direction—"thought if you got pushed enough you'd do it sooner, like tonight sooner."

"But only because you both looked like you were going to combust every time you looked at each other by the grease trucks this whole week, and you know, that would have deprived the rest of us of coffee. And when I found out for sure you hadn't asked her out, I figured you needed…assistance," Bennie added helpfully.

I shook my head, more amused than anything because as much as I hated to admit it…well, I did have a date with Jean the next night. But still, I couldn't let them get completely away with it, either. "You guys suck. And you both kinda lose, 'cause I didn't ask her out."

"That's right, you didn't," Bennie agreed. "You were just practicing rescue breathing, borrowing each other's lungs, vertical fu—"

"That's enough. I'll call you guys Sunday to work out the week," I said as I got out of the car. "And just so you know?" I told them through Roy's window, "You both still suck."

"That's what friends are for." Roy grinned at me.

"Yeah," Bennie said, leaning over to the window. "Just remember, we suck in the right way."

I rolled my eyes. "Good night." I walked the path behind the house to my apartment, kicking the snow as I went. I'd take care of that first thing in the morning, I thought, but first, I was going to take a shower, as cold as I could possibly stand it, and hope it cooled the fire Jean had set ablaze under my skin.

❖

After clearing the snow, then sparring with Samantha in the morning, I decided to get a haircut so I'd look presentable when I showed up at Jean's folks' place. I preferred my hair to skirt my collarbone rather than flow past it.

The Scanlon home was a three-story brownstone not far from Peggy's in Bay Ridge, and I was glad I already knew how hard it was to find a parking spot or I'd never have gotten there on time.

Several young men in leather jackets and kilts lounged along the stairs that led to the front door—two police department and two fire department, from the colors of them, and the music that poured out of the door was distinctly Irish.

"Hey, Scotty!" One of the young men detached himself from the cement railing and became Pat in the early twilight as he bounded down the steps. "Welcome to the *ceilidh*!"

He grabbed my hand and dragged me up the steps. "Ignore these dirty layabouts. They're just here for the free beer."

"What's a *ceilidh*?" I asked Pat as he took my coat from me.

He stared at me, mock horror on his face. "Your last name is Scotts and you don't know what a *ceilidh* is?"

"Nope," I shook my head, "I don't."

"Don't let my da hear you say that!" He grinned. "Or you'll be listening to a Scanlon version of Celtic history for the next hour!"

"And who's needing a history lesson?" A distinctly male rumble cut through the noise and I knew, without a doubt, that this burly man, with his shock of thick gray hair and barrel chest, wearing the same tartan Pat wore with a navy blue fire-department polo shirt, was none other than Pat and Jean's dad. She had his eyes, a sparkling warm brown, and I realized what they made me think of: cider. Dark, hot, cinnamon-spiced cider.

"Mr. Scanlon," I held out my hand, "I'm Tori Scotts, and I'm glad to finally meet you."

He smiled, a huge smile, and instead of shaking my hand, he pulled me into a bear hug.

"We're all family here, all nine-one-one, and I'm glad to meet you too. Pat, where's her beer?" he asked as he released me and tucked my hand in his arm.

"I was just getting her coat and—"

"Beer, man! Get her a beer! What the hell kind of host are you to your sister's"—he gave me a sidelong glance and the tiniest of grins— "friend?"

I grinned back. I didn't know what Jean and I were, either, but I knew that friend was somewhere in there.

"I'm all right," I told him, "fine. But," and I craned my head about, "where's Jean?"

Mr. Scanlon led me through the hallway. "Come meet Mrs. Scanlon before I let you go into the living room. One drink and they're all happy, two drinks and they're deaf, three and they're all the lord of the dance in there. It's frightening, I tell you," he said with a grin and patted my hand as we walked into what was clearly the dining area.

Pat shoved a large mug into my free hand. "It's Guinness, not that crap stuff, so no complaints and drink it all—it's my job to see your mug doesn't run dry."

"It'll be slow going for you, then, buddy. I'm driving tonight." I grinned at him as we all neared what I assumed under all that food was a dining table. A group of nine or so had set up a circle of chairs before it and were chatting animatedly over the music.

"Megs!" Mr. Scanlon called above the din. "Tori's here!"

When she turned her head and smiled, I recognized Jean, what Jean would be in another twenty years. Beautiful. Her mother was beautiful, and Jean had her coloring, her smile, and even her tilt of head, though Mrs. Scanlon had a few streaks of silver in her short hair.

"So," Mrs. Scanlon said as she stood and kissed my cheek, "you're Tori. Jean's told us a bit about you—"

"About twenty thousand things, twenty thousand times, Jean has," her brother quipped from my elbow where he refilled my mug.

"Hey, who's taking my name in vain?"

My head snapped at the recognition of that voice, and nothing could have stopped the smile I felt spread across my face. I watched what must have been a mirror expression grow on Jean's as I handed my mug back to Pat.

"You're here," she said simply and the next second was in my arms, a warm and solid presence.

"Told you I would be," I answered and breathed in everything about her: the fresh-soap smell of her hair and its silken glide across my cheek, the strength in the arms that surrounded me and the comforting spread of her hands across my back, and the very welcome feeling of her chest pressed against mine, the thud like it was my own.

"You look great," she said quietly.

"Thanks, you too," I answered just as softly. "Can I kiss you now or do I have to wait and find a quiet space outside?" I murmured into her ear after pressing my lips to her neck. I felt the pulse jump under her skin.

Her hands smoothed down my spine. "Only if you want to make that sort of declaration in front of my *entire* family. Not that *I'd* mind, but I warn you, my mom and aunts will be planning the wedding, naming our kids, and picking the wallpaper."

"Really? Will it be plaid?"

"Is what plaid?"

"The wallpaper. I can't live with plaid wallpaper, and I'm dying to kiss you."

"We'll paint, I promise." Her lips were a soft brush against my ear before they became a gentle fit on mine.

"Oh, great, now she'll *never* dance with me!"

We both laughed as we broke apart, and Pat shoved my beer right back at me as one of the guys from out front saluted us with his.

I spent the rest of the night meeting aunts and uncles and cousins, husbands, wives, partners, boyfriends and girlfriends of aunts, uncles, and cousins, as well as friends *and* friends of friends, and I was thankful for the varying tribal insignia people wore; otherwise I wouldn't have been able to keep track of anyone.

I learned to recognize not only the PD and FDNY tartans that I already knew, but the Scanlon tartan, which more than half of those in attendance wore, and the McCabe attire, which identified Jean's mother's side of the family.

"They were originally from Scotland too," Mrs. Scanlon told me with a twinkle in her eye as I met her brother and her nephew, Shaun.

"Too bad Shannon won't be back from Ireland for another few weeks," Pat turned and said to Jean with an unmistakably evil grin. "She'd *love* Tori."

"Shut up," Jean said with a scowl as she elbowed him.

I gave her a questioning look, which Pat answered instead.

"Ah, Shannon, Shaun's sister and our cousin…she has a thing for Jean's—"

Jean clapped her hand over his mouth and wrestled him into a headlock. "He's had way too much to drink, and I think it's time for cake."

He waggled his eyebrows at me from under Jean's arm, but I got the picture: watch out for Shannon. I gave him the okay sign to let him know I'd been duly warned, but I wasn't really worried about it.

Once Pat had been pardoned and paroled after Jean extracted his mute promise of no further outbursts, we admired the cake, complete with a reproduction of Jean's new city-issue shield and her new badge numbers on it. After that, we had more beer, more food, and more music.

Mr. Scanlon had been right: everyone thought they were lord of the dance, including Mr. Scanlon, who taught me the steps to a reel and made sure to take me on a tour around the living room where I ended up dancing with everyone.

"You know what they say, don't you?" one of Pat's friends asked with a laugh as we tried not to collide with innocent bystanders.

"What's that?"

"A man in a kilt is a man and a *half*!"

I chuckled as we went through the next step in the reel; it hadn't been hard to learn. I just had to remember to take one large, turning step every fourth.

"Ah, you're a nice guy, but I'm not interested in any of your parts," I said with a grin.

"And that's because she likes her men with boobs like mine," Jean added as she and Pat whirled behind me.

"Yeah, and she doesn't want any of your half, either," Pat added.

The two of them, combined with the friend's mock wounded expression, made me laugh so hard I almost spilled the beer.

"Now *that's* alcohol abuse," Pat cautioned as he saved my glass, "and it can't be tolerated."

I turned to Jean. "What say you help me find a safe place for me and my beer?"

"Hmm…" She tapped her chin. "I know just the spot—c'mon." She took my hand.

Although we barely let go of each other the rest of the night, her mom presented me with a plate that seemed to never empty because everyone kept trying to feed me, while every time I put that mug down, true to his word, Pat kept it filled, no matter how much I protested. After a while, I stopped protesting, only because I was sitting on the sofa with Jean and we didn't notice much else but each other.

It was really late: the revelry had died down, the music had softened, and Jean and I were the only two people not in the kitchen or the dining room.

"I should get going," I said finally. It had been difficult to simply sit there and hold hands, to give her occasional little kisses, when what I really wanted to do was…anything, everything. I wanted her so badly my stomach hurt and my skin felt numb from the overload. And it wasn't just sex, either, because I wanted to feel her skin against mine, just to hold her, close and warm, feel the whisper glide of her hair against my cheek when I pressed my mouth to her neck.

"Do you have to? Are you all right to drive?" Jean asked, her breath almost as much a distraction as the tender lips that brushed my skin.

"I'm fine," I said, feeling very regretful as I untangled from our embrace and stood, "and it's getting very late."

Jean stood with me, her hands gentle on my arms. "You *can* stay, you know."

I smiled at her. I wanted to stay, I wanted to stay with her, but for once in my life, I didn't want to rush…I wanted to take the time to explore whatever this was, this growing thing between us that had such strength, that felt so important and yet so fragile. Besides, this was her *parents'* house, and I couldn't stay that close to her and not touch her, and just the wanting seemed disrespectful somehow. And…I had to talk with Trace; I owed her that.

"I can't," I said instead, "but thank you."

Jean caught my hand up in hers as we walked toward the front hallway to get my coat and kissed my fingers. "Can I see you tomorrow?" She nibbled slowly against the skin, a move that nearly weakened my resolve to go home with my dignity intact as I dug with my free hand along the hooks on the wall for my coat.

"Please…" I cupped her cheek in my hand. "I don't…" Her lips moved so invitingly over my skin I needed to…I needed to think. I couldn't think at all, because all I *wanted* was to feel her skin against mine.

"Call me tomorrow, okay?"

"That I can do." Her words were a low burr in my ear as we caught each other up again because I was leaving, I was really and truly going to leave this time.

Mr. Scanlon stood at the top of the steps as I stepped out the front door, waving off the other departing revelers.

"I had a great time, Mr. Scanlon, and please tell Mrs. Scanlon thanks for having me."

"Will do. Are you sure you're okay to drive?"

"Yes, absolutely. I've managed to pretend not to see Pat's refill attempts for the past hour or so."

"Are you sure? You're welcome to stay, you know." He smiled at me as his hands engulfed mine.

All I could think as I gazed at that kind man was that I couldn't stay, I simply couldn't look into his eyes, stay in his home, when the only thing that echoed in my head was how much I wanted, I needed to love his daughter—now, later, for as long as she wanted me to, and maybe even if she didn't.

I repeated those words in my head. I loved her. God help me, that's what this had to be, because the thought of Jean drove me to distraction, her proximity made me shake, and leaving her now made me feel physically ill.

I either loved her, or I had the flu. The recognition of that probability caught me up short as I gaped at Mr. Scanlon, not knowing what to say. Holy shit…I loved his daughter.

"I love your…house," was all I could manage to blurt out, catching myself before I said anything else, now that I had the words to match my feelings. My scalp felt numb.

"Well, you're welcome here anytime, young Scotty, anytime," he said, and gave me another hug. "Hope we'll see you soon."

I don't know what I said as I extricated myself and said my final good-byes, but I was very focused on trying not to fall down the steps as I walked to my car.

As I drove home, I wondered at myself, at the strange, new sensation that filled my chest. This was so…different, different than anything or anyone.

Kerry and I had dated about four months before we'd lived together. After a couple of nights of running into each other at the same bar and some heated flirting, we had sex before we'd even gotten halfway through our first official date—but we did at least date. We fucked a lot, but we went out and did things too. I'd already been taking the EMT class by that time, and living together, well, it had seemed like the next logical step: we really liked and cared for each other, we got along well, and the sex was great. It was too bad we hadn't had much besides that.

Trace and I, well, we'd never dated at all; we didn't live together either, and the sex, well, that simply had to end—completely. Things had already slowed down considerably, but still, it wasn't fair, not to anyone, and especially not with the way I felt about Jean.

I pulled into the driveway at exactly midnight, and the phone rang in my back pocket as I fumbled for the keys.

"Scotty," I answered as I managed to grab the right one and fit it to the lock.

"Hey there," Jean's voice cheered in my ear, "it's tomorrow."

"Yeah, it certainly is that." I laughed.

"So…you still want to do something?"

"Sure," I answered, glad to know she was interested. "Got anything in mind?"

"How about…since you came out to Brooklyn, I'll come over to Staten Island?"

"Sounds great. What do you think about noon?"

"What do you think about five minutes?"

"What?"

"Well, I'm just about to pull through the toll plaza. What's your cross street?"

I laughed again and gave her the address. I knew she wouldn't really need directions, since she'd worked on the Island, but I did have to explain how to reach my place behind the house. I checked my watch when we hung up: I had about ten minutes before she arrived.

A quick apartment inspection revealed it as pretty neat, probably since all I'd been really doing lately was studying, and I figured a cup of coffee or two couldn't hurt so I put some on.

The idle of her vehicle sounded through the quiet street as she parked outside and the engine cut to silence just as the brew cycle started. I was glad I'd shoveled the walk after yesterday's light snow. "Hey," I said from the open door as she came up the walk. "You *know* you're out of you're fucking mind, right?" I couldn't help smiling as I said it.

"Yeah, yeah," she agreed when I folded my arms around her. "I'm psycho, but you're the one driving me there."

I kissed her exactly the way I'd wanted to through the long hours of the party, an agonizing blend of sweet sensuality and shyness with a growing undercurrent of need as we stepped in and I managed to close the door behind her.

"Mmm…wanted to do that all night."

"I wanted you too," she admitted, her tongue and voice a low buzz in my ear.

"There's fresh coffee," I stuttered out finally, because between the way I felt and the way she held me, I could see this going in only one direction, and I had to slow it down before it raced away from me, out of control, without my knowing or understanding what it was or where it came from.

"Sure, yeah. Coffee sounds good," Jean agreed, her words almost faint, her breath as ragged as mine.

As we got caffeinated, we sat and did our best to talk about the station and battalion Jean had been assigned to. I had difficulty focusing: I couldn't stop admiring the graceful line of her neck, or the way a tendril of hair curved just so over the sharply defined tendon there and ended over what I knew were probably the most magnificent breasts I'd ever seen.

I did manage to understand that she had been put into B Company and would start on Tuesday as vacation relief, meaning that she would fill in for absent members or work at the station itself, from two p.m. to ten p.m., until she was assigned to a regular unit.

"Are you happy with those hours?" I asked as I shifted closer to her along the sofa. Somewhere in the back of my mind, I realized that Jean was gracefully allowing me to set the pace and tone, and I appreciated that. I'd already done the let's-not-talk, let's-get-right-to-the-fuck thing, as well as the oh-baby, I-want-to-do-whatever sex talk. I wasn't sure of what I did want, but whatever happened between us, I knew I didn't want *that;* I wanted this to be…right.

"Well…it was actually my second choice, stationwise," she

admitted, "but the other available choices would have brought me to the Bronx, and that would have been a crazy commute, and Brooklyn would have ended up in an overnight rotation."

I caught the slightest shake in her hand when she put her mug down.

"I'm a little tired of those overnights," she continued, then grinned at me. Her gaze moved from my eyes to my mouth, and the shift of her grin, from humor to a frank sensuality, made my heart stop for one painful second before it throbbed back to life, a heavy beat in my ears. "There's this girl I really like—she prefers a three-to-eleven shift."

"Funnily enough," I said, hardly able to hear myself past the beat in my head, "that station was *my* first choice. And I did, in fact, request a three-to-eleven shift."

"I know." Her voice was barely audible. "I remembered."

I was stunned. Jean had based a major career decision on *my* preferences, on the chance that I would get both the station and the shift I wanted. Granted, she could always transfer, but we'd been repeatedly warned at the academy that transfers were hard to get, especially as newbies. "Depends on the needs of the service," our instructor had said. "You could get one right away, but you're more likely to wait anywhere from one to fifteen years."

I put my cup down. "Jean, you didn't do that, you didn't throw away a chance at a station you want for a girl."

"I didn't throw anything away." She brushed the hair away from my forehead. "I'm taking a chance on something I really want."

I forced the air and the words out past the knot in my chest and the tightening of my throat. "So tell me more about this girl you like."

"She's beautiful," Jean whispered. Her eyes were the color of burnt sugar as she carefully cradled my face in her hands, then stroked my cheeks. "She's break-my-heart beautiful."

I'd been told I was cute, and I'd been told more times than I could remember that I was pretty in so many ways, by so many people, I even knew it in an objective, almost logical way, the same way I knew my hair or eye color. But in the same way those other things were simply embedded facts I never consciously thought about, so was the idea of being "pretty." It was a concept that had no real meaning for me, just another fact among so many others—until I heard Jean put it that way. Her words…they meant something to me, because the way she said them had meaning, more meaning than just my face.

"And she's very, very special," Jean continued as I found myself thinking I felt the same way about her. "She doesn't know how special she is."

When her mouth met mine, I was more grateful than I can ever remember feeling for the taste of her lips, the return pressure of her hands wherever they roamed.

"I'll bet," I said when we took a breath, "she really likes you too."

❖

When we finally got to my room, I hesitated. Not because I didn't know what to do, but because I was afraid—afraid that after Kerry, and especially after Trace, I wouldn't know how to touch her. Not that I couldn't make her come, but that I wouldn't remember how to be gentle, caring. I knew how to *fuck*, that was easy. But I didn't know if I could show her how I felt, how she made me feel for her, about her.

I decided to take the risk and tell her. "Jean, I know this might sound…silly or something, but…I don't want to rush things, I don't want to just—"

Jean shushed me with the gentle pressure of her lips on mine. "It's okay. I don't want to rush us, either."

"Could we…would you…just stay with me? Is that okay?"

Her eyes, a fiery henna that triggered a line of combustion along my internal geography, fixed on mine.

"I would be very happy," she kissed my neck, "to do *exactly* that," she concluded, the words a rumble that tumbled against my throat.

I forgot all my fears as we settled around each other, shedding each concern with each new brush of freshly revealed skin—silky, soft, and drawing me, drawing her, onward, closer, the incandescent meld wrapping us around one another as we explored new terrain: the channel of her spine down her lightly muscled back, the jut of her hip that fit my palm precisely, and the yielding firmness behind it as I drank of her breath, the wine taste of her mouth, the tender sensuality of her lips and tongue again and again.

Her hands, hands I'd seen carefully palpate for a vein or a pulse, measure drugs, soothe the sick and the scared, take tension from mine to set broken bones, hands that I knew for a fact were competent, capable, strong, those same hands now set that combusting line into a series of fiery sparks that made every cell in my body pulse with awareness, the awareness of Jean and how much, how very much I wanted her hands on me, to explore her with mine.

The growing heat took us from separate sparks to a joined blaze, fueled a magnetic heat I wanted to sink into forever; and her body molded to my hands, held me firmly, told me the truth behind every single one of her joking declarations, all of them.

"Jean...you...are *so*...fucking...beautiful..." I whispered into the tender skin at the junction of her jaw as I moved within her. I had no other words to describe how incredible she was, she felt, how she made me feel. For once, the fire didn't threaten, didn't frighten, but warmed me instead with its steady light, a joyful, heady peace that made me feel complete.

My name, choked from her lips, a soft cry in my ear, made me tremble against her, the sound surging into my body, through my blood, until I couldn't tell who we were anymore when her free hand pulled me even closer to hold my beating chest against hers.

"Tori?" Jean whispered as the glide continued, setting flames dancing in the just-banked fire.

"Hmm?" The delicate vein in her throat lay under my tongue.

"Happy Valentine's Day."

It was the best one I'd ever had.

EXTREMITY/EXTRICATION

After life threats have been treated properly, the decision to transport immediately and continue evaluation en route, or to delay transport and continue the evaluation, must be made.

Despite my mother's rather obvious and occasionally very pointed disapproval of my new profession, something about her recent hospital experience had changed her perspective. When I stopped by to say hello and drop off my check, she asked about my graduation date, and as I half ashamedly admitted that there'd be an actual ceremony and answered her questions of when and where, I was shocked to realize that she wanted to attend.

After the brief ceremony I learned that not only had I received the station and shift I'd wanted, I'd been assigned, along with Bennie and Roy, to the same battalion as Jean, which meant we'd have the same days off, and was further pleasantly surprised to discover my mother had arranged for a small dinner party at one of my favorite restaurants, Real Madrid.

She'd also invited Nina and Samantha. I promptly turned around and invited Jean, and this time, I didn't care what my family or, rather, my status-conscious mother thought.

There's no denying that I was more than slightly relieved to learn after I introduced her to Nina and Samantha that none of them had met before—well, not really, anyway. Sam remembered Jean's father and mother from her own father's funeral.

I actually called Trace about three days before that, as much as I dreaded it, but I didn't want to leave things unclear between us, and I didn't want to lead her on in any way. I had decided to meet her at the hospital after her shift and tell her face-to-face that, yes, I found her attractive, yes, we were friends, but no, I couldn't continue sleeping with her, because I really didn't share, and I couldn't share myself, not like that, not anymore.

I still didn't know what Jean and I had, but I wasn't going to let anything stop us from discovering.

When Jean and I had touched, really and truly touched, for the first time when I tasted her wine-sweet skin and filled my hands with her curves, I wanted more: to taste the line of her neck and the curve of her breast, those beautiful curves she carried so proudly. She was beautiful: shining in my eyes, moving with my hands, gliding under my tongue, and I was happily shocked that she explored me with the same eagerness.

I reluctantly tore my lips from the light chocolate kiss of her hardened nipples to return to her mouth, and Jean explored me, fingertips rolling and kneading my breasts, making me catch my breath as I eased my leg between hers.

She made me aware of my body—not just my arousal, but my heartbeat, my skin, my fingers as she drew them between her lips, made me sigh over the slip of her tongue along my neck and made my breath catch again when that same tongue teased across my chest to bathe one hardened point, then the other, slowly, deliberately, meant only for me to savor in the moment.

I'd known, in the same way I'd known that rain was wet and fire burned, that I was female. It meant I had to wear a bra, had to deal with the same physiological occurrences approximately every four weeks, and that I could, assuming all systems were fine, bear live young someday; my gender was simply a fact, like the continents or the oceans, apparent and *genetically* incontrovertible, nothing to have an emotion or an opinion about.

Sex had always been a combination of lust and mechanics, biological drive coupled with the artistry of technique, where my needs were secondary to my partner's as a matter of consideration, manners, and, I have to admit, pride.

But Jean…Jean made me *know* in a way I never had before that I was not only female, but that I was also a *woman*—a concept I hadn't considered before, not in any way, not in this certain fullness; it simply didn't figure into my equations.

In Jean's eyes and hands, next to her skin, I was desirable, *because* of my genetic inheritance, my body built to receive the same pleasure it gave and for the same reasons, not as an afterthought or a tool, not even as part of a contest of wills or to prove anything other than this: she desired me, she found me beautiful, and she wanted to show me.

"Tori...sweet, sweet Tori," she groaned, "I love the way you feel." Her hands traveled along my sides to grip my ass and shift us so that we lay next to each other, and I trailed my fingers down the tense muscles of her stomach, through the velvet down that covered her.

It was a smooth glide between lips ready for my touch, the hardness of her clit slick under my fingertips. I was moved, so moved that my heart ached.

Jean slipped an arm around my waist, pulled me closer, and delivered a kiss that revealed me, left me equally ready beneath her hand as she pushed herself harder against me.

Nothing, but nothing, had ever felt as erotic or as stirring as my tongue playing against Jean's while we teased each other.

I'd never been so naked; I'd never felt so free.

"I want...I need to be inside you," I managed to say against her lips, her clit sliding along the groove between my fingers before I eased my thumb there instead and let my fingers edge closer to her wet invitation.

"Wait," she breathed against my mouth as I felt her fingers shift, press, and tease against the body hunger she created, "do it with me."

Her tongue filled my mouth as we filled each other, a slick and ardent merge that made me surge against her, on her, in her, and she felt so *right*; it all felt just so very *right*.

"Perfect," I could barely groan out at the honey-sweet fullness in my cunt, the lush embrace of her liquid heat, the finesse of the stroke on my clit, and the amazing pulse that throbbed under my thumb.

I read the cues of her breath, of her body, the shift of her hips and the slide of her cunt on my fingers to discover what she liked and what she loved, turned on even higher by every whispered request and half-gasped urging as I learned her rhythms.

I was again surprised when instead of merely thrusting inside me, she swam within me and touched me, really touched me, like no one ever had—and I loved it, loved the way she stirred me. She took my body and my mind places they had never been, and I was continually stunned by just how much her responses sharpened mine.

"Feel that, baby?" she asked as I felt her cunt tighten on my fingers. "You're gonna make me come...I wanna show you..."

My body reacted so intensely to hers, to her voice, that when she moved in me, I experienced her feelings not just in my cunt, but in my chest, in my throat. We met each other stroke for stroke, and when her body pulsed around me and she sang my name into my ear, I was floored by the intensity of feeling her come, the flame that shot through my veins and burst through my skin almost deafening me to her name on my lips in that final fusion.

❖

I met Trace at the entrance to the nearly empty cafeteria with its view of the ER bay, and as we settled down with our coffees, I didn't waste time; I cut to the heart of it immediately. "Trace…I can't do this between us anymore, the casual thing. And…I know me too well, I can't, uh…I can't sleep with you and date someone else." It was a little embarrassing to say, but at least I had finally said it.

"We're just friends, Tori, friends with fringe benefits. What…are you in love or something?" Her expression was friendly, maybe even slightly smug.

It had been just under thirty-six hours since I'd seen Jean, and it would probably be at least another six before I saw her again…and I missed her. I could still feel her in me, on me, the taste of her breath on my lips and the rhythm of her life a haze that rode just over my skin. I felt like I was missing something—an arm, a leg, my head—until I could feel her next to me again, and I wanted her so much my entire body ached.

"I don't know…maybe. Could be the flu." I didn't want to discuss it, not with anyone really, not while this was so new, so *us*, ours alone, and especially not with Trace, because we'd slept together, because I knew she and Jean had…been involved.

And besides, my mother had been, probably still *was*, in love with my dad, and *that* had been a disaster that had left a lot of damage, damage she was still recovering from. On the other hand, when I looked at Nina and Samantha, I couldn't help but see how much they loved each other, it was a palpable aura that surrounded them, and if that was "in love" then maybe, just maybe…if I discussed Jean with anyone, it would be my cousin. I trusted her.

"Have you ever been in love?" I asked Trace, out of curiosity.

She stared down at the table and played with her napkin. "Almost.

Once," she said with a little sigh. She folded the napkin flat and smoothed it. "She told me I couldn't handle her—she was right." Trace gave me a smile, the one I liked so much, though her eyes shone too brightly. "I...I wasn't really comfortable with...things...yet, and she's, well, she's always been out, and that's really that. So...anyone I know?"

I hesitated, but the medical community was a small one, and it was better if she found out from me than from someone else. Besides, I had nothing to hide. I'd certainly done nothing wrong, not by Trace, not by myself, and not by Jean. Not telling Trace felt like I'd betray all of us, which was dishonest. I didn't want to be that.

"Uh...you probably do." I temporized a bit, because I didn't know how to make this any less awkward. "Her name's Jean. She's a paramedic, worked the privates for a while, has a per diem at Saint Vin's, and at University South, so—"

"Jean Scanlon?" If she was surprised, she didn't show it. "She's a beautiful girl. I can see where you'd suit each other." Her eyes shaded to a deeper gray. "It's funny," she commented, with the tiniest twist to the corner of her mouth, "you never, ever, know what life is going to bring."

I agreed and we finished our coffee with the promise to keep in touch from time to time. After all, we'd surely run into each other, and we _were_ still friends, albeit without the fringe benefits.

"Well," Trace smirked at me as I got up to leave, "if things change, you know where to find me."

"I'll remember that." I had nothing else to say.

❖

My rotations as vacation relief weren't terrible at all. I liked the shift, I liked the different people I worked with, and soon I was settled into a unit of my own. The schedule suited me fine; I had five days off out of every fifteen.

Despite our determination not to rush things, Jean and I spent quite a bit of our free time together, but not in a crazy way; she had her apartment, and Dusty, and her family, whereas I had my place and my family too, but we had this unspoken knowing that sooner or later things would change.

However, I was finally able to spend more time with my family, with my mother and sister, whom I'd drop in on in the early afternoon before I left for work. My mother might not have been pleased with my job, but she didn't mention that; she'd instead ask me if I was "being careful." On one of my visits she insisted I bring my dress uniform, then sewed on not only the patches and insignia, but also had it tailored.

She surprised me with my uniform when I came back from a food shopping expedition with Elena, and I have to admit, my dress blues looked super sharp. Elena then showed me her new favorite T-shirt. "An EMT loves me," it stated in an arch above a star of life with its caduceus emblazoned in the center. I gave her a big hug.

I also spent more time with Nina and Samantha. Samantha and I hadn't stopped our sparring lessons yet, and as Nina grew more and more obviously pregnant, I didn't want to stray too far.

Jean understood, and she probably visited Staten Island more than I did Brooklyn, for which I was thankful.

Staten Island celebrated Saint Patrick's Day with a huge parade on the second Sunday of March so that it wouldn't interfere with the "real" day, or the larger parade in Manhattan, and I thought Jean might enjoy watching it.

Besides, it took place maybe three whole blocks from the house, and Nina and Samantha were going, a tradition they'd enjoyed for several years, and we customarily said hello to all of the neighbors who'd been sequestered during the cold and snow of winter.

That, and the bars offered free drinks on the sidewalks, while the bakeries handed out all sorts of great pastries. The entire thing was just plain fun, and Jean's heritage—from the claddagh ring she wore on a chain around her neck and under her shirt on the job, or on her right hand as soon as she was off duty, to the funny and fierce arguments around her parents' table as to whether or not the Irish really had tartans—was evidently very important to her.

Combine that with the fact that Sunday would be exactly one month since we'd started dating, and it just seemed like a perfect combination. Besides, I thought she might enjoy the local experience, especially since I suspected her family would have some sort of tremendous cultural celebration that Wednesday, March 17.

"Can I wear a kilt?" Jean asked me when I called during our last shift before a three-day weekend to make plans.

"Sure."

"Can I wear one of those huge foam leprechaun hats?"

"Fine." I started to laugh at the image that arose in my mind.

"Can I wear just that to bed?" she asked in a throaty purr.

The radio went off in the cab of my rig. "I've got to run—I'll see you at end of shift, and we can debate the hat thing later."

"Okay, later, then." I heard her laugh as we hung up.

I'd been moved from a line unit that generally responded in a particular area, to a tactical one that roamed wherever we were needed; we spent about half of our calls backing up medics. My rig was call-signed "Ten David," or "One-oh David," but my partners, Janet Diaz, a pretty Puerto Rican girl with a ready laugh and sharper wit, and Isbjorn Rygh, who told us all repeatedly that *isbjorn* meant "polar bear" in Norwegian, and occupied over six feet of deceptively soft-looking solidity—we called him "Izzy"—had nicknamed our bus "One Over Dose."

It was a rough night. We'd finally had a few warmer days, and for whatever reason, this hint of spring and the warmer weather that would inevitably follow meant that weapons got...exotic. Not one, but two patients had been shot with crossbow bolts, the first in what had appeared to be a random incident on the West Side, and the second almost an hour later on the East Side.

Actually, we had three patients on the East Side: The first was a seventeen-year-old male who'd been grazed across the scalp with an arrow tip as he crossed the parking lot we were in. The head wound was bloody, but not deadly, and he was already being packaged and about to be transported for stitches by Bennie's crew. Another patient, a male approximately the same age, had received a bolt through his left thigh and was already being stabilized by another crew on scene.

The police were there, searching for the perpetrator, and our own supervisory patrol was present as well. Diaz and I eyed each other and the area warily as we slipped our gloves on. We'd pointed out to each other the three or so loose arrows that littered the ground and were both aware that if the cops were still there, so was the psycho William Tell. Neither of us felt particularly secure.

"You've got medic backup coming," our supervisor said as he directed us to the third patient, also male, of similar approximate age, who'd moments ago received a bolt through the chest, just above the first floating rib.

Each shaft we'd seen previously had been at least fifteen inches long, and a good six inches of this one were lodged in the patient's thorax.

He was conscious, aware, and understandably panicked as we went through the drill and evaluated him while he received supplemental oxygen. Next we stabilized the penetrating object. We absolutely wouldn't remove it in the field because such an attempt could cause further damage to the nerves, blood vessels, or muscles, as well as result in uncontrollable bleeding.

Besides, his breaths were fast and shallow, his pulse was weak, and what alarmed me most as his eyes fluttered open and closed were the muffled heart sounds and the distended veins in his neck, combined with the diminished lung sounds on the penetrative side of the injury. I was certain the patient had a pneumothorax, which was causing his lung to collapse, but I didn't know if the muffled heart sounds were from the increased pressure in the chest cavity or, and this is what had me really worried, a pericardial tamponade—blood filling the sac surrounding the heart—if the tip of the arrow had penetrated it.

Either way, as soon as the patient could be moved, he would be. There was no way we could wait for the medics—seconds counted and they were fast flying by. Diaz and I decided to load and go. Everything this guy needed, namely a sterile field and a surgeon, was in the hospital, not out here on the dirty asphalt.

Additionally, another patrol car had arrived while we worked, and shouts had gone up as another arrow had come flying by; we could hear the smash of a cruiser's window as the bolt found its mark not ten feet away from us. Still, Diaz and I did what we had to before we could take our patient to the relative safety of the emergency room.

Just as we had settled back into the rig and were trying to decide on whether we wanted pizza or fried chicken, "One-oh David, what's your twenty? Over."

"This is one-overdose. We are exiting Bellevue and proceeding to our COR. Over."

"We have a call for a male, approximately twenty years old, unresponsive, located at…"

I wrote down the information as Diaz flipped on the lights.

"Do you copy?" the anonymous voice asked.

"Ten-four, dispatch, we copy. One-oh David en route. Over."

The moment I clicked the mic and entered our status into the computer console, Diaz flipped the sirens.

We didn't have a lot of information to go on, and when we got to the location, an old brownstone that was probably the local "shooting gallery," as the addicts called them, as we radioed in our status I noted another rig parked out front.

It had rained lightly while we'd taken care of our last call, and the ground shone back up at us, almost reflecting the streetlights.

"Must be another patient," Diaz said, hefting the O$_2$ bag as we walked up the crumbling steps.

"At least it's on the first floor." I shrugged nonchalantly, but I had a bad feeling about this call—maybe it was the street, which was quiet, too quiet, like the bricks and the cement were holding their breath, as if something more than the rain had subdued them. That strange sense didn't ease as I shifted my bag over my shoulder and my fingers grazed the radio clipped to my waist.

The front door had been left open, either to let in air or by the last entering crew, and we walked down a dim hallway to find the apartment we'd been sent to.

Light flooded out into a narrow beam as a door opened, and the looming figure of a member of service—Lukaski, one of Jean's partners—ran out, waving a hand at us.

"Go!" he shouted as he ran. "Get out of the building—call PD, call patrol! Go!" He grabbed Diaz by the shoulder and was about to grab me too.

"Where's Scanlon?" I asked through dry lips as a band tightened around my chest.

"Right here," she said from behind his arm as they both rushed us out.

"Supposed to be an OD, but we've got a shooter too," Jean said, her hand firmly on my shoulder, but that band around my chest wouldn't ease as we almost tripped down the steps.

"He's fuckin' dusted, waving a gun around—he went into the bathroom with the OD, and that's how we're out here now."

Fuck. PCP users were probably among the most dangerous and unstable of the overdose crowd. There was every chance, every strong chance, this could get very ugly, very fast. We had just passed the curb and hit the asphalt, maybe six feet from the rig, as I keyed the radio.

"Fuckin' Rico! You piece of shit!" a male voice screamed.

I looked over my shoulder and past Jean's hand to see a young man, approximately twenty, dragging another to the stoop by the hood of his stained sweatshirt and waving a gun in his free hand.

"You fucked my *sister*!" he screamed, and as I opened my mouth to request PD backup, Jean threw me to the ground.

The world slowed to a cartoon-like crawl as three shots rang out, the first two almost simultaneously. The sound shut off. The radio skittered from my hands, and I watched the word "Motorola" flip over in the air before it delicately bounced on the ground; noted the position of my hands, realizing the bulk of impact would be on my forearms; and knew that it was inertia that kept my bag suspended above my hip before the strap that ran over my shoulder pulled it forward and down.

I saw Diaz gracefully twist to protect the O_2 tank from crashing to the ground and potentially exploding, while Lukaski reached out over her like a catcher stretching for the play at home base.

I felt Jean's body slide against my back and the medic box hit the ground half a heartbeat after I did.

Then the sound came back.

"How do you like that, motherfucker? Huh? How do you like that?" the perp screamed as Jean, Diaz, and I crawled under the rig.

Diaz got the radio first, and as I twisted and peered out from under the bus, I saw Lukaski, flat on the ground. He hadn't moved, and I didn't notice the cold or wet of the choppy asphalt that seeped through my pants as I belly-crawled back over to him.

He glanced up at me, and his eyes gleamed in the streetlight. "Got my leg," he whispered hoarsely, surprise etched across his cheeks.

I thought I heard Diaz call the ten-thirteen into the radio and glanced to my left when a sheen caught my eye: dark and shiny, like oil on her pant leg. Jean had gotten sprayed with Lukaski's blood.

"I gotcha, buddy," I said, even as that band squeezed harder, not just my chest, but my head too, and it sent icy heat through me, a strange burn flowing up my neck.

The perp was yelling something as I seized the shoulders of Lukaski's jacket.

"Can you crawl?" I asked him as he shifted onto his elbows.

"Yeah." He nodded. "I think so."

He propelled himself forward with his arms as I inched backward, dragging him by fistfuls of his jacket, and just as he was close enough for me to hook my hands under his armpits, he pitched headfirst.

Jean crawled over me, and together we got him under the rig.

Diaz had already set up the O_2 and was taking care of his airway and breathing, and she passed Jean a flashlight as I sheared through the bloody remains of Lukaski's left pant leg and boot.

What a bloody mess. I had no pedal pulse, which meant there was very little if any blood flow to his foot. I found the entry and exit wounds, and the visible cavitation, the damage caused by the bullet's trajectory, was ugly; the bullet appeared to have entered his boot just above his ankle. The leather had probably deflected the bullet's trajectory enough so that it had traveled up the bulk muscle of his calf to exit below and behind the knee; the fibula reflected starkly back at me under the glare of the flashlight. I now knew what "blown away" really meant: Lukaski's gastrocnemius, the visible main muscle of the calf, was splattered on the inside of the cloth I'd had to cut away.

Stop the bleeding. Jean handed me bandages and Kling tape, and after a quick rinse with saline and a quicker "Hail Mary" that no bits of asphalt remained in the wound, together we applied and secured a pressure bandage. We didn't have room to elevate his leg or to move anywhere else except to try to get Lukaski and us between the tires, as two more shots rang out and sirens wailed in the distance.

We needed to get out of there; we needed to get Lukaski to an ER, and fast, and as the sirens came closer, the perp screamed again.

"Ten, Rico, ten fucking years old! Mom, I'm so sorry, I'm so fucking sorry—God!"

I could see tires of responding vehicles surround the bus on three sides.

"Put the gun down!" a voice commanded, and despite Jean's warning grip on my arm, I peered out around the tire, hoping to find a clear path between us and another vehicle to get Lukaski out of there and onto one of the rigs I knew had to be close by.

"My fault, my fucking fault!" the gunman wailed. "What, you want me? You fuckin' want me?" he yelled, incredulity obvious in his voice as he turned to face wherever it was the cop had shouted from.

I glanced quickly and saw the original patient, or what I assumed had been the original patient, who lay slumped in the doorway, the stain that had covered his sweatshirt now soaking through his jeans.

"Fuckin' take him, take *him*, he fucked my sister—God," he wailed again, "my baby sister..." He took the gun and raised it to his head, and before anything else could happen, another shot rang out.

I saw the millisecond of shock register on his face before it seemed to disappear into a wet haze.

I don't remember how we got out of there, although I do recall being forced to sit with Jean and Diaz on the back step of the bus so we could get quickly checked as other units loaded up Lukaski, the original OD, the wounded gunman, and his sister, who had been found huddled in a room somewhere in the apartment.

I don't even know how we got back to the station, but when we did, a patrol supervisor, whom I'd never met before since he worked the shift after mine, politely asked us to accompany him to the precinct as soon as we'd stowed our gear.

"Bo heeka, baby, bo fuckin' heeka," Diaz muttered as she slammed her locker shut next to mine.

"What?"

"Bee oh aitch, eye cee aye. BOHICA," Diaz repeated as we walked toward the Suburban. "Bend over, here it comes again. Got it?"

We sat through what felt like hours of questioning as my wet pants first chafed, then dried on my skin, and I occasionally fussed with the newly frayed spot on my knee.

Who drew first, who shot what, did the perp shoot himself, could the shot have come from another direction—those were the questions we were asked, over and over, in every conceivable fashion. I couldn't understand why the officers asked, since I figured ballistics would show whose gun it had been.

We were finally free to go, and as Diaz and I marched out of there back to the Suburban that would give us a ride back to our station and back to my car, we passed Jean in another small office being interrogated by yet another officer. I gave her a tight smile and a thumbs-up as I walked by, and she nodded back.

An idea occurred to me. "Hold up a sec," I told Diaz. I fumbled in my pocket for my key ring and unhooked the ones to my apartment, then knocked on the door of that little office.

"I'm sorry to interrupt," I told the detective when his head swiveled toward me, "I'll just be a second. Hey, Scanlon?" I focused on her as she sat there, all coiled energy contained in a chair that was probably older than both of us combined.

"Yeah?"

I held out my key ring and gently tossed the keys to her. "Later."

"Yup," she agreed as she caught, then held them in her hand. I gave her the barest ghost of a smile, which she returned as I left.

"What a skell show, huh?" an officer asked, smirking at us as we passed. Colgano, I noted, his name tag said Colgano.

Skell. That word brought back some very fresh memories of one of our instructing lieutenants screaming in a student's face that were he ever to hear *any* of us use that word, a word that technically meant a homeless derelict but was used as a catchall to mean "subhuman," he would have that person's shield.

The word was meant to be both dehumanizing and degrading. I wouldn't use it, and it bothered me that anyone would be so free with it, but considering how tired and stressed I was pretty sure we all felt, this wasn't the time or place. I nodded politely at Colgano as we passed, but he had more to say.

"Fuckin' junkie gets his sister screwed up, shoots another junkie, and injures an MOS. People fuckin' care who blew his fuckin' head off? He was killing himself anyway and taking others with him."

I felt more than saw with my peripheral vision the grim twist that crossed Diaz's face, and I reached for her forearm, arresting her motion. I didn't know what she was going to do, but heat bled off her in waves, and that wasn't a good sign.

"It was a rough night," I said mildly, "and we've got to get back to our station." I smirked back at Colgano, then walked out the station door.

Diaz caught up to me on the steps and tapped my shoulder. "Thanks for that," she said, gesturing over her shoulder with her thumb.

"Hey, no worries." I grinned at her. "I've got your back, you've got mine. Right, partner?" I held out my hand.

She gave me a slow grin in return as she shook it firmly and agreed, "Right, partner."

I called Jean's cell right before I left the station and couldn't believe it was two in the morning. "They've got some more paperwork for me to fill out, and a new team wants to talk with me because Lukaski and I were first on scene," she told me, sounding tired and frustrated. "Turns out the OD? He's probably gonna live—might not ever walk again, probably pee into a bag forever, but—"

"And they want to find out as much as they can to see what kind of charges they can press against him?"

"Yeah, exactly," Jean confirmed, then sighed. "Anyway, figure another hour before I'm out of here, and give me twenty minutes after that to get to you."

"Hey, I heard Lukaski's pulled through surgery. Won't know for a while about the leg, but you know how that goes." I didn't know if anyone at the precinct had thought of telling Jean, or if they even knew, and *I* knew Jean had to be worried.

"Yeah? Good, good," she said, and I heard her swallow. "Thanks."

"Yeah, no problem, and as for later? Just get there when you get there, don't kill yourself. We can wait until tomorrow if you want."

"Hell, no!" Jean answered with a slight chuckle. "We still need to have our hat debate."

"You got it."

I didn't know what to do with myself once I pulled into the driveway. I took off my boots and left them by the door, hung up my jacket—dry-cleaning would take care of that—and carefully stripped off my uniform. The shirt was fine but my pants were ruined, and as I bagged them and tossed them right outside the door so I could remember to put them out in the morning, I wondered why I hadn't changed at the station.

Must have been the rush to simply get home after filling out an incident report, I mused as I took a long shower. The lieutenant had tacked another three comp days off to our scheduled swing weekend, but I'd save them for another time, I decided as I dressed again.

I *still* didn't know what to do with myself. I was exhausted but restless and trying very hard not to see Lukaski's leg in pieces under my hands. I shuddered as the band that had crushed my chest earlier came back, an icy grip this time as I once again saw the blood on Jean's pant leg. The part of my brain that does nothing but calculate estimated how close to her the bullet had come.

"He'll be all right. Patrol said he was gonna be fine," I muttered to myself, my voice too loud even to me in the empty garden house as I paced from room to room.

I didn't think the gunman had shot himself; I was pretty sure a cop had got him first. I knew what my mother would say about that: the victim had rights, and even if he *had* been about to shoot himself, that would have been his decision, a suicide, just as he'd been doing, albeit slowly, all along with the drugs.

But to have been shot down…was it murder? A suicidal person was a danger to all, and yes, he'd shot Lukaski, although strangely enough, I wasn't sure he'd meant to. Not that it would have made a difference to Lukaski, I supposed, or to any of us, had it been someone else.

That Jean could have been hurt was enough to make me wish that I'd been armed…and he'd shot that other guy for hurting his sister. Who was the criminal, then? The abusing OD, or his shooter? Or the cop who shot him?

If that had been my sister, my sister who'd been hurt… There'd be *no* place on this planet safe to hide, I thought grimly, and I would've taken great pleasure in watching the person who'd done it hurt, then hurt some more. Same if it had been Jean. Or one of my partners. Hell, Lukaski, too. Lukaski hadn't deserved that; he'd just wanted to help, that was all, just being a good person.

So what did that make me? Normal people, reacting in normal ways, to abnormal circumstances. That's what we'd been taught in the academy. But what was normal, anyway? That…was the average of deviance. And I wasn't feeling anything close to "normal," whatever that was.

I ran my hands through my hair in agitated frustration; I couldn't take what was going on in my head anymore, questions that brought up more questions and the smell of Lukaski's blood that could have so easily been Jean's still in my nose.

It occurred to me that sometimes, just sometimes, Nina and Samantha were up extremely late, and even if they weren't, well, I just didn't want to be alone at the moment, and simply knowing other people breathed nearby…it appealed to me, and I'd be able to hear Jean's car when she pulled up, anyway.

Tomorrow, we'd do something normal, and good, and fun: we'd go and enjoy the parade, say hellos to everyone, then go to the local pub with Nina and Samantha for dinner.

It was dark as I made my way inside their house, but as I approached the top of the stairs, I could see a soft light at the end of the hall where their room was.

Though thinking I'd say hello or something equally banal, I stopped three feet away from the entry, arrested by the sight before me.

At first, I couldn't tell what I saw, but as my eyes adjusted to the half light, I realized that my cousin moved slowly, languidly, over Samantha. There was such intensity and grace in the curve of her back, the fall of her hair, the proud line that followed her now-fuller breasts, then led down the slimness of her rib cage to the gentle swell of her belly before she disappeared into the blankets that covered them, I caught my breath. She was so mind-blowingly beautiful, beautiful in her love for the woman who moved beneath her, beautiful in her body that changed because of the love within it.

And as close, as physically *joined* as she was at that moment to her love, clearly she—they—reached for still more, in the fingers that quested for and captured Nina's face, then drew her nearer still, the clutch and clasp of hands that revealed taut lines of muscle, the strain of the work of devotion laid bare as together they built, they created... something I had no words for but I understood, in a place I'd only just discovered.

When Samantha softly called her name as she arched up under her, only to gather Nina in her arms, the kiss they shared reverberated through my soul, a chest-clenching throb, a sublime, radiant ache that threatened to bring me to tears, and I turned away as she gently rolled them over.

I quietly walked down the hallway to my room, the room they both had said would always be mine. It was strange, I mused as I turned the knob on the door, that thing, that desperate thing that had crawled in me had quieted.

It hadn't completely disappeared. I could feel it, awake and alive, but like a cat that for the moment sits next to you and purrs quietly, content to just be there, it had settled and curled on my chest, sated for the moment.

I flipped on a low light and grabbed a book from the shelf as I adjusted myself on the bed. I really wanted to take the next medic class, and it would do me no good if I forgot the things I'd learned.

How amazing, I thought as I flipped through the pages with my head full of the feelings that my unwitting voyeurism had brought me: they loved each other, they really and truly loved each other so much they wanted to have a child together. Utterly, fantastically amazing. And so beautiful. Perfect. At least one kid would have all the love it deserved.

My phone woke me just after three a.m. I'd fallen asleep in the house after all.

"Scotty."

"Hey, there," Jean said across the airwaves.

"Hey, yourself, what's up?"

She sighed. "I had a flat just as I crossed the bridge. I managed to get to..." and she named the cross street.

I was on my feet in seconds.

"I'll be there in under five minutes—we'll take care of it in daylight," I promised as I grabbed my jacket and left as quietly as I could.

❖

The temperature had dropped significantly, and when I pulled up not more than three minutes later and cut the engine, Jean stepped out of her Chevy Blazer.

"Yo."

"Hey," I returned and suddenly, as I crossed the several feet that separated us, everything crashed down on me: the fear and the stress, the pressure from the grilling at the precinct, the unfairness of Lukaski's injury, and the poetry, the absolute, silent, powerful clarity of what I hadn't meant to witness for even those few seconds between Nina and her Sam, and I had no doubt that's exactly what Samantha was, *Nina*'s Sam, just as Nina was completely, unconditionally hers: she'd put her own body on the line to prove it. And that's when I realized that was exactly what Jean had done—she had put herself between me and certain harm, something no one other than my cousin or my grandmother had ever done before.

I needed her, needed *Jean*, with an urgency that pounded and scraped through me as my head filled with the knowledge of what she'd volunteered to sacrifice, my ears with the hyper-reality of gunfire, and my face with the scent of a friend's blood.

Close, she was *so* close, and the deepest pit of my gut clenched with the unmistakable new knowledge that the most miraculous thing I'd ever witnessed was two people building the ineffable together, their bodies translating what their hearts held. It was Beauty in a world gone mad, something good, something *wondrous*, and I held on to that as the world shifted into hazy shades of red, blinded by rain and smoke and fire as I curled my fingers into the collar of Jean's coat and pulled her to me.

Her tongue fucked my mouth with electric intention, the lightning crack of warning, as her hands spread on my hips with near-bruising demand and I rocked her on my thigh.

We fell into my backseat and kept falling as the door crashed behind us, the ghost replay of thunder, a clouding echo that filled my sky as I dropped through it while she ripped at my shirt, left me gasping as the air hit my bare skin, her lips, her tongue hard and fast with unmistakable intent on me.

Her leg eased up between mine, and I sighed, grateful for the pressure as the scud of her zipper sliced through the air.

"Oh, I need you…" she said, her voice barely a whisper as her fingers gently gripped my wrist and urged my hand on.

I was lightning in the sky, a burning brand tossed away and discarded by a forgetful god, then Jean's mouth caught mine. It was a desperate reach that *hurt*, my chest *hurt* as her cunt wrapped around my fingers.

"Stay with me, Tori," she breathed and shifted, twisting to reach me, touch me. Her hands drew lines of cool blue fire down my back, eased along my ass, lines that wove around me even as I fell, a whirling tumble as I cut through Lukaski's pant leg, spinning and falling in a red wet haze, falling and spinning as Jean fell too, her body between me and deadly thunder.

"Look at me. Tori…look at me," Jean said, her voice thick, low, and sure, and I did, I looked into her eyes, those beautiful eyes that arrested my frantic, pathless drop through the clouds and carried me in their cinnamon-and-sugar sight.

"God, Jean…" I choked, the words fighting against gravity, the words that would weigh me, smash me down into cold, wet ground unless I released them. "You *know* I love you, don't you?" I had to tell her, I had to let her know because tomorrow…tomorrow *anything* could happen. It could be her, or it could be me, and I would never, ever, get the chance to tell her, to let her know because—

"You're not there, it's over," she whispered, "it's over, baby. You're here, and I'm here, and it's *us*, Tori…it's *us*, right here, right now."

She kissed me—her lips, her mouth the net that caught me as her body cradled me. "And I *love* you," she said as she entered me, filling me with fluid grace that guided me safely home, "I love you so…damned…much…"

She was crying when we got back to the bed that waited for us, and the first tear hit my skin as I lightly rubbed my thumb against the scar that marked the edge of her beautiful breast. I caught the next tear on my lips before it fell. I planned to catch all the rest of them too, for as long as she needed me to.

"I'm right here, baby," I murmured to her as she caught me up in her arms and her rhythm. "You're safe...I'm not going anywhere. It's just us...you and me."

We spent the rest of the night proving that to each other—every movement, every shift and turn a restatement of emotions we had no words for. I tasted and touched every high plain and low valley of the wondrous living creature that was my Jean, kissed the tender skin that covered defenseless pulse points, sucked on the birthmark that crowned the hill of her bicep, and my lips painted the immunization scar that rounded her shoulder.

I reverently savored the tiny taut ridge that topped her navel, then continued exploring until she was pulsing under my tongue, the force of her life, the life she'd shielded mine with, blending with the beat of my heart as she came for me.

Not long after, she knelt above me, thighs embracing my hips.

"I want...I hope you like this, Tori," she said, her voice low and hoarse as her hands gently unfurled me. "Hold yourself open for me, baby."

I did as she asked and was struck dumb by how beautiful she was when she did the same, the tender, vulnerable parts of her open to my hungry eyes.

I couldn't breathe as I watched her lower herself upon me, and the first hot contact found me half seated. Jean wrapped her legs around me, and I closed my arms about her as her cunt ground against mine with an intensity of touch I'd never felt before. We edged closer and closer to that final burst of cunt-fire and I *knew*, with a certainty that painted my very marrow with its brightness, that as much as Jean was mine, I was hers too, for as long as we had each other.

By the time we were fully convinced of each other's realness, the satisfying solidity of presence, nothing was left as we wrapped around each other—not the fear, not the sorrow. Nothing was left but us.

❖

We woke relatively early to repair that tire and bring her truck back to the neighborhood before the parade made that impossible, and as we stood on Forest Avenue watching the cycling O'Something family perform all sorts of fancy whirls and weaves on a variety of odd-pedaled vehicles, including an old-fashioned velocipede, Jean nudged my elbow.

"Have you ever thought about that?"

"What?" The hat debate hadn't even happened; she wore one of those huge foam things on her head and a temporary tattoo of a shamrock on her left cheek. This gear, however, did not make her stand out from the local crowd, who wore not only similar hats and tattoos, but also the traditional "Kiss me—I'm Irish" T-shirts and buttons, and one colorful fellow wore a T-shirt that read "Unrepentant Fenian Bastard."

"That..." She tilted her head toward Samantha and Nina where they stood two feet away from us in the human crush.

A MacCrae tartan blanket draped over Samantha's shoulder and arms, which were in turn wrapped protectively around Nina. Sam's hands rested under the blanket on the now-obvious swelling that meant my niece or nephew was comfortable, snug, and growing well.

"I can't wear the MacCrae tartan," I said and grinned back at Jean. "I'm not married to Samantha."

"Ha ha," Jean mocked. "I meant," and she gestured, "that."

Ah. Nina's pregnancy. Hmm. I knew family meant a lot to Jean, it meant a lot to me too, and while I really liked kids, I'd never thought much about having them or, at least, how they'd arrive.

"I've never discounted it. I just sorta assumed, well, it would happen somehow, sometime, I guess. How about you? You thought about it?"

Jean flushed and glanced down. "Yeah, I've thought about it. I, uh, I think it would be very cool."

I closed the slight distance between us, put my lips to her ear, and touched her cheek carefully. I could feel the flush under my fingertips. "If they look like you? It would be."

"Really?" she drawled, putting an arm around my waist as I turned to see her face. "That *could* be arranged, though I'd rather they looked like you..." She smiled that gentle smile that told me so much. "And that? Could also be arranged."

I pulled the brim of that ridiculous hat down lower over her head. "I'll make you a deal," I said as I stroked the sensitive line of her nose and the profile of her lips, then rested on the tip on her chin. "We discuss this in depth after I finish the medic class, and in the meanwhile? We can…practice."

"I like that," Jean murmured against my finger and kissed it. "When can we start?"

"How fast can you walk three blocks?"

❖

In the end we headed back to the house with Nina and Samantha: it was still very cold, and Nina was tired. As we walked, Jean pulled me tighter and slipped her hand under my jacket, warming it by tucking her fingers into my waistband and tickling my skin.

We all spent the afternoon together, and instead of going to the pub, we ordered in some Italian food. I insisted on paying the delivery guy when he arrived—it was the very least I could do in light of everything Nina and Sam had done for me.

I left Jean chatting with Nina in the living room and joined Sam in the kitchen to play with the pizza, the only thing Nina could tolerate lately; baked ziti, which was Jean's request; and the eggplant parmesan, which got both Sam's and my vote.

"Got that?" Sam asked as I carried the plates and glasses to the counter.

"Yeah, no problem." I grinned as I settled the glassware safely and intact on the sleek amber marble.

"Hey, I…I need to ask you a favor," Sam said finally into the companionable silence as we opened the various containers and divided the food according to everyone's preferences.

"Sure. Anything." I carefully put the serving spoon down so I wouldn't spatter sauce everywhere. "What is it?"

I gave her my full attention, only to find her eyes wide and deep dark blue, a color I was suddenly certain my cousin loved drowning in.

"I have to travel, and I was hoping you wouldn't mind staying in the house instead of the apartment while I'm away."

"No problem. When are you leaving?"

"Three days. Oh, and, uh, I don't want to…cramp your style or whatever. Nina and I both like Jean, and she's welcome to stay here too, you know?" she added, quickly hiding the tiniest of smirks.

I hadn't thought about that, but now that Samantha mentioned it... I could feel a slight tinge of heat rush up my cheeks. "How long will you be gone?" I asked instead and returned my focus to the eggplant before me. I cut it very carefully.

"About ten days," she answered with a sigh. "Ten long days, and hopefully not any more than that."

I glanced up at her again. "Why go, then? Do you have to?"

"Work," Samantha said matter-of-factly. "Germany for a few days to check out a new band, then I have to stop in London and iron out some business details with my uncle for about a week. But I *will* have my cell phone with me and on at all times, in case you need me."

I saw something desperately sad in her eyes, something that made them shift to an even deeper, darker hue, and I understood that she didn't want to go, not at all, but she trusted me with the people she cared for most. If it made her feel better...

"Good, very good. Hey, send a postcard, huh?" I joked in an attempt to lighten her mood as we each balanced a tray with two drinks and two full plates and headed for the doorway.

"Sure." She tossed me a half smile over her shoulder. "Besides, you're an EMT and Jean's a medic. Things'll be fine, I'm sure."

"Absolutely," I assured, giving her a grin of my own. "Just don't forget those cards."

"You got it. I'll even bring back a bunch of those Kinder Eggs you love so much." She smiled, and as we walked carefully to the living room we both laughed at the memory of the chocolates with the toys inside she and Nina used to send me from Europe when I was a kid.

It happened while we all sat eating our dinner, talking, and ignoring the TV that played as background noise.

Nina put her hand on her stomach, then quickly grabbed Sam's and held it in the same spot. The motion jumped me into alertness, a shoulder and neck tension that relaxed when I watched the smile break across Sam's face.

"Is that—"

"Yeah." Nina nodded and smiled back. "You feel that?"

"I do," Sam said, her voice thick. She cupped Nina's face with her free hand. "You're amazing," she said softly and kissed her.

I glanced at Jean as her hand slipped into mine and couldn't help but look down again: the way they kissed before us was no different than how they made love, and I felt my face grow warm at both the memory and at again witnessing what seemed so very intimate, so very private.

"Tori, c'mere," Nina said, and I looked up to see her waving me over. She smiled so brightly my eyes almost hurt when I watched Samantha wrap an arm around her.

I stood, unsure and uncertain, and Jean loosened her hand from mine and pushed me lightly, urging me forward.

After I crossed the few steps around the table, Nina grabbed my hand, gently pulling me the rest of the way.

"You've gotta feel this—it's wild!" She tugged me down before her.

"Yeah?" Still hesitant even as I crouched down, I looked into her eyes, that brilliant beam of blue, and she nodded.

I glanced back over my shoulder at Jean, who smiled at me, then up at Samantha, who smiled too. "Go ahead."

At first I felt the pulse, the strong line of force that ran up the center line and ended at her navel, and as I eased my hand over where Nina guided it...there. A tiny bump that disappeared almost as quickly as it came. Nina was right. It *was* totally wild to feel the thump under my palm that could mean only one thing.

My grin broke free as I looked up at her again. "You're having a soccer player."

❖

Saint Patrick's Day in the Scanlon household was everything I thought it would be and then some. When we walked in, Dusty's mass of fur, muscle, and whip-accurate tail threatened everything within its scope, so Pat rescued both our uniforms and our bags and took them to Jean's room.

We both knew this would be a long party, and I'd already stayed over before; it would be simpler for us to just go to the station from there the following afternoon. Besides, her parents expected us to stay, and we really didn't have any reason not to.

"So...*you're* Tori," a voice with a sensual drawl similar to Jean's said. "Or is it Scotty?" she continued as I rounded the bottom of the stairs.

My first impression was of a woman almost, if not exactly, as tall as Jean, with shaggy gold hair that skirted her shoulders. Her face resembled Jean's as well, though her eyes, light brown and somehow sharp, held the same humor but not the same warmth.

"Shannon, when did you fly in?" Jean asked from a step behind me.

"Hey, you! Yesterday, cuz, yesterday. Sorry I missed your official day of assignment, but I doubt you missed me much," she said with a smile that lightened her expression considerably.

"Hate to tell you, but you're right," Jean answered as she joined me on the landing and took my hand lightly within hers. "I haven't been missing much of anyone."

Shannon laughed. "So this *is* Tori, then?"

"I guess I am," I interjected and held out my free hand.

She tossed her chin at me as she attempted to crush my fingers.

I relaxed my grip, something Nina had taught me a long time ago and something Samantha repeated during sparring sessions: the truly strong never, *ever*, had to show it. I had no idea what Shannon's beef was, but I had no desire to get into a contest with her over it.

Her eyes widened a bit at my lack of defensive posture.

"Nice to meet you," I said with a smile. "Good to have a face to go with the name. Hey, Jean?" I turned to her and asked, "Didn't your mom specifically say she needed us a few minutes ago?"

"Oh yeah, she did."

"See you later," I said to Shannon and we went to find Jean's mom.

❖

Dusty settled contentedly and quite literally under our feet when we joined everyone in the main room for the American version of traditional Irish food, which included the requisite corned beef and cabbage, as well as Mrs. Scanlon's fabulous mashed potatoes.

Chatter was lively throughout the room, and Shannon studiously ignored us, or at least I ignored her. When one of Jean's aunts suggested we live in her parents' house so we could save for a place of our own, Mrs. Scanlon gracefully steered her into the kitchen and threw us an amusedly exasperated smile.

Jean shrugged. "I did tell you they'd make plans," she whispered and gave me a half-embarrassed grin.

"It's worth thinking about," I mused aloud.

"What, living *here*?" Jean's eyebrows almost disappeared under her hair where it fell over her brow.

"No…living together. That's worth thinking about."

Jean took my hands and stood abruptly. "Come with me," she asked simply, her eyes spiced-cider hot on me as she waited.

With all the people, kids, pseudo-kids, and Dusty flying in, out, and about the room, no one would notice if we left, not for a little while anyway, especially since *everyone* was going out to the yard to witness Pat's first bagpipe performance, so I rose and followed her. "What's up?" I was slightly concerned as we went to the front hallway by the stairs.

Jean stopped at the bottom of the steps, then dropped my hands, only to catch me up in her arms and kiss me so thoroughly I thought I might either come right then or fuck her against the wall. "We're going upstairs. I want you so badly I'll beg if you want me to," she whispered heatedly as she gripped my hips. "I want you in me, on me, around me, any way you *want* to be," she told me as she pulled me up the steps after her. "I love you, I want you, and I want you *now*."

I knew two things as we tripped up the stairs, then wrestled just inside the room with the door closed while Jean pulled at my zipper. I loved Jean, and that love was heavily intertwined with desire, a want so deep that I couldn't tell the difference between the love and the lust because both thrummed through me, the one setting my chest on fire, the other spurting through my veins, taking the fire with it, spreading it bodily.

I *had* to touch her, all the time. It didn't matter where, when, or how, just so long as the contact was there, and I almost tripped out of my pants when she slipped her fingers between my folds, then pulled me down on top of her.

As I kicked off my boots and the remnants of my pants, I couldn't help but reach for her, fastening my lips to first one gorgeous breast, then the other. God, she had the most fucking beautiful tits, and I was so lucky that they were so sensitive…

For one hot moment, I wished I had my dick on so I could give her tits the attention they deserved, so I could fill her, fuck her, feel her move beneath me while my hands, my mouth, stirred her further so that when she came, when her clit bounced against my cock jammed deep in her cunt, she'd feel it—*everywhere*. When I thought of coming inside her like that—

"God…you're *so* wet," Jean whispered throatily as we shifted on the bed. She stroked my clit slowly, firmly, driving me wild, making me burn. "That for me, baby?"

"Just for you," I assured her, and her mouth pressed against my neck, a hungry suck on skin that drove any other thought out of my head as I teased her pussy lips apart with my fingers.

"Mine?" I asked, loving the creamy feel of her cunt as I slicked along her folds, tweaking her hard-on, playing, ready, waiting.

"Yours," she murmured, a hot affirmation in my ear, "so take me."

God, how that one little phrase, the affirmation of belonging, of possession, seared through me: I wanted to, I *needed* to. I did.

"I *love* you," I whispered as I eased my fingers into the slick warmth of her cunt's embrace, "and I love *fucking* you."

Jean wrapped her leg over my hip, pulling me even closer, deeper. "Love *you*," she returned, her words choked into my mouth between breaths as I groaned out a welcome to her when she drove into me, "love fucking *you*."

We slipped in and against each other, the intensity heightened that much more by the sweat-smooth pressure of her body against mine, the frenetic expression of ardor through carnality.

The feel of her, thorough and full, the beautiful fuck-heavy ache in my cunt because she loved me, loved me and fucked me with a purity of intention that spoke to me in a way no words ever could as I loved her, loved her in heavy wet rhythm, my heart in my hands, and my hands sliding and gripping her skin, buried in the pulse of her gorgeous pussy, the constant push into the endless pull, and it was…all…just…so—

"Oh…I love that," she sighed when the flood of sensation made me surge against her, gently shove her onto her back, increasing the pressure for both of us as her long legs pressed against mine, then encircled me. Her free hand skated along my spine to rest on the curve just above my ass in a none-too-subtle urging that made me throb around her.

"Fuckin' nice!" she gasped when I eased another finger inside her. "So…fuckin'…yeah…"

I kissed her neck, an open-mouthed brush of my lips against the straining muscle before I rubbed my face against it, glazed in lust and love as she drove so hard, so fucking good inside me, the beat of her heart wild under mine, breath short and hot, and when she eased her hand down and around my ass to slide another finger into my cunt, I was so fucking full and it was so much, too fucking much as the pressure built and drove through me, through her.

"Baby…" I managed to choke out as the feeling magnified, swelled through and rippled under my skin, "that's so fucking…mmph." I bit my lip, unable to speak as the tremor ran through me, the first hint of the explosion that would rip me apart.

"You gonna come?"

"Uh-huh." I sucked on the soft, sweet, skin of her throat.

"Tori, let me see you, baby, let me see your eyes."

It took effort, but somehow I managed it—to lift my head, to look into those radiant eyes that dazzled me with their clarity, the unquestioning love and primal need that shone in them.

"Come deep," she told me, "deep and hard inside me."

I could barely breathe as I felt my body tighten around her just before the blast hit. "With me, baby…please," I begged those eyes that shone at me while I did as she asked, body pushing harder when her pussy clutched at my fingers, in the thrust and the pull and the burning, burning light and the "love-you…" breath that tore out of me, almost soundless.

Nothing could be more miraculous or magnificent than this, her soul that beamed at me in all its naked glory, embracing my totality—my body, my heart, and my mind—the blaze that raced outward from her touch, the simmering acceptance of mine. This *was* love, and I knew that I was in it as I lay myself on its pyre.

"Tori…you're so…fuckin'…beautiful…" she gasped out between lips that I wanted to devour as she shook under me, making me come harder as she came, blasted by the intensity and the stunning sensation of the hot, wet gush against my hand.

"Stay?" I asked quietly as we shifted again, because my body still pulsed, a strong, repeated contraction that flared deliciously through my belly, and I couldn't bear the thought of not having her in me.

"Of course." Her lips brushed my chin before she tucked her head under it, and I reveled in the feel of her in me, her skin softer, smoother, as she rested on top of me, beloved and safe for now, in the circle of my arms.

It was this time, all sleepy and easy, that I cherished most, the traded soft kisses, caresses, the murmured endearments even more important now, after such raw proclamation, as we lay together in the warm afternoon sun that filtered in through the curtain. Dust motes glimmered like tiny diamonds in the beam.

"You're...like an angel," I murmured, surprising myself with that word as it came out, unbidden but perfect, that word from me, who didn't really believe in God or any of the representations of heaven.

Yet Jean, in her humor, in her love, in the complete giving of herself with an unalloyed, honest blade-sharpness that sliced past my logic and my doubts, knifed into my very sense of self, leaving me open without hurting, without bleeding, led me to not only consider, but to *see*, really see for just those eternal moments, that this...this between us...was immortal. She brought me face-to-face with the flesh-bound divine.

"And you're my heart," she whispered back, her breath a scatter across my throat, down my chest.

"So...it's not a myth," Jean commented finally after we were resettled under the blanket and snuggled up against the headboard.

"What?"

"Female ejaculation. Not a myth."

I stroked the line of her neck and kissed her head as she again rested on my shoulder. "What was it like?"

"Oh...my God." Jean rolled her eyes at me. She flipped over and climbed up me, a sexy, playful smirk on her lips. "Want to find out?"

I slid beneath her as she parted my thighs. "I'm willing to try," I said and wrapped an arm around her shoulder, drawing her down for the incendiary caress of her lips on mine.

"Your family...might...hmm...miss us," I got out in between choking heartbeats as she tasted her way down my body, lips and hands, teeth and tongue, all conspiring to rob me of my voice. The blatant hunger on her face as her lips moved on me lifted me, thrilled me, made the hardened end of her tit playing against my hard-on an exquisite torture.

Jean stopped for one agonizing second to glance up, her gaze as heated as her touch upon me. "We're in love," she said gently, reverently, then kissed the spot right below my navel. "They won't mind."

"Then bring your hips up here, baby," I told her in the same tone. "I want to taste you...feel you on my lips."

We were in complete agreement as she balanced on the tip of my tongue and she took me with her mouth.

❖

I learned Jean's ring size after dinner and, with that knowledge, decided to take the good lieutenant up on his offer and use one of my comp days the next day. After I got back to Staten Island I went immediately to the Claddagh Shop on Forest Avenue. If they didn't have what I wanted, they'd know where I could find it.

I lucked out: it would be ready in an hour, so I had time to wander about, then pick up something to eat before I went back to the house. Besides, Samantha had just left and I wanted to spend a little time with Nina, maybe talk with her about what I had in mind over lunch. I'd speak with my mother later.

"So…how are you gonna do it?" Nina asked, her eyes sparkling at me as we sat down at the table in the kitchen over a huge meatball hero that we split and Cokes—normal for me, caffeine-free for her. "This… tastes *really* awful," Nina commented as she pushed her can away.

"Hey, your kid bounces around enough in there," I joked. "Doesn't need any help."

"I know, I know, *believe* me, I know." She smiled back. "Now spill."

I stared down at my food, momentarily self-conscious. "I was just gonna ask, I guess, and then, you know, give it to her."

"Simple, straightforward," Nina answered, nodding thoughtfully. "Sounds fine."

"You think?"

"Yes," she said emphatically, then covered my hand with hers. "You'll be fine."

I blew out my breath. "I have to tell Elena…tell my mom." That had me nervous.

Nina's fingers squeezed sympathetically. "Just remember that she loves you, and it'll all work out, I promise."

I was puzzled by that statement and cocked my head. "What, my mom? I know that."

"No, I meant Jean."

She got up from the table and came over to give me a hug, then kissed the top of my head. "Don't let your mom rattle your cage too much, tough guy. You're going for the prize here, you know?"

I leaned my head against her. That's when the baby kicked, a solid little thump against my cheek.

"I guess that's my second opinion," I said, and gave the bump a little rub.

Nina ruffled my hair as I stood. "Yup. Go get 'em, tiger."

I decided there was no time like the present, as the saying goes, and as soon as I picked up my order from the shop, I went to see my mother.

"You're kidding. The ambulance driver?" My mother stared at me with unmistakable incredulity as we faced each other across her living room.

"Paramedic, Mom. She's a paramedic."

"Hmph." Her face clouded, and she gave me her inscrutable look. "When are you going to ask her?"

"I don't know. Soon, probably in the next few days."

"And if she agrees, where do you plan on doing this?"

"We'll figure that out together."

She glanced down at the floor and took a deep breath. When she fixed her attention on me again, I realized I should have known that this discussion couldn't have happened without the usual interrogation. She folded her arms across her chest. "Where will you live?"

"I don't know."

"You have obligations, *family* obligations."

"I know, Mom. I'm not forgetting them. I've been coming by, taking care of things. I'll still do that."

"You are going to *legally* bind yourself in ways that are more difficult to take apart just to get four rights, two of which are valid only in this city."

I knew that. I swallowed the anger that rose in my throat. "I'm aware."

She nodded. "Good. School?"

"What about it?"

"When are you going back?"

I glanced at the ground before I faced her again. "I don't know. I want to become a paramedic. We'll see where it goes from there."

Her breath huffed out harshly. "What are you *doing*? You're destroying your life—for what? A pretty face? I can understand that she might please you, I'm sure the sex—"

"Don't even say it." My voice felt thick as I waved my hand and cut her off. I loved my mother and respected her, but I wasn't going to let her speak about Jean like that. "I love you, I won't argue with you, but I will not listen to you talk about her like that."

"My apologies," she said, coldly, "but Victoria, you're still a *child*. You don't know what you're *doing*. At least Kerry had a very bright future, wanted more out of life and you—"

"No." I shook my head vehemently. "Kerry would have never—"

"You're talking about sex, *hija*. Why can't you just wait and see? Why do you have to do this...this drastic thing?"

I'd reached the limits of my temper. "Would you just *listen* to me? I love her, Mami. I love her. I don't want to spend another extra minute that I don't have to without her."

Her eyes were almost ice light, and I realized they had tears in them. I gentled my voice and took her hand, then sat on the sofa and she followed.

"Mami, she loves me. She put herself in harm's way for me. Kerry would *never* have done that."

"Ah, *querida*," she said, and this time, her tears fell. She brushed the hair away from my face with her free hand. "You put yourself in harm's way every day. I don't want you to get hurt. Don't you understand?"

"Look." I took my hand from hers and reached into my pocket for a tissue. Beneath it was the little box I had safely tucked there. "This city...it trusts me, *me,* Mami, with the life of its citizens. Don't you think you can trust me with mine?"

I wiped her eyes and she took the tissue from my hand. "This," I said, and took the box out of my pocket, "this is what I'm giving her."

She sniffed and took it from my hand, staring at the black leather cover. Finally, she opened it, then nodded.

"It *is* beautiful," she said quietly after considering it from different angles. "You respect her and her heritage—I've managed to teach you that much, at least. Does her family know?"

"You taught me a lot more than that, Mami. And yes, they know we love each other." I smiled, because the memory was so very fresh. "They don't know about this. I...I did speak with Nina, though."

My mom closed the box, gently placed it in my hand, and gave me a surprised glance.

"Oh? What does she say?"

I grinned as I carefully tucked it back into my pocket. "Nina said to go for it."

My mother accepted that statement with another small nod. That Nina approved...it carried weight with her. It always had. For once, though, Nina's importance didn't bother me.

"I just wish...you would take a little more time," she said, as she brushed her fingers through my hair once more.

I nodded. I understood what she meant, but as I thought of how to answer her, all I could see in my mind's eye were the dead, killed by accident, the innocent maimed by circumstance, and Lukaski, looking at a year of rehab and needing to re-create his life at the ripe old age of twenty-seven, and lucky, *lucky*, to be able to do it.

"Mom?" I said softly, "time's the one thing no one has. I'm not wasting any more of it."

It took four weeks, that was all, to set a date and get it all arranged—Jean and I were on the same page: love may be immortal and the spirit divine, but the body is neither. Why wait? We just wanted to be together.

After Samantha came back from her business trip, Jean and I went to city hall and waited in a room that had been around since President Madison for a bored clerk to charge us a dollar more than a marriage license cost so we could receive approximately one thousand nine hundred some-odd *fewer* rights than one of those would grant. But the four rights we did get, two of which were, as my mother had reminded me, only good in a city jail or a city-run hospital, enabled us to do things I'd never really thought about before, like have insurance.

We had additional benefits, though: working as city employees meant we could do quite a few things, things my cousin and Samantha couldn't without jumping through a lot of hoops, then hoping someone might overlook something or make an exception. It pissed me off, but I had to let it go—who could live with that kind of anger all the time?

Because I still gave my mom about forty percent of my paycheck, Jean had no issues with us staying on Staten Island as opposed to living in Brooklyn, and I really did want to be around Nina and Samantha, especially with everything going on.

Besides, Nina was thrilled about the dog, Dusty, who instantly parked at her feet and followed her everywhere. I also strongly suspected that Samantha liked the idea of having a literal watchdog around her wife.

In no time at all, I was in an anteroom of the Unitarian church, with Mr. Scanlon waving Mrs. Scanlon inside so he could speak with me.

"Scotty, I know..." He stared down at his shoes a moment, the shiny dress black ones with the fringe over them that matched his tartan. "I know your father's not here, and I'm not asking you to—" He placed a warm hand on my shoulder, and took a deep breath. "Tori, I'd be honored if the young woman who loves my daughter so well would let me be her da too."

I stared at him, into the warm eyes his daughter had inherited, this man with his barrel chest from breathing in too much smoke from all the fires he'd run into over the years, his voice low and slightly gravelly for the same reason, this man who loved his family so much that he had room in his heart to add to their number.

"I think...I think the honor's mine," I told him as he pulled me into a bear hug. I returned his hold until we both got embarrassed.

"Good, then," he said as we separated. He clapped me on the shoulder. "Well, young Scotty, I'll see you inside." He smiled, then walked through the door.

My throat was so tight and my lips so dry I couldn't imagine breathing, never mind speaking the words I knew I had to as we walked up to the minister and then...seconds later we stood before him, exchanging promises that duplicated word for word what her parents had promised each other and rings that went with them.

"With these hands, I give you my heart and I crown it with my love."

I wasn't sure if I could honestly tell if our parents got along or not, but everyone seemed happy enough at the reception/party Nina and Samantha both insisted be held at Nox, although both Jean and I in return insisted on paying for as much of it as I could talk them into allowing. My cousins had already given me enough.

At some point during the night, Bennie bumped my shoulder.

"Hey, you guys registered at Toys in Babeland or something?"

I eyed her smirk and decided to ignore the comment.

It *was* funny in a way, because the topic of adult recreational toys had come up just recently.

"You know, baby," I had said several nights before, between kisses as Jean and I fooled around on her sofa instead of packing (she had a comic book collection to rival Nina's), "all those jokes about showing me your pee-pee..." I bit down on her nipple through her shirt as I tugged it out of her pants.

"Uh...yeah?" Jean opened my zipper and twisted so that I was on my side when she slid her hand down and parted me.

Her lips were fierce on mine and I pulled her closer, intent on reaching the same goal. She was wet and hard...which always stoked me higher.

"Well," I murmured into her ear, "we're getting married...and I haven't seen it yet."

"What's the matter, baby?" she said in a syrupy low voice, her lips against my throat, "are you bored already?" She began to jerk me off, deliciously slow and hard, ensuring that I'd be so very ready for her to fill me.

"Nuh...no," I breathed against the onslaught, "I love...love the way...you touch me." That was very true. Nothing had ever felt better than her touch or her riding me. I loved the way we felt together: wherever, however. "It's just...I like to...play," I told her as I stroked along her slick entrance.

"Toys, huh? Okay, baby," she agreed, the last word a sigh from the pressure of my thumb along her shaft, "bring on the Barbies."

We negotiated careful territory as we loved each other, discussed, discovered, and stretched new boundaries in an exchange that was part confession and part demonstration. Jean had never been penetrated in that way, which surprised me, while I'd never let anyone else "drive," as Jean had put it. By the time we had both come, fueled by word and touch, we knew what we were going to do.

I loved that Jean was so playful about the whole thing, even if she had done her best to make me blush on that particular shopping expedition.

"Well," Bennie said, as she gave my back a solid thump that took me away from my reverie, "if you need advice, demonstrations, you know you can always count on me."

"Ya know what, *Benadette*?" I stressed her given name to tease her and thumped her in return. "I think I've had all the help from you I need."

I knew I was right when Jean walked up half a second later and Bennie, the room, the whole world disappeared in her lips.

The service recognized the legality of our new relationship, and Jean and I took the two weeks off from work that was granted to any newly married member of service.

"What a *waste* of a vacation!" Pat had jokingly complained at the table when Jean's parents had suggested we visit the Florida Keys, the night we took them out for dinner to officially inform them of our plans. "You know they're never going to even *see* daylight, they'll be so busy—"

It was the dark look that Mrs. Scanlon threw his way that made Pat stop and mumble apologetically into his dinner.

"We'll see the sun, Pat, don't worry," Jean assured him. She took my hand and smiled at him sweetly. "We do have to get to and from the plane."

❖

We spent ten days in a beautiful resort called Ocean Key, not caring about the weather one bit.

While Jean took a shower after I did to relax from the long day, long night, and our flight, I sat in a chair by a floor-to-ceiling window that overlooked the water or, at least, promised to during the day, and flipped through the assorted brochures of things to do: shopping, walking, scuba, sailing, a restaurant every other building, swimming—

"Baby?" she called lightly.

I looked up and dropped whatever dumb thing I'd been reading. Her hair, still wet from the shower, was brushed sleekly back, curled around her neck and over a shoulder, while the shirt she'd put on over a pair of faded jeans that hugged the length of her legs hung open to her navel, a white chambray veil over her perfect curves. She leaned casually against the door frame.

Her body was against mine before I'd even become aware I'd gone to her.

"Are you hungry?" she murmured against my lips as I caught my breath and her hands wreaked havoc along my waist and hips.

"Room service," I answered as I pulled her closer to me and pressed her up against the doorjamb, "later."

"Tired?" she asked before scraping her teeth against my ear. She unzipped my pants and eased them down my hips, and I let them fall a little farther before I stepped out of them.

"Not at all." My hands were already slipping up the silk of her skin, reaching for the places I wanted to touch and...

"Good," she whispered back as a practiced hand unsnapped my bra and stripped my shirt off me. Jean walked me backward toward the bed. "It's our first official night as a family...I thought we'd do something...a little different."

I got the first button of her jeans open. "We can do anything you want," I told her as I planted a kiss on the bare skin I'd revealed and released the rest of the brass buttons. I knew what she meant, though, even before she leaned over me to reach for her flight case. I didn't mind at all, because it meant I had the length of her body arched above me, and I slid the denim that still covered too much of her lower. She kicked the rest off as she leaned on an elbow, black satin bag in hand.

I took it from her hand and set it down to the side, then cradled her face. "Are you sure you want to do this?" I asked her seriously. "We don't have to...I love the way we are."

I meant every word as her beautiful luminous eyes searched mine. I was very, very satisfied, and more than, with the way we made love, and if this was something she wasn't sure of or comfortable with, we didn't need to—

Jean smiled at me, a smile I'd never seen before, a gentle quirk of her sensual lips, then kissed me in answer. "Baby," she said into my ear, a sultry purr that set my blood on track, "don't you dream about fucking me?"

She eased her leg between mine and pressed against me; her strong fingers scratched along my ribs. "I do," she whispered and laid hot kisses against my jaw. "I dream about it...you *fucking* me...about fucking my *wife*."

I savored her mouth, the taste and the skill, the lush fullness of our kiss as we adjusted on the luxurious expanse of the bed.

We had nowhere to be later, or the next day, or for a few days after that, and I wanted to enjoy every single moment as I reached for the hardness that lay under the silk at my side and held it in my hand to warm.

"Angel baby," I murmured between sensual attacks, "are you sure?"

"Yes. Absolutely." Gently encircling my wrist, she guided me to her. "I want to feel it when I fuck you."

Thus encouraged and so aroused I didn't know how to think anymore, I edged the head of the toy against her, parting her, letting it slide along her cleft as if it were my tongue, for the first time in my life envious for a moment that it wasn't, that it wasn't "me," that I wasn't tasting her. I couldn't resist sucking her tit into my mouth as I played her.

"You're so very, very good with that," she sighed as she shifted in response to my stroke.

"You'll like it even more," I promised and kissed her deeply as I pressed the very tip against her waiting entrance.

She gasped, and her breath caught again as I gently worked the head past that initial tightened ring.

"You okay?" I asked, pausing slightly, ready to stop if she wanted.

"God...yes..." she got out between her teeth, and she lifted her hips as it entered her, taking it deeper. She pushed on my hand.

"Easy, baby...I've got you," I told her, still moving slowly, letting her get used to the feel of it inside her. I very, very gently began to jerk her off.

Her fingers wrapped around mine, around the dick that was partially in her, waiting for me as I straddled her thighs and leaned over to suck on her tongue.

This had been our discussion, and our decision. It wasn't about position, or power. It was about pleasure, expression, love. It was something that had new elements for both of us, something we could explore together.

Jean's eyes were hazy and wide, smoldering copper and honey, as they gazed at me.

"Tori," she groaned as she jerked her dick off against my cunt, playing me from hole to head so damned good, and I was ready, so fucking ready. "I want...I need to—"

It wasn't my words that stopped hers. I raised my body and held myself open before I lowered myself again so she could watch the head of her dick slide into me.

A hushed "oh..." escaped me and I eased up again, shocked at the difference in sensation the position made.

"God, baby, you're dripping on my dick," Jean said in a hush, and she reached for my hips.

"Watch, baby," I told her as I put my hand over hers, "just watch."

"Oh…that's it…yeah," she encouraged in a throaty growl, "I want to jerk it off in your cunt, baby." She licked her lips, then swallowed, hunger on her face, in her eyes as they focused on my pussy easing over her cock. "Let me in you."

I settled down against her, unable to help closing my eyes at the feel of her dick fully nestled within me.

"Jesus Christ!" she exclaimed, a sharp burst of breath as the full weight and depth of the cock we shared was now completely inside her.

"That's just so…oh, Tori, your face…you are so fucking beautiful with my dick inside you."

The hand that held my hips now gripped firmly as she rocked me slowly against her, and I couldn't speak against the feel of her body, those perfect tits under mine, her dick filling me beautifully while I rode her in easy rhythm.

"I love you, I fucking love you," she mouthed against my throat when our rhythm changed from ease to urgency and the different sensation, the sensation of being fucked by her dick, first diffused through my body, then coalesced into an intense thrum that filled me. I could only wrap my arms, curve my legs around her, hold her to me as close as I could because the thrum had become a throb, became a wordless, worldless movement as the shiver of Jean's body beneath and next to me was the tremble I felt within me, and I knew she was going to come with her cock buried deep inside me and I *knew* it, could *feel* it and—

"Come, please…" I urged, a desperate gulp, a whisper over her head, uttered against the rising fire and blood that threatened to tear me away from myself, to erase me, remake me, an image I didn't know if I'd recognize.

Despite that, I couldn't keep the wonder and the awe I felt out of my voice, because I got it, I understood the fascination with having sex, with making love, in exactly this way.

"Oh, soon…" she groaned, and with a strength that shouldn't have surprised me, she caught me around the waist and with a quick twist of her back and hips gently deposited me on my back, her dick lodged fully and firmly within me.

Jean always gave herself to me completely when we made love, the surrender of her self, total, complete, and I knew it in every possible way, how much she loved me, how much she wanted me. And today? Today, she had declared it not just to me, but in front of family, friends, and God. Jean had placed her life, her faith, her heart in my hands.

I hadn't realized until that moment that I'd held back anything. I gave up all pretense that this was anything other than what it was, a claiming—in love, in flesh, in mind. Jean was telling me, with her body that shuddered above me, with her dick that trembled with even greater urgency in me, that I was hers—and hers alone.

I had faith in her, faith in love. I had faith in us—I'd let her take me anywhere she wanted, and as she rocked in me, loving me, fucking me with pure grace—I hadn't known there were deeper levels of surrender.

"Let me make this good for you," she begged, her eyes hot on mine as she changed her rhythm and her method, "let me make you come." Her cock slid even farther in me with practiced, skillful ease that played its length against my clit, and despite the incredible intensity of sensation I smiled, because I knew that trick too, the sliding rock that was a glide as opposed to a straight thrust—I planned on doing it to her the first chance I got—oh, she was good, so *fucking* good. God, she worked my pussy beautifully and when I moved with her she knew it, too; the satisfied smile she returned before her tongue fucked my mouth the way her dick moved me said so.

"Angel...you're incredible," I told her with what little breath I had left, ragged as her cock filled me over and over. "I love you," I whispered against her neck before I pressed my face against it, and I could only wrap myself around her again.

I gave her everything, the only thing that was left, the words she needed to hear, torn from a place hidden, even from myself.

"Yours, angel. Always."

She embraced me, pulled me to her chest, and tucked her legs against me. "God, how I love you..." she said, the words a gentle gasp as her cheek smoothed against my neck.

We clutched at each other against the slip of sweat-slick skin, in the desperate drive of her dick in me, in us, pushing, climbing, with the shudder that became the fuckin' gorgeous hard thrust, and I dug my fingers down along her back, felt the straining muscles, the flex of her perfect ass that molded under my hands. I reached back just a bit farther and touched against hot slickness, the wet cock that filled us both as it slid under my fingertips and I pressed it into her, played a steady tattoo against it, begging her to fuck me.

"Harder...oh, please, baby...fuck me, fuck me deep...hard."

"Yes, baby," she murmured into my ear as she did exactly that, "I'm gonna fuck you...fuck you good and hard."

The last of the restraints either one of us held was gone. "Gonna come, baby, gonna come in your beautiful cunt...gonna come all over you." Her voice strained on the last few words and I urged her on.

"Angel, come, please," I gasped, because she felt so good, and she felt so right, and she clasped me to her as she came, good and hard while her cock twitched and jerked beautifully as she sank it in me, and I let my body move with hers, any way I needed, she needed.

"Yeah...that's...oh..." was all I could choke out, unable to even tell her with anything but the arch of my back and the baring of my throat that I loved her because I burned, burned with liquid gold flame, the white hot of steel in the forge, the deliverance of earth as it burst forth, destroying, erasing everything that had come before it, creating fertile new land.

"You're my heart, Tori," Jean said into my ear as she held me close and I shook beneath her. "My precious, precious heart."

Later when I reverentially slid my cock inside the loving warmth of her and she wrapped her arms and legs around me, she growled, "I love you," as we rocked together.

She'd been right earlier; I *had* dreamed about it, dreamed about fucking my wife, and I don't know who cried harder when she came: Jean, because this was all so very, very new, or me, because she *was* my wife, and I loved her so much, in ways I could only express with my body—and hers was so beautifully open to me.

It didn't matter whose the tears were, though, because I held her to me tightly and used all the words I did have, kissed every tear, and simply loved her, loved her with tone and touch, until she knew she was on solid ground again.

Over the next hours and days, Jean and I together explored the fresh terrain before us, the new internal geography that we would spend the rest of our lives learning to landscape; and then it was time to go back, back to the reality of moving Jean's stuff over to what was now our place, time to really learn how to go from living by myself to living with another person, secure in the knowledge of today, tomorrow, and every day that followed.

Living together was easier than I expected. I loved waking up with Jean next to me every day as much as I loved falling asleep with her every night. I'd never been happier.

❖

It was a classically beautiful May day when my cell went off. Since Jean was comfortably sleeping with her arms and legs draped across me, Nina and Samantha were both safely ensconced in their home, and I had spoken to both my mother and sister the night before, I was pretty certain of who it wasn't.

I grabbed it off my nightstand before it woke Jean and flipped it open. "Scotty."

"Hey, how you doing?" Trace asked in the early morning light.

"Fine, just fine. What's up?" We hadn't spoken more than a few times since our whatever-it-was-called had ended, although I'd seen her on crash teams when I'd done overtime in Brooklyn or Staten Island and we'd chatted here and there. I'd even told her about the wedding over a quick cup of coffee while our rig got decontaminated and had received a congratulatory hug. She'd sent a card.

"Uh, Tori…" I heard her breath catch and, much to my astonishment, I heard her sob, "My grandmother died, and I…I didn't know who else I could talk to and…Tori, please, you're my friend. Would you come with me to the wake? I need you."

I hesitated only a moment. Yes, okay, we weren't any sort of sleeping together anymore, but we were still friends, weren't we? What we had shared, even though it was over, *had* been intense, even if it had been occasionally alarming. Besides, I knew what it was like to lose a beloved grandmother; I couldn't abandon anyone who reached out to me for something like that. "Yeah, sure, just give me the time and the location, and I'll see you in a little while."

"Thanks, Tori, thank you so much. You…this means a lot to me," she said after she gave me the information.

I checked the clock and knew I had to move fast. After kissing Jean I carefully got out of bed to shower and get dressed for the wake.

"Hey, you look like you're going to a funeral," Jean said, smiling at me when I walked out of the bathroom.

"Actually, it's a wake," I answered, then took a deep breath and explained the whole thing to her, a little nervous that she might misinterpret it.

"Look, I understand, you guys are, were, sorta friends. I respect that."

I put my arms around her and kissed her. "Why don't you think about those colors we're going to paint over the plaid?" I teased. "We can start making those kids when I get back."

"Is that your way of telling me you love me?"

"That's my way of telling you I like your taste." I tugged her closer and placed gentle kisses on her neck before I reached her lips again. "This…is my way of telling you that I love you."

"I think I need to be told again," Jean murmured as her hands began to wander.

"I'm going to be late," I sighed, reluctant to leave her, "if I don't get going."

Jean looked at me closely. "Tori, do you want me to go with you? I will if you do."

I considered that possibility. Part of me really did, because I was nervous, but it probably wasn't a good idea, for a variety of reasons, including the fact that I thought the whole thing was probably upsetting enough without—well, it didn't seem like the right thing to do.

"I'll be all right. Just…*be* here, okay?"

"Always, baby, always." Jean pulled me back to her, and I let the sound of her breath and heart under my ear soothe me for a few more moments before I had to leave.

When I met Trace at the funeral home, she was composed if pale, her eyes reddened, but she held herself together through the hours of meeting and greeting, and when she asked me if I'd attend the funeral service with her the next morning, I couldn't look into those pewter eyes with their unshed tears and say no.

Jean once again offered to accompany me, and once again I told her I'd be all right.

I'd lied. The funeral was horrible. I instantly flashed back to being a kid and relived the gut-tearing loss of Nana, so much so that my heart ached, at the memory, in empathetic sympathy for Trace and her family, and it was in that spirit that I held Trace's hand during the service and let her rest her head on my shoulder during the burial.

I drove her home after the whatever-it's-called food thing at her parents' home, and despite my own misgivings, because this whole thing felt so strange—the loss and sorrow that wasn't mine but so echoed my own—when Trace asked me to come in for a bit because she didn't want to be alone, I agreed.

I held her while she cried, shared and listened to stories about the woman who had been buried, and finally, I had a glass of wine with her, because I thought it might help her calm down and relax.

When my neck started to itch, I assumed the sulfurs in the wine were to blame, so I asked if she had any Benadryl, which she found and gave me with a glass of water.

I wanted to get home soon, despite it being merely late afternoon. It had already been a long day, and when Trace said she was exhausted, I didn't mind walking her into that bedroom I had walked into so many times before. I had absolutely no intention of staying, but when Trace asked if I would hold her until she slept…I felt so bad for her, I made the biggest mistake of my life: I said yes.

I rocked her until the crying finally eased into a sleepy cadence and promised myself that I'd leave in a few moments, as soon as the world stopped spiraling around me.

I was flying with Jean, who was a string of neon purple light spread across a midnight starless sky, and I reached for her, an aqua blue streak that blended with that light, amazing, intense, how incredibly wonderful it felt, an electric float, and then thunder roared in my ears, but it started in my head and I hurt, God, I hurt, and then I disappeared until the pain returned, stronger, sharper, like a pinpoint, precision bruise.

I had a body, and now I was stuck in it—heavy, thick, and unresponsive as I tried to shift, to get away from that spot that hurt and back, deeper into the dream, the dream where Jean and I loved each other, but everything was so heavy I couldn't move, and I resigned myself to the discomfort that had resolved into a small, dull ache.

A fierce punch of almost agonizing flame shot through my groin and reverberated through my thighs and back, almost making my heart stop with its ferocity. My breath caught hard and fast in my chest, and

I would have sat up except I couldn't: I could barely open my eyes because they were so heavy too, and I felt more than saw Trace, her lips close to mine.

"We needed this, baby," she said and kissed me, slick and rough, as her legs slipped along mine, and it hurt, God, it hurt, but it also didn't matter, because my eyes were so heavy, and I was tired, so fucking tired…my head was so damn heavy…and all I could think was how did I end up having sex with Trace when I was just with Jean? How was I going to tell her about this? And I passed back out.

❖

I experienced no transition whatsoever—one moment everything was black, and the next, my eyes opened and I was awake. Judging from the light in the room, the sun hadn't gone down yet but probably would within the next hour, which meant I'd been out of it about three, maybe four hours. I had to get home; it was later than I'd either anticipated or communicated before I'd left. What a bizarre dream I'd just had.

I *was* still muzzy-headed, but without the bone-deep weariness I'd thought I'd imagined. Then I sat up. My muscles ached, the tendons in my thighs felt like I'd worked a double shift, and my arms burned. Then a cramp knifed through my belly, unlike anything I'd ever had before. And finally…it didn't matter, not at all, because despite the pain, despite the confusion, I wasn't there, not really. I was just floating through this heavy sack of meat I called a body, and the pain was strange, because it was absurd; I was a meat puppet.

This meat sock had to go home, because Jean was there and I wanted to wrap myself around her and breathe in the scent of her skin, feel her hair slide against my face, let her know how much I loved and appreciated her.

I glanced over my shoulder, a slow movement that noted every shadow cast by the sheets and the pillows, the hills and valleys of the various textures, but Trace was gone; and as I looked back at the chair next to the bed, I noticed my pants neatly folded over the back.

Strange. I'd gone to bed fully dressed; in fact, I was still wearing the blouse and bra I'd fallen asleep holding Trace in, but wasn't that weird? I stood up and could feel every individually fuzzy carpet fiber under the soles of my feet.

The next cramp swamped over me like a wave at high tide, with an accompanying head-spinning nausea, and when it knocked me to my knees I noticed a faint gleam on my thighs. Blood. A light sheen of blood. That meant this meat sock was alive, and I would have laughed if the pain hadn't taken my breath away, because I remembered the last time I'd felt like this, only…I glanced at my left arm, at a faint white line where I'd gashed myself months before, and the texture felt different, smooth, under the fingertip I ran over it.

When I got dressed, I noticed I was bleeding. Two slowly falling deep red drops seemed to expand as one closed in on the carpet and the other hit my thigh.

The nausea came and went like a giant glove that gripped me from my knees to my head in a spasmodic rhythm, but I managed to walk to the main hallway. Trace had left a note on the table there:

> *Sorry to leave—I have to go to my parents' house. Make yourself comfortable. I left you something in the fridge, and I'll see you later.*
> *Trace*

The paper had tiny bubbles and bumps in it as I rubbed it between my fingertips and considered the black ink of the words, tracing the dents on the paper. I couldn't stay. I had work the next day and a lot to do to get ready for it. Besides, I wasn't really feeling well and I wanted to go home, curl up next to Jean, and not think about the ache that was the loss of my grandmother these past few days had brought back to me.

The doorknob was so cool, so bright, the brightness translating into a message I couldn't understand as I held it in my hand and twisted it a few times to understand until I remembered I had to go home.

The ataxic pain and the accompanying nausea again forced me to the floor, and I suddenly realized, with an unblinking clarity, that I was definitely *not* okay. Sheer will got me through the door and forced me to my car.

That same clarity that resolved itself into a small, faint voice between my eyes told me there was no way I could or should drive, and I pulled my cell phone out of my pocket and hit the "last-dialed" button.

Three rings, four rings. "Please answer," I prayed silently as the fifth started.

"Tori, are you okay?" Jean's voice, the one I wanted to hear. Thank God.

"Jean…I don't feel very well," I said through another round of pain and sickness. "I think I took too many Benadryl or something—I need someone to drive."

"Where are you?"

I gave her the address. "I'm just going to curl up in the passenger seat, and I'll leave the driver's side unlocked, okay?"

"Baby, I'll be there in a few minutes. Hang up now and I'll call you back in a minute, but don't go to sleep, okay?"

"Okay. Wait. Jean?" I asked, hoping she hadn't hung up yet.

"Yeah, baby?"

"I love you."

"I love you too," she answered, her voice a soft reassurance in my ear as I climbed over the gear shift into the passenger seat. "Now don't go to sleep. I'll call you right back, okay?"

"Okay. I won't go to sleep."

I wasn't, I really wasn't going to go to sleep, but that light, fuzzy float was crawling up my legs, up my stomach, approaching my neck, an inexorable march to my head as I curled against the fleece cover of the seat, each whorl of softness a tiny hand on my face as I waited for the phone to ring.

"Hey," I answered when it did, and the sound came from so very far away.

"Baby, what are you feeling?" Jean asked me.

As I tried to find the word to describe my signs and symptoms, memory hit me like a blow to the mouth. Trace. Trace on top of me. She had said something, something…I couldn't remember, but I recalled a quick flash of light and then the sharp sting that cut into my skin just below my navel, and I lifted my shirt to touch it as I remembered Trace fucking me, the way she'd always said she'd wanted to. Oh, shit. Holy fucking shit. I could feel the lines she'd cut into my skin. "Oh, my God…you're gonna hate me…" was all I could say.

My fault. This was my fault, I realized as light glanced off the ring I wore on my left hand, a ring that symbolized vows I'd shattered in one stupid moment. I should have never had that glass of wine. I'd led her on, let her think this was okay, and now, now I'd ruined my relationship with Jean because she'd never forgive me—how could she? I couldn't. The whole situation started to spiral through my head, twisting me with it, and I started to shiver uncontrollably, my teeth rattling in my head. I could feel each one as it hit another.

"I'm not gonna hate you, baby. I'm never gonna hate you. Now look out the window, because I'm walking up to your door now. I brought a little help, okay?"

I curled up tighter on my seat, the caress of the fleece changing to a coarse sting as my face rubbed against it.

The door opened and I saw her pants before her knees flexed and her beautiful face was in my line of sight. "Hi, baby," she said softly and smiled.

Samantha peeked around her arm. "Hey, Tor. Jean's gonna drive you, and I'm gonna drive Jean's car."

The skin of my face was cold and I realized I'd been crying, because I was pretty sure I'd slept with Trace, and if I felt sick, I deserved it.

"It's all right baby, it's all right," Jean said as she tried to put her arms around me.

"No," I said and struggled to push her away as the nausea kicked up with a vengeance, and she stepped aside just in time for me to heave my guts up onto the sidewalk, leaving my throat sore and my head light. Jean was holding me in a nanosecond, one hand against my face, the other grasping my wrist, and as sick as I felt, I tried to pull away. I wasn't at all worthy of her.

Jean's expression changed from gentle concern to the professional look I knew so very well. "Sam, you drive, we'll pick up my car later," Jean said as she counted my pulse, and I heard the driver's side door pop open.

"Tori, are you bleeding?" Samantha asked.

"Yeah, yeah, a little," I said muzzily. "There wasn't anything, you know…" The words disappeared from my head as another wave engulfed me. "I'm gonna throw up…"

Jean caught me before I fell out onto the sidewalk, and once again I tried to struggle free of her embrace, the embrace I so wanted and didn't deserve.

"It's me, baby. I'm not going to hurt you. I just want to check you out. Let me see your eyes."

I lifted my head and leaned it against the soothing fleece of the seat as Jean's serious brown eyes evaluated mine by shading them with her hand, then removing it to watch my pupil reaction.

"Take the seat cover off carefully and throw it in the back," Jean said over my head to Sam. "It's evidence. Tori, you have to go to the hospital."

"I don't want to. I just need a ride home. Please."

The unmistakable sound of my car engine roaring to life rang through my head, and the vibration settled into my gut, a shake that matched the tremor I felt bodily.

Jean sighed. "Tori, your pulse is slow and erratic, you're pale, your pupils are sluggish, you're vomiting *and* bleeding. You *have* to get evaluated."

I shook my head in the negative. "Jean, I'm Ay and Oh times three. I know your name, my name, and Sam's, I know it's almost dusk, and we're in my car in front of Trace's—"

I had no warning before I threw up this time, but nothing was left, and Jean climbed into the seat next to me, crushing me against her, an arm wrapped securely around my shoulder.

"Sam, the closest ER," Jean directed. "I've got my badge if we get pulled over."

I tried to protest. I wanted to go home, home to forget this whole thing had ever happened, to be sick in the privacy of my room and bath before I had to deal with the inevitable reality of having slept with Trace, but I was starting to drift again, and my only thought as I floated away into nothing was that I finally hated someone as much as I hated my father—myself.

❖

I didn't get to make any decisions at all, because I opened my eyes to the cool white light of a hospital room, and the painful twist of my head revealed a drip on the right side and hooked into my forearm, and the distinctive vitamin smell of O_2 rushing up the plastic in my nose. The needle itched and someone held my other hand.

"Colposcopy with toluidine blue dye showed tears in the fossa navicularis as well as the posterior fourchette. And here…okay. She needed a few stitches, too." The voice was male, clinical and subdued, and as I looked for its source, I spotted a TV screen on the wall showing an image of pink flesh with some extensive purplish blue markings, then some deeper-colored viscera that seeped blood. I watched as a pair of small-tipped forceps pushed a curved needle into one end and out the other, closing the tear.

"That…had to hurt," I thought, "wonder *what* it is."

"Hey, you're with us." Jean's voice cut through my thoughts and I oriented on it instead.

"Hi," I said as I found her face right above the hand she held. Her eyes were warm as always on me and I smiled at her. "What are we up to?" I tried to sit up.

"Relax, stay there." Jean leaned over and pressed gentle fingers against my chest. "You passed out."

"Really? I did? Why?"

"I'm Dr. Petrossi. How are you feeling, Ms. Scott?" the same male voice I'd heard before asked.

I thought about that question before I answered. Better. I wasn't nauseous, and the cramp that had knocked me silly seemed to be gone. "I feel better."

"I'm glad to hear it. Ms. Scott, I have to ask you a few questions, and I need you to be really honest, even if it's embarrassing, okay?"

"Sure," I said, not really caring much about anything, because I was feeling light, drifty, like everything was made of gossamer and about to float away.

"Are you on medication for anything?"

"No, not at all."

"Do you use recreational drugs, like Ecstasy, K, or GHB?"

Why in the world would anyone ask me that? "No, I don't do drugs."

"Okay," he answered, "you should know you're testing positive for ketamine and for GHB."

"What's ketamine?"

Jean smoothed my forehead. "It's an anesthetic and a hallucinogen, and GHB is Liquid X."

I struggled to think and wondered what the doctor was talking about; I didn't do that shit. "Benadryl," I said finally. "I had Benadryl because the wine made me itch…and some water."

"Well, it's not Benadryl alone that made you *that* sick," Dr. Petrossi said, "even with the wine, Ms. Scott."

"It's Tori. Jean, tell him to call me Tori?" I asked and squeezed her hand.

"Tori it is, then," the doctor answered. "Tori, do you remember what you did or where you went earlier today?"

"What?"

Jean's grip on my hand tightened almost imperceptibly as he repeated the question, and the floating, drifting feeling started to crumble as I remembered the funeral, the amazing amount of grief that had hit me in waves as Trace held my hand and pressed against me at the burial.

I'd driven her home and she'd cried some more, and then I'd had the glass of wine and the Benadryl about fifteen minutes later, which I supposed had knocked me out, and then we…toluidine blue, that's what the doctor had said. It was used to detect abnormal cells in cervical cancer, and a low-percentage tincture was used in the ER because it clung to damaged tissue and was especially useful during colposcopy in evaluating for—

Once more nausea raced through me, but my head was perfectly clear when I sat up and ripped the damn tubing off my face. "What's that on the screen?"

"That's the colposcopy exam," Dr. Petrossi answered.

"You didn't ask me if you could perform that exam," I said tightly. I might not have been feeling my personal best, but I knew my rights.

"I just did the immediately necessary, Tori. You were passed out and bleeding. It's up to you if you want to go through the rest of it…and you might be a little light-headed," he added as I shifted and swayed. "I did administer a mild anesthetic so the exam and the stitches wouldn't be painful."

"I gave permission for that, Tori," Jean said quietly. Her thumb brushed across the back of my hand.

I nodded briefly. Of course. She had the legal right to do that for me, as I did for her.

My heart started to pound as I stared at the image on the screen. That…was me. My body, the toluidine clinging to the damaged tissue like it was supposed to, making what would have been varying shades of pink, some of the tears invisible, a vivid portrait of bruised blue. What the fuck had I done to myself?

"Get this line *out* of my arm, stop *whatever* the fuck you're doing. I want my clothes, and I want to go home."

"You're almost done, baby, we'll be out of here soon," Jean soothed, but that familiar heat had flamed up my neck, and though I was trying very hard not to flip out, I was hand over hand on a very thin line.

"Don't fucking touch me. I don't want *anyone* to fucking touch me," I snapped and swung my legs off the bed.

"Just a moment, Tori," the doctor said, "you're gonna hurt yourself. Let me—"

"Fine. Whatever. Just let me out of here. Can you take this out of my arm, please?" I asked, holding up the arm with the line in it.

I got a good look at Dr. Petrossi as he clipped, closed, and carefully removed the needle that was sunk into the vein of my arm. Had I not been so scared and angry, I would have said he looked both kindly and intelligent, with salt-and-pepper brown hair and a close-trimmed beard.

But I was both those things and more, so it was a great relief for me when he didn't try to smile as he put a piece of gauze and tape over the insertion site, then asked me to hold pressure on it for a bit.

"Tori," he said, and his voice was serious and steady, something I could listen to without reacting, "this is all recorded if you want to press charges, because considering your urine, bloods, and my findings, I'm finding it hard to believe this was consensual," he stated quietly as I stared back up at the screen.

Consensual. It was an adjective we learned well in 911, because consent had legal ramifications for all patient-care providers, especially at the pre-hospital level. My brain seized on that word. Consensual: by mutual agreement of all the parties involved, legally. Medically, biologically, it meant the reflexive response of one part of the body to the stimulation of another, such as both pupils reacting to light even though only one is being directly evaluated.

"You're gonna need to come back and see me in two weeks. I would like to make sure that you're healing properly. You'll also want to avoid penetrative sex for about that long too, or at least until you've been reevaluated."

I shook my head, staring at him in disbelief.

"You're going to be fine," he said reassuringly, misunderstanding my reaction. "There's no permanent damage, everything should clear up in a few weeks, you'll be able to have sex, have kids, you're young and healthy, you'll be okay."

I nodded curtly. Now I felt completely humiliated. "I'd like to go home now."

"I understand, Tori," he said sympathetically, "I really do, and you can if you really want to, but please wait for at least another twenty minutes before you leave. Settle down a bit, let the anesthetic wear off, let your system normalize before you go running out of here. You blacked out earlier, and while you're okay right now, you might again, and I'm sure you don't want that."

Jean stirred next to me and reached for my shoulder, then dropped her hand. I felt instantly guilty.

"So…another twenty minutes or so?" she asked him instead.

Dr. Petrossi nodded. "That sounds about right. In fact, I'll make sure I'm back in twenty minutes. Tori, you and Jean just relax here for a little while, okay? I promise you, as soon as I come back, I'd like to speak with you because I'll have a few more lab results, and then you can leave."

"Where are my cousins?" I asked instead. I remembered that Samantha had driven my car, and I was sure that Nina knew by now just how far I'd fucked up. I looked at the walls, I looked at the ceiling, I looked at anything but the doctor with his kind eyes or Jean with her loving ones because I wanted to scream, rip that damn screen off the wall and fling it until I could feel the muscles in my shoulders tear and hear the glass shatter in that ultimately satisfying way. I wanted to curl up into the tightest ball I could and cry, I wanted to shred the skin off my body with my hands so I could feel clean again, and I didn't want either one of them to see how I felt, read it on my face.

"Samantha picked up Nina to get my car and some clothes for you a little bit ago. They should be back soon," Jean answered. "Do you want to see them when they get here?"

I found a ceiling tile to fixate on as I nodded yet again because I didn't trust myself to speak.

"I'll tell the nurse to send them in when they return," Dr. Petrossi said. "You and your…Jean…should probably take a few moments to talk. I'll see you in a few," he concluded and left the room, the door a quick breeze with a smooth click as he closed it behind him.

"Tori, baby, look at me."

I shook my head because I couldn't. I had really fucked up. This was beyond all fucking recall. It was like the more senior techs and medics said: A M F, YOYO—*adiós*, motherfucker, you're on your own.

"Why?" I countered.

She took my hands in hers, and though I tried to draw them away, she wouldn't let me. "Tori, baby, this isn't your fault."

I kept my eyes focused on that spot of tile. "It sure is," I chuckled bitterly, "it sure as hell fucking is. I went to the funeral, I went to her place. I should have known better than to drink with her, I shouldn't have let myself fall asleep there. I just didn't think—"

"Think what, baby? That she…that something would happen? Why would you have thought that?"

This time I looked at her directly. "Jean. I shouldn't have let it happen. And…" My throat squeezed so tightly I thought I'd never get the words out, but I had to, I had to tell her. The expression she wore was killing me—her heart in her eyes for me, the way it always was, and I didn't deserve. "And if you want to move your stuff—"

Jean put her arms around me. "Don't you *dare* pull that shit on me, Tori, don't you *fucking* dare."

I rested my cheek against her chest as she held me closely and the steady thump under my ear became a strong, hard beat.

"I am *not* going anywhere, you're *not* going to lose me, and I will *not* let you push me away."

I slowly put my arms around her and let myself believe her, even if just for a little while, because it was nice to hear, even if it might not be true, and she rocked me lightly as she smoothed my hair.

Nina and Samantha did come in with the promised clothes, and I have to admit that when Nina unhesitatingly threw her arms around me I spent all of about five seconds wanting to cry helplessly, but I stopped myself—she was pregnant, and I didn't want to add to her stress.

Between the discussion with the doctor and Jean, it wasn't too hard to put together all the missing pieces and even easier to privately conclude that it probably hadn't been the first time I'd ingested an interesting chemical or two at Trace's. It definitely explained a lot.

I learned that the severe vomiting and the hallucinations, as well as the out-of-body experience, were typical of ketamine, while the GHB had caused the increased sensation and the sudden transition from blackness to alertness.

Add the Benadryl and the alcohol, and the effects magnified. I was lucky that I hadn't gone into a coma or respiratory arrest; the doctor told us GHB had been known to cause temporary coma-like states that lasted two to three hours. That news scared me, terribly, because a whole lot more things might have happened—not just earlier that day, but at other times—that I didn't remember.

I must have shivered because Jean withdrew the hand I hadn't realized I was crushing in mine and put an arm around my waist so I could lean into her.

By mutual agreement we all returned to Nina's, and Jean was no more than an inch away from me at any given time while I told my cousins what I did know and everyone made suggestions about next moves.

From what Jean and I had understood from our discussion with Dr. Petrossi, the options were slim: both drugs were legally available, the perpetrator was also female, and...we were in Richmond County. The laws were slightly different here than in any of the other counties of New York City; in this county lesbianism was a defense for, well, only crimes of this sort by a male perpetrator, since the law didn't mention this specific type of incident involving a female perpetrator— which meant it didn't legally exist. The doctor had clippings from the local newspaper of trials where he'd testified as a medical expert for the prosecution. That specific defense, "she was a lesbian, it made me temporarily insane," had cleared more than one offender. And because I had at one point been in a sexual relationship with...*her*, as he'd stated matter-of-factly, we couldn't do a lot.

After I shared that information with Nina and Samantha, Nina walked into the kitchen and I could hear her speaking with someone on the phone.

I sipped the glass of water Sam had brought me earlier.

"Although," Jean said quietly for my ears alone, "with the, uh, the knife cut, it might be possible to get an assault and battery conviction, if nothing else. I could ask Pat."

I gaped at her. I didn't want to talk with anyone more than I already had, and the thought of telling anyone else, especially a member of Jean's family...I couldn't bear it. "Jean, I can't. I don't want to have to tell—"

"Kitt—Fran will be here in two days," Nina announced with a grim smile when she returned to the room.

Samantha stood and stared. "You're kidding."

"No. Not at all. If we can't do something on the criminal level, there's got to be something on the civil, and she'll find it."

"I'm not sure I want to do anything just yet," I said into the silence that met that statement. "I'm not even sure I can say that this whole thing isn't just a big fuckup on my—"

Jean shifted next to me on the sofa "Don't even say it, Tori," she took my hand, "because you didn't do anything voluntarily that landed you in an ER, okay? You have to understand that, baby," she said, her gaze steady and serious on my face. "You didn't do *anything* wrong. You should never, *ever*, feel guilty, ashamed, or embarrassed for something someone else does."

I tried to understand, I really did, but I suddenly realized how tired I was, and tomorrow? Tomorrow was a workday.

"Jean, do you mind if," and I turned to Nina and Sam, "is it okay if we stay in the house tonight?"

An almost overpowering case of nerves descended on me. I was shaky and unsure, edgy. I felt like I might fly apart at any moment; a good strong wind would come and tear me away, tear me into a thousand pieces, scatter me like sand. I loved the home Jean and I shared, but there was something to be said for being on the second floor of a house that had the kind of security setup my cousins had.

"It's always okay, Tori," Nina said. "This is always your home, both of you."

"Absolutely, and bring Dusty in too," Sam suggested and smiled. "I'm sure she'll love being able to visit with everyone."

I smiled at that myself, because I knew that Dusty always sat as close to Nina as possible, so much so that I was surprised she didn't think *her* name was Samantha.

I stood suddenly, tired, sore, and drained. "Do you guys mind if I go take a shower? I just, you know, need…" I waved my hands in the air.

"Of course not," Nina said, and I moved toward the stairs.

Jean stood too. "I'll go pick up a few things and bring them over, okay?"

"Thanks, baby." I smiled at her, because I loved her. "I'll see you in a few?" I touched her arm.

"Yeah," she said softly and kissed my forehead. "I'll be right back, and I'll bring Dusty too."

❖

Once in the shower, the hot water running down my head, I took stock of myself: the blood had dried on my thighs and the cut just below my navel was a duplicate of the one Jean had, maybe slightly larger, and although it had been cleaned and bandaged in the ER, to my eyes it was large and ugly, the lines clear, dark pink and topped in red. They stung as the water sluiced over them.

"I'm finding it hard to believe this was consensual," Dr. Petrossi had said, his words echoing in my ears as I once again saw the image onscreen and felt the slick rough kiss of Trace in my mouth as I rubbed at the stubborn rust that stained my thighs.

Nothing, from the image that still shone from the playback in my mind to the fragmented memories in my head, had anything even remotely close to my participatory agreement. I'd never even had the chance to say no. She had taken that—forcibly taken it—from me.

The realization shattered me. I could feel my internal structure crack, a spiderweb stretching across a windshield, as the knowledge leaked into my bones.

In that moment I was filled with an almost blinding black rage. I couldn't fucking *believe* this had happened, couldn't fucking *believe* I'd fucking let her *touch* me; I had stitches—*stitches*—inside, stitches that had to be checked and removed in two weeks.

And now, I had a fucking mark across my stomach too, a mark where Jean liked to kiss me after I'd come in her mouth, a fucking scar where Jean would splay her hand over me as we lay together, her fingers stroking gently on the skin there, right *there*, before or after we made love, or absently in her sleep.

How could she ever want to touch me again, our beautiful warm embraces, the heavenly feel of us as we slid along each other—God. Damn. It.

I slammed my hand against the tile, the pain of contact forcing one word into my brain. Trace. Fucking Trace. I had *let* her fucking touch me. I slammed the tiles again. I was such a fucking idiot. I'd known better, I'd fucking *known* better. Trace cried, and Trace fucked—that's how it had always gone down.

A part of my brain was ready to supply excuses for Trace—the grief, the wine, the familiarity of "us"—but the pain I felt in my body, coupled with the specific damage report…Trace hadn't merely fucked me, she'd ripped me apart—in every way she could.

Had she fucked my wife like that? Had she drugged her, taken away her free will, and cut her while she—I couldn't complete the thought; the picture in my head made me nauseous. No. Jean had told me, quite clearly, that she had never...before we...I had to believe that, didn't I?

How could I ever touch her again without thinking, without wondering, without remembering Trace?

"I don't care who you fuck," she'd said, "just think of me when you do." Yeah. That seemed pretty guaranteed, assuming I ever wanted to again.

Jean had warned me, had *told* me Trace would take what she wanted.

Numbness jumped and fell along my arms, each burst begun by the sting I ignored every time I hit the wall. I could never be clean enough; I would *never* be clean enough to touch anyone, ever, again.

The tiles slipped under my hands, and I could barely see the red-now-pink-now-red-now-pink streaks that flowed down the wall as I beat it repeatedly, a steady tattoo that matched the pulse in my head, the blindness of the steam, and the sting of my eyes.

"Baby, what are you doing?" Jean's voice cut through the fog.

"Baby, stop," she said as I wrenched away from the touch on my shoulder, "stop."

She wrapped an arm around me, heedless of the water that cascaded over her, and hauled me to her chest as her free hand closed the taps. I struggled for a moment, the heat in my body threatening to explode, and just as quickly as they came, all the anger and the strength vanished, leaving my body as suddenly as the air would if I'd been sucker punched.

Nerveless, almost boneless, I leaned back against Jean, gasping for breath as she eased us down onto the floor of the tub, and I was in the safe cage of her arms and legs.

"Here, wait a second, baby," she said and stripped her shirt off.

It was the right thing to do; her skin was soft, warm, and soothing under my cheek as she once again held me securely and rubbed her face against my head.

"You're gonna get cold," she murmured softly as she released her hold slightly, and I could feel her reach over the side of the tub. She draped a towel over me. "C'mon baby, let's get you out of here."

Once inside the room, Jean inspected my damaged knuckles.

"Remind me not to get in your way if you wanna throw a right hook," she joked.

I stood still, a curious blankness enveloping me as she bandaged the skin that stretched and oozed across my knuckles. *That'll probably hurt soon,* I observed with the same strange detachment.

"Oh hey, I brought you some pj's," Jean said and pointed to the folded clothes on the bed. "I'm gonna go grab a shower, okay?"

"Yeah, fine," I agreed, numb as I walked over and sat on the bed, pulling the T-shirt and the lounge pants onto my lap. So it had started: we never slept clothed; it was one of the things I loved about us, the way we felt together in those hazy moments before sleeping and waking.

I shivered and pulled the towel tightly. I hadn't wanted to lose that intimacy, not ever, and especially not now when I so needed the reassurance of her skin, to breathe it in and feel like home. But I didn't blame her.

I was still sitting there when Jean came back into the room, dressed in a T-shirt and the "light" version of the plaid loungers she so loved. Dusty followed her in, and Jean closed the door as the dog settled by my feet.

"Aren't you cold in that towel?"

I stared at her a long moment. "Jean…we don't wear pajamas," I said finally.

I watched as she came over and sat on the edge of the bed next to me. She gazed down at the space between us.

"I thought…" she began, then lifted her eyes to mine. "Tori, I thought you wouldn't…you wouldn't want…" She gestured helplessly, at a seeming loss for the first time since I'd known her.

"I'm okay with that, I…" I didn't want to tell her how much I needed the reassurance of her body close to me, how necessary to my survival it felt; I didn't want her to do anything simply because she felt obligated. "It's okay, never mind." I sighed and turned down the blanket so I wouldn't have to look into those beautiful eyes and find the distance I expected.

"Tori," she said quietly, "I don't…I don't—I'm making a mess of this, aren't I?" She touched my hand so gently I wanted to cry. "Baby, what do you need? What do you want? That's what I want to do, and I don't know what I'm doing right now."

That light touch, that small bit of skin on skin, gave me hope that something could be saved. I curled my fingers around hers. "I want us to be okay, I want..." I felt desperate as I twisted to look at her and moved her hand so that the palm pressed against my sternum. She delicately stroked my skin with her fingertips. "I want you to be the way you always are with me, Jean, I—" I took a deep breath. "I'm not feeling very normal right now, and I very much need for us to be normal, even just a little bit."

"Okay, that I can do," she said softly. "Can I kiss you?"

"Sure."

She did, first my forehead, then a gentle sealing of her lips to mine that made my chest grow warm. "All right," she murmured and pulled the blankets further down, "get under there and I'll join you in a moment."

I climbed under the blankets, and once I was fully covered, I unwrapped myself from the towel, then handed it to her. Yes, I needed Jean next to me, her skin on mine, but I felt vulnerable for asking and ashamed of the lines etched into my skin, the faint bruises that marked me in other places. I couldn't bear to let her see that, to see her reaction, because I didn't know if I could take it, no matter what it was.

It was seconds before Jean slid in next to me, and the fear that I wouldn't accept her touch disappeared when I felt the so-familiar glide I didn't think I could live without. In that instant of contact, I could breathe again.

"Thank you," I whispered as I pressed my back against her and her arms wound around me.

"I thought you wouldn't want me to hold you," Jean said softly into my hair.

I faced her, secure now in her grip, and pressed my lips to the pulse in her neck. "I think I'd break if you didn't."

"I won't let you—I swear I won't let you." The urgent whisper played in my ear and soothed me.

But still, it took forever to fall asleep. Every time I closed my eyes and drifted, I'd jump upright, because I thought I was falling, panicked I'd dissolve and die. Every single time, Jean would gently draw me back down and I'd shake—I couldn't help it.

Finally, Jean retrieved a few extra pillows from the hallway linen closet and placed them between me and the wall. We shifted with her around me until I finally felt secure. I ended up lying on my stomach with Jean literally on top of me and was finally able to really close my eyes.

When I woke, Jean was still half draped over my back, the warmest, most comforting blanket I'd ever have. "Holy shit, I'm gonna be late for my shift!" I struggled to sit up.

Jean again gently pressed me back down. "I called us both out for the week last night. We've got almost a dozen comp days we haven't used," she said as she drew me back into the warmth of her body, "and you're staying here, with me, for the rest of the week."

"Yeah?" I asked, oddly grateful for the reprieve, and even more so for the continued reassurance of her warm presence.

"Yeah," she kissed my neck, "now close your eyes and dream of those paint chips that we'll go pick up later."

I settled into her contours and laced my fingers through hers as I drew her over me again. "I love you," I said simply and kissed her hand.

"You better," she sighed, then kissed the back of my head. "I'm giving up plaid for you."

❖

I couldn't look anyone in the eye over breakfast later that morning. I felt like my skin had been ripped off, making every glance, every word, no matter how kind or mild, sting and scald, a whispered reproach, a litany of shame that weighted my head. I couldn't look at Nina at all, afraid that even the slightest glance would…contaminate her or something, somehow.

I jumped at the tiniest of noises: the scrape of a chair on the floor, the solid thunk of a coffee cup on the table. And every time I placed a fork to my mouth, my appetite completely disappeared. Even Samantha's home fries were tasteless.

"Hey, Tor. Gonna spar with me today?" she asked casually. She made no comment about my bandaged hands.

"Yeah, sure," I said, glad to do something normal. I practically jumped out of my seat. "I just need to grab my sneakers."

I was sore, still spotting a bit, but I didn't think it would matter much; it wasn't like the stitches were in my stomach or anything, I thought as I wrapped my hands for sparring. Besides, the sweat would purge anything left out of my system.

The session started as they normally did: stretches, footwork, push-hands techniques that forced the mind to act, not just react.

Then came the combinations. "Harder, Tori. Faster. C'mon," Samantha urged as I almost missed ducking a strike-pad coming straight for my head.

Jab, jab, duck, reverse punch, then switch to the other side. A few more rounds, and it was time for the next combination, this one a mix of hand and footwork. The first roundhouse kick went fine, as did the second, though I did feel a burn across my belly. The third caught me short, a lick of fire that went deeper than skin, and I instinctively pressed my hand against it. The flame settled, and when I took my hand away, I saw a smear of blood. Closer inspection of my T-shirt showed a red cross that had leached through the cotton.

I lost it. I let loose a volley of kicks and blows until I found myself on my knees, crying and choking and puking on the grass, with Samantha's arm across my shoulders.

"I'm sorry, Tor, I am so very sorry," she soothed, rocking me as I fought to breathe. "The world is full of things that take…take things they have no right to. I *know* you hurt, I know *how* you hurt, but I swear, Tori, she didn't take *you*, didn't touch *you*. You're still Victoria Scotts, still my cousin, still Nina's favorite little sister and Elena's big one. You're still the beautiful young woman, the beautiful person Jean loves."

"I don't know about that," I said, choking still on the bitter taste that filled my mouth.

"I do," she said firmly and kissed the back of my head. "No one can touch or take your heart away from you, Tori, not a heart like yours. And I bet Jean's just waiting by the door, giving us a moment before she comes out."

She let go of me and stood up. "C'mon," she said and stood before me, her hand out. "See, just like I told you"—she looked past my shoulder as she pulled me up—"here comes Jean now."

I stood and before I could even fully turn, I was already firmly enclosed in Jean's arms. Samantha said something about checking with Nina about Fran's arrival time, as Jean kissed my head. "I want to take you inside, take care of your hands, take care of that cut, and then we're gonna go lie down for a bit, okay?"

"I'm not tired," I murmured into her shoulder.

"Humor the psycho dyke, please," she said, and I could hear the smile in her voice. "You don't want to mess with my I'm-always-right delusion, do you? Besides, if you're really not sleepy, we'll go see a movie or rent one or whatever, okay?"

"Okay, fine," I chuckled, "but only because I don't want to mess with your delusion."

About fifteen, maybe twenty minutes later I muttered, "Medics," as I lay down exhausted, with Jean stretched securely over me.

"What about 'em?"

"You guys think you know everything."

"Ah, that. Well, you know why, right?" she asked and kissed my cheek.

"Why?"

"Because, in fact, we do. Hey, two years of med school crammed into one has to count for something, you know."

"Hmm," I answered with a yawn. "That all?"

"No," she said, and kissed me again. "I know *you*, Tori. Go to sleep. I'll be right here when you wake up."

"Promise?"

"Always," she swore as she curved her arms over mine. "For better or worse, baby. It only seems worse right now. It'll get better, I swear."

I snuggled a bit more under her and, thus assured, I slept right through to the next day.

❖

The next morning, Jean didn't let me out of her direct line of sight, not outside playing with Dusty or sparring with Samantha, not even in the shower, really, because she wanted to "check that cut again" before we went downstairs to meet Nina and Sam's friend.

I recognized Fran instantly—she had that same lucky gene quirk that both Samantha and Nina had and appeared to be in her twenties, not her early thirties—she'd stood by Samantha at her and Nina's wedding.

I remembered, too, her smile, which struck me as somewhat familiar as she shook my hand with friendly and firm warmth. Good shake, I thought as I noted the texture of her skin, a slight paperiness to it that her tan couldn't hide. I knew what it meant instantly, the leaching effect of chemo, of radiation therapies, that took so long for the body that survived the treatments to recover from. I would have asked her questions about it had I not been trying so hard not to feel anything about why we were meeting in the first place.

"We'll need about two hours," Fran said as Nina and Sam ushered us into the den off the living room.

"Take all the time you need. We're just gonna run a couple of errands and come back with lunch, 'kay?" Nina turned to me and said.

"Yeah, sure," I agreed through dry lips.

Nina put a very light hand on my shoulder. "You'll be okay, *querida*," she said softly, "you're in good hands—I trust her with my life."

I swallowed and nodded as I put my arms around her. Hers was a vote of confidence I couldn't ignore.

Reintroductions aside, the resulting discussion as we sat around that desk was difficult at best, and humiliating at worst, with the same questions Dr. Petrossi had asked, and more: specific, detailed questions that made me want to crawl—when was the last time Jean and I had made love before my visit to the emergency room (it was the morning of the funeral), what could I remember of that afternoon, what was the nature of my interactions with Trace, before and after we'd...ended.

Fran paid careful attention and asked to see the mark on my arm but didn't ask to see the one on my stomach; there were already medical records on that. A few times during the deposition, because that was exactly what this question-and-answer session was—the report that would go to court if I pressed charges, the record that would accompany me to the precinct—I thought I'd explode, implode, or merely retch.

At one point, right before we got into the detailed history, Fran asked if I wanted to do that part alone. Jean stood to leave.

For some bizarre reason, my mind seized on the first night I'd spent there, the night I'd tried to argue with Nina about Kerry. "There's nothing you don't know," Nina had said to Sam when she'd gotten up to go.

That...was some amazing trust. I might not have told Jean some things, but there was nothing that she couldn't, or shouldn't, know: if everyone was right, as they kept assuring me in every way they could, then I'd done nothing wrong, nothing to be ashamed of.

I reached for Jean's hand. "I don't have anything to hide," I said to Fran. I looked up into Jean's pale face. "If you want to stay, I want you to."

She crouched down until we were eye to eye and folded my hand in both of hers. "I want whatever you want. If you want me to stay, I'm right here with you, but…" She took a breath and let it out slowly. "This is really private, really personal stuff, Tori. Don't do it just because you think you have to."

"I know I don't have to," I said as Fran shuffled papers. "I'd feel better, though, if you stayed." It was true, I would. And I didn't want Jean to have doubts about me, either—think I'd lied or held something back.

"You got it," she said and kissed my fingertips. She held my hand through the whole thing.

❖

"Tori, why haven't you spoken with your mother about this?" Fran asked as we sat around the table in the kitchen swapping cartons of Chinese food. She'd had amazing timing, because it seemed the very second she'd said we'd gone through enough, Nina and Samantha had returned—bearing food.

"She was an absolutely brilliant prosecutor, she'd be able to help, I'm certain," she added.

"Tor, that's not a bad idea," Jean seconded.

"No fucking way." No way did I want to discuss this with my mother because she'd go one of two ways, either devastated and tragic, and then I'd be responsible for her next heart attack, or she'd be exactly what Fran had said, the prosecutor, the judge, and I couldn't face that.

"It's like this, Tori. This isn't California," Fran said, her eyes a kindly amber glow. "The law is very clear about this exact sort of situation there, but right now? New York, neither state nor city, has any law regarding this directly, but this isn't my specialty. Tori, even if your mom hasn't practiced in years, she's going to know what to look for, criminally or civilly. You should think about it."

Nina must have known what I feared when she spoke up. "Tori…I know…look, in the clutch, your mom? She can be pretty amazing. I'll talk with her." She covered my hand with her own. "Would you let me do that for you?"

I couldn't say no to the expression in her eyes, the combination of love and pain in them. She hurt for me, and the knowledge of that…it threatened to break me. I didn't want anyone to hurt for me, because of me. I didn't know what good speaking with my mother would do, but if it made her feel better...

"You can try, I guess."

Nina nodded as she removed her hand. "I'll do better than that." She excused herself to make that call, and about twenty minutes later, Samantha left.

She returned in less than an hour carrying the mail and accompanied by my mother. For the first time since I could remember, for a situation that was not a family gathering of some sort or one of her organizational functions, my mother had really dressed: she wore a suit and had pulled her hair severely back. I remembered that look, my strong mother who had faced down desperate, conscienceless thugs and corrupt governors.

Sam handed Jean the mail as my mother held me to her firmly. "Let me help you, *mi hija querida*, okay?" she said before she turned to Jean and gave her a big hug too.

"You have to remember, Tori, Jean," she said, her tone gentle as she observed us both, "you're *both* going through this, okay?" Her tone shifted, became brisk and matter-of-fact. "Have you found a therapist yet?"

Jean and I looked at each other as I held her hand tightly.

"I, uh...no, Mom, haven't thought about that, honestly."

"I didn't think about it either," Jean answered.

"Well, that's your next task," my mom said, "but for now, it's a beautiful day out there—why don't you two go see a movie or go to the zoo, and—"

Nina came into the living room, Fran beside her. My mother beamed at her niece and at her friend as they approached.

"Nina...Samantha's taking wonderful care of you two, I see," she commented as they hugged each other and my mom took a second to do what everyone did, which was pet the belly.

"*Tía*, you remember—"

"Francesca? Of course, but it's always wonderful to see you again," she said as she shook her hand.

Jean swore under her breath next to me. "Fuck." She held two envelopes in her hand and stared anywhere but at me as I took them from her.

I examined them. Both were cards, one from the Cayden family, thanking me for attending the wake, the other from Trace. I stared at the handwritten name and address in the corner. Whatever composure I'd had left was gone.

My mother turned back to us. "Give that to me," she said, her voice gentle as she took them both from my numb fingers. "Victoria?"

My head snapped up at her voice speaking my name. "Huh?"

"Give me your cell phone."

I automatically reached into my back pocket for it. "I haven't had it on since…" I couldn't finish that thought as I handed it to her. My chest began to squeeze, and I wondered if I'd ever be able to breathe normally again.

"I know. I left you a message yesterday."

My mother's eyes snapped like lake fire as she took my phone from me. "I need this," she said, waving it at me. "It's going to help. I'll find something—*te lo juro.*" *I swear*, she promised.

"I…I still have her stuff from…from the hospital," Jean said to her. "Bagged it and tagged it. It's in the car."

"I'll get it," Samantha offered and slipped out.

My mother nodded at Jean with approval. "Good. That will help. Girls, please. Go out, do something nice, let the lawyers"—she grinned at Fran, who gave her the same grin right back—"take care of it."

She stepped away and tucked Nina's hand in her arm, and Nina smiled reassuringly at me over her shoulder as we were dismissed.

"You don't need to ask me questions or anything?" I asked, finally able to speak around the painful buzz that filled me.

My mother walked back to me. "Victoria, *querida*," she said quietly, and she brushed the hair behind my ear, "it's better for both of us if I read it, okay? Let me be a lawyer now, and later, when this is all done, I can be your mother, you can be my daughter." She glanced up at Jean and smiled. "You can both be my daughters and we can talk about this, any way you'd like to."

I understood, I really understood her need to be objective at the moment; I wished for that ability myself. "Okay, Mami."

A thought struck me. "Mami, should I talk to Elena?"

I could see her hesitate, think before she spoke. "She's your sister, and she loves you," my mother said finally. "It's your decision, *hija*. I'd advise you…give her a chance to be there for you, to…to…you know what I mean."

She smiled at me and chucked my chin. "But don't worry about that right now. Go out, girls. This might take some time."

Jean and I opted on Ralph's Ices, where they served over twenty different flavors of combinations of milk, ice, sugar, and flavors, and a gratifyingly stupid movie, followed by the promised trip to the hardware store for paint. We didn't speak much. I was still numb, and Jean was giving me room.

"Hey, Jean?" I asked on the way home. "Can we go somewhere?"

"Any place you want. Where to?"

"I want..." I hesitated. I felt a little silly asking, but it was a compulsion, a directive I had to follow. "I want to see my grandmother."

We stopped so I could pick up some flowers on the way.

"It's all right, I'll wait here if you want," Jean said as I stepped out of the car. I smiled at her in thanks and made my way among the headstones.

I cleaned out the old flowers, carefully put the new ones down, and pushed away the grass from the marker.

"Hi, Nana," I said quietly as I sat on the grass. "I'm sorry it's been so long, but I think of you all the time."

I traced the engraving on the polished granite, following the whorls and the curves with my fingers over her name, Sophia Del Castillo Monte Negron, past the date of her birth and the date of her death. The anniversary of the first would arrive in a few days; the anniversary of the second had already passed.

It was so strange, I mused, how two days, two different days separated by years, could follow one another in reverse of their events in each twelve-month cycle.

"Nina's pregnant, she's due in about twelve, thirteen weeks, but you probably knew that," I said, then laughed a little self-consciously. I was talking to a stone, but I continued anyway. "I got married, Nana, to Jean, right after Easter. She's a paramedic, and you'd love her, you really would, everyone does. I..." and my breath caught.

My fingers dug into the grass, letting the blades wrap around them as I combed along. "Nana...I feel so lost. I miss you so much and I'm scared, so scared, Nana, that I've fucked everything up. Everyone's back at the house, trying to figure something out, ready to go do I don't know what, and I don't even know why. Why do they care? If I hadn't gone there in the first place, nothing…"

I swallowed and wiped my eyes. "And Nana, I feel so strange… it's like I had a whole life before two days ago, and that day? That day is a wall, separating me from everything, like there's a field of grass behind it, and ahead? It's all gray stone. I hurt, Nana. I didn't tell anybody, everyone's stressed enough, but it hurts, and…and…" I wiped my eyes again.

"I can't even *feel* you anymore. You're completely gone, and I can't feel anything but the hurt, and the gray…"

I couldn't continue. I buried my face into my hands and wept, part of my mind surprised I could even do that.

"I just wish I knew where you were," I said quietly through the tears, "that you could tell me somehow that it's all gonna be okay."

I sniffed as I stood. I could hear someone approaching through the field of stones and knew, without looking, that it was Jean.

"Hi," I said softly and held out my hand for her. "There's someone I want you to meet," I told her as her palm met mine. "Nana, this is Jean."

❖

We spent the next few days moving things around and painting in the apartment, although I still slept in the house with my Jean blanket.

"You still interested in diving?" Jean asked on the way back from one of our many trips to and from the hardware store.

"Yeah, definitely."

"All right, then." Jean nodded as she drove. "Let's go down to my favorite dive shop."

We crossed the Narrows and went to Sheepshead Bay near Manhattan Beach, where we walked along the piers and the promenade hand in hand. When we got to the shop, we picked up some basic books on equipment and technique, decided on a wet suit—"It's all cold water around here," Jean informed me—and I registered for a class that would start in two weeks. Jean would attend as well, so she could make sure "all my stuff is current," she said.

It was after one of those busy painting days, following a shared pizza with Nina and Samantha, that Nina convinced me to go for coffee and dessert at the local coffeehouse with her and my mother while Samantha took Jean and Fran with her, destination unknown. Mission? "Just some stuff to take care of," Samantha said.

I tried not to think about what they were doing, though I noticed my mom cast occasional sharp and worried glances my way while she asked Nina if she and Samantha had already picked out a name for the forthcoming niece or nephew (they had some ideas, but Samantha thought it was bad luck to name a baby before it was born), whether they knew if it was a niece or a nephew (they didn't want to know, and those procedures weren't always reliable anyway), and what was new with the label and the club. I understood none of that part of the conversation, so I just let myself enjoy the rhythm and enthusiasm of their voices as they spoke and I savored my cappuccino.

When Jean and I got ready for bed later, I asked her what that had been all about, and she told me that she and Samantha took Fran to take care of a few things with Trace. I asked her what that meant.

Jean carefully caught my shoulders. "It's taken care of," she said softly. "You won't have to deal with her."

Her expression was so somber it alarmed me.

"You guys didn't make her take a long walk off a short pier with heavy shoes or something like that, did you?" I asked, half joking, half afraid they'd done something unrecoverable, that could put them at risk. Then again, considering the 911 connections we all had, it was unlikely that they would get in trouble, but still...I didn't want *anyone* to do *anything* unethical, not for me, not because of me, not ever. And if anyone was going to do anything, it should be me.

Jean studied me intently. "No. Nothing like that." She carefully caught my chin in her hand. "Would you want that?"

My entire body flushed as I thought about it and stared back up at Jean. "Yeah," I said finally, "yeah, I would, but I'd want to be the one to do it."

I didn't know how she'd react, but she had to know how I honestly felt.

Jean sighed and wrapped her arms around me. "Me too."

❖

We both woke suddenly to Nina's voice calling for Samantha in a tone I'd never heard before, and as I jumped out of bed and slipped on a pair of jeans and a T-shirt, Sam knocked on the door as she passed. I could hear the rapid tread of her feet across the hallway as she ran to the bathroom.

"I'm right behind you," Jean said as I popped on a pair of loafers, grabbed my bag, and slung it over my shoulder, then ran out into the hallway, Dusty leading the way.

The dark red blood on the floor prompted action without thought: bleeding in a pregnant patient was considered a true emergency, especially past the first trimester. While Jean ran down to the truck to grab an O_2 tank and her medic bag, I had Samantha get a sheet and lay it out on the floor in the hallway while I guided Nina down into a left-lateral recumbent position. I then asked Samantha to call 911, and she held the phone for me so I could speak to dispatch while asking the questions involved in the initial assessment.

We had a thirty-one-year-old female whose history revealed this as a second pregnancy in its twenty-eighth week with a previous miscarriage in the sixteenth, a blood pressure that just skirted excessively low, and who had started to bleed—deep, dark red blood that was thankfully progressing slowly. She said she had reached "the wrong way" and had felt one, terribly painful, "tearing" sensation. The abdomen was very tender, the uterus felt tightly contracted.

I could hear the screen door slam shut when Jean returned.

"I left the door open so the responding team can walk in," she said as her head topped the stairs. The tank was set to high-flow O_2 with a non-rebreather mask, SOP for pregnant women, and Jean dropped a line for Ringer's lactate to prevent Nina's blood pressure from dropping too severely and to open a passage for other meds to be administered, if necessary. Samantha held it over her shoulder.

"What the…?" Jean asked under her breath as she tried to monitor fetal tones. "Tori, give a listen."

I listened but heard a strange, rapid off-beat. I listened for another few seconds, then it hit me: it wasn't one strange rhythm, but *two* non-synced ones.

Two. "Are you guys expecting twins?" I asked, looking from Nina's face to Samantha's.

Samantha swallowed, then nodded.

That explained quite a bit about things I'd seen in the past few months.

"You got this for a moment?" I asked Jean.

"Yeah."

"Great. Give me four seconds," I said as Dusty began to bark, letting us know the response team had arrived. I ran to the room and grabbed our wallets—so we'd have our shields on us.

"Down, Dusty, friends!" Jean called, and Dusty stopped barking immediately. I could hear the scatter of her paws as she flew back up the steps, leading the response team behind her. She settled herself by Nina's head as I tossed Jean her shield, then reevaluated the vitals.

"Hey, Tori, Jean," Roy greeted us.

Jean presented as they loaded Nina onto the stretcher and Roy put the Ringer's bag over his shoulder.

"You're coming, right?" he asked her.

She had to go; there was a live IV running, and as competent as Roy was, his unit was BLS, not ALS. Also, even though Jean and I were both off duty, at that moment, legally, we represented the city, while Roy, while off duty for the city, was on duty for a contracted hospital, which meant, in essence, this was *our* scene, and even more so Jean's, since she was the highest medical authority as well as senior to at least me and Roy.

"Who's coming with us?" he asked as they got to the top of the stairs.

"I am," Jean said, and she whirled back and grabbed Samantha, "and she is."

"Which hospital?" I asked as everyone walked carefully down.

"St. Vin's has a NICU," Jean said, "and it's closest. Roy, have dispatch contact the hospital and tell them what we've got."

"I'll meet you there. Nina, I'll see you in two minutes," I assured her as they loaded her in. She waved at me before they closed the doors and Samantha was escorted to the front passenger seat.

I don't know how I got there before them, but I did, and when the guard who sat by the vestibule tried to chase me off, I popped my shield out of my back pocket and into his face. He backed off immediately; I'd seen him a thousand times before while working the privates, and he'd always been an officious prick.

In the end they tried to bar Samantha from entering, but one of the receiving nurses was Kathy, my instructor. I caught her on the side. "Kathy, don't make her leave. They're her kids too, and my cousin shouldn't go through whatever's going to happen by herself."

Kathy nodded in understanding and gripped my shoulder, pulling me closer so no one could overhear.

"Scotty, this is a *Catholic* hospital. Half the staff will be cool, the others will be"—she tightened her lips—"official. Tell her to tell *anyone* that asks that she's her sister, get me? She can't be refused entrance then—I'll get the word to anyone else."

"Okay. Thanks, Kathy." I patted her arm and she smiled at me.

"No problem, Scotty. I have a cousin too."

I stopped by Nina's bed where an orderly was preparing to wheel her away. She was still on high-flow O_2 and was now attached to a few portable monitors.

I curled my fingers around hers, reached over to brush an unruly strand of hair behind her ear, then kissed her cheek. "Nina, tell them Samantha's your sister," I whispered to her in Spanish, "so they'll let her go with you, okay?"

Nina squeezed my hand lightly. "*Gracias, hermanita.*" *Thanks, little sister.*

Kathy brought Samantha back to Nina's bed. "You know the deal?" I asked her quietly.

"Yeah, I do. Thanks, Tori." She hugged me briefly but fiercely. "And tell Jean the same." She handed me her cell phone. "Do me a favor?" she asked as they began to move en masse.

"Sure. Anything. Name it."

"Call Nina's doctor. Tell him what's going on, then call Mom, call Uncle Cort, and call Fran? Their numbers are all in there." Sam's eyes darted back to the stretcher.

"Go, Sam, I've got it covered," I told her, "and we'll see you upstairs."

They disappeared around the corner into the corridor, and I stepped back out through the vestibule to the bay to make those calls.

Jean came out and split a cigarette with me while I left a message with the doctor's answering service, a message for Samantha's uncle, another one for Fran, and then...I was rather certain that other than my mother and possibly Elena, no one else in Nina's family knew yet. I called my mother, because I didn't know how to step into that breach.

"Victoria, *qué pasó?*" *What happened,* my mother asked. "Are you and Jean okay?"

"Mami, we're fine, it's Nina," I began and reached for the comfort of Jean. "She's in the hospital..."

I explained to my mother what I knew before I handed the phone to Jean to fill in the blanks. "She'll be here in twenty minutes," Jean told me as she returned my phone.

I took it from her and tightened my arm around her waist, and she draped hers across my shoulder.

"What do you think?"

"Abruptio, hopefully a partial," she added as we walked around to the regular entrance.

"I was thinking the same thing," I sighed.

It was a harsh diagnosis; any of them could die, since it basically meant a sudden separation of the placenta from the uterine wall. If it was a complete abruption, it was possible for the little ones to die, possible for Nina to die if she'd bled too much internally. If it was a partial... there were options: if it wasn't too severe, the recommendation would be complete bed rest, either at home or monitored in the hospital.

If it was severe, or worse yet, a complete abruption, the docs would probably opt for an emergency caesarean section and hope they could save everyone. This had risks too. At twenty-eight weeks, and twins no less, well, the neonates would be small, not much more than a pound each, more than likely, maybe two at most. They'd be about the size of apples all curled up, and their lungs were probably not developed enough, and different systems were probably incomplete.

"Jean," I said as we walked, "do you think this happened because she was so stressed out over...the last few days?"

Her arm tightened around me. "No, baby. I don't. Sometimes things just happen."

"I hope they'll all be okay," I said, then stopped walking as it hit me. "Twins, Jean, twins. I *knew* something was up. Christ..."

Jean rubbed my shoulder. "We did everything that could be done, I think," she said, then reviewed everything aloud. "And we got her here fast, *really* fast. We had a rig in less than two minutes. Up to the surgeons and whatever else from here."

I pulled her closer in silent agreement and we went up to Obstetrics, and once there, we were told to go to Labor and Delivery; they were bringing my cousin in for the emergency C-section.

"Victoria, where is she?"

Aunt Carolina's voice broke the silence that reigned in the waiting room where Jean and I waited to hear anything about what was going on.

I sat up straight, not letting go of Jean's hand as I watched my aunt walk in, hand in hand with my mother, while my cousins and Nina's father trailed behind with Elena.

My aunt, plainly put, looked like hell, and my mom patted her hand repeatedly as Jean and I explained what we knew.

During the wait that felt like several hours, although it really couldn't have been, because these things are supposed to go fast, Fran showed up, and after greeting everyone, she refused to sit and instead waited by the door until Samantha walked out into the waiting room, her face so very pale over the scrub gown hospital staff had put on her, and obviously exhausted.

Everyone stood and Samantha buried her head on Fran's shoulder and wept. "Nina's still in surgery…she lost a lot of blood, they said, and…" Samantha took a deep breath, then straightened, but didn't let go of Fran. "One girl, one boy, both in NICU…they're so tiny, so fucking tiny…"

It took three days for Nina and the little ones to be stabilized enough to be transferred to another hospital, the one where Nina's doctor was, where there would be no issues about whether or not Sam could stay with her family. Since it was our last day off before we returned to work, when the private ambulances that would transfer them came, Samantha and Nina had absolutely no issues with Jean's and my insistence that we each ride with one of the infants to the other hospital in Manhattan.

Fran rode with Nina and Samantha—she barely left Samantha or Nina's side the entire time, once visitors were allowed.

It was hard riding in that rig with that plastic case and the machinery that helped my niece breathe. As feared and expected, both neonates lacked surfactant, the protein that would enable their lungs to stay open so they could breathe on their own, and had to be fed intravenously.

Her skin was red and translucent; I could see the fine network of blood vessels that ran under it. She had no name. Samantha was reluctant to name either one of them yet, and, much to my surprise, Nina went along with her choice.

"Give her a week," Nina said to me privately right before we left after the transfer was complete, "she'll come around."

❖

Jean and I stayed in the apartment that night, for the first time since everything that had happened. "You sure you're ready to go back to work?" Jean asked as I pulled out our uniforms and she made some coffee.

"Yeah, sure, I'm fine." In fact, I was looking forward to it because I really enjoyed it.

"Okay." She handed me a mug. "Are you all right with sleeping here tonight?"

It was a strange question, and I stopped what I was doing so I could read her face. She kept her expression carefully neutral as she sipped and watched me over the rim of her cup.

"What do you mean?"

"It's just that…you seemed, you know, like you felt comfortable there, and I don't—you just seemed happier, I guess." She shrugged casually.

Her controlled casualness didn't fool me. This was something serious, and I carefully put my mug down and stepped closer.

"Baby, the only thing I'm not happy about is that I'm not going to be with you all day tomorrow," I said and put my hands on her waist. "That, and I'm a little worried about, you know, things."

I closed my arms around her, and Jean hesitated only a moment before she buried her face in my neck and murmured into my hair.

"What was that, baby? I didn't hear you."

"I just thought that maybe," her breath caught as she raised her face to mine, "you didn't feel safe with me, like I can't—"

"Can't what, baby?" I asked gently. Her eyes shone brightly, filled with emotion, with the threat of tears, and I couldn't help but stroke the long strands of hair behind her ear. "Come on," I said and led her to the sofa, "sit with me. Can't what?" I ran my thumb along her cheek.

"Like I can't protect you," she said finally, her voice hoarse, "because I should have been there."

"Jean…I'm the one who asked you not to go. I thought it would upset you, that it would be the weirdest sort of wrong to show up with someone's ex-girlfriend to a wake or a funeral and…you…I've really fucked us up, haven't I?"

Jean hugged me tightly. "You're not the fuckup here," she said, the words choked as she spoke them. "I knew better than you who she is, how she is. I should have gone with you."

I could feel the tension in her back as she tried not to cry, and while I held her closely and murmured, "It's not your fault, Jean, baby, it's not your fault," all I could think was that my mother had been right—this was something we were both going through. The question now was how did we both get through it?

❖

Although I got a clean bill of health at my follow-up appointment, it forcibly reminded me why I had to go in the first place and it left me jumpy and shaken. I was glad every time I hit the station and got to work; it kept me focused, busy, and so long as I wore a T-shirt, nothing rubbed against the constant itch that were the lines that slowly healed under my navel.

"You and Jean must sure be enjoying the honeymoon," my partner, Diaz, teased me with a bright grin as we reloaded the stretcher into the rig after a routine my-chest-hurts, I-just-smoked-crack call and my cell had gone off.

I grinned back at her as I answered. I felt no compulsion and hadn't shared the events of the last weeks, at least not my personal situation, with either of my work partners, although we did discuss my cousin and my still-unnamed niece and nephew.

"Scotty," I answered my cell.

"Hey, baby."

"Hey yourself, what's up? You get banged with overtime?"

"No. Just ran into Pat while I was on a call, and? My dad phoned. He called me Sinead and spoke in garlic. Dinner day after tomorrow at my parents'?"

I winced. Sinead was Jean in Gaelic, or "garlic" as Jean called it, and if her father was using it… We hadn't visited them in a few weeks, and no matter what the reasons might have been, they were Jean's family, and it wasn't fair for her not to see them.

"Sure, no problem."

"Great! Oh, and he asked if we'd bring Dusty and stay the night."

"Sure," I said again. I didn't mind, not at all. I just felt a little guilty that we'd neglected Jean's parents.

We had a great time. Mom Megs made her absolutely fabulous mashed potatoes, while Jean's da insisted that a barbecue wasn't working right if the flames didn't jump out of the grill.

We ate in the yard, where Jean and Pat's playful verbal sparring amused us all until the first threat of flung food.

"Don't disrespect the mash!" Jean warned, eyeing Pat carefully as he loaded his fork a little too fully.

"You disrespected the piper on Saint Patrick's Day! And I *know* where you were while I was playing!" he retorted, waving his cutlery with menace.

"Paidrig!"

Their da's voice cut through the bickering like a clap of thunder, and we all looked at him.

"Patrick," he said, and his voice lowered, "you...*killed*...the trees. The grass? Has not recovered, and my ears *still* hurt. Jean and Tori's absence during your murder of tone and all things green has at least ensured that your mother and I will have grandchildren. Put the fork down...and after dinner, you get to seed the lawn, again."

"You would have made a hell of a hostage negotiator, Da," Pat muttered as he returned his attention to his plate.

Jean's da reached behind for the cooler, then handed us each a beer. "Speaking of grandkids, how are Logan's?" he asked, focusing on me and Jean.

We caught everyone up on the latest. Jean's parents remembered Samantha as a girl, as Fire Captain Logan Cray's daughter, and I learned that in a firefighter's household, a 911 household, the memories of the fallen are honored forever.

❖

When Jean and I curled up together that night upstairs in the Scanlon home, I had a hard time falling asleep. Jean held me carefully, her arm curled over my waist, but as I listened to her breathe over my shoulder, I wondered if it was the not completely healed mark on my skin or the fact that it was Trace who'd left it there after she'd…if that was the reason behind why Jean and I hadn't really shared more than hugs and the occasional tender kiss.

I could understand why in those first two weeks, given the shock, the stitches, and the concern over Nina, as well as the surprise and fear for the twins, we had refrained, but I was fine now. I'd been fine for a few weeks.

I wondered if maybe something was wrong with me. I'd always enjoyed sex, and I loved making love with Jean. It was literally the best thing I could think of doing, since I loved her so much and we felt so good together.

Maybe I wasn't supposed to want to yet? Or maybe Jean thought I wasn't interested? What scared me more than anything was wondering if maybe Jean simply didn't want to, didn't want me.

The more I thought about it, the more this seemed like it had the makings of a huge misunderstanding one way or another. I knew Jean loved me; I just didn't know if she still desired me. The only way to find out for certain was to ask.

Tomorrow, after we left here, we'd planned to stop by the hospital and visit Nina and the twins. Since the last update we'd learned they might be released in another week or so (Nina had been released after the first six days, but she and Sam practically lived at the hospital). Jean and I, in conjunction with my mother, my aunt, and Fran, who spent almost as much time at the hospital as my cousins did, had picked up everything Nina and Sam might need for the nursery, and it was amazing what "everything" meant for twins. After we visited the hospital, Jean and I planned to stop there in the afternoon and put it all together.

I'd discuss it with Jean then, I mused, because it would be just the two of us, and with our hands focused on the tasks before us, we'd have time to talk, time for me to ask the important questions.

If things were still okay between us, then fine, wonderful—perfect, even. And if we weren't okay, if Jean felt differently about me, about us? I would improvise and adapt. I didn't know if I could overcome, but I would definitely try. First, though, I needed an answer.

❖

Once at the hospital, I was shocked, and Jean equally so, to find that neither twin had yet been named. They had reached what would have been thirty-four, almost thirty-five weeks gestational age, had slightly more than doubled in weight, were breathing on their own, and while they still needed a little help eating, they'd learned to swallow. They finally had eyelashes over their little new-baby blue eyes, and their skin had lost that frighteningly delicate translucency. They looked much more like tiny babies than the weak chicks that had been transported to the hospital more than a month before.

I found myself alone with Samantha in the hallway as the nurses and doctors did whatever it was they did behind the lowered curtain.

"Sam, can I ask you something?"

"Yeah, go ahead."

"Why haven't you named them yet? Nina could, but she's waiting for you. They're healthy, they're going home soon. They need names. Besides," I said in as light a tone as I could muster, "I'm tired of describing them to my coworkers as simply my niece Baby A and my nephew Baby B."

Samantha shook her head. "It's too soon, nothing's certain yet."

I touched her arm gently. "Sam…" I started. How did I explain that some children lived and died nameless, unloved, unwanted, young and old? That no matter whose child or what age, live or die, everyone deserved to have an identity?

I thought of Mr. Wheeler and of the seemingly countless patients I'd had since then, of the bodies I'd worked on, fighting for life as it poured out, the hands I'd held of the dying who had no will to fight and no wish to be fought for, those who fought and lost anyway, and those who knew it was simply their time. How did I explain that I loved them, every single one of them, even though I'd never met them before, that those moments together bound me to them and them to me? They were strangers, complete strangers, yet each one became the entirety of the universe to me, my whole purpose for being, and I hoped, I so deeply hoped, that each one knew they hadn't left this world for the void—or for whatever else might exist—unloved, unknown, in those last breaths.

How much more would I feel for these tiny, innocent beings, beings I shared blood with, had watched grow in Nina's body and Samantha's heart, had felt kick and shift under my hand? I knew, because it was so obvious, that Samantha loved them. The fact that she was so fiercely afraid of losing them screamed it, but that fear…they needed her more than she needed it.

"Samantha, they're your babies, and they deserve to know that you love them. Name them so when you hold them, they know who they are, no matter what happens."

She twisted her face away and jammed a hand into her pocket.

"There are no guarantees, Sam. I know you know that. They're missing out on you, and you're missing out on them, for however long you're all here."

The silence was so absolute I could hear the sound of the cloth moving as Samantha shifted a shoulder.

"You're hurting your wife," I added softly, because I had read the pain that flashed in Nina's eyes when the subject came up, and I knew Nina: she'd forbear and forgive only for so long, and the damage it might do between them…Samantha had to realize that. "I know you don't want or mean to do that."

Samantha faced me then, her mouth set, a tight, thin line. "Really?" she said dryly. "You're neglecting yours."

Stunned by the harshness of her delivery as well as the words that plucked at the strings of my own self-doubt and played its exact tune, I merely stared.

I wasn't sure what Sam meant, but I knew my own misgivings. Maybe, just maybe, Jean and I had spent too long being loving, but not sensual. And maybe…that change was obvious. If it was? Then I didn't think it was something that we could recover.

Or maybe Sam meant that I was spending too much time concerned about her family and not enough with mine. Either way, it seemed like I had really fucked up again.

"Hey, there you are!" Jean said as she ambled up and clapped a friendly hand on my shoulder. "Hey, Sam."

"Jean."

The guarded friendliness in that touch did something to me, and I snapped to a new awareness.

"I've gotta go," I said abruptly as I stepped out from Jean's grasp. "Got some stuff to take care of. Jean, you can stay if you want. I'll see you later."

"Tor, what…?" Jean asked with that same friendly tone, a slightly puzzled look creasing her forehead.

It cut me to hear it, that tone that was so clear in my new ears, to see that expression with my eyes opened this way.

"Yeah, you know, stuff," I told her. "Later, Sam. Tell Nina I said good-bye." I strode to the elevator quickly, and I didn't look back.

I took a subway down to the ferry that would take me back to the Island. From there, it was a short bus ride to the house. The first thing I did after letting Dusty out of the apartment to play in the yard was to go inside the house and upstairs. I scanned the room that had been mine, removed anything that was still there, then after another inspection to make sure I'd left nothing, I stripped the bed and put up the laundry.

I'd promised to put the baby furniture together, so I did that next—two cribs, one changing table, and two drawer sets—then went into their room and attached something called a "side along" to the bed frame, a three-sided crib that would allow Nina and Sam to keep the infants next to them at night. It was quick work; altogether it took perhaps an hour, maybe an hour and a half. I owed them that, at the very least.

Thanks to the vagaries of traffic versus public transportation I was done and able to take off in my car before Jean even hit the Island; I knew that because she'd called my cell a few times and left me messages that I played as I drove.

I thought I drove aimlessly, but instead I automatically headed to the beach, the same beach I always went to. Despite the early summer weather, school wasn't out yet, so no one was around, at least not now, not before the sun set.

My phone rang two more times as I walked to my favorite spot, one call from Nina, the other from Samantha. I didn't answer those calls, either.

What the fuck did anything matter, anyway? I wondered as I aimed my feet toward the pier. I hadn't been there in months, the pier since I'd broken up with Kerry and the beach since I'd hooked up with Trace.

Trace. I'd really, truly, just wanted to help her out, and instead...I would have loved to be able to pretend that it was just sex gone bad or, better yet, that nothing had happened, because the word that I was supposed to use to describe the event, hell, the memories that I did have, made me want to puke. Jean didn't want to touch me and, really, what the fuck did I care.

It wasn't as if there wouldn't come a day when I'd probably walk in and she'd either tell me we were done, or, better yet, I'd probably have the joy of discovering she'd been fucking someone else. I held no illusions; we were both very sexual people, and the field, hell, the world was crawling with people who would be more than happy and available for her if I wasn't. Christ. The first time Jean had come on to me it was because I wasn't wearing anyone's ring—not a distinction too many would care about.

A variation on that reality had happened to my mother. It had already happened to me once; the only difference was that Kerry and I were still fucking even when she'd been cheating.

And…it was time I moved on. I'd very obviously overstayed with my cousins. Well, so much for that. It just fucking figured. Hell, it probably was my fault that Nina had suffered the abruption; one stupid fucking decision and I'd screwed up a lot of lives.

Nothing, absolutely nothing lasted forever—not love, not family, certainly not people. Even the bloody evidence of life and death was washed away with soap and water, run over by cars, flushed sans regard down toilets every day, burned and boiled away, recycled, either by humans or nature.

Tomorrow, I'd go back to work, and as rough and even downright terrifying as it could be sometimes, I never had to worry about anything except whether or not I remembered everything I had to, if the results of my actions would prolong life, promote health, or not. If I forgot something, someone died; if I didn't, they might anyway, but at least I'd try, I'd give it my best and hope it was good enough, hope it wasn't me or my partner that got hurt.

If I remembered the schedule correctly, I'd be working with Izzy for the first three days, Diaz for the second two before my three-day break. That would give me a few days to find a place, three days to help Jean move her stuff if she wanted my help, and move my own wherever I was going. I'd apologize to my mom about not being able to help out for the next week or so, but then again, she'd started doing some consulting work, so maybe she wouldn't need it quite so much for that little bit of time.

I kicked at the crumbling concrete of the pier as I stood at its edge. The tide was out, so the rocks that formed the jetty showed clearly, rising about eight feet above and for another fifty feet out, a long, dark finger into the bay. For the first time in years, I scrambled off the edge and walked along the rocks and broken slabs of concrete, picking my way carefully to the end. I sat on the ledge of the one closest to the water and picked at the loose stones with no conscious thought in my mind as I threw them, one at a time, slowly, deliberately, with intense precision as I aimed for certain waves.

Dig, pick, throw. Dig, pick, throw. I hit a rhythm that worked for me until the sun had fallen low enough in the sky to blind as it blazed back at me from its reflection in the water, the bay now lava gold with black shadowed waves.

I should have never gone to Trace's. Throw.

I should have never fucking even mentioned living together to Jean, never mind everything else. Throw. That one hurt; the thought of not knowing her parents as Mom Megs and Da, of not being teased by Pat…thinking I had to give up Jean's smile, the warmth of her arms, the feel of her heart beating next to mine as we breathed the same air. To lose the almost achingly sweet taste of her mouth, the honey and copper of her eyes when they shone on me, hurt even more.

Why did I think I could do anything useful in the medical field? Throw.

I'd thought maybe I'd be something like a knight in a tin can riding around, helping out, and maybe even saving the day every now and again. Throw.

What a fucking joke—I couldn't even fucking save myself. That was my last rock, and I dug my fingers into the crevice between the boulder and the slab for more.

"I owe you an apology."

Samantha's voice was low and carried over the splash of fire that smashed itself into molten globs and white foam on the rocks and the occasional keen of the gulls. I ignored her. Dig, pick, throw.

After Samantha settled on the ledge next to me, I placed a few rocks between us and kept going. Dig, pick, throw.

My peripheral vision caught the edge of her arm as she picked up one of the missiles I'd set aside for her and tossed it right after mine. "You were right," she said finally. "You saved their lives, you and Jean, and you saved mine, twice."

I shrugged. "Part of the job." I tossed another rock.

"It was an almost complete abruption, Tori. She could have, she probably would have bled to death before we even knew what was going on, and the kids…" I could hear her swallow, hard, before she continued, "our kids, they would have died with her. If you hadn't been right there, knowing what to do—"

"Glad everyone's okay." Throw.

"You were a very big part in that," she said quietly.

Silence reigned as I let my fingers scrabble around for more things to throw.

"I lost my mom when I was two," Samantha said with a sigh. "I barely remember her, and when my dad…I was a teenager. For a long time I thought the one person besides him who meant more to me than anyone else was dead too, and when that wasn't true—Tori, I never want to lose anyone again."

I understood that. My father was worse than dead. He had disowned me, my mother, my sister, and we'd had nothing to do with him for years, while my Nana? She'd been my world, the living rock of my faith until the morning I'd heard a faint cry from the hallway and run out of my room only to trip over her as she lay there, facedown on the floor.

I'd called 911, told them my grandmother wouldn't wake up from the floor, and recited my address as every schoolchild is taught to do while my mother stared in horrified shock, unable to dial, unable to speak, and I opened the door to let the paramedics in. And then I was gently pushed aside to watch, helpless, powerless, while a terrified seven-year-old Elena huddled in my lap as the crew worked on my grandmother right there in the hallway, unable to stop the process that had already started. She'd never wake up again.

When they pronounced her dead, the medics were kind enough to move her mortal remains carefully, respectfully, back to her bed, and they called the police department before they left. I don't remember what they said to me as they walked out, but as soon as they had gone, I went to Nana's room.

Her hands had still been warm, her face still soft, like always, and except for the dark bruise on her forehead where she'd hit the floor, she seemed to be sleeping. I leaned over and kissed the bruise, then crawled onto the bed and put my arm over her. I snuggled my Nana the way I always did, and I told her I loved her, that I would miss her, the last time I could ever remember crying so freely, crying on my Nana, until someone, I don't remember who, either my aunt or Nina, found and removed me so Nana's body could be taken to the funeral home.

I didn't cry again until after the funeral. It had snowed, and I wondered if Nana was unhappy, buried in the cold ground, under the snow, so very far from the warmth of the land she loved and never forgot.

My mother had never been the same.

"I know a little bit about loss, Sam."

"I know you do, Tori, I know you do. I didn't realize how much it was going to *hurt*, the first time Nina miscarried, not her, not me, and this whole thing—" Samantha sighed. "I thought if they had no names, if something happened, if we lost them…" Samantha tossed her final rock, wiped her hands, then stood.

"Your niece and your nephew have names, Tori, names of heroes, real flesh-and-blood heroes. Victoria. Victoria Jean Cray, and we're gonna call her TJ just because we can, and your—"

"What?" I twisted my head over my shoulder to look at her, and Samantha's smile gleamed at me, a flash of white in the setting sun. That seemed so…so…unreal. *Did she and Nina really name their daughter that?.*

"Well, I'm pretty sure everyone will simply call them the baby and the babies for the next two years, but eventually…" Her smile grew even wider for a second, then her face turned somber again.

"Your nephew is Kitt Logan, Kitt Logan Cray. Come home, Tori," Sam said and extended her hand. "That was a shitty thing for me to say and I'm so very sorry. I was angry because I knew you were right. I wasn't being fair to those little lives you saved or to Nina, and I took it out on you."

"Wasn't any of my business."

"It sure was," she said firmly. "You saw something, you did something. It's what you do—and we're family. Who else would care that much about us?"

She held her other hand out as well. "Nina needs you, the little ones need you, *I* need you, little sister, and Jean's pretending she's not worried sick. Come home."

I took the hands. Samantha pulled me to my feet, then wrapped me in a fierce hug. "I'm sorry. I was an ass, a complete ass."

"How'd you know where I'd be?" I asked finally. I could feel my heart pound as I returned the embrace.

She chuckled in my shoulder, then let me go. "Where else does anyone on this Island go when they want to think? That and"—she flashed me another grin—"Nina told me."

I shook my head. Of course Nina knew. She'd been the first one to bring me here when I was a kid; in fact, she'd brought me here the spring following Nana's funeral.

"Are we okay?" she asked softly.

"Yeah, we're okay."

"Oh, this is for you." Samantha reached down for the small gift bag that she'd set down when she arrived and handed it to me.

"I know…you know a few things about loss," she said as I reached through the paper and found the smooth plastic contours of a bottle. "I know a few things about scars."

It was scented almond oil from the Body Shop. When I gave Samantha a puzzled glance, to my surprise, she dropped her eyes and shifted uncomfortably.

"I, uh, I know you've… Look. That cut thing, if it's bothering you, this stuff works great. The marks get softer like, after the first time, and if you use it for a while, well, see?" She showed me her forearm.

Curious, I looked closely. Even with the glare of the falling sun on her skin, I noticed just one faint line that disappeared into the crease of her skin. "I don't really see anything," I told her as she took her arm back.

"Yeah, well, that's the point. They're gone now, and I'd had them for years before that. So, you know, you might—"

I understood, I got it. "Thanks, Sam."

"Least I could do," she said, "least I could do," and we walked in silence back to the parking lot.

❖

Jean waited in our apartment for me and embraced me with all her strength before I could even say hello.

"Tori, don't ever fucking do that again, please," she said, her voice thick and raspy. "You scared the shit out of me." She burrowed her face against my neck and I realized she was crying.

"I'm so sorry, Jean," I told her and held her just as close, "I'm so sorry for everything." We stayed in that embrace a little longer, and Jean rubbed my back through my shirt. When her fingers traveled down across my hips, just above my ass, she froze. I grabbed her hand and held it in place before she could move away.

"I am *so* sorry." She tried to shift her hand. "I didn't mean—"

"Jean, we have to talk about this," I told her, still holding her in place. "This is not us." I deliberately reached for her hip with my free hand and pulled her closer to me. "This," I whispered against her neck before I pressed my lips against the pulse that suddenly flared, "this is us."

I heard her inhale sharply. "Tori, I don't, I mean, you shouldn't..."

I leaned away to look at her. "Tell me you don't want me, and baby, I promise we'll make this easy. You don't owe me anything, you don't..." I tried to find the right words. Everyone had the right to pursue happiness. If Jean wasn't happy, I loved her enough to let her go seek it, whatever or whoever would take her there, no questions, no regrets. I wanted her to know that. "You're not obligated."

"Jesus Christ, Tori—no!" She freed her hand and caught my face. Her eyes sparked, turned the color of tea. A single drop shone in the corner of her eye like a diamond, her birthstone, a diamond like the one that was the heart of her ring, the ring I'd asked her to marry me with, the ring she wore as a wedding band. "Tori, I love you. I want you, but it just didn't seem right, you know?"

"See, that's why we need to talk." I smiled and carefully wiped the tear from her eye.

"What didn't seem right?" I asked as we faced each other on the sofa.

Jean took my hand in hers. "It didn't seem right for me to want to...to want to touch you, to feel that need, after...everything," she said earnestly, "especially when I knew what you did remember of...you know."

I listened. I could understand that. "I've felt a little bad over that too," I admitted, "like maybe I shouldn't want to, that you might think...I don't know." I shook my head.

"Do you think it's wrong?" I asked. I wanted to know what she really thought, how she really felt. I touched the angle of her cheek. "Does it bother you...that I want to touch you, want to make love with you?"

Jean kissed my palm before she spoke again. "But what if...what if I do something that reminds you of—"

"Trace?" I said, using her name deliberately. I could no longer allow that name to have power over either of us. "Trace Cayden? There is nothing, absolutely nothing, you could do, I promise you," I told her and cradled her face in my hands, "that could ever, *ever*, remind me of her." I scooted closer to her on the sofa. "Nothing, angel. Nothing."

I kissed Jean softly before I teased her lips with my tongue. When she granted me entrance and met me more than halfway, her hands gripping at my waist, I knew, with the same bone-deep certainty I'd known when we made love, how much we belonged to each other, just how much Jean wanted me. I tried to show her exactly how mutual that desire was as she surged against me and pressed me beneath her.

"I miss you," I said into her ear as we stretched out along the couch. Her leg eased between mine. "I miss your hands, the taste of your skin. I miss the feel of your cunt around me, your dick inside me." I smoothed my hands along her back until I held her ass, pulling her solidly against me before I reached for her waistband and unsnapped the top button.

"Is that what you want, baby?" Jean asked, her voice a gruff rumble against my throat. "You want my dick inside you?" She palmed my tit, the hardened end scraping against her hand as she opened my shirt with the other. Her tongue trailed behind it and air escaped me.

"Wear it, share it, I don't care," I answered through the haze that built, was about to overwhelm me as she moved against my thigh. "Ride or drive—whatever you want. Don't you miss my cock inside you, baby?"

She groaned against my skin, then suddenly stilled. "I don't want to hurt you." The words were so soft I barely heard them, whispered right above my heart. She rested her cheek against my sternum.

"Angel baby, look at me." I ran my fingers through her hair and tipped her chin. "It's okay."

Jean raised eyes that shone almost new-penny bright with tears. "That's what…that's what—"

"Trace," I supplied firmly. I wouldn't let her be the ghost that haunted our heads, or our bed. The thought of her *did* upset me, could still wake me up from a sound sleep, shaken, panicked even, sometimes, but I simply refused to let it stop me, or Jean, from being "us."

Jean nodded. "Trace." She swallowed. "That's what Trace did to you. I don't want to remind you—"

"Shh, baby," I said and stroked along the delicate line of her jaw. "That's not what she did. What she did do," I told Jean as I sat up and took her with me so I could focus on her lovely face and those eyes with the dark lashes that glinted at me, "what she did…was try to take something she couldn't have, and when she couldn't have it?"

I ran my thumb along her cheek. "She tried to break it. And all she did, Jean, the only thing she really did? Was to prove that she couldn't."

I smoothed my fingers along her lips. "Angel baby, I love you more right now than I did the first time I told you. I'm gonna love you more tomorrow."

Jean kissed my fingers, then caught my hand. "Do you mean that?"

Once again I cupped her cheek and gazed into eyes that burned me in cinnamon-and-sugar sight. "With my whole heart."

I kissed her again and took her hand in mine. "Let me take you to our room, to our bed. Let me show you."

I almost tripped over the bag I'd forgotten I'd brought in.

"What is that?" Jean asked.

I laughed a little self-consciously as I tried to pick it up while still holding on to her hand. "That was a gift from Samantha."

"Yeah?"

"Yeah." I felt awkward, but I explained anyway.

"Well," she said and took the bag from my hand, "let's see if it works."

She hesitated for one heart-stopping moment as we reached the threshold. "Promise you'll tell me if you're hurting?"

I squeezed her hand. "Yes, I'll tell you."

"You didn't last time."

I stared at her. "What?"

"When you were in pain." Jean took a deep breath and brushed the back of her fingers along my stomach just under my navel. "With the stitches and the cramping—you didn't tell me."

I could hear the hurt in her voice, and I gazed down at the floor. "You're right," I said finally, looking up at her. "I'm sorry."

She dropped my hand to brush the hair back from my forehead. "Were you trying to protect me?"

I nodded.

"Please don't," she asked softly. "It hurts me more if you shut me out. I'll let you know if I can't handle something."

"Okay."

"Good. Thank you," she said, then kissed me and drew me into the room.

For the first time in almost two months, we undressed each other, a careful peeling of layers that revealed her to me freshly and where my eyes traveled, my hands followed. "I missed you," I whispered into her throat before I tasted her skin, before I kissed her and felt the return of her tongue, its carnal promise leaving me breathless and high, dizzy with the need that burned through me.

"Want you," she murmured as we shifted, and I was blown away again by the press of her lush breasts against mine, the tips already hard. I needed to touch her, to taste her, to fill her, to watch the flame burn in her eyes as I heard her call my name.

The feel of each breast as it filled my hands, the taste of each hardened point between my lips sent a thrill through me that was second only to the joy and the clit-hardening rush that finding out how hard—absolutely hard and lusciously wet—she was when I slid my fingers between her lips and around her clit.

"Tori," she groaned as my fingers played right at her entrance, "I want...I need...to *touch* you." Her eyes were wide, a smoldering copper as they looked back into mine. "Baby...can I touch you?"

"Please," I answered, the word barely a whisper as it floated out, "please touch me." I shifted so she could slide her arm under my ribs, and she touched my face as she did so.

"Are you sure?"

I looked into those eyes, at the gentle quirk of her lips, the faint sprinkle of freckles across her cheeks, and the fine strands of hair that flowed like burnt sugar from her face and over her shoulder. My Jean was beautiful.

"I might break if you don't."

"I promised you I wouldn't let that happen," she said, then smiled. Her fingers traveled down the line of my neck and across my shoulder, and she kissed me as they skated across the lines of my stomach. "Do you know I love you?" she asked in a throaty, low tone as her fingers quested lower and found me, aching, hard, and she ran a fingertip along the highly sensitive underside of my clit.

I gasped, then kissed her in answer to the question, to the touch that robbed me of speech, but it was the shift of her hand, the thumb that grazed along the same edge she'd just stroked, the fingers that played with me, waiting to enter me, that pushed me forward.

"Please, baby, wait," she said, halting my slide. "Do it with me?" I breathlessly agreed.

"You sure you're ready?" she murmured into my ear before catching the tender skin between her teeth while her fingers skillfully teased. "I don't want to—"

"I need you," I told her, and pressed my fingers just that much harder against her. "Please." The wait to bury myself in her, to feel her close around me as she filled me in turn, was maddening. I twisted my head to catch her mouth with mine and let my tongue fuck hers until it was done, the ache of want replaced by the gorgeously snug glide of her pussy on me, clit hard and straining under my thumb, the burning need met by the almost-too-much stretch of my cunt around her fingers.

There was one bare moment of doubt, of pure fear, but I knew I was safe, I was loved, I was with *Jean*, and I quickly pushed it aside.

"Feel me, baby?" she groaned as her cunt bore down on me. "Feel how much I love you?"

The slide of her leg up my arm until her knee hooked over my shoulder opened her to me in a gesture of trust and need so profound, and so goddamned hot, I felt my entire body respond as I moved willingly, happily, freely into the deeper invitation.

I sighed with the pure pleasure of plowing my baby so completely. God, I loved her, and the hand that had held on to my waist now grabbed my ass as I edged my body over her, and Jean fucked me the way I liked best, a full and steady pressure deep inside as she moved within me.

"I feel you, baby…so *fucking* amazing…" Christ, I meant it, it was…fucking beautiful…just…so… "Yeah, baby, just like that," I begged, and when her lips found mine, we shifted again, Jean's body surging against me until…I was…so close, so *fucking* close and I loved her so much, and I could feel how absolutely she loved me from the way her pussy embraced me, the elegant slick of her skin on mine, to the God-so-perfect touch inside me.

"Gonna come," I told her, needing to let her know what she was doing to me.

"Show me." Her words were throaty and low, robbed of air, filled with emotion. "Please show me. Fuck me the way you feel it."

"Jesus, baby…" I choked against the tightening in my cunt, the throb that was the hard-on she stroked, the love and lust that pulsed around my fingers and I…was… "love you…" there.

I went beyond the burn and the fire to the glowing gold center of the earth. I melted into it, joined it, discovered *us* at the heart of the furnace, tempered and pure as I came, then came again when she showed me over and over how she felt it too.

❖

It was hours later, time enough for sleep, for rest, before we had to rejoin the real world to face the daily dragons of death and despair before coming home, then do it all over again, and Jean and I lay together, enjoying the skin to skin as we finally got around to trying out the helpful suggestion.

"Jean?" I asked tentatively as she lay on top of my legs and carefully massaged the oil into my belly.

"Yeah?" She kissed the spot she had rubbed, then glanced up from her ministrations. I couldn't help but smile—I'd missed that too.

I took a breath. "What did you guys do to Trace?" I didn't realize how much that question had been on my mind, tugging at an ugly dark corner, because even though I hadn't gone out of my way to avoid her, I'd still done the occasional overtime shift and...I needed to know, for me, so I knew what the future might hold.

Jean raised her head farther. "Do you really need to know?"

"You know you're scaring me, right?" I said, half joking, because it was partially true—the not knowing was getting to me. Maybe they *had* dropped her off a pier somewhere...

"I swear it's nothing to be scared of," Jean sighed, then scooted up the bed and gathered me in her arms. "It really wasn't anything big or bad at all."

"Oh, yeah?" I asked, and shifted so that I faced her. I draped my leg over her hip and gently pushed her onto her back. "And why's that?"

She kissed me. "It was really simple, baby, and totally legal. Your mom and Fran basically drew up a list in that weird lawyer-language they both speak of all the things that she could be sued for on a civil level and—"

"Yes?"

Her fingers cradled my face. "She had to basically get out of Dodge or be slapped with a suit for damages it would take generations for her to pay." Her eyes were steady on mine, a rich, deep coffee color. "We had to do something, Tor."

"Is that all you did?"

Jean shifted under me and dropped her gaze. "I, uh…I let the air out of her tires."

I leaned up in surprise. "You did not."

"Actually?" She opened the top drawer of her night table and rummaged about until she found what she was looking for.

She took my hand in hers and placed something in my palm, then closed my fingers over it. "Yeah, I did."

I opened my hand and stared. Four little plastic caps. Tire caps.

"You're fucking crazy, Scanlon." I smiled and shook my head. "Out of your fucking mind."

She took the caps from my hand and placed them back in her drawer. "Oh, yeah?" she drawled, then rolled me over again. "Just remember…" She kissed me, then nudged her leg between mine and I wrapped my arms around her, smoothing my hands along her shoulders, molding them against her.

"I'm *your* psycho dyke," she said softly into my ear, then let her tongue travel down the length of my neck.

"I'm a little crazy about you too," I admitted freely, "maybe more than a little."

"Maybe?" she asked, and raised her eyes to mine, an expression of mock surprise across the face I so loved. "Just maybe?"

I stroked the silky skin of her neck. "You know I'm playing, right?"

The smile that crossed Jean's mouth shifted from silly to sexy, and her eyes smoldered as they traveled down me. "I'd love to play with you right now," she purred.

"Really?" I caught her fire and shifted in response. "Any special requests or preferences?" I drew her to me so I could feel the electric connect of her mouth to mine. Whatever she wanted, however she wanted it, she'd have.

"Yes," she said finally, halting our progress long enough to reach over for my night table, "anything. Everything…with you."

FOCUSED ASSESSMENT

After all life threats have been treated and stabilized, a full head-to-toe examination of the patient should be performed, either on scene or en route, with specific focus on each area...

When the twins finally came home, we had a party at Nina and Samantha's house, Del Castillo style, impromptu, joyous, and overfull—which meant the whole family, including Sam's uncle, my cousin's friend Fran, Nina's parents and siblings, and Jean's brother and parents.

I was gladder than glad for the joy of the day; my shift supervisor had given me a comp day because I'd had the unfortunate good luck to be on a call where my partner Izzy and I had felt the need to slam our helmets on our heads, slide on our turnout coats, and run into a fire right behind the responding firemen to pull out a homeless vet who'd been so far gone on "'die land tin' for my epilepsy," that he hadn't known he was moments shy of becoming barbecue. And that? Smells a lot like cooked chicken.

Calls like that always made me and Jean seek out each other and our family; this was the perfect way to forget the things that upset us and to remember why we did it.

"Family puts the 'fun' in dysfunction," as Jean said. I agreed.

"Hey, you know, you never told me how you figured out the twins thing," Nina said as she handed me my niece.

"It was the rhythm, you know, when I listened for tones? Just something about the sound," I explained as I carefully shifted the baby in my arms.

"Good ear, good hands. You would have made a great musician, Tori," she said with a smile.

I laughed. "Thanks, Nina. You would have made a great EMT. But," I said, still smiling, "ya never know what the future holds. Maybe I'll play the drums or something when I get tired of playing knight in a tin can. I'll probably learn to play a bagpipe."

She chuckled. "Ethnic color, not a bad thing."

"Actually, Jean's got a nice voice."

"Yeah?" she raised an interested brow. "I've never heard her sing, though she's got a great speaking voice. Maybe you guys should drop by the studio sometime."

I tried hard not to blush. "Well, she does kinda only sing for me."

"You might want to keep it that way. Ask me or Sam about that sometime."

We both glanced over to where Sam stood, trying not to look too anxious as Nina's father held her son.

"I've got to go give her a hand," Nina said. "My dad always makes her tense."

"You okay with my holding her?"

Nina put a hand on my shoulder. "You held my life in your hands, Tori." She kissed the baby that slept in the crook of my arm, then kissed my cheek. "I'll always be okay with you doing it again."

I stared at her, stunned at the magnitude of what she trusted me with, as she walked away, and I watched as she kissed her father and her son, then handed the baby back from her father to her wife, who put an obviously relieved arm around her.

A warm hand clasped my shoulder. "Are you hogging all of our niece's attention?" Jean's voice was liquid and low.

I turned to find her smiling at me. "You want to hold her?"

"Yeah, I do."

We found a vacant spot on the sofa, and I carefully passed the baby over before I sat down next to them.

"Of all my nieces," Jean said softly as she cuddled her close, "I like *you* best."

"That's because she's named for you," I teased. I brushed the hair off her cheek and behind her ear.

"Well, there's that too," Jean conceded with a grin, then kissed me.

We both focused on our niece, playing with the reflexive grip of her toes when we pressed a finger right below them, examining the tiny,

tiny nails and the perfect joints of her hands, the typical Del Castillo long lashes that lined her tightly closed eyes.

"Now there's a sight I'd like to see in my own living room one fine Sunday."

Jean and I both looked up to see her da smiling as he came over, camera in hand. This time, I couldn't stop the blush I felt crawl warmly up my neck, and I think Jean flushed too, as he snapped a picture.

"Now, granted, you're both young, you've got some time, but don't make an old man wait too long."

I glanced at Jean, observed the way she held our niece, the gentle way she played with that tiny fist curled tightly around her pinkie, and the smile I'd bet anything she didn't know she had while she did it.

"I don't think you'll have to wait too terribly long, Da."

Jean glanced over at me, surprised.

"Yeah?"

"Yeah." I smiled. "After the medic class."

The smile she returned was so delighted, so radiant, it made my chest hurt.

"Not too long at all, Da," Jean seconded.

❖

About two minutes later, someone got the idea for a group picture. "Come on, three generations of Del Castillo women? How often are we gonna get that?"

"Well, that's my excuse to get up from this comfortable seat," Jean said. "I'll be over there, on the *other* side of the camera."

"Thanks, thanks a lot," I said as she transferred the baby back to me, then stood.

She kissed my forehead and chuckled. "Anytime."

I glanced down at my niece, who seemed oblivious to the noisy circus of her family as her grandmother, aunts, and cousins gathered around. Just then, she opened her eyes and looked straight into mine, a strong, searching glance, before she held her hand up to me and smiled.

My heart caught in my chest, a pained and joyful throb, because I instantly recognized those eyes, that hand gesture, the expression on that little face.

"Nina, look!" I said, and Nina leaned her head over my shoulder.

"It's Nana!" I gazed up into my cousin's eyes, which shone with the same happy tears mine held.

"I know," she said, and smiled her beautiful smile as I put her daughter in her arms. The flash went off. "Isn't it wild?"

Jean and I hung that picture up in our living room, between our certificates from the academy and below the photo from our wedding.

"Hey, come take a look," Jean called and pointed at the picture as she finished straightening it. "Did you notice this before?"

I came closer to see for myself. "That's just artifact from the flash."

"You sure?" she asked. "Look closely."

I did. A quick glance showed an arc of light behind the group that clustered about the sofa, but as I studied it...

"You see her, don't you?" Jean asked softly from behind me and put her arms around my waist.

"Yeah," I answered just as softly and covered her hands with mine, "I do."

Jean rested her chin on my shoulder and stared with me.

It was an outline etched in light, an outline with the unmistakable curves of a woman. She stood behind the group, her arms outstretched to hold us all.

GENERAL IMPRESSIONS

May, earlier that year

"Did everything work out the way it was supposed to, mission accomplished and all that?" Nina asked Samantha as they readied themselves for sleep.

"Yeah, I think so. Kitt delivered the papers, and I stayed by the car with Jean."

"Uh-huh," Nina answered with humored skepticism. "Is that all you did?"

Samantha shrugged as she pulled the blankets down. "Well, I did help Jean let the air out of her tires. I think she kept the caps as a trophy."

"She deserves something, at the very least," Nina sighed as she sat on the edge of the bed.

Samantha stretched along the mattress. "Come here, love, lie down. Don't think about it right now—it's not good for you or the littles."

"I know, you're right," Nina answered as she slid onto the bed. She eased herself onto her left side, and Samantha automatically wrapped her arms around her.

"It's just, I can't help but think…Samantha, we should have told her, we could have *stopped* this, *prevented* it."

Samantha sighed and pulled her wife even closer, knowing how close to tears she was. She was on that edge herself. "Love, what were we supposed to tell her? 'Trace Cayden's a human hound turned soul-sucker, and while she may have been astrally restricted oh, about ten years ago, she's still got plenty of power on this level, so you might not want to date her'?"

"She tried to bind her, Sam."

"I know," she answered quietly, remembering the cross over Tori's heart chakra, representing the pain that's slow to fade. A bruise like that could have been a simple mark to begin the binding, but this particular pattern was a combination of symbol and initial; Trace had been attempting to create a complete thrall. Then there was the night Samantha had followed the trail of bright red dots to the smear on Tori's doorknob and had found Tori half awake but clearly out of it, a neat, straight, and slightly too deep gash on her arm—the left arm, the side traditionally associated with stronger flow from the heart...

She'd known in that instant several things: Had Trace not known before, she had discovered Tori's relations then, for if Tori hadn't revealed it herself, it had been scryed through her blood—and it was no secret who Nina was married to.

Samantha herself had bandaged the cut, had recognized the second mark of the binding ritual, the trance state, probably drug induced...and she'd also performed the unbinding, shed her own blood, to break it.

The Law was the Law: to interfere not in another's free will, to give aid when asked, unless clearly, clearly, free will had been violated. Samantha had done that, by performing the unbinding, but she was still bound by other aspects of the Law; she was forbidden from interfering in any way.

And...what could she really have said to Tori, anyway? How could Nina or Samantha have told her about Trace, especially after her reaction when she'd heard of Kerry's past association with Nina?

The Law had been followed, respected: Tori had been unwillingly bound, then freed. Her choice, her free will had kept her from being bound again, from becoming a vessel, or a thrall. Perhaps Samantha had skirted the edges of the Law by offering Tori alternative ways of spending her time, but they were offers only, not directives, and Tori had made those choices freely, without prompting. Samantha had thought they were safe; Tori had broken free, perhaps with a little help, but still free, whole and healthy after, and not too long later so very clearly in love with Jean.

Nina sat up and buried her face in her hands. "She...she raped her. God, Sam, she *hurt* my little sister." The words were anguished, torn, and Samantha's heart ached for both of them, for the wife she so loved whose heart bled for Tori's pain, and for Tori herself, whose own goodness had been used to betray her, for what Samantha knew from experience Tori had yet to go through.

She held Nina carefully as she schooled her own mind against the memories. Nina, whether she wanted to admit it or not, was an empath. She literally felt not only textures, but emotions, thoughts, through her skin. Bound as closely to Samantha as she was... Nina's aura carried her sorrow, which Samantha could tell she was trying so very hard to not let touch the energy field that surrounded their children.

"She's marked two chakras on her, one over her heart, where she hurts most, where you'd hurt most if something happened to her, and the other—she knows you're pregnant." Samantha felt the first hint of ice in her heart as she realized what it meant. "Nina, she's blood linked to you through Tori."

Nina nodded against her chest. "That's what I thought. What do we do?"

Samantha kissed her head, then cautiously released her. She walked over to the dresser she'd folded her pants on and took her cell phone out of the pocket. "I have to call my uncle," she explained as she dialed. "I'm gonna need backup."

Samantha watched Nina shift on the bed. She seemed oddly calm, even knowing what the dangers to her, to all of them, were.

Perhaps...Samantha considered. Perhaps Nina was still in shock, mourning even, over what had happened to Tori. She'd cried for hours, silent tears the first night, her head pressed firmly against Samantha's heart, and again after the deposition, unable to take comfort from her or from Kitt. Her stillness now worried Samantha.

"Uncle, it's me," she said into the phone as soon as the message beep sounded. "Get the soonest flight if you can. It's hungry and coming our way." She clipped her phone shut with a nervous snap.

"Are you okay?" she asked as she sat next to Nina on their bed. She ran her fingers through the shiny, rich length of her hair.

Nina turned eyes that shone with tiredness in the half-light of the room. "I'm fine. You know what? I'm just gonna get a glass of water."

Samantha jumped up. "I'll get that for you."

Nina stood and stretched her arms above her head. "I'm not a veal, you know," she said with a smile, "and it's good for me to move around, remember?"

"Yeah, yeah, I know, you're not a veal," Samantha responded. "I just, you know."

Nina kissed her gently. "I do know. It's one of the things I love about you. Besides, nothing bad is allowed to happen today, you know that, right?"

"Really? Why's that?" Samantha murmured softly against her lips.

"Because," Nina answered after taking another moment to savor the softness of the mouth that pressed against hers, "tomorrow is my grandmother's birthday, so nothing bad can ever happen. I'll be right back."

Once Nina had left the room, Samantha paced.

She'd thought—probably wishfully, she realized ruefully—that it was over. She was mistaken. She would have berated herself but had no time. She had to *think*, to find the clues, because there was more: the last cut, the last symbol, a direct strike in so many ways to the seat of life, an actual bleeding cut both inside and out...

Oh, Tori, she thought in empathic sympathy, *I should have found a better way—I'm so sorry I didn't protect you better.*

Dammit, what phase was the moon in? she wondered frantically. This had happened how many days ago? It had been a blood spell, cast in the waning moon, and tonight—Samantha calculated quickly—tonight it reached its nadir.

That bitch had had ungodly good luck with her timing, assuming it had been luck at all, Samantha thought grimly. Dammit it twice, because Trace had apparently found a way to get around the restrictions placed on her so long ago, to manipulate the energies in a different way, a dirtier way.

And the door had been opened with compassion, augmented with the power of death behind it, and all tied to the blood that ran through Nina and Tori's veins, and Samantha's as well, since that too was part of the lives Nina carried.

Samantha felt the ice that had touched her heart seep through her. This series of actions wasn't simply directed at Nina for refusing Trace so many years ago, or anger—jealousy, even—at Tori for breaking free.

It all came down to the knife cut, she thought, the representational severing at the seat of life—it brazenly bore Trace's initial, a challenge to Samantha, a threat to her children. As the final piece clicked into place, Samantha knew one solid fact with almost blinding clarity: in failing Tori, she'd failed them all.

The numbers on the clock face shifted, catching Samantha's eye. Midnight. On the nadir. It was already too late to stop, or even deflect, Samantha realized as she started walking automatically to the door. She felt the gathering of power tingle on her skin, raising the hairs on the back of her neck. She felt the wood under her feet and gathered energy from the earth, breathed in slowly and drew it from the air, tried to center and draw it from aethyr, before she surrounded herself, then blew it out toward her wife, the only shield she really had time for. All she could hope was to blunt its impact, to—

"Sam?" Nina called in a tone that Samantha knew meant nothing good. She tore out of the room in a dead run, knocking on Tori's door on the way.

She could smell the blood before she saw it, knew before seeing that this was it, was dangerous for her wife, for their children.

All she could hope was that they might all get through it, that that unholy glorified hound hadn't finally gotten everything she'd wanted in one blow, Samantha thought as she caught her wife in her arms.

Tori stood beside her out of seemingly nowhere, helping her, helping Nina. There was a time to lead, and a time to follow, and Samantha followed whatever orders she received.

No matter what happened, Samantha swore to herself as she followed the stretcher that carried her world on it down the stairs and to the ambulance that waited outside, as soon as this was over? The hunt was on.

Author's Note

If you are in a situation and you think you may need help, please visit this Web site: http://www.thenetworklared.org/english/resources/natl_intl.html

Ketamine became a Schedule III drug in August 1999, and GHB was outlawed later in the same year. Both were legally available before that; however, GHB is easily made, while ketamine is still available via prescription.

In 2001, the state of New York passed SARA, the Sexual Assault Reform Act, which, among other things, created new provisions for crimes previously undefined and therefore unprosecutable under the law. In 2006 the statute of limitations on rape was eliminated.

About the Author

JD Glass lives in the city of her choice and birth, New York, with her beloved partner. When she's not writing, she's the lead singer (as well as alternately guitarist and bassist) in Life Underwater, which also keeps her pretty busy.

JD spent three years writing the semimonthly *Vintage News*, a journal about all sorts of neat collectible guitars, basses, and other fretted string instruments, and also wrote and illustrated *Water, Water Everywhere*, an illustrated text and guide about water in the human body, for the famous Children's Museum Water Exhibit. When not creating something (she swears she's way too busy to ever be bored), she sleeps. Right.

Works in progress include *American Goth* (Bold Strokes Books, 2008).

Further information can be found at www.boldstrokesbooks.com and at www.myspace.com/jdglass, where you can check out the daily music plays, blogs, reviews of all sorts of fun things, and the occasional flash of wit.

Books Available From Bold Strokes Books

Red Light by JD Glass. Tori forges her path as an EMT in the New York City 911 system while discovering what matters most to herself and the woman she loves. (978-1-933110-81-3)

Honor Under Siege by Radclyffe. Secret Service agent Cameron Roberts struggles to protect her lover while searching for a traitor who just may be another woman with a claim on her heart. (978-1-933110-80-6)

Dark Valentine by Jennifer Fulton. Danger and desire fuel a high-stakes cat-and-mouse game when an attorney and an endangered witness team up to thwart a killer. (978-1-933110-79-0)

Sequestered Hearts by Erin Dutton. A popular artist suddenly goes into seclusion, a reluctant reporter wants to know why, and a heart locked away yearns to be set free. (978-1-933110-78-3)

Erotic Interludes 5: Road Games, ed. by. Radclyffe and Stacia Seaman. Adventure, "sport," and sex on the road—hot stories of travel adventures and games of seduction. (978-1-933110-77-6)

The Spanish Pearl by Catherine Friend. On a trip to Spain, Kate Vincent is accidentally transported back in time—an epic saga spiced with humor, lust, and danger. (978-1-933110-76-9)

Lady Knight by L-J Baker. Loyalty and honor clash with love and ambition in a medieval world of magic when female knight Riannon meets Lady Eleanor. (978-1-933110-75-2)

Dark Dreamer by Jennifer Fulton. Best-selling horror author Rowe Devlin falls under the spell of psychic Phoebe Temple. A Dark Vista romance. (978-1-933110-74-5)

Come and Get Me by Julie Cannon. Elliott Foster isn't used to pursuing women, but alluring attorney Lauren Collier makes her change her mind. (978-1-933110-73-8)

Blind Curves by Diane and Jacob Anderson-Minshall. Private eye Yoshi Yakamota comes to the aid of her ex-lover Velvet Erickson in the first Blind Eye mystery. (978-1-933110-72-1)

Dynasty of Rogues by Jane Fletcher. It's hate at first sight for Ranger Riki Sadiq and her new patrol corporal, Tanya Coppelli—except for their undeniable attraction. (978-1-933110-71-4)

Running With the Wind by Nell Stark. Sailing instructor Corrie Marsten has signed off on love until she meets Quinn Davies—one woman she can't ignore. (978-1-933110-70-7)

More Than Paradise by Jennifer Fulton. Two women battle danger, risk all, and find in each other an unexpected ally and an unforgettable love. (978-1-933110-69-1)

Flight Risk by Kim Baldwin. For Blayne Keller, being in the wrong place at the wrong time just might turn out to be the best thing that ever happened to her. (978-1-933110-68-4)

Rebel's Quest: Supreme Constellations Book Two by Gun Brooke. On a world torn by war, two women discover a love that defies all boundaries. (978-1-933110-67-7)

Punk and Zen by JD Glass. Angst, sex, love, rock. Trace, Candace, Francesca…Samantha. Losing control—and finding the truth within. BSB Victory Editions. (1-933110-66-X)

When Dreams Tremble by Radclyffe. Two women whose lives turned out far differently than they'd once imagined discover that sometimes the shape of the future can only be found in the past. (1-933110-64-3)

Stellium in Scorpio by Andrews & Austin. The passionate reunion of two powerful women on the glitzy Las Vegas Strip, where everything is an illusion and love is a gamble. (1-933110-65-1)

The Devil Unleashed by Ali Vali. As the heat of violence rises, so does the passion. A Casey Clan crime saga. (1-933110-61-9)

Burning Dreams by Susan Smith. The chronicle of the challenges faced by a young drag king and an older woman who share a love "outside the bounds." (1-933110-62-7)

Fresh Tracks by Georgia Beers. Seven women, seven days. A lot can happen when old friends, lovers, and a new girl in town get together in the mountains. (1-933110-63-5)

The Empress and the Acolyte by Jane Fletcher. Jemeryl and Tevi fight to protect the very fabric of their world...time. Lyremouth Chronicles Book Three. (1-933110-60-0)

First Instinct by JLee Meyer. When high-stakes security fraud leads to murder, one woman flees for her life while another risks her heart to protect her. (1-933110-59-7)

Erotic Interludes 4: Extreme Passions, ed. by Radclyffe and Stacia Seaman. Thirty of today's hottest erotica writers set the pages aflame with love, lust, and steamy liaisons. (1-933110-58-9)

Unexpected Ties by Gina L. Dartt. With death before dessert, Kate Shannon and Nikki Harris are swept up in another tale of danger and romance. (1-933110-56-2)

Broken Wings by L-J Baker. When Rye Woods, a fairy, meets the beautiful dryad Flora Withe, her libido, as squashed and hidden as her wings, reawakens along with her heart. (1-933110-55-4)

Combust the Sun by Andrews & Austin. A Richfield and Rivers mystery set in L.A. Murder among the stars. (1-933110-52-X)

Sleep of Reason by Rose Beecham. Nothing is as it seems when Detective Jude Devine finds herself caught up in a small-town soap opera. And her rocky relationship with forensic pathologist Dr. Mercy Westmoreland just got a lot harder. (1-933110-53-8)

Grave Silence by Rose Beecham. Detective Jude Devine's investigation of a series of ritual murders is complicated by her torrid affair with the golden girl of Southwestern forensic pathology, Dr. Mercy Westmoreland. (1-933110-25-2)

Too Close to Touch by Georgia Beers. Kylie O'Brien believes in true love and is willing to wait for it. It doesn't matter one damn bit that Gretchen, her new and off-limits boss, has a voice as rich and smooth as melted chocolate. It absolutely doesn't... (1-933110-47-3)

Carly's Sound by Ali Vali. Poppy Valente and Julia Johnson form a bond of friendship that lays the foundation for something more, until Poppy's past comes back to haunt her—literally. A poignant romance about love and renewal. (1-933110-45-7)

Passion's Bright Fury by Radclyffe. When a trauma surgeon and a filmmaker become reluctant allies on the battleground between life and death, passion strikes without warning. (1-933110-54-6)

Tristaine Rises by Cate Culpepper. Brenna, Jesstin, and the Amazons of Tristaine face their greatest challenge for survival. (1-933110-50-3)

Of Drag Kings and the Wheel of Fate by Susan Smith. A blind date in a drag club leads to an unlikely romance. (1-933110-51-1)

100th Generation by Justine Saracen. Ancient curses, modern-day villains, and a most intriguing woman who keeps appearing when least expected lead archeologist Valerie Foret on the adventure of her life. (1-933110-48-1)

The Traitor and the Chalice by Jane Fletcher. Tevi and Jemeryl risk all in the race to uncover a traitor. The Lyremouth Chronicles Book Two. (1-933110-43-0)

Whitewater Rendezvous by Kim Baldwin. Two women on a wilderness kayak adventure—Chaz Herrick, a laid-back outdoorswoman, and Megan Maxwell, a workaholic news executive—discover that true love may be nothing at all like they imagined. (1-933110-38-4)

Erotic Interludes 3: Lessons in Love, ed. by Radclyffe and Stacia Seaman. Sign on for a class in love…the best lesbian erotica writers take us to "school." (1-9331100-39-2)

Punk Like Me by JD Glass. Twenty-one-year-old Nina writes lyrics and plays guitar in the rock band Adam's Rib, and she doesn't always play by the rules. And oh yeah—she has a way with the girls. (1-933110-40-6)

Forever Found by JLee Meyer. Can time, tragedy, and shattered trust destroy a love that seemed destined? When chance reunites two childhood friends separated by tragedy, the past resurfaces to determine the shape of their future. (1-933110-37-6)

Sword of the Guardian by Merry Shannon. Princess Shasta's bold new bodyguard has a secret that could change both of their lives. *He* is actually a *she*. A passionate romance filled with courtly intrigue, chivalry, and devotion. (1-933110-36-8)

Sweet Creek by Lee Lynch. A celebration of the enduring nature of love, friendship, and community in the quirky, heart-warming lesbian community of Waterfall Falls. (1-933110-29-5)

Wild Abandon by Ronica Black. From their first tumultuous meeting, Dr. Chandler Brogan and Officer Sarah Monroe are drawn together by their common obsessions—sex, speed, and danger. (1-933110-35-X)

The Devil Inside by Ali Vali. Derby Cain Casey, head of a New Orleans crime organization, runs the family business with guts and grit, and no one crosses her. No one, that is, until Emma Verde claims her heart and turns her world upside down. (1-933110-30-9)

Chance by Grace Lennox. At twenty-six, Chance Delaney decides her life isn't working, so she swaps it for a different one. What follows is the sexy, funny, touching story of two women who, in finding themselves, also find one another. (1-933110-31-7)

Turn Back Time by Radclyffe. Pearce Rifkin and Wynter Thompson have nothing in common but a shared passion for surgery. They clash at every opportunity, especially when matters of the heart are suddenly at stake. (1-933110-34-1)

Promising Hearts by Radclyffe. Dr. Vance Phelps lost everything in the War Between the States and arrives in New Hope, Montana, with no hope of happiness and no desire for anything except forgetting—until she meets Mae, a frontier madam. (1-933110-44-9)

Innocent Hearts by Radclyffe. In a wild and unforgiving land, two women learn about love, passion, and the wonders of the heart. (1-933110-21-X)

Protector of the Realm: Supreme Constellations Book One by Gun Brooke. A space adventure filled with suspense and a daring intergalactic romance featuring Commodore Rae Jacelon and a stunning, but decidedly lethal Kellen O'Dal. (1-933110-26-0)

Course of Action by Gun Brooke. Actress Carolyn Black desperately wants the starring role in an upcoming film produced by Annelie Peterson. Just how far will she go for the dream part of a lifetime? (1-933110-22-8)

Coffee Sonata by Gun Brooke. Four women whose lives unexpectedly intersect in a small town by the sea have one thing in common—they all have secrets. (1-933110-41-4)

The Temple at Landfall by Jane Fletcher. An imprinter, one of Celaeno's most revered servants of the Goddess, is also a prisoner to the faith—until a Ranger frees her by claiming her heart. (1-933110-27-9)

Rangers at Roadsend by Jane Fletcher. Sergeant Chip Coppelli has learned to spot trouble coming, and that is exactly what she sees in her new recruit, Katryn Nagata. The Celaeno series. (1-933110-28-7)

The Walls of Westernfort by Jane Fletcher. All Temple Guard Natasha Ionadis wants is to serve the Goddess—until she falls in love with one of the rebels she is sworn to destroy. The Celaeno series. (1-933110-24-4)

Erotic Interludes 2: Stolen Moments, ed. by Stacia Seaman and Radclyffe. Love on the run, in the office, in the shadows…Fast, furious, and almost too hot to handle. (1-933110-16-3)

The Exile and the Sorcerer by Jane Fletcher. First in the Lyremouth Chronicles. Tevi and a shy young sorcerer face monsters, magic, and the challenge of loving. (1-933110-32-5)

Force of Nature by Kim Baldwin. From tornados to forest fires, the forces of nature conspire to bring Gable McCoy and Erin Richards close to danger, and closer to each other. (1-933110-23-6)

In Too Deep by Ronica Black. Undercover homicide cop Erin McKenzie tracks a femme fatale who just might be a real killer…with love and danger hot on her heels. (1-933110-17-1)

Hunter's Pursuit by Kim Baldwin. A raging blizzard, a mountain hideaway, and a killer-for-hire set a scene for disaster—or desire—when Katarzyna Demetrious rescues a beautiful stranger. (1-933110-09-0)

Erotic Interludes: Change of Pace by Radclyffe. Twenty-five hot-wired encounters guaranteed to spark more than just your imagination. Erotica as you've always dreamed of it. (1-933110-07-4)

Justice Served by Radclyffe. Lieutenant Rebecca Frye and her lover, Dr. Catherine Rawlings, embark on a deadly game of hide-and-seek with an underworld kingpin who traffics in human souls. (1-933110-15-5)

Justice in the Shadows by Radclyffe. In a shadow world of secrets and lies, Detective Sergeant Rebecca Frye and her lover, Dr. Catherine Rawlings, join forces in the elusive search for justice. (1-933110-03-1)

A Matter of Trust by Radclyffe. JT Sloan is a cybersleuth who doesn't like attachments. Michael Lassiter is leaving her husband, and she needs Sloan's expertise to safeguard her company. It should just be business—but it turns into much more. (1-933110-33-3)

Fated Love by Radclyffe. Amidst the chaos and drama of a busy emergency room, two women must contend not only with the fragile nature of life, but also with the irresistible forces of fate. (1-933110-05-8)

Storms of Change by Radclyffe. In the continuing saga of the Provincetown Tales, duty and love are at odds as Reese and Tory face their greatest challenge. (1-933110-57-0)

Distant Shores, Silent Thunder by Radclyffe. Dr. Tory King—along with the women who love her—is forced to examine the boundaries of love, friendship, and the ties that transcend time. (1-933110-08-2)

Beyond the Breakwater by Radclyffe. One Provincetown summer, three women learn the true meaning of love, friendship, and family. (1-933110-06-6)

Safe Harbor by Radclyffe. A mysterious newcomer, a reclusive doctor, and a troubled gay teenager learn about love, friendship, and trust during one tumultuous summer in Provincetown. (1-933110-13-9)

shadowland by Radclyffe. In a world on the far edge of desire, two women are drawn together by power, passion, and dark pleasures. An erotic romance. (1-933110-11-2)

Love's Masquerade by Radclyffe. Plunged into the indistinguishable realms of fiction, fantasy, and hidden desires, Auden Frost is forced to question all she believes about the nature of love. (1-933110-14-7)

Honor Reclaimed by Radclyffe. In the aftermath of 9/11, Secret Service Agent Cameron Roberts and Blair Powell close ranks with a trusted few to find the would-be assassins who nearly claimed Blair's life. (1-933110-18-X)

Honor Guards by Radclyffe. In a wild flight for their lives, the president's daughter and those who are sworn to protect her wage a desperate struggle for survival. (1-933110-01-5)

Love & Honor by Radclyffe. The president's daughter and her lover are faced with difficult choices as they battle a tangled web of Washington intrigue for…love and honor. (1-933110-10-4)

Honor Bound by Radclyffe. Secret Service Agent Cameron Roberts and Blair Powell face political intrigue, a clandestine threat to Blair's safety, and the seemingly irreconcilable personal differences that force them ever farther apart. (1-933110-20-1)

Above All, Honor by Radclyffe. Secret Service Agent Cameron Roberts fights her desire for the one woman she can't have—Blair Powell, the daughter of the president of the United States. (1-933110-04-X)